SOULS OF MALAPACE: BOOK 2

THE BOOK OF QUEENIE

THE SCALE OF LIMBO

BY SEON JUNG

CONTENTS

To Jush

A good friend who stays true to his heart

"Do I need a reason to talk, to love?
Do I need a reason to sacrifice, to cherish?"
-Zanshin, the man of forced isolation

PROLOGUE

Did burnt tobacco count as litter? Geralt had always pondered the question every time he lit up a cigarette, but being honest in his answer would mean he had desecrated numerous towns. Hell...even the *concept* of litter felt so idiotic. What would the moral high ground mean to the masses when no one knew where their next meal would come from? So, he shut up and lit his hand-rolled cigarette.

He had always wondered about the old world. From the small bits of books he had read, even the peasants lived like kings. Guaranteed food every day, pressurized plumbing, and even mechanized transportation. It seemed skeptically luxurious. Had Geralt himself not come across the ruins of the old world, he would write off all these numbed whispers as pure fiction.

The well-suited man sat down on a nearby tree stump, brushing his tidy hair with groomed fingers with one hand, scanning a worn map in the other, and holding up his tobacco with his blessing. Blessings were the manifested power of each individual's desires that everyone had. Geralt had come across numerous blessings: ranging from lifeblood manipulation to turning yellow tulips purple. Using your blessing required soul, and using too much of your soul meant death. So, soulbearers had to maintain a healthy balance of using their blessings, resting up to recharge, rinse and repeat.

It was exhausting. It was no different from stopping a jog to catch your breath, then running once you were rested up. To think humans traded so much safety and splendor for...this? A nuclear war...to change the color of flowers? It was so idiotic that his malignance almost reset back to sheer humor.

Geralt used his blessing to tuck away his lighter into his jacket pocket, glancing at the leathery map in his hand. He had scouted out about five villages over the course of seven days, hopefully without catching the attention of the supposedly omnipotent Overseer.

There wasn't much news about the Overseer. The only guarantee that *anyone* knew was that the Overseer rested somewhere amidst the walls of Malapace, the damned grand city, while they peered over every village in the vicinity. Depending on their mood, the Overseer would send aid or hindrances to the various communities. Geralt looked up from his map to scowl, his grimace flicking some ashes onto his map. He blew the debris away with his blessing as he focused on the looming city walls. Inside, people had guarenteed food, shelter, and joy.

Of course, only 'useful' people could reside in Malapace's walls. The city barely glanced at anyone else, only stepping in when their own leisure was disturbed.

The thick tar that bubbled in Geralt's veins was warm...and he wasn't the only one who shared that rage. Father had adopted numerous likeminded individuals into his Family, with the sole goal in tearing it *all* down. Geralt was one of Father's strongest fighters...so it was up to the smoker to put it all on the line for his commander.

He blew out his last puff of smoke before dropping the butt onto the floor, quashing it into paste with his blessing. Geralt took out a sliver of jerky and grinded on it between his molars, glancing to his left. Just as the parchment stated, over the yellow hill lay a village. Zanshin really outdid himself; the map he had crafted was precise.

Geralt packed away the map and resumed his walk. Limbo was crashing down soon...and Geralt needed all the advantages he could get.

It had been one year, eight months, twenty-two days and six hours since Taba, Queenie, and Hush were held captive by the Gatekeepers. Time to pick up those damn kids: Malapace kept them hostage long enough.

CHAPTER I

Q ueenie tilted her head back, slamming down the flask of luke-
warm water. She burped under her breath before glancing over
the city's stone walls, trying to determine exactly the species mutant
she was looking at. Well, it didn't help that she didn't know much
about the "old world", so even if she knew what the thing *was*…it really
wouldn't help.

It was the size of a wagon, had an armored shield-no, a *shell*, that
was blinding to look at. The limbs that protruded from its main body
cracked the dry dirt under its weight, implying that the thing was
probably dense as hell. The biggest concern, however, was the mutant's head. It spent its time peeking out with bubbled eyes, ominously
staring at them as it approached the city slowly. When a soldier got
close…

A man squinted as he charged with a nerve wracked battlecry, only
for him to suddenly fall over in surprise as a portion of his torso
vanished. He lay on the floor, too stunned to even scream before the
rest of him suddenly vanished.

Taba crouched next to her, cursing. "I can't track the damn thing when it's popping out. At the very least, we can determine that it's a physical ability, nothing really soulbased."

Queenie glanced at her close friend, Taba. He looked as though he had just rolled out of bed, donning a basic t-shirt and shorts. Hell, he probably *was* sleeping, seeing as he entered the battlefield with horrendous bedhead. His face was rugged from his daily exercise routines, with subtle bags under his eyes from constant exhaustion. Taba was well-built, standing a few inches taller than most men...but always acted as though he were a lesser person. Ironically, Queenie thought more highly of him than most. If Taba led the charge, victory was guaranteed. If Taba assured you, that meant he did not see a world where you failed.

...and if Taba stood against you? Well, Queenie didn't want to think of such a possibility. It was like imagining fighting a tsunami or an earthquake: where would you even begin?

Queenie nodded as she offered a fistbump. "Yeah. I think it's some mutant turtle of sorts, but that wouldn't explain why the damn thing is so fast. I tried shooting at it with the sniper rifle, but the bullet only chipped the shell."

Hush, Queenie's older brother, stared at the mutant as he joined the two. He had shoulder-length hair, tied to in a tiny ponytail with a few traces of silver due to his...stressful upbringing. He wore his usual olive jacket, his build slightly more lanky than Taba. However, her brother could hold his own in most fights, despite not being a frontline combatant. Though she would never admit it...Queenie *heavily* respected her brother and loved him to death.

"Well, you try using soul manipulation?" he asked.

Her eye twitched. "Look, I never had to use soul manipulation for my sniper shots. That's like the equivalent of coating a steak with ground beef. Plus, where the hell were *you*?" she asked in annoyance.

Hush tilted his head inwards to Malapace. "Alexandria's mom was caught outside the city on the opposite side. We had to hold ground till Sana could step in."

Sana. One of the three Gatekeepers of Malapace...and one of the strongest hurdles that the three Misfits had to overcome. Initially, the trio tried to assassinate the Gatekeepers...but they failed. After some negotiations, the Misfits were spared the death penalty in exchange for loyalty. Though the trio openly expressed their allegiance with the Family...the leaders of Malapace didn't seem to mind. In fact, they were...kind to them. Malapace had taken the time to converse and nurture the three of them, like a mother bird orphaning three chicks.

Taba's subtly darting eyes softened as they settled. He then nodded to the two of them in confidence. "We can win. You guys ready?" he asked.

Queenie raised an eyebrow. Taba's blessing had the ability to simply ask questions regarding others, receiving definite "yes" or "no"s on how each scenario would play out. It was a weak blessing, but Taba utilized his ability to such a fascinating degree that to bystanders, he seemed like an omnipotent god. If Taba said they could win, victory was assured...as long as they followed Taba's instructions *precisely*.

Hush frowned. "You want to explain your plan first? If Queenie's bullets aren't piercing the thing, I don't see a world where we have the firepower required to take the thing down."

The disheveled boy rubbed his mouth as he stared at the thing. "The *shell* is dense...but the neck is very tender. It has to be, or it wouldn't be able to achieve such speeds. All we need to do is cut it while its neck is exposed," said Taba, nodding to Queenie. "I can get you a clear shot of its head. You'll have about two seconds, can you do it in that timeframe?"

"Well...yeah. That isn't hard. How do you plan to do that?" she asked.

Taba grinned. "I need a spear. One that's about six feet long. You have one, right?"

"Do you just need a long, pointed weapon?"

"Uh...yeah. I guess so."

Queenie rolled her eyes. Her blessing allowed her to store and withdraw items (and to an extent, living beings) in an other-dimensional storage...like a space backpack. As a former thief, she had amassed a lifetime's worth of items, ranging from weapons to groceries. The blessing wasn't *bad*, but juxtaposing it against things like elemental control or immortality? The ability to pull out a normal dagger whenever she wanted felt a bit underwhelming. Without further question, she withdrew a slender pike and passed it to Taba. "I have spears, but I figured you'd want this more."

He took it gratefully then turned to her older brother. "Can you blind the thing?" Taba asked.

Hush's blessing allowed him to augment the senses of any living being by flexing his fingers, be it amplification or nullification. If he wanted, he could deafen Queenie, increase Taba's voice...or blind the mutant turtle, all dependant on which fingers he flexed. Her older brother nodded. "Yeah, I can. Do you need me on the ground, too?" he asked.

"Mhm, but stay on standby till I give the okay. Queenie, chamber a round. Fire when you see the opportunity."

The two guys scrambled down the city's walls as Queenie set up her rifle with slow breaths, loading a round as she squinted at the shiny mutant's general area. It seemed to reflect light at a one-to-one conversion. For the average person, this would likely make accuracy an impossibility. However, Queenie enjoyed a good challenge here and there, so she welcomed the hurdle. She kept the mutant in her peripheral vision to avoid fully blinding herself, but stared the the blob in the corner of her vision down intently so as to not miss the opportunity that Taba would provide.

The Misfit stood a fair distance away from the mutant, taking a slow inhale as he did. He nodded to Hush, who flexed a finger to blind the creature. In turn, the thing flinched, tucking its head deeper into its dome, blind eyes darting around frantically.

Taba exhaled slowly, quietly picking up a stone from the ground with his free hand and taking cautious steps toward the mutant. If Hush undid his blessing, Taba would die. If Taba made the slightest noise, he would die. If Queenie or Hush failed to do their part, he would die. If he failed executing his plan, he would die. Queenie scowled as her calm hands dripped the slightest bit of sweat down the rifle's grip. Not wanting to risk anything, she squeezed her hand to disperse the sweat, patiently waiting for an opening.

Suddenly, Taba dropped the stone a few feet to his right. The second it clattered against the floor, the mutant's head darted out on reflex, jaw opened wide as it searched for the source of the sound. The thing's mouth snapped shut a mere foot away from Taba, who flinched slightly before ramming the pike through the turtle's exposed neck. In response, the creature yelped as it suddenly retracted…only for its head to be stopped from fully ducking into its shell due to the length of the pike.

Taba glanced back towards Hush, who sprinted forward to back his friend up. Together, the two of the Misfits dove to the bending handle of the weapon, slamming into the polearm to prevent it from splintering. The turtle flailed around, a pathetic whimper cracking around the battlefield-

…before the force of Queenie's bullet hollowed out a portion of the mutant's head. After her shot cracked throughout the sky and splattered onto the floor, the turtle slumped onto the floor, her brother and friend now coated in "turtle juices". The two of them silently groaned as they attempted to wipe the matter from their faces with Queenie offering a bold thumbs up from her perch. Oddly enough, the mutant's shell still shone brightly, making it difficult to properly make eye contact with her allies. Still, the danger was gone from *this* portion of Malapace: she needed to check in on the others.

Queenie stored away her rifle and jumped off the city walls, catching herself with a summoned chain and zipping away to the next loudest commotion. She whirled around the massive city, trying her best to not get distracted by the fascinating architecture. Malapace had crafted their buildings out of natural stone with a steel base: an unfathomable marvel. Roads were paved and sprinkled with rolled pebbles, with the path adorned with streetlights that held candles for long nights. In modern times, it was common to have smithies craft buildings with soul, which would usually result in imperfect, squishy wood or stone structures. So, to see such a massive civilization maintained with natural materials? Queenie couldn't help but feel jealous.

She heard the sounds of a scuffle, so she changed her trajectory midair, swinging around the corner to assist in whoever was in trouble. As she approached the sound of the fight, it slowly became evident that the mutant had breached the city's stone walls, with some bald man boldly fighting what appeared to be an extremely buff, hairy, and four-armed man.

She blinked. Huh? Four arms?

Queenie touched down onto a nearby building, staring at the fight unfolding. What she had mistaken for as a four-armed man also had three tails, with a mouth full of sharpened teeth. It was bulging with veins, its eyes twitching everywhere as the being screamed ear-piercing incoherence. Furthermore, the being's hands and feet were clawlike, the fingers not showing any resistance as it easily gripped into the floor and flesh of its opponent.

Yet...the mutant's opponent did not fall. In fact, for all the blood that was flung in the air and splattered onto the floor, the man seemed uninjured. His face had the unsettling expression of ravenous blood-lust. His mouth was twisted into a sickening grin, eyes scowling dully in the fight, similar to how one's gaze might turn sour upon witnessing roadkill. Despite being overwhelmed likewise, the man kept up with a complete disregard of self-preservation, taking fatal blows and returning punches of equal devastation. Queenie was so stunned at the sight that she couldn't even consider stepping in to help the fighter, instead choosing to be mesmerized at his tenacity.

After a few minutes of constant blows, the mutant stumbled back, one of its arms bent an incorrect way, some teeth broken off, and stomach slightly hunched with raspy breaths. The man, on the other hand, stood up calmly as he tucked his arms in close to his chest.

Queenie scowled. The fighter was none other than G, one of the city's Gatekeepers...and one of the targets that Queenie had failed to takedown months ago. The same bullet that had taken out the mutant turtle from before had failed to even render G unconscious. Due to his fighting style and spotless body, there was heavy rumor that his blessing was simply immortality...and this fight further pushed that narrative.

The mutant stumbled forward, screaming a piercing screech as it threw a punch towards the Gatekeeper's head. G's head popped like a red balloon, before his body weaved downwards and uppercut the creature with a sickening *crack*. The being fell onto the floor, its arms slightly going limp as it tried to reorient itself. G wasted no time to jump onto the beast, pinning it to the floor, and repeatedly slammed his fists into the mutant. The thing attempted to defend itself with its tails, but each attempt of blocking proved to be unfruitful as G simply twisted his arms into unnatural directions to land endless blows. With each sickening *THOCK* that reigned across the battlefield, the mutant's defenses grew weaker and weaker until it stopped responding to G's attacks. Confirming that his opponent was dead, G got up with a groan, stretching his back before locking eyes with the dumbfounded Queenie.

The bloody bald man wiped his face with an equally bloody hand, smearing the blood around head. "Well. Thanks for the assist, dipwad," he snapped.

Queenie flipped him off. "You had it, piss off," she scowled.

G glanced around the arena, looking for any other threats. "I don't see any other mutants here," he frowned. "I imagine Sana and Patchy are done with their fights, too...so go to the town hall. I'll be there in a second."

. . .

The town hall was littered with scattered mentors of varying sizes and abilities. From her time staying at the city, Queenie genuinely wasn't too impressed by them. They were *capable*, but she couldn't imagine any of them putting up a solid fight. Well, barring Juliette, the Gatekeepers, and a few others.

Though there weren't many mentors in Malapace overall, the amount that conversed in the town hall was fewer than expected. A good chunk of mentors were probably still out patrolling, with another chunk getting their injuries treated. Queenie instinctively unsheathed a dagger and nervously unraveled/retaped the handle...before flinching and tucking it away, opting to pull out a wooden hairbrush instead. She wasn't sure where Taba and her brother were. Maybe they were cleaning the gunk off their faces. She hoped they would hurry up: Queenie hated being surrounded by these creeps.

The murmurs suddenly quieted down as the conference room doors swung open. All heads turned to watch as a withered woman draped in white slowly sat down at the head of the table. She quietly took the blindfold that was loosely wrapped around her knuckles and gently placed it in front of her, her white irises glaring sharply at the room. Immediately, the other mentors took their seats in silence, awaiting her words.

Queenie's nose twitched as she remained standing in the corner of the room. The elderly woman who entered the room, Babs the

Overseer, was the head of Malapace. If she was taken out of the picture than the Family's goal would be drastically easier. Despite this, Taba couldn't bring himself to kill the queenpin. Queenie didn't get it. Hell, she flat out *hated* his hesitation...but if Taba made a decision, then who was she to go against it?

The blind woman cleared her throat. "Good to see you, mentors. Before we proceed...have we lost anyone?" she asked.

Silence filled the room before a scrawny mentor cleared his throat. "Uh...we didn't *lose* her, but the Dancing Painter is hospitalized again."

The Dancing Painter. The Drunken Fox. Juliette. *Their* mentor was working overtime to cover up the weaknesses of her allies. Though she hid her expression with her ceremonial fox mask, even Queenie could see the bags under the woman's sharp blue eyes. A few months ago, she had taken a heavy blow to protect Queenie. Though Juliette was *technically* an enemy...Queenie couldn't help but feel tremendous guilt since that day. The female Misfit struggled to even meet her mentor's eyes before the attacks began. How was the girl supposed to ever hold her head up now, knowing that...that...

The Overseer's sigh snapped Queenie out of her delusions. The elder tapped her fingers on her blindfold, pondering the scrawny mentor's statement. "Damn brat keeps overworking herself," she muttered. "I'll talk to her later. The rest of you: step it up so she doesn't have to pick up your slack." Many mentors hung their heads in shame as the rest grit their teeth and nodded. Babs glanced around the room with a monotone gaze. "Guessing the Gatekeepers are still out? Bah, kids are getting sloppy."

14

As she said that, the conference room door was kicked open by a lanky man with raggedy hair, immediately turning everyone's heads. He scratched his stomach with an unsuppressed yawn, slumping in a chair as he nodded to the other mentors. Queenie stared at the new visitor while also subtly glancing at the newly dirty footprint in the middle of the door. The man who had entered was the last of the city's Gatekeepers, Patchy. According to what Taba had mentioned a while ago, there was a good chance his name was correlated to the weird skin he had...though she had personally never seen it. He was a laidback man, sloppy in everything, barring combat. She still had no idea what his blessing was, but from what she could tell it appeared to be some sort of teleportation. At best, he was annoying. At worst? He was an untouchable genius who blinked around the battlefield. He raised a hand to the Overseer. "Hiya, Babs. Sorry I'm late, was taking care of things."

The Overseer, Babs, pursed her lip with a heavy sigh. "I know, but still. Would it kill you to at least *pretend* to show shame in being late?" she said.

"No idea if it'd kill me, but I don't intend on finding out." He said with a shrug as he leaned his chair back, stuffing his hands into his pockets.

"What about the others?" asked Babs.

"G was punching a dead monkey, which in turn made some child cry...so now he's trying to soothe the kid while covered in monkey guts...so that was fun to watch. Sana was taking on a weird....ladybug? No idea, some kinda beetle. She insisted she was fine and told me to go on ahead, so here I am," said Patchy.

The blind woman sighed as she hung her head with exhaustion. "Now I *wish* you didn't show up. You left Sana to fight a mutant by herself?"

"Hey, she was winning."

"That's not my complaint, you absolute mongrol. I meant...never mind." She turned to Queenie, causing the girl to flinch. "And what about your 'Misfits'? Where are they?"

"Covered in turtle guts," Queenie shrugged. "I think they're cleaning up."

"...Right. Well, let's get to assessing property damage."

Queenie zoned out the bland talk and conversation, choosing to paint her focus on her hair brush, fiddling with it however she could. Unpeeling and peeling the tape on the handle, twirling it between her fingers, juggling the bristles with small flicks, so forth. She only snapped back to focus when the grinding sound of chairs being pushed out rang through the air. She quickly stored away her hairbrush as all the mentors shuffled out. One of the mentors stopped a few feet in front of Queenie, frowning at her as she stared back blankly. He looked familiar. Queenie raised an eyebrow. "Can...I help you?"

The man crossed his arms over his chest, his forearms unconsciously flexing as he did. "Young girl, it would serve you well to pay attention to the meetings. Information is power, after all."

She dismissed his advice, simply squinting as she tried to itch the recognition she felt upon staring at the single vein that bulged on his forehead. After a few seconds of silence, she clapped her hands as light beamed across her face. "Ah! Alexandria's mentor! *That's* where I remember your receding hairline! What was your name...Bogus?"

16

The mentor looked slightly taken aback by her comment about his hairline, but kept his composure. "First off missy, it's Banase. Secondly, my hairline hasn't shrunk whatsoever. Lastly, I do mean what I said. Everyone's out here trying their best to help the city, you should too."

Queenie rolled her eyes as she stared at the stocky man with a disapproving gaze. "Ok. First off, 'Base', I really don't care about your name. Secondly, I'm not exactly 'allied' with you guys, remember? I don't really care about Malapace: you clean up your own mess." She then stepped up to the mentor. Though she was a solid foot shorter than him, she gazed up with listless eyes. "Lastly, preparation or not, doesn't matter. I could beat you in a fight with one hand tied behind my back. Know your place."

Banase's eyes slightly widened in intrigued surprise, but overall seemed indifferent. "I don't doubt you could beat me in the average fight. Still, stay complacent and that's how you let others down. Your friends. Your Family. *Juliette,"* he said.

She flinched upon hearing the last name, a twinge of guilt and anger flaring up as she subconsciously withdrew a revolver. Banase tightened his lips as he stared at the manifested weapon. "If shooting me will change the condition of your mentor, then by all means: fire away. Just remember *why* she's suffering as she is...though I suppose you wouldn't give a damn, right? After all, we're you 'enemy'," he snapped.

Queenie's jaw locked as her eyes trembled with contradictory emotions of fury and shame. She wasn't sure if she should burn holes into the man's skull or curl up into a ball and sob. So, she held a respectable middle ground and angrily contemplated into the man's taut suspenders. He huffed, seemingly satisfied with her emotions, then left the room silently until it was just Babs and Patchy staring at the fuming girl. Patchy whistled as Banase quietly exited the room. "That man sure has guts. Still, he's pretty strong, I wouldn't go provoking him," he said.

The girl fired her gun towards the ceiling in frustration. Patchy chuckled, his eyes slightly flickering as her bullet was thrown off course and exploded in the soil of a nearby potted plant. Queenie threw her gun to the ground: she couldn't even *vent* properly without intervention. She pulled out a chair and slammed into it, kicking her feet up onto the table. "So, why am I even needed for these meetings? They feel so pointless and none of them really address the main issue," she groaned.

The Gatekeeper raised an eyebrow as he scratched his stomach under his shirt. "Eh, as boring as they are, meetings are important because it makes us look like we're doing something. Right, Babs?" he said.

The Overseer ignored Patchy's comment and turned to Queenie. "What do you reckon is the 'main issue' then, you Misfit?" she asked.

Queenie pulled out a bullet and absentmindedly began to throw it around. "Why are mutants suddenly attacking the city? Once is already rare...but what has it been so far? Two weeks of consecutive attacks? At that point, it isn't a coincidence: why aren't you guys addressing *that*?" frowned the female Misfit.

"I...have a slight idea why we're suddenly being bombarded, but it doesn't explain everything. I'm more focused on protecting my people over investigating a solution with no leads," said Babs.

"Actually, girly has a point," Patchy said. "Whatever happened to the soulscale? It was working wonders for a while now."

Queenie's ears perked up. "Soulscale?"

18

The Overseer hesitated for a few seconds before standing up from her chair. She nodded to the two of them. "I can show you. Follow me."

The Gatekeeper and Misfit exchanged small glances before shrugging and following the woman. They entered her chambers before she uncovered a rug on the floor, revealing a small trapdoor. Queenie blinked in mild surprise but Patchy didn't bat an eye. Babs opened the hatch and the three of them slowly descended down an uneven stone path.

After a few seconds of awkward shuffling, they turned a corner and revealed a small opening that couldn't have been much larger than the room that Queenie slept in. Towards the center of the room was an oddly shaped fragment that glowed a...color. As familiar as it seemed...her mind couldn't fully grasp what she was looking at. The shape seemed to slightly change but Queenie wasn't sure of when the "change" happened. From one second, it looked like a small stone. It would slowly morph its shape until it suddenly looked like a seashell. Then a beetle. Then some...blob. No, calling it a blob was misleading: that implied it had a shape or form. What really confused her, however, was the thing's color. It wasn't anything on the spectrum that she recognized. No, it was as if a shadow were shining a bright color that was the opposite of the rainbow. Not an inverted color, but a "negative rainbow" of sorts. It lit up the room while simultaneously dimming the lights, a contradictory impossibility since the room didn't even carry the light from the Overseer's chambers.

Babs pointed a thin finger to the shard. "The soulscale is a small bit of fifth dimensional soul that's given as a reward from...an ecliptical being, if you want to call it that. It's something we can't comprehend or fathom, so our mind decyphers it into something we can somewhat grasp. Even then, its impossible. Its a densely packed soul bit that kind of acts like a 'wall' to mutants, serving to dissuade them from approaching anywhere near the city, like how a wasp will flee from smoke," she said.

Queenie stared at the Soulscale, her hand subconsciously reaching to it. Patchy caught her hand, snapping her back to reality. He cautiously shook his head. "Don't recommend touching this. It's...not pleasant," he advised.

Babs sighed. "No, it'll be fine. That's the issue: the soulscale is losing its...soul. A better description is that the soulstone's essence is returning to its dimension."

"I don't get it. Does that mean its gonna just '*fwoop*' out of here randomly?"

Patchy scratched his head. "Eh...not quite. Think of it like an air bubble in a glass of water. You can try to keep the bubble submerged with your fingers, but sooner or later it'll disperse to the surface. The fifth dimension already exists 'here' in this world, if you will: we just can't perceive it. So, the soulscale is gradually returning to that plane of existence."

The Misfit crossed her arms as she fixated her eyes on the morphing impossibility in front of her. "Well, that doesn't make sense. Does that mean the fifth dimension is overlapped with our dimension?"

"There's just 'one' dimension, if you want to get technical," corrected Babs. "Depending on how much you can observe the reality, however, determines what 'dimension' you exist in. So, due to the limitations of humanity, we exist in the third dimension...but really, it's just our brains unable to decipher what exists around us."

"This is making my brain hurt."

Patchy chuckled as he ruffled Queenie's hair, causing her to flinch and scowl. "To sum it up: that thing isn't from this realm and it serves as a repellant for mutants, but its losing energy. When it fully fades, we're boned."

"Don't touch me," Queenie snapped as she slapped the Gatekeeper's hand away. "Do you guys have a solution to fixing all this, or is the end of days nigh for Malapace?"

Babs rubbed her chin as she blindly stared at the soulscale. "Well, we could get a new one."

Before Queenie could question the proposal, Patchy interjected with a strong cough. "Whoa, Babs. Last time, it took me, Sana, and G. The three of us can't exactly leave the city at the moment. The second we do, Malapace crumbles."

"I know. I wasn't thinking of sending you guys." The Overseer then turned her gaze to Queenie with a crooked grin. She and Patchy exchanged confused gazes before the proposal clicked with him.

"Uh...yeah, *no*. The brats? *Seriously*? Have you gone mad?"

"Child, I've *been* mad for quite a while. They'll b-"

Queenie took a small step back. "Shockingly, for the first time, I'm with Patchy. Why should we help out? What do we gain from this?"

The old woman took slow, but oddly malicious steps towards the girl. Queenie instinctively unstored a pistol, holding it to her chest in self defence. Undeterred by this, Babs continued her slow pace until she was able to lean into Queenie's ear.

"The soulscale could also help heal Juliette. You feel remorse? Regrets? You could repair your faults and weakness by getting the soulscale."

21

Queenie jolted back, sweat clammed up in her hand. "You lie. Shut up."

The withered lady cackled as she waved a dismissive hand to the shaken Misfit. "If you think I'm lying, ask anyone. The Gatekeepers, Juliette, or even Taba. It's truth. I won't force you onto this mission...but could you live with yourself if you walked away from such an opportunity?"

She hated this. The Overseer had planted hope in Queenie's fragile heart. This wasn't an idea that she could so easily ignore or turn away from. She swallowed with dry saliva, her trembling hands storing her weapon before she scampered from the room. She burst out of the Overseer's chambers, taking long strides past the reception desk and frontdoors. The nearby pedestrians all turned to look at this random girl who slapped the tears out of her eyeballs with her hoodie sleeve as she scampered up the rooftops.

After a few minutes of fleeing and ensuring she was alone, Queenie simply curled up into a ball next to a chimney and took rapid breaths, her heart pounding in her throat. It made no sense. She was being held hostage in the city of her enemy. By doing nothing, the city would grow weaker and weaker until her Family could easily siege the place. All she had to do...was...abandon the debt of someone who saved her life. It was an easy choice.

It should've been an easy choice.

One of the first things Queenie remembered seeing when waking up was Juliette's porcelain back being cracked and bloodied beyond recognition. Her mentor's mouth was covered with bile and blood, her sharp blue eyes heavy with exhaustion. Both of the Dancing Painter's ankles were crumpled incorrectly, and sh-

Queenie suddenly felt her throat retch, forcing her to hunch and vomit off the side of the building. She didn't get it. The girl had seen worse things during her times with the Hush clan. She had *done* worse things at such a younger age.

So...why did Queenie carry such regret? Why did she eagerly want to jump at the opportunity Babs had provided her, knowing how it would harm her Family in the long run? Why was Juliette's condition tormenting her?

Why couldn't it have been Queenie who got harmed instead? Why was Queenie the reason that her childhood hero was on her deathbed?

CHAPTER 2

H ush dried out his hair with a towel before throwing on a shirt. The mutant turtle had oily blood that had soaked *deep* into his clothes. Even after three rinses, he could still smell the juices. Ugh. He stepped out into the hallway, only to catch Taba quietly sniffing his shoulders. The two men noticed each other and tapped fists, exchanging slight glances at each other's wet hair.

"Couldn't fully get the smell out, huh?"

"Yeah."

The two of them turned the corner of the hallway and peeked their heads into the conference room. However, the two of them exchanged slightly confused glances at the empty table.

"Huh. Guess they ended early?" Hush turned to his friend. "Where do you think they're at?"

Taba closed his eyes, muttering to himself as he seemed to be in deep concentration. After a few seconds, he opened his eyes with a raised eyebrow. "No idea about Queenie, but Babs is in her room. Let's pay her a visit," he proposed. The two of them walked down the hallway before politely knocking on the door of the Overseer's chambers. After a few seconds, the door swung open and they were greeted by a disheveled face.

Patchy nodded to them. "Mm. Where were y'all in the meeting?"

"Turtle blood."

"Ah. Well, what did y'all need?"

Hush quietly peeked through the door to reveal an empty chamber, lacking even the Overseer herself. Hm. That was odd, considering that Taba's blessing had contradicted what his eyes revealed.

The older brother pulled back and tilted his head. "Well, we're here to give off a report. Also, we were hoping to find Queenie: did you see her?"

Patchy rubbed his neck with slight discomfort. "Well, kinda. She had a meeting with Babs a while ago before running off somewhere. No idea where she is now."

"Why'd she run off?" Taba asked.

"Ask her yourself when you find her. I don't know."

Taba turned to Hush with a nod. "What did you wanna do? We both don't need to be here for a report. Did you want to find her while I give Babs a recap?" he asked.

Hush stuck one of his hands inside his jacket pocket as he lifted the other towards Taba, slight unease filling his gut. "Sure. We'll catch up later." The two of them tapped fists before they went their individual ways. Taba ducked under Patchy's arm and into the chambers while Hush turned on his heel and walked down the hallway. He gave an awkward wave to the guild receptionist, Tabitha, and pushed past the heavy doors into the brisk open air. The more he walked through the town square, however, the more whispers and murmurs he heard of.

"Did you see her…"

"...was she crying?"

"...with the chains..."

"...onto the rooftops..."

His gut wrenched as he picked up his walking pace. Hush flexed his fingers in his jacket pocket to activate his blessing, allowing him to enhance (or nullify) a chosen sense. Using his blessing, Hush amplified his sense of hearing to scout out any sounds. As his ears perked up, he quietly ducked around the city to follow the trail of whispers until he caught the hint of a sniffle from above him. He quickly looked up to the building where the sound dripped from, grabbed the drain gutter attached to the wall, and began to hike up. Onlookers gave him odd stares, but he didn't give a damn. Hush quietly stepped over the roof's railing and his heart sunk upon seeing his sister sniffling in a ball, fists balled into her eyes. He quietly approached her and sat down a few inches away from Queenie. The ball of sadness flinched upon hearing the crunch of nearby gravel, immediately getting up to a knee with a pistol in hand.

Her puffy eyes glared at her uninvited guest, before her gaze softened a bit. "Oh. I..."

Hush said nothing but simply lifted up his arms. Queenie, in response, said nothing and quietly received the hug. As she sniffled snot and slobber into his jacket, he simply pat her back with a soft rub, humming a low tune that their mother had sung as a lullaby. The two of them had long forgotten the lyrics, but found tender comfort in repeating the same eight measures. He wasn't sure how many times he had repeated the hum, but after a while, Queenie leaned deep into his shirt and blew her nose. He slightly flinched at this, looking down at her with an annoyed, yet relieved, expression.

26

She wiped her nose on his shirt for good measure. "This never happened."

"I have permanent stains on my clothes that prove otherwise, idiot."

"Shut up...and thanks."

"Mhm."

Queenie pulled out some rags from her storage to wipe her face, trying unsuccessfully to rub away her sorrows. Hush stayed silent, not even bothering to ask any questions. Should the situation ever arise, she would talk to him. If she never wished to, that was also fine.

After a few minutes, his younger sister took a deep breath and slapped her cheeks, her weapon being stored as she did so. Queenie hopped to her feet and took a deep breath. "No idea what got over me, whew. I'm hungry, let's go eat something," she said with forced energy.

Hush looked down to the mess that littered his shirt. "Ok, so...I'm down to eat. But...are *you* ok wi-"

Queenie's face flushed velvet before reaching into her storage to pull out a spare shirt. He chuckled as he took the shirt, quickly changing into the comfy fit. Since his jacket was still smudged to high oblivion, he passed it along with his sullied shirt to his sister. She chucked them in her storage before she peered over the building side. "Alexandria's place is like...a few minutes from here. You wanna grab some wings?" she asked.

"Sure, I need to check up on her mom anyhow." Queenie raised an eyebrow. Hush realised a bit too late on the phrasing of his sentence, choking on his spit to backpedal. "No, like...we saved her earlier. I don't mean...like...oh shut up."

27

She cackled and jumped from the rooftop, rolling as she landed to disperse the landing impact. Hush did the same, and the siblings strolled on over to Alexandria's bar. After a few minutes of small chatter, they ducked into the gloomy bar. Alexandria's dad, Hutch, looked up with a stern glare. Upon recognizing his patrons, his piercing gaze softened drastically, gesturing to any of the open booths. The siblings waved awkwardly before ducking into the furthest booth as an armless woman with goggles sauntered over.

Alexandria slowly leaned her serving tray onto the table, allowing gravity to slide the drinks awkwardly in front of them. She smiled warmly at Hush, who turned away with slight embarrassment. "Thanks for earlier, man. Really. Don't know what we would've done if you weren't there," gushed Alexandria.

Hush hadn't planned on helping her mom. No, what had really inspired him to act was seeing the armless woman fighting back against a swarm of mutant beetles by herself. All of her reinforcements had fled into the inner city, Alexandria alone holding the line. She was both outnumbered and overpowered, the mutants buzzing wildly as they each took turns biting away at her blessing's arms. Despite the odds, as he watched the bloodied woman stand over her small mother with furious exhaustion, how could he *not* act?

He had only meant to help buy time for the two to allow them retreat, but he had unintentionally stalled long enough for Sana, one of the Gatekeepers, to step in. From that moment, he had no idea what became of the fight as the city gates closed behind him...but he couldn't really imagine Sana losing *any* fight. Hush turned back to the waitress with slight hesitation. "Well...glad to see you're patched up," he admitted. "Was it G?"

"Yeah, it's as though nothing ever happened. Dad wanted me to rest up, but I think that's a waste of time. So, what can I ge-"

Suddenly, a tiny woman emerged from the kitchen, locked eyes with Hush, then dove onto him with a tight hug. Between him and Alexandria, it wasn't clear whose face was more crimson.

Alexandria choked out a mortified cry. "*Mom!*"

Hush wriggled slightly, not wanting the hug but also not wishing to be rude. "I...uh...Miss...?" he wheezed.

After a minute of tight hugging, she pulled away with a warm smile. Alexandria's mom patted his cheek with warm taps before skipping back to the kitchen, humming as she did. Alexandria stood stiffly with tightened shoulders, unsure of what to say. After a few seconds of thickened embarrassment, Queenie broke the atmosphere with a brash laugh. "Holy crap, that was great. Looks like you have her mom's approval," she roared.

Alexandria shot a humiliated glare at Hush's younger sister, the waitress's leg already raised to deliver a swift kick. Before violence could ring out, he clapped loudly with a strong cough. "*Alright.* Can you get us some chicken? Twenty-four pieces, please, and thanks. Feel free to get some more for yourself."

Alexandria lowered her leg and itched her neck with a shoulder. "I'd love to...but the main reason mom went outside the city was because we were low on stock. I think we have about fifteen wings...or something. You cool with that?" she asked.

"Sure, whatever. As much as you can bring out."

As she scampered away, Hush noticed the tips of her ears were still flush. Huh. Go figure. He turned back to his sister, and though her face was still puffy from her crying, she grinned madly. "Aww, you care for her? Would be a sha-"

Her voice suddenly cut off as Hush flexed his fingers directly in sight of his sister. She scowled and flipped him off in return, reaching into her storage to pull out trash to chuck at him. Within a few minutes, Alexandria returned with a small tray of chicken balanced on her serving tray, cautiously tilting it from the platter hooked around her neck onto the table. Only then did she glance up to Queenie's face with a frown. "You been crying? Why?" She glared at Hush, who blinked in confusion. "...Is it because of *him*?" she scowled.

"First off, I wasn't crying. Second off, yes: it's his fault."

"Wait. Relax. I promise you I'm just as lost as you are," Hush said, hands up in confused surrender as he leaned away from Alexandria's raised leg.

Alexandria raised an eyebrow as her leg lowered. She gestured to Hush, who scooted over subconsciously, as she plopped down next to him. She leaned forward as she stared at Queenie's eyes with a frown. "Mhm. In the months I've known you guys...never seen her face that puffy. So, either she was bawling due to a reason you guys refuse to disclose...or she has an allergy. Which is it?" she asked.

As Hush opened up his mouth to reply, Queenie cut him off with an over dramatic sigh. "You got me. Hush yelled at me for not taking out the trash. Made me cry. He's treating me out as hush money."

Alexandria shoved into Hush with her shoulder, causing him to flinch as he shuffled uncomfortably. "That...really didn't-whatever. Can we eat?" he asked.

The three of them silently ate before Queenie gestured a drumstick to Alexandria. "So, how has your family been faring for the past few days?"

Alexandria quietly bit off a chunk of meat from her chicken onto her plate, sighing as she leaned back into her chair. "Rough, in all honesty. We usually sustain the shop with a combination of foraging and bartering...so it's a bit tough when we can't leave the city walls," she admitted. "I think we'll have enough to last a few days before we have to close shop and wait 'till this all blows over."

Hush chewed his wing with slight concern. From the time he's spent around the city, there seemed to be more rationing that occurred in even the biggest restaurants or stores. Sure, that behavior was typically normal outside the city...but for *Malapace* to go through such a state? If the constant barrage of mutants didn't blow over soon, money would be the least of everyone's issues: hell, the city could very well run out of food. Of course, Babs was doing what she could to scavenge the leftover mutant meat from each invasion to disperse onto the needy...but even that was running thin. After a few wings, he stopped eating so the others could eat more: what was a little bit of hunger going to do? Queenie took subtle notice at her brother's behavior, but knew better than to protest against it, shrugging as she bit into one of the last wings on the platter. Once the platter was a forgotten memory of poultry, Hush cleared his throat as he gestured to his sister. "We need to check in on Taba, he's probably a bit lost in all this. Thanks for the food," he said to Alexandria.

Queenie pulled out a sack of coins from her storage, plopping it on the table. Alexandria frowned at the overpayment. "We can't take that. Don't be dumb," said Alexandria.

31

"It's a loan, pay us back when this all blows over."

"...Whatever. I'm paying you interest. Thanks."

The siblings scooted out, waved goodbye to the entire family, then left the bar with half-full bellies, the sun slowly setting beyond the city walls as the duo went off to the town hall.

. . .

Sana knelt in the ground as she reaped wheat, her left hand tugging at the grain as her right hand sliced the stalks with her trusty sickle. Her sugegasa blocked the harsh sun from cracking into her eyes, the light breeze ruffling the hem of her white sundress. Maybe not the *best* outfit to be harvesting in, but she had grown up harvesting in this attire to the point where it felt unnatural to reap in anything more appropriate, like overalls.

After chucking the last batch into a basket, she wiped non-existent sweat off her brow as she felt her curse flicker. Someone was staring at her from behind. Sana glanced backwards and her heart fluttered slightly as G approached the fields, a jug of water in his hands.

A lot of people were intimidated by G, and for good reason. He was always shirtless, exposing over-exaggerated muscle definition. The only clothes he wore were green pants, held up with a purple belt. Due to his innate toughness, he walked around barefoot as no shoe was tougher than his calloused feet. His bald held reflected the sun, his jawline sharp enough to cut through diamonds.

...and yet, when people got to know G? His soft eyes? The way his nose twitched when he was worried about someone's health? The soft personality hidden behind crass words? Oh...what a *man*.

Sana immediately stood up and smoothed her dress out, taking off her hat to comb it with nervous fingers. G dismissed her actions as he approached, handing her the jug of water. "It's been a while since we could breathe. How are the fields?" he asked.

Sana wasn't thirsty, but she gratefully took the water just to have an excuse to touch his fingers. She drank a small sip and corked it. "Yeah. A bunch of the crops died, but that's sadly expected." She nodded to him with a raised eyebrow. "No one injured in the medical ward? That's...unbelievable."

"It's just people resting up. Wanted to stop by to give an update: Patchy is heading out soon to scout out the nearby villages," said G. He then shuffled his feet, his eyes not making eye contact. Sana could feel his emotions with her curse. G felt...uneasy. She took a step forward with a frown. "What are you uneasy about?"

G flinched, but sighed. "I...don't know how to feel about the Misfits. I don't think trusting them is...right. You know?"

Though Taba, Queenie, and Hush were very useful...Sana understood G's concern. *Technically*, they were enemies of Malapace. In fact, the trio had tried (and failed) to assassinate Sana, G, and Patchy: the Gatekeepers of Malapace. The only reason they hadn't been executed was because, well, Taba showed no malice in his actions. It was bizarre: he was precise with his movements, but carried no hatred in his heart. In fact...he had a tinge of sorrow in his soul. Sana was perplexed by this, and convinced Babs to let Taba, Queenie, and Hush into the city to nurture them under the watchful eye of Sana's good friend, Juliette. Sana believed the trio were just misguided, but the more time they spent in Malapace, the more the Gatekeepers got to understand the Misfits. They were kind souls, loyal to the people who raised them, and all three strived towards a goal larger than themselves. It...was hard to hate them. Hell, Sana *admired* the Misfits, and she suspected even G held some level of respect for the trio.

And yet...at the end of the day? The Gatekeepers were trusting enemies of Malapace to protect the city. They were trustworthy...yet *could* they be trusted? Sana could read their intentions with full transparency, but it made complete sense for G to be a bit skeptical. Realistically, there would be a time and day when the Misfits departed from Malapace...but her heart ached to consider that possibility. She would never force them to stay, nor could she bear to cut them down, but to protect the children behind her? The safety of Malapace's citizens triumphed over everything...even Sana's personal feelings.

Sana had no doubt G, Patchy, Babs, and Juliette shared that sentiment.

The female Gatekeeper tucked her sickle into her waistband as she quietly contemplated G's feelings. "Yeah. I...get it. I suppose it isn't right to trust them, from a pure logical view. Still, they're good people. After a year, even *you* have to admit it, right?"

G stared at the milled soil, silently.

"Sometimes...logic isn't the best metric," Sana said softly. "I trust them wholeheartedly, and I know you do as well."

"...they're probably using us. Getting information for the Family."

Sana smiled. "Even if that were true...*you* don't believe it yourself. Sure, they could easily be betraying us...but I doubt they would do it with malicious intent. If they were to backstab us, they wouldn't take pleasure in it. You could see it too, right? The world where they're standing against us, the pain in their eyes?" she asked.

"...I...yeah. I could see that."

Sana hugged G, her heart jumping as she felt his slight jitters. "Trust them. Even if it means we get betrayed, trust them. The regret of treachery is far more insignificant than the regret of forced apathy," she said.

G opened his mouth, but the Overseer's voice rang in their heads. *"I'm sorry to interrupt, but four-o'-clock: two mutant serpents. You two are the closest. Please...take them out."*

Sana sighed. "Let's continue our talk later, ok?"

"...alright."

.   .   .

The Misfits sat in Taba's room, Queenie sitting on his pillow, Taba sitting in a rickety chair, and Hush standing in the corner. Taba went over the events of his report with the Overseer as he ate a banana, only taking small pauses between each bite to swallow.

"...so yeah. Nothing really too new, but apparently more and more mentors are getting exhausted because they don't have enough time to actually rest up between invasions. G's pill apparently doesn't fully recover fatigue, so Babs says its only a matter of time before the city gets overwhelmed."

"Technically, isn't that a good thing?" Hush asked. "Means Father could just waltz right in without resistance."

"Well...they *could*, but that's the thing: why aren't they invading *now*? It just doesn't make sense. I don't think the Family would lose if they attacked right now.

Throughout the discussion, Queenie stayed oddly silent. She shifted uncomfortably on the bed, though whether it was due to an internal issue or the rigidness of the mattress, Hush had no idea. After a bit of discussion, Queenie spoke up with a slightly cracked voice. "Hey, guys?" she whispered.

The two of them turned to face her, causing her to flinch as she stared at her lap. His sister was acting...*oddly* uncharacteristic today. "Yeah?" responded Hush.

She took a slow breath before slightly raising her eyes. "So...do you guys trust me?"

"I don't see a reason not to."

"Yeah, why?"

"Cool, cool. So...could you hear me out?"

Queenie then quickly rambled into the floor, with mentions of how the soulscale existed, could completely bolster the defenses of the city, and how Babs wanted her to get it for them. Throughout it all, her eyes darted slightly, occasionally peaking up before looking downwards immediately, her hands slightly trembling as she spoke rapidly. A few minutes passed before silence flooded the room. The two guys exchanged glances as they tried to communicate non-verbally. Queenie had made no request: she simply laid out a fact of something Babs told her...but his sister was not the kind of person to divulge random information. Hell, he hadn't seen her *this* vulnerable in a long time...not even while she was on death's door. It was obvious what she was asking for: she wanted their approval to betray their Family. He had no idea why, but she wanted to get the Soulscale for Malapace.

Hush quietly nodded to Taba. "My turn. Do *you guys* trust *me*?" he asked the others.

"Duh."

"...I guess."

"Good enough. Taba, talk to Queenie for a bit: I need to take a piss."

"Bathroom is all yours, man," said Taba, nodding to the bathroom door.

"No, I'm using the one in my room."

"I...huh. Sure."

The two of them stared at his back as he left the room, turning on his heel to immediately power walk to Bab's room. Without knocking, he barged into the room to stare at the blind woman staring at him with welcoming intent. The Overseer had the smallest of smirks as she sat kneeling on the floor. "Figured you'd be the one to show up," she chuckled.

"Oh...that right?" he scowled.

The silence between the two was palpable, Hush gritting his teeth as his instincts screamed at him to be rational. After a few seconds, he let out a soft exhale as his muscles relaxed.

"So...about the soulscale."

"Yes?"

"...Not gonna ask me how I know about it?"

"Should I? Please, there's only one reason you'd know about it right now, we both know that. So...?"

"You're...crafty. Hell, borderline cruel," Hush bit sourly.

She chuckled as her dull eyes reflected hollowly. "Yeah. I know."

"Glad we're on the same page. We'll get your stupid soulscale. Any directions or guidelines you have for us?"

"I have *some* info, not much," Babs shrugged. "The soulscale shows up on Limbo's peak."

"Is…is that symbolic? Like a metaphor or something?" asked Hush with a blank face.

"Not at all: Limbo is…well, it's an imaginary mountain."

"Babs, you aren't making sense."

The Overseer shrugged as she loosely tightened the blindfold on her arm. "It might not make sense, sure…but that's on par for Limbo. It's a mountain that appears based on the amount of soul in the world, with the location changing every appearance based on soul density. I know it's a bit tricky to explain…but the only thing you need to know is that it's a mountain that teleports onto Earth every few years," she explained. "The other thing we know is that the soulscale's lifespan seems to align with the solar eclipse."

"That seems random. Is that a coincidence, or is there a correlation?" asked Hush, his brain struggling to fully wrap around all this new information.

"Could be a coincidence, could be correlated. Doesn't matter." The Overseer twirled her bony finger in the air with a weird glint in her dull eyes. "The last world war really threw the world for, well, a loop. Inconsistent day and night cycles slowly became a thing, whether due to some weird science with planetary revolution or soulbearers with unique abilities, we don't know. Maybe it's both. All we know is that the eclipse is quite difficult to track now. By the time we see the eclipse…it's too late to get the soulscale. So, we need to prepare for Limbo before the eclipse comes."

"So…eclipses are a response to the Soulscale?"

"Not necessarily, no," said Babs. "Think of the eclipse schedule kind of like a timer. When one eclipse begins, the next eclipse is already set in motion and destined to happen: we just don't know when."

Hush unfolded his arms and placed his arms in his lap with a frown. "Does that mean the lifespan for each soulscale is different, if each eclipse's timing varies?"

Babs smiled a cracked grin. "Bingo, kid. They all last varying timeframes. The question is whether or not it lasts four months of forty years. We don't know ourselves until the Soulscale runs out of steam. The soulscale *I* retrieved lasted about two decades. The ones the Gatekeepers got only lasted for four years. There's no pattern, rhyme, or reason with it." She stood up and dusted off her white gown gesturing to him with an elegant nod. "Follow me, brat."

Hush got up silently and trailed the Overseer as she walked down a hidden trapdoor and into an oddly small chamber that revealed a...thing. Was it a shape? Object? Illusion? Hell, he couldn't even comprehend the color of whatever he was looking at: even *with* his blessing activated. It was bright and dull, horrifying and attractive. Here and there, Past and future. It was as though someone had gathered up all the contradictions possible and slammed them into one little..."it".

She nodded towards the object. "*That* is the Soulscale in its diminished form. Fascinating, no? Don't touch it," she advised.

The older brother hesitated between averting his eyes and not breaking eye-contact with the soulscale. "Don't worry, I have no desire to go anywhere near it," he muttered uncomfortably. "What madman would *want* to touch that?"

She turned around and grabbed the boy by the hems of his jacket, dragging him back to her chambers. Once she closed the trapdoor, she sighed. "Unfortunately, there are many madmen...and mad*women* out there. I can't tell whether or not those with that instinct are brilliant or idiotic."

"Let's assume idiotic," said Hush with distaste. "Now that I know what it...*feels* like, tell me more about Limbo. If the eclipse is a sign that says it's 'too late', how do we begin climbing beforehand?" he asked.

"Limbo appears moments before the eclipse, but *only* to those who have mastered their blessings to a certain point. If you're chosen, you can choose to enter Limbo: the entrance looks like a fragment of broken glass floating in front of you. If you aren't chosen, you won't see anything," said Babs. "Seeing as you Misfits can defeat mutants, I don't see why Limbo wouldn't choose you all."

"That somehow makes less sense than the soulscale. Is the soulscale like, a clump of soul? What exactly *is* it?"

"...for simplicity's sake, let's just say the soulscale is a way for the third dimension, us, to experience the authenticity of the fifth dimension."

Hush leaned back on his hands, his head spinning fuzzily as he tried to process all the new lore. Soulscale? Limbo? Eclipse? It all made his head hurt...but at the end of the day...

"So... we can't 'plan' for Limbo: instead, it just happens moments before the eclipse, which tells us that it's too late to get the soulscale. So, see shattered 'air-glass', climb Limbo, and by the time we reach the top...we get the soulscale as the eclipse happens in the real world. Is...is that the gist of everything?" he asked.

"It's far more complicated...but you got a good idea of the situation, yes. I should mention: there's a time limit."

The older brother groaned. "Of course there is. Why not. How much time do we have?" he asked.

"Same thing as the eclipse and the soulscale duration: we don't know until its too late. Just climb, *really* fast. Run frantically, even if it seems like you're just trying to survive for one more second. As long as you keep scrambling forward, you'll eventually reach Limbo's peak."

"So, abandon all dignity and run for my life. Wonderful. Out of curiosity, what happens if we don't make it to the peak in time?"

Babs leaned in, the light blinking dully in her dead pupils. "Imagine bringing a shovel to hell to dig deeper, the walls of a room shrinking while you're inside it, or your soul being stretched to threads while your brain struggles to form a coherent thought. Impossibilities stack up. Sometimes, it's good. Mostly, it's bad. Don't stay in Limbo when the gates close, trust me," she said bitterly.

"This doesn't seem worth it. Me, Queenie, and Taba don't gain anything from helping you in this."

Babs shook her head. "You, personally? No, I don't think you do. However...for your sister? This could be the one piece of redemption to help her back up on her feet. You know that more than anyone, don't you?" she said.

Hush was being used. He had nothing to gain from this climb. Logically, it made sense to walk away from all this...but all logic crumbled away when he remembered his sister earlier, fists balled in her leaking eyes, her heart's creaks and cracks hollowing out from her mouth.

Damn it. Damn. It.

Hush flopped onto the floor with a groan. This all seemed impossible. He wasn't sure if learning all this new information was valuable or a waste. Babs noticed his frustrated exhaustion and chuckled, "Relax. Though it is impossible to precisely predict Limbo's arrival...we *can* greatly increase the odds of when it stops by. Get some rest for now,

I'll let you Misfits know the fine details when you're more rested up," she said.

.   .   .

The blind woman stared outside the window, watching as the sun crept below the city walls. Once crickets began to chirp, the Overseer quietly opened her door, careful not to make any sound. Ensuring Tabitha and the Misfits were sleeping soundly, she tiptoed down the hall and softly exited the town hall. She stepped into the night sky, sighing as she inhaled in the cool night mist. Her bedroom got damn suffocating: a breath of fresh air was good once in a while.

She glanced around with her white pupils, quietly scanning for any beings. As expected, no soul stirred in the dead of night apart from a few energetic moths. Babs took a slow long detour through her city, delaying her walk to her destination and slowly sinking in the glory of Malapace…or what little she could *feel* of it. Sadly, her eyes were only good in detecting beings with soul: it did very little against stone. Regardless, she traced her withered fingertips against the walls, doing her best to blindly navigate various pathways.

Steel foundations. Stone walls. Dusty accents. Paved roads. Whispers of crickets. Minty air. Rustling of wind through the alleyways. Without her blindness, the Overseer doubted she could fully appreciate each minute detail of Malapace.

It was odd. Taba, Queenie, and Hush were enemies of Malapace, yet they were the first to run to the front lines when the mutant bombardment began. Since then, they had silently joined rotation with the other mentors, actually *outperforming* many of the other adults, as their coordination allowed them to consistently take out mutants.

They were...enemies. Even when Babatiya shared bland, mediocre meals with Taba, the day would come where they would leave the city to rejoin their Family. Even when Queenie argued with the smithies on the cost of ammo, there would be a day where she would point that barrel to the same shopkeepers. Even when Hush would help Alexandria forage the wilderness for food...there would be a day where he would raze everything to the ground.

It wasn't a matter of personality. The ideals of Malapace and the Family simply didn't align. Babatiya knew this, and she knew that the Misfits knew it as well. When war would inevitably begin...she knew their betrayal would carry no malice. *That* was why she was ok with picking Queenie back up with the soulscale: Babatiya's heart had softened over the past year to consider them family.

The problem was the void the trio would leave behind upon scaling Limbo. Someone would have to pick up their responsibilities...and unfortunately, the best candidate for the job was also the one in the weakest condition. The Overseer hated to stack more burdens on her fragile shoulders, but the Drunken Fox would hate it *far* more if someone died instead.

Time was hard to track, but Babatiya eventually got to her destination. She opened the creaky wooden door and past the unattended reception desk. Within the building were rows of rooms, full of beings with weak souls. Babs felt her heart tighten in pain as she forced herself to look straight forward.

'One problem at a time, Babatiya.' she thought. *'Focus on what you can do.'*

She ignored the silent whimpers and snores of the various rooms and eventually approached the largest soul of the room. It took the shape of a bald man resting in a chair in front of the Dancing Painter's room. Even with the Overseer's quiet steps, the sleeping man roused and stared up at her with half-alert eyes.

"Babs? What're you doing here?"

"You know why I'm here, G," Babatiya said with a dismissive wave. "Go rest or allow me some privacy: let me speak to her in peace."

"She's all yours, Babs. Just don't take too much of her energy, alright?" G said with a stifled yawn.

She bowed in thanks to the Gatekeeper and entered the room he guarded. There was only one occupied bed in the ward, positioned next to the only window. The woman had a cold personality, her frigid eyes striking fearful awe into any who witnessed her. She usually stood in solitude, with people simply observing her from afar...like a sparrow admiring a patrolling stag. Yet despite the exuded atmosphere of superiority...this same woman dove to protect her enemy, Queenie, and suffered a fatal wound as a result. More than a year later, the Drunken Fox continuously reaped the consequences of her actions.

She rested on her stomach, because sleeping on her back was still too difficult due to her recovery. Next to her bed was a wooden box with a festive fox mask hanging off its corner. The box itself was about seven feet tall and two feet wide, containing her weapon of choice: an oversized paintbrush with sharpened steel bristles.

As the Overseer approached the patient, the wounded woman immediately roused from her light slumber and struggled to her elbows, beads of sweat instantly emerging from her temple as she did. Her messy bun slowly unraveled as she turned her head to the guest of honor, her infamous crimson lips gritting in frustration as her immobility rendered her from properly showing respect.

Over the years, the woman went by many names. Only after her heart was torn from her body was she able to shed the fear people felt from her approach. Some called her "The Drunken Fox", from how she was constantly seen sipping spirits from her flask while donning a festive fox mask. Others called her "The Dancing Painter", for the way her movements in combat mimicked an unrestrained artist. Very few knew her by her real name, a name only used by close comrades.

...and *everyone* knew her as one of the strongest defenders of Malapace. A woman who could grind atoms to nothingness, all while fluttering around the corpses of her enemies.

Babatiya kneeled next to the bed. "Relax. You don't need to get up. Lay back down," she gently ordered.

Juliette shook her head in defiance, her azure eyes flickering in the dark. "As though I could show such disrespect. To what do I owe the pleasure, ma'am?"

CHAPTER 3

Taba quietly entered the jail and sat across the holding cell. The room, as musty as ever, couldn't hide the beaming grin of his good imprisoned friend. Toukie smiled widely with an outstretched fist. "Taba! Hey! It's been a hot minute, how's the outside world faring?" he asked.

Taba couldn't help but crack a grin as he sat on the dusty floor, extending his own arm to meet Toukie's fist bump. "Hey, Tooks. Sorry, the fighting's been a bit rough recently: it's all the city can do to fortify their defenses. You holding out yourself?"

The powder monkey groaned as he flopped backwards in his cell. "It's so *boring*. I had a little pebble before to kinda throw around, but I accidentally chucked that outside the cell. All I can do to pass the time is sleep and read the labels of some of the boxes from outside the cell. I'm going to lose it if I read the nutritional facts of salted jerky one more time."

Taba scratched his head with a sigh. "Yeah…I'll see if I can get them to give you a book or something out of pity."

"Ew. See if they'll spare a broken watch or something instead. I'll repair guns and stuff for them if they're willing."

"As if they'll just pass along damaged tools and weaponry to the city's hostage-taker: be real Tooks."

He scratched his fluffy afro with a chuckle. "Whatever, worth a shot. Anyhow...what can I help you with?" he asked.

Taba leaned on his knees with a frown. "I know Dad told you about the chimera...but why? I was just curious if he had any ways of controlling the chimera...sorry, *Linda*. It just doesn't really click to me that he would throw out a wild card with no backup."

Toukie scratched his stomach with a frown. "Well, I don't think the Big Papa really planned on making the Chimera part of his assault squad. Something along the lines of 'harumph, it would be swell but da city won't let it happen.'."

The Misfit's ears perked up. "That wording is...specific. Wouldn't that imply that he had a way to control Linda?"

Toukie rocked his butt on the floor. "Well yeah. I mean don't you know...well, I guess you *wouldn't* know since she only joined us *after* you guys got captured."

"Who?"

He shrugged impishly. "I guess I shoulda mentioned it. A new Family member that can control mutants...kinda."

Taba blinked before scrambling closer to the holding cell with a hushed whisper. "I'm *sorry*? *What*? And you didn't think to tell me this bit of info in all your time here?"

Toukie pouted with crossed arms. "Well, sor-*ry*. You rarely visit, so forgive me if the random new recruit isn't the center of my attention twenty four-seven."

The questioner sighed with a shake of his head. Unfortunately, Toukie was always a bit absent on specific details...this wasn't new. "Whatever. So, what's her blessing?"

The powder monkey bit his thumbnail. "I think calling it a blessing is misleading. The Big P called it a 'curse'. It isn't that she controls mutants, but becomes a magnet for them. On default the 'magnet' is on her body...but she can transfer that 'attraction'...or something like that. I wasn't really paying attention."

Taba's eyes darted wildly. This changed things drastically. Curses were an anomaly among blessings, akin to someone being born with a third arm or without a lung. While blessings could be manually activated...curses were passive, like a blessing that could never turn off. Someone who was cursed could amplify the strength of their curse with their soul...but they would *never* be able to suppress it. It would explain the sudden influx of mutant attacks...but when had she snuck in the city? Where was the "magnet" transferred to? How co-

His eyes stopped flickering as a slow realization dawned on his face. The soulstone's expiration. Mutants. Attraction. Could it be...?

He raised his head to his friend. "What details do you remember about it?"

Toukie shrugged. "It's like cooties. First person she touches gets the attraction until they die. Then it goes back to her. I think that's it: she doesn't really get to choose to pass along the 'magnet', it just happens by touch, whether she likes it or not."

"Touks, this is *very* important. Did she touch you before the Family's invasion?"

He frowned. "Well...yeah? She hugged everyone. So...oh."

Taba groaned as he rubbed his face. "Touks...what order did she hug i-"

He tightened his lips. "Yeah, she hugged me first. Whatever, big whup. I thought it was because she thought I was a stud. Damn."

"Are you *dense*? Why would you hug the person who could-"

He rubbed his newly clammy face with a trembling hand. "I...look, they didn't tell us until *after* she hugged us. I only learned about her blessing slightly when we were walking over here. I didn't pay it much attention because I was trying to focus on Zanshin, alright? Sue me." Toukie swallowed heavily. "I mean...do you think I'm cursed now? No way: the timeframe from when she hugged me and the mutant invasion is too big. Mutants would've swarmed the city so much sooner if I were cursed...right?"

The Misfit slowly shook his head with tight lips. "No. No, they wouldn't...because the soulscale's protection was still going strong. They're only swarming now because it's dwindling in power. The weaker it gets, the stronger the attraction becomes."

The frizzy boy stared blankly at his toes. He was daft, yet even he recognized the looming danger before his eyes. "I...does...am I going to die, Taba? I...I don't want to die."

The questioner grit his teeth and shook his head. "No. I'll make sure of it, ok? Keep your wits about you. Now...did Dad tell you *any* information about a soulstone?"

· · ·

Taba sat on a tree stump in the park, his eyes darting wildly as he silently asked questions in his head. His blessing allowed him to ask questions to obtain the definite answer for many things...but even that had limits. The people involved, how he asked questions, tim-

49

ing, specificity, so on. The more lax he was in regards to asking his questions, the more likely he was to miss vital information and fail in executing his plans.

Still...Toukie had given him nearly nothing to work with. The only information that was divulged was that the soulstone existed and that Dad was looking to get it...for reasons. Plus, there was a *very* good chance that Dad wasn't involved in Toukie becoming a mutant magnet, which just baffled Taba further. Hell, where should he even *begin* to ask questions? All he co-

Boy, your questions are bland. Where is your creativity?

He flinched and scowled, rubbing his head. Again, that damn voice was back. Ever since the chimera mission, this booming....*thought* just slammed into his skull from time-to-time whenever he tried using his blessing. It wasn't his own...because every time it happened, Taba had the hejeebies scared out of him. The first few times made him jump. After the thirtieth time? It just irritated him. He couldn't even tell the others about it, because that would just make them concerned. Ironically, his blessing confirmed their hypothetical reactions.

He closed his eyes with a scowl. "Seriously, if you're just going to criticize my brain, could you at least *tell* me who you are? It's been months and it feels like I'm going insane."

A minute of silence passed...as usual. Taba cursed under his breath before getting up with a stretch. It was frustrating: his blessing couldn't seem to read the voice that echoed in his head, implying it wasn't a person. Still, the irregularity made it impossible to just be random schizophrenia or whatnot. Taba kicked a stone from the ground, spitting on the dirt as he did. Whatever, one thing at a time: he was better off fixing this soulscale issue first.

Taba glanced up at the setting sun with a frown. Time flew quickly, he should return back to his room. Right as he turned to head out of the park, he locked eyes with the familiar void of a fox mask, its wearer leaning on a massive paintbrush as a crutch.

He chewed his lip with a small nod. "Rare to see you outside of battle. Shouldn't you be passed out in a bed?"

Juliette, his mentor and supervisor, sighed as she took a small sip from her flask. "My thoughts, exactly. Sadly, I figured I should talk to you in regards to your friend," she said.

"Toukie? Oh, odd coincidence: he was asking for something to do in his cell to pass the time. Could you giv-"

"No, not the terrorist. I'm talking about Queenie. How's her mental state?"

Taba blinked, slightly surprised. Juliette took note of his brief pause. "Have you been slacking on your questioning? The old you would've known that I was approaching the park, not to mention the subject of what I planned to talk to you about."

She...wasn't wrong. The voice that boomed in his head was dissuading him from asking questions as normal. He rubbed his neck. "I'm sleepy, bite me. What about Queenie's mental state?" he asked with slight confusion.

The Dancing Painter leaned on her weapon with a sigh. "The girl has yet to look me in the eye...and it's been months. Didn't take her as someone who carried guilt," Juliette muttered.

It wasn't just towards Juliette, though. Queenie seemed to be much more hesitant towards Taba and Hush, her normally brash nature suddenly mellowed out by fighting from the backlines. At first, he thought it was a coincidence that she was sniping in all her fights...but Queenie was rarely seen using a dagger as of late.

"I'm not going to lie, she's...well, her confidence is a bit shot," he admitted. "Can't really blame her though, not after the whole Chimera scuffle."

Juliette nodded as she tied the flask to her hip. "Glad to see you still have situational awareness at least. Well, I'm certain you know about Hush accepting the whole soulscale mission from Babs, right?"

"Yeah. Why?"

Juliette nodded with a limp. "Well, unless Queenie comes to me alone and talks to me, I don't plan on helping the city out. That's all."

Taba opened his mouth...but he was a bit baffled. The injured woman, who was technically still their enemy and captor, refused to help in a mission that would only benefit Malapace. It was the most backwards threat he had heard that *actually* held some ground. He knew well that if Juliette denied the mission due to Queenie's incompetence, what was left of the female Misfit's pride would shatter.

Taba frowned. "You guys are all messed up here, you know that right?"

She shrugged. "I think I've quite earned the right to be a bit mean. Now go coax her into being annoying again, you Misfit."

With that, she limped out of the park as onlookers quickly moved out of the way with respectful bows. As he stared at her kimono, Taba couldn't help but wonder how such an immobile lady could waltz across the battlefield during wartime.

What a weird lady.

. . .

Taba quietly chewed his sun dried eggplant with a slight grimace. He was never a fan of the fruit, but beggars couldn't be choosers. Who was he to turn down food when the entire populace faced uncertainty for their next meals?

Across from him, the Overseer sipped her tea with calm fingers. A bit over a year ago, Taba, Queenie, and Hush had failed an assassination attempt on the Gatekeepers. Now, they were sharing dinner solely out of Malapace's goodwill. Despite the fact that they were supposed to be enemies...he oddly enjoyed his small meals with her. Babs tended to be exhausted after all of her "Overseeing" sessions, whereas Taba's brain always felt fuzzy as the day approached its end. One day, Babs had offered him a few steamed carrots on a plate, and from then on, the two had made it an unspoken habit to eat a light dinner with each other every other day.

Taba didn't want to think about the very real possibility that the Misfits would one day have to betray this kindness. It hurt him deeply. So, he buried that guilt by downing bitter tea.

After her cup of tea, Babs turned to face the tired boy. "Your mind looks busy. What's got you in a twist, brat?" she asked with an oddly considerate tone.

He dismissed her offhand comment with a sigh. "Doubt my plate is as big as yours: friend is facing imminent death, another friend is struggling with her own things, and I got some guy jumpscaring my thoughts on a random timer."

Babs cackled with a small snort as she stabbed a piece of wilted asparagus on her plate with a fork, lifting it to her mouth before scowling as it slipped off her utensil. "What lousy smithy crafted a fork that fails to properly stab?" She daintily picked up the asparagus with her fingers and chewed on the end before nodding to Taba. "I imagine it will work itself out. The problems of today become the memories of the future."

"Stop trying to sound so wise, that feels weird."

She smirked as she finished off her food. "Glad you think I sound wise, boy." After chewing silently for a bit, she nodded at him. "One thing at a time. How do you plan to help out...Toukie, was it? Toukie and Queenie. How do you plan to help the pair?"

Taba blinked. "How-"

"Boy, I have eyes across the entire city. It's half the reason why I'm always so damn tired."

"...Right. That's fair."

He leaned back on his hands as he stared at the wide ceiling. What to do, indeed. Protecting his friend from a lifetime of mutants was, well, impossible. Furthermore, Queenie's guilt seemed to be killing her confidence. Taba couldn't help but wonder if there was some magical answer to fixing both problems.

Babs stared at him with blind eyes, clearing her throat. "The soulscale could absolutely fix all your worries, by the way."

Taba continued to stare up into the white ceiling. "Incredible. The one thing that your city needs is also the solution to my unrelated problems. How convenient!"

The Overseer leaned into the table with both elbows. "Dead serious, boy. Think about it. Your terrorist friend only *recently* started attracting mutants since our current soulscale began to fizzle out. On the other hand, Queenie had her confidence shot because of her weakness causing Juliette's injury. The soulscale helps in both of those cases." She held up two fingers. "We can refresh the protection of the soulscale, since covering Toukie with soul would hide his presence from mutants while he's in the city. Plus, we have a means to use the soulscale to heal Juliette. The process isn't direct *healing*...but rather, injecting her with so much soul that it converts into healing. Your blessing should confirm that."

Taba stared at Babs and decided to go with her suggestion. *Would the soulscale hide Toukie from mutants?* **O** *Could the soulscale heal Juliette?* **O**

He sat up with slightly twitching eyes. This...could work. Still, a nagging part of him couldn't help but feel suspicion towards how perfectly everything clicked. The soulscale began to fizzle out, and *coincidentally*, two problems that were unrelated to each other would get fixed. His gut felt off, but he couldn't tell if that was because of a nagging instinct or the eggplant from earlier.

The Overseer shrugged. "I won't lie: it *is* odd how your problems get fixed with something that would benefit Malapace...but do you have a choice? The other alternative is that we kick your friend out of the city and watch as a good chunk of the place blows up with his departure. Believe it or not, I would rather not have my people blown up."

Taba sighed as he ruffled his hair. Toukie's blessing allowed him to embed his soul into objects, then expunge said soul to make the object blow up. Before he was apprehended, Toukie had turned a good chunk of the city into a ticking bomb. Should he die or be separated from the city without deactivating his blessing, the city walls would explode. His friend, though lovable as a goober, was an absolute impulsive idiot.

He closed his eyes and slowly exhaled. For now, Taba would have to go with it. "Fine. Looks like we both benefit from all this. I heard a bit from Queenie and Hush, but do you have any guidepost on where to start?" he asked.

"Maybe I do, maybe I don't. The first step is to get Juliette's approval, no? After all: I doubt the city would last long without her aid. Have her acknowledge Queenie, *then* we can talk about hypothetical starts. Whether or not Queenie has the guts to face her failures is up to her: nothing we outsiders can do about that." Babs then clapped her hands and stood up slowly, shuffling to her bed. "While Queenie works on that...go talk to Patchy in Alexandria's bar. Tell him to bring you along to his surveying under my orders."

. . .

"But I don't wanna," Patchy whined.

"Look, I'm not really the most thrilled about this, too. You technically still haven't apologized for trying to kill me during your fight with Nancy," said Taba.

"Well, I *knew* you'd be safe. Probably. It worked out in the end, right?"

"Whatever. Look, let's just...go. The sooner we do this, the better."

Patchy kicked a rock down the road with a grumble as he shuffled along the dirt road, Taba following closely behind. After a few silent minutes, Taba cleared his throat. "Hey, so..."

"Hm?"

"Why don't you, like, teleport? Wouldn't that be faster?"

Patchy frowned. "Technically...I guess I could? Well, it's *way* more complicated than that. So... let's just say I like walking. If you have any more questions, go ask your blessing."

Taba frowned. It wasn't like he *wasn't* trying to reverse-engineer Patchy's ability. However, the two rarely had time to interact within close proximity, and even when they *did*, Taba couldn't figure out anything in regards to Patchy's blessing. It wasn't teleportation, repulsion, illusionary, and so on. The only thing Taba was able to deduce was that Patchy's blessing *did* use soul, and that it was a very active blessing. So, the pair quietly strolled over to the neighboring village, Taba muttering questions with little success and Patchy yawning as he scratched his sides.

Upon reaching the shoddy village, Patchy gave nonchalant greetings with mock formality as Taba gave polite nods. The villagers gave their praises and slight complaints to the Gatekeeper. While it seemed as though Patchy was ignoring their concerns, Taba noticed how Patchy always turned his head towards those who voiced complaints and would actively propose solutions.

"Our rabbit ran off!"

"That's probably for the best," said Patchy. "You guys shouldn't be having pets while your village is starving."

"The roof of our house is caving in. Can you fix it?"

"Why...why would you lace the roof of a wooden house with stone?" Patchy frowned. "There's no foundation under the roof. Scrap the top, rebuild it with a foundation of pinewood coated with hay if you have to."

"The village well is dry. Could y-"

"There's a river half a mile to your village's left. Walk."

Patchy's stroll was slowed down by someone tugging the hems of his coat. He turned around with a frown, only to see a little boy grasping the leather jacket with thin hands. Patchy sighed as he crouched down to make eye contact with the child. "What do you want, kid?"

"Grandpap's cough is getting worse. Can you...?'

The voices hushed down around him. After a few seconds of tight lips, Patchy sighed. "Where does he live, little man?"

The small child dragged him to the house furthest from the village center, leading Patchy and Taba to a rundown shack that couldn't have been big enough to hold more than a single bed. Patchy turned to the little boy with a nod. "Wait here, ok?"

The little boy sniffled with a nod. Patchy opened the door and squeezed in. Before the Gatekeeper's body could block the sight of the crumbled shed's interior, Taba caught a glimpse of a spotted old man, visibly stifling a cough as he noticed the visitor. Taba turned to the child with a small smile. "Can you go to the village center? I think Mr. Gatekeeper would *love* a small flower as a souvenir."

The toddler waddled off as Taba stood against the door in silence. The shelter did nothing to muffle the conversation...and he was certain that sending off the child was the correct move.

"Give it to me straight, good Gatekeeper. I'm dying, right?"

"I...I don't have enough medical knowledge. I wouldn't kn-"

Raggedy coughs cut off Patchy's words, before the sound of a loogie hitting the floor resonated out. *"Please. In your line of work, I'm sure you've seen tons of death. You know what a dying man looks like."*

Silence. After a few muffled coughs, Patchy softly sighed. *"Yeah, To be honest, you're a walking miracle. Surprised you haven't died, like, last week."*

A small cackle rang out before it erupted into a violent coughing fit. After a little bit, the coughs turned...watery. *"Well. Looks like I jinxed it,"* said Patchy.

"Oh, I would love to crack a laugh at that...but I fear my body would crumble if I did. Listen...I have a favor to ask of you. Could you-"

Taba stepped away from the shelter. A dying man's request wasn't one to be shared. Better to keep the little boy away for the time being. As he stepped into the town center, he scanned the area to look for the child. Maybe he could play with him.

Taba shortly noticed the little boy talking to another man in a suit. The man's finely dressed attire stood out tremendously from the other villagers, so much to the point that Taba was astonished that he had missed the man. As the man ruffled the child's hair, the well-suited man looked up and locked eyes with Taba. Taba took slow steps towards the familiar visitor with cautious steps, a bit stunned at this unexpected encounter.

"...Geralt?"

"Hey, sport. You're still alive...somehow." Geralt took off his shades to reveal his mismatched pupils, his scarred eye staring blindly into Taba. "Slightly surprised you're here, what are the odds?"

Did Babs know Geralt was here? **O**

Taba sighed. "No, this wasn't a coincidence. The Overseer knew you were here, I think she wanted us to talk," he said. "Why are *you* here? This village is a bit aways from the base."

"Well, it's nearly time for the next soulscale, and I think it would really help Father t-"

"Wait, the soulscale? You *know* about it?" asked Taba.

59

Geralt frowned. "Well, yeah? Last time it appeared, Father didn't wish to contest it against the Gatekeepers. I figured that since they were all cooped up in the city this year, it would be much more free to take." he said.

"Do you have any hints? The city is kinda looking for it too."

"Whoa, kiddo. As much as I love you, can't have you be giving Malapace extra fortification. Sorry." He squinted his eyes. "On a similar note...why even side with the city? If you wanted, I could probably take you back right now."

"No, that'd be dumb," said Taba. "If I vanish, the city will just tighten up their hold on Queenie and Hush...and the Family would probably be in a worse-off position. Plus, one of the Gatekeepers is in the village right now. I don't thi-"

"What, you don't think I can take him?" Geralt asked with a slight frown.

"No...it's more like you don't really have a way of *forcing* him to fight. If he senses risk, he's just going to flee to warn the city. I don't think securing me again is worth that position."

The crunch of dirt crept up behind the two. "He's right, you know. I'm a coward."

The pair whipped around to lock eyes with Patchy, one pinky digging into his ear as he yawned loudly. The scraggly Gatekeeper opened his droopy eyes to reveal a faint glow. "Like...I *really* don't wanna fight. Can we just share a cup of tea and giggle together?" he asked.

Geralt scratched his slight stubble, genuinely seeming to consider the idea. To Taba's slight surprise, Geralt nodded as he gestured to a crummy log that had been split in two to form a makeshift bench. "Sure. Don't have tea, but I'm ok with talking." he said.

"I...uh...huh. Eh, sure. Why not."

The two powerful men walked over to take their seats. Patchy flopped down onto the log while Geralt dusted off his seat before sitting with folded hands. The two representatives quietly sat down, a bit unsure of what to really say or do. Patchy decided to break the silence with a small cough. "So...you're one of the big shots of Taba's Family, right?" he asked. "What brings you to this dinky lil' village?"

Geralt opened his mouth to respond before Patchy held up his hand to cut him off. "Wait. Before you answer...we're *technically* still at war, right? Why even hold a tealess teatime with me?" he asked.

The air tightened around the bench as Taba sharply inhaled, anticipating the worst. Geralt raised his hand into his jacket, instinctively putting Patchy on edge.

Geralt withdrew his hand to reveal a paper container. He unfurled it to pull out a hand-rolled cigarette, quietly lighting it with a lighter as he deeply inhaled, sighing smoke into the sky. After the drag, he nodded to the wary Gatekeeper. "Yes, we're at war...but there's always time and hope for civility, no? Oddly enough...the war is partially why I'm scouting the village." Geralt tapped out a few ashes before taking another drag. "Whew. Also...it feels narcissistic to call myself a 'big shot'...but I guess Father *does* trust me a smidge more than others. Anything else?" he asked

"Hm. I can kinda respect the balls to, well, *admit* you're planning for war. You should be lucky G isn't here: hell, if he heard this...he would've probably punched you."

"Mhm. And the reason you aren't punching me is because...?"

61

Patchy shrugged. "I would obviously lose if we were to fight. I'd say I'm the weakest of the Gatekeepers. Against someone like you-"

"...you'd hold your own. Cripes, you don't need to downplay your strength: just sitting this close to you is making me nervous." muttered Geralt as he inhaled some more tobacco.

Patchy blinked, a bit taken back by the reaction. "I gotta say...you're one of the few ones to get nervous from me. That feels weird. Ick." He cleared his throat. "Anyhow, I overheard a *wee* bit of your conversation with..." he jutted his thumb to the silent Taba. "Would *love* to get the coordinates for the next Limbo. You have any clue of it?" he asked.

This was the first time Taba had heard of the term Limbo. He guessed it was related to the soulscale. "Oh? Do you mean to tell me you found two soulscales by *chance*?" said a slightly astonished Geralt.

"Only the second one. The first time? Well, the Overseer won't tell us how she got it."

Geralt's arm froze just as he was about to take another drag. "So...the Overseer is female," he said. "Guess Father was right."

Patchy winced at the slip of his tongue. "Ah. Crap. Please forget you heard that."

"No. Now...it looks like we each have information that the other side doesn't. How about a little deal? We each tell each other the honest truth of what we know, and whoever gets the soulscale first, keeps it. That sound fair?" offered Geralt.

"Well, the thing is...how can I trust you?"

Geralt grinned widely as he nodded to Taba. "The boy will be a mediator. If either one of us lies, he is to announce it. Fair?" the dapper man proposed.

Patchy scowled. "No, *not* fair. The kid is on *your* side. He's just going to lie," the Gatekeeper said.

"No...he wouldn't. We raised him better than that. Plus...there's no way you *don't* trust the boy after all this time...especially after the most recent Malapace attacks, no?"

Patchy crossed his legs and balanced on the log-bench as he stared at his dusty feet. After a few seconds of silence, he sighed and looked at Taba. "Kid, I don't like you. I think we both know this."

"Thanks, Patchy." muttered Taba.

"You're welcome. That being said...can I trust you to be an honest moderator?"

Taba clenched his fists in frustration. Though he was normally fine with sitting on the sidelines...this situation just rubbed him the wrong way. Ignoring the itch, the Misfit sighed as he nodded slightly. "Yeah. I'll be impartial." he said.

Geralt clapped with a smile. "Wonderous. On that note, I'll start with what I know. Limbo is activated by having someone's blood drain into a river during the reflection of a full moon." He nodded to Taba. "Can you back me up, kiddo?"

Was Geralt's statement true? **X**

The blood slightly drained from Taba's fingers. Was this a test? What did Geralt want from him? Did he want Taba to lie as well? However he stared into the strong, trusting, gaze of his former mentor...he found all thoughts of deception fading away. "No. That's a lie, Geralt. You know that," said Taba.

Patchy raised his eyebrows as he glanced at Taba. Meanwhile, Geralt roared with pride as he wrapped Taba's torso in a one-armed hug, the other arm holding a smoking cigarette. After a tight hug, Geralt turned to Patchy with a nod. "And there you go. Proof that the kiddo won't lie. I'm so damn proud of him." he said with a grin.

"Well then," frowned Patchy. "Glad to know that an answer I didn't know was false was false. Doesn't really do much for me, since I can't exactly fact check anyone here but...care for some honesty?"

"Yeah. Well, Limbo is directly correlated to the soul that's naturally dispersed when anything dies. The soul is then ebbed from 'this' dimension into the 'other' dimension," said Geralt. "After a certain threshold of soul seeps back into its 'normal' state...Limbo appears. You can calculate where it appears and *how* it appears based on when and where you choose to dissipate the soul."

Was Geralt being truthful? **O**

Taba nodded to Patchy. "He was being honest. I swear." he said.

Patchy chewed his lip as he contemplated whether or not to trust these words. "That's the extent of our knowledge," said Geralt. "We only know the conditions of summoning Limbo. We don't know much about Limbo's terrain, the soulscale, or how to transport it. I hope you can help me out on those subjects." said Geralt.

The scraggily Gatekeeper sat with crunched legs, furiously scritching at his head as dandruff snowed onto the floor. Geralt frowned at the grimy display yet said nothing. After a few seconds, Patchy sighed as he wiped his hand on his jacket. "Ah...cripes. Whatever. Not like you guys have a way to actually transport the thing," muttered Patchy. "Fine. Limbo is fairly close to a mountain that changes its landscape when you aren't looking at it. If you're able to navigate to the peak of the mountain, ...some...*thing* just kinda appears and hands the soulscale to whoever can take it. If you aren't prepared, you'll *never* be able to take it from the being." he said.

"What do you mean?" asked Geralt, slightly puffing his tobacco.

Patchy shrugged. "I genuinely don't know. I wasn't the one who took the soulscale: that was G. When he reappeared, it was my job to move it to Malapace. I never bothered asking for further details." he said.

Geralt stepped on his fizzled cigarette with a frown. After ensuring his smoke was completely out, he looked up at the Gatekeeper with a frown. "Hm. That's the bald one, right? Why couldn't he transport it?" he asked.

"Simple. G is strong...but strong enough to carry the concept of a folding infinity? That's not his forte. So...transporting it with my blessing was my job, due to the process of elimination." said Patchy.

"So it's impossible to transport it without a blessing?"

"Well...it might be. I don't recommend touching the soulscale in full force, though: you'd probably go drunk with power. Oh, also: there's a time limit. There isn't really a way to track the time, so you gotta just climb as fast as possible. If you're stuck in Limbo when it closes, then..."

It was odd. After the first confirmations, the two men stopped asking Taba if the other party was being honest or deceitful. Seeing them bounce off each other's statements was...unnaturally comfortable. It was so seamless, as though they were coworkers, or even *friends*, who were simply speaking to each other. To an outsider, it would've been unfathomable to consider these men enemies on opposite sides of a war.

Geralt kicked some dirt over his cigarette butt with a nod. "Thanks for the info. As a show of respect, I'll give more info in regards to 'summoning' Limbo." he said. Geralt glanced around before slightly leaning in, the smell of tobacco still on his breath. "So...Limbo can't really 'appear' off of nothing. No, the best way to describe it is to say...Limbo uses structures or landmarks that exist in our dimension as a rough skeleton to form around. Even when it *does* appear, those without a strong resonance with their soul won't be able to interact, hell, they won't even be able to *see* Limbo."

"I know this," Patchy said with a frown. "I saw G climb Limbo before. I know how it looks from the outsider's perspective. To them...you just *vanish*, right?"

"Correct...but you're missing my point. Limbo is summoned by *building* around something."

"You're losing me," whined Patchy. "Dumb it down for me?"

Geralt sighed. "Fine. Let's put it like this. Do mutants have soul? Yes or no?" he asked.

"Well...yeah. That's how their traits are enhanced."

"Correct. So...what happens to that soul when the mutant is killed?"

Patchy stayed silent, his calm eyes betrayed by the twitch in his nose. Geralt continued his explanation. "Good. You get it. Now...let me reemphasize. Limbo is summoned by *building* around something. Where did Limbo appear last time?" he asked.

"...the ocean. There was a tsunami that year full of various fish mutants. Babs dispatched us...and Limbo appeared on the sixth day."

"You starting to see the picture?"

Patchy rubbed his face with slightly shaking fingers. "Crap. Crap. Crap. *Crappp.*"

"I'm...sorry?" said Taba. "I'm a bit lost. What's happening?"

Geralt looked up at him, a bit of confusion on his face. "The questioner is lost on a subject? I always thought you to be the smartest guy in the room. You getting rusty?" he asked.

"My questioning has been a bit...weird as of late. Sue me."

Patchy looked up to Taba, stress behind his usually laidback eyes. He immediately jumped up with glowing eyes and grabbed him. "We're heading back to Malapace, kid. *Now.*" said Patchy through gritted teeth.

Before he could voice a protest, Taba and Patchy suddenly began blinking through the landscape until they appeared in the Overseer's chambers. Babs calmly looked up at the two with concerned eyes. "Patchy, relax," she said to the wheezing Gatekeeper. "No need to push yourself."

Patchy caught his breath, obviously winded from overusing his blessing. Once a few minutes passed, he looked up with a furrowed brow. "*Relax?* Babs. You were eavesdropping that conversation, right? How could you be so calm about this?" he asked.

"I'm sorry," said Taba with a slightly loud voice. "Can *anyone* explain the sudden random urgency?"

"Taba. The soul of mutants dissipates into the other dimension with their death," Babs said calmly. "What has been happening to Malapace as of late?"

His mind raced slightly as the dots slowly clicked into place. Limbo's summoning conditions. Malapace's constant siege. Patchy's sudden stress. Geralt's surveying of the villages surrounding the city.

Taba suddenly looked up as everything connected. "No... Do you mean-"

"Limbo's next appearance will be around Malapace," Patchy said through huffed breaths. "With each passing day, the odds of Limbo building around the city grows. If Limbo appears while we're unprepared, the entire city will be wiped out."

CHAPTER 4

Queenie sat in the park, simply holding a dagger as she stared at its handle. She hadn't used a melee weapon in a while. It had gotten to the point where even the tape rubbing on her palm felt weird. She swished her wrist around a few times to try and get a feel for the weight of the weapon once more before her heart froze as the numerous eyes of the chimera flickered in her mind. She swore, flinging the blade towards a nearby tree stump as she took shallow breaths, trying to remove the image from her mind.

A few months ago, the Misfits were sent out to dispatch the chimera...a mutated failure of a project that was once someone from their Family. Whenever Queenie tried to swing a weapon, the mental flashes of eyeballs that darted towards her just made Queenie...*freeze*. That wasn't even mentioning what had happened to Juliette when she dove in front of-

Queenie pulled out a pistol and shot it into the air, the crack of the bullet slamming into her ears as it fizzled into the sky. She slowly exhaled as she put her gun away, turning to walk back to her room. As she turned around, she locked eyes with her brother...simply standing there, staring.

"How long were you there for?" she asked.

"Enough to see you miss a stationary target," he replied, nodding to a dagger that lay embedded into the floor next to the tree stump. He walked over and picked up the blade, tossing it to his sister in an underhanded throw. "You're getting rusty."

She snatched the dagger out of the air without making eye contact. "Shut up," she muttered as she rubbed her elbows.

Hush knelt down next to the tree stump and nodded to his sister, who stared at him with an odd frown. "Arm wrestle me," he said.

"Why?"

"Humor me."

She rolled her eyes as she knelt as well, propping her arm on the tree stump. This was pointless. They both knew that Hush was far more stronger than she was. Still, she listened to his request as she clasped hands, straining to push his arm down with beaded sweat dripping down her temple. After a few seconds, Hush slowly pushed his arm down gently, but firmly, making Queenie's hand tap the tree trunk. She let go with a mutter, rubbing her hand while rubbing her head with her shoulder. "Cool, you're stronger than me. Is your ego inflated enough?" she asked.

"Not yet. Give me a gun." said Hush.

Queenie wrinkled her brow as she pulled out a small pistol to hand over. He gently took the gun before nodding to another tree in the park. "You see those big flowers?"

"The red ones? They're kinda ugly."

"Well...not really what I'm getting at. You think you can hit those?"

Queenie rolled her eyes before pulling out another pistol from her storage. She exhaled slightly as she took aim before firing two times. The first shot nipped the flower from the tree as the second one made it explode in a red puff as she sniped it midair. Hush gave a low whistle as he gave his best shot as well. However, after five bullets...he failed to even hit the tree trunk.

"You're ass at this." she said with the slightest of grins.

"I guess I am," Hush said with a shrug. "Despite that...you still lost that arm wrestling contest."

"Duh. you're way stronger than me...physically, anyways."

"Oh...so you *do* get it."

Queenie frowned as she turned to face her brother. "Huh?"

Hush placed his gun on the tree stump. "We all have our strengths and weaknesses. Even *with* my eyesight being enhanced...I'm nowhere near as good as you in terms of shooting. Hell, I imagine in terms of actual hand-to-hand combat, you would beat me," he said. "Doesn't matter if I'm stronger than you if I can't actually catch you, right?"

"I guess...? I don't really get wha-"

"So...why beat yourself up over Juliette?" he asked.

She flinched, her mouth drying up as the pistol in her handle fumbled out onto the tree trunk. Hush noticed her surprise and quickly caught it before the weapon landed. "Careful, this thing is still loaded," he said.

"What...what does individual strengths have to do with what happened to Juliette? I failed. If I were str-"

"No. You did your best and so did she. Juliette only protected you because she wanted to, not because she was forced too. You know that."

She blinked back wet eyes as she stared into the dirt. "If...if I were faster...I could have dodged-"

"But you weren't. Sure, your exhaustion might've been the reason she had to take a protection hit for you...but without you, we wouldn't have even been able to *get* to Linda," said Hush. "No one is blaming you for Juliette...and even if they *were*, would beating yourself up for months really help anyone?" He ruffled her hair as she stared at the floor with watery vision. "We got permission to get the soulscale. All that's left is to get Juliette's approval before we head out," said Hush.

Queenie stared at her brother with humiliated, yet infuriated, intensity. Did he truly expect her to ask for forgiveness from an enemy she had permanently scarred? As she opened her mouth to speak her complaints, her voice failed to escape her lips. She blinked before scowling harshly, flipping her brother the bird. Hush smiled as he removed his hand from her head, putting it in his jacket pocket. "Relax. Doesn't need to be today. Let's go grab dinner at Alexandria's bar later, then slowly work our way up to talking to Juliette. Cool?" asked Hush.

She waved him off with a mute grumble, stomping away from the park. Whatever...guess she was having dinner with Hush tonight.

. . .

Juliette sipped from her flask with a casual nod. "Hey."

Queenie froze in the bar's entrance, instinctively darting her eyes downwards to avoid eye contact. Why was Juliette here? Where was Hush? What? Should she run away? Hell, *could* she allow herself to run? While questions continued to flurry around her mind, she felt a gentle push on her back, causing her to stumble into the bar. She turned around to meet eyes with her brother, staring at her with gentle, yet firm, eyes.

72

Intentions be damned, it felt as though she had just been back-stabbed with a frozen, rusty dagger. Queenie wasn't sure if she could portray her level of raw disgust, rage, fear, and disappointment with a single phrase or glance. So, she simply stared at the floor, unsure of where to direct her emotions. While she stared at the slightly sticky bar floor, she flinched at the sound of a bar stool being pushed out, with slow and clunky steps approaching her location. Sweat beaded across her neck and forehead, slowly dripping across her clammy cheeks. She was torn between trying to crawl into a smaller ball, or staying still and praying she wasn't being approached.

The uneven steps stopped a few feet before Queenie's head. The bar was pin-drop silent as the Drunken Fox hissed with slight pain as she knelt down to Queenie's location. Once her knees touched the floor, Juliette cleared her throat.

"Still disappointing, I see."

Queenie bit her lip as her head lowered further, not bothering to respond. After a few seconds of silence, Juliette sighed. Because Queenie wasn't looking up, she was completely caught off-guard as the handle of Juliette's weapon slammed into the side of Queenie's head, causing her to tumble to the floor with clunky rigidness. A small welt slowly formed on her head as she looked up with a wince.

"Good," said Juliette. "You're finally looking at me in the eyes."

A mix of anger and shame flipped in Queenie's eyes as she turned away. "Are you done? If you're just here to get revenge, just get it over with," she muttered.

"Revenge? Revenge for *what*, exactly?"

"Stop mocking me."

Juliette sighed as she turned to Hush with a slight nod. He nodded and quietly stepped out of the bar, with the bartender coughing into his hand and stepping into the kitchen. Once it was just the two girls, Juliette slipped off her kimono to reveal a sarashi. She turned around to reveal her back, though heavily scarred, was fully healed. She nodded to Queenie. "Touch my back," she commanded.

Queenie hesitated but laid her hand on her mentor's spine, feeling calloused skin. "Do you feel any wounds?" asked Juliette.

"Well...barring the...the scars...not really, I guess."

"Mhm. Do you know why I have a limp? Why I'm still 'recovering'?"

Queenie blinked, a bit taken back by the question. She had always blamed herself for Juliette's wound that she hadn't bothered to even question if Juliette was still wounded. After all, she had always walked around with a limp. However...if the limp wasn't caused by the injury...

"Alright, you Misfit. How much do you know about ascension?" asked Juliette.

"It's...something Taba said he was looking into," Queenie replied. "Nothing much that I know or care about."

"Good. Let's keep it that way. Nothing good comes out of learning how to ascend," said Juliette. "All you need to know is that it requires an insane amount of soul to use. Typically, with a few exceptions, a person can't ascend multiple times in short succession. If you do...it's the equivalent of trying to lift a boulder after running fifty miles. Your body will just...collapse onto itself. Your soul will implode, your body will lose its bedrock, and your brain shuts down in an effort to preserve energy. In short, overusing ascension is akin to self destruction." Juliette lifted an arm, turning it every way she could. Though clear muscle definition could be seen through her porcelain skin, she winced with even the slightest movement. "Me, being a hypocritical fool, tried to ascend twice in a row to kill your Father. It was a foolish decision, but a decision I would make again and again, if presented the choice." she said.

Queenie frowned. Taba had told her that Juliette and Father fought...but he said nothing about ascension. Well, of course he hadn't: he still didn't *know* what ascension was. Juliette slipped her kimono on once more, tying it on firmly as she continued to speak. "The injury I received from protecting you? Horrendous. Even with G's help...it took a while for me to fully recover from that ailment. The problem is that I overexerted my soul in that fight...and *that* is on me. My body is essentially trying to work at normal capacity with a much more fragile structure," said Juliette. The Drunken Fox finished fitting her clothes and nodded to Queenie with a monotone gaze. "You aren't impactful enough to permanently impede me. Stop trying to take credit for my own faults, numbskull."

"...but if I were faster-"

"Misfit. Stop throwing yourself a pity party and *think*. My end goals are *not* your end goals. Though we are circumstantially together now, there may be a day where our arms are drawn against each other. If you were faster, and I *didn't* get injured? I would be more healthy in fighting your Father. Would you have forgiven yourself if I had killed him? Furthermore, without you, we wouldn't have even been *able* to approach the chimera," said Juliette. "Seriously, *that* is why I find you to be such a massive disappointment. If it's your fault, do what you can to atone and fix your mistake. If it *isn't* your fault, hold your head up high." Juliette stood up with a wince and extended a hand. "Stop thinking of hypotheticals and work with what you got. That's the best you can do."

"I still feel bad, though," muttered Queenie subconsciously as she grabbed Juliette's hand to pull herself up.

Juliette pulled Queenie to her feet and rested an arm on a nearby table, sighing in slight relief. "That's fine. Feeling miserable at the suffering of another is empathy. That isn't a bad trait to have," said Juliette. "What *is* bad is refusing to act on that emotion. If you feel responsible, then *do* something to fix it, even if it's only a tiny step in the right direction. Until then, I'm willing to be patient with you. Ok?"

"...I hate your guts, you know that right?"

"Mhm."

"Cool, cool. Glad we're on the same page."

Queenie took stiff steps towards a booth to slide in, clenching her jaw as she forced herself to make eye contact with her mentor. "Let's eat, then. We can talk about how to fix this stupid mistake over some chicken," she said.

Juliette softly smiled as she limped over to the booth to sit across from her. "Welcome back, you Misfit."

A gentle knock rang from the front door of the bar. Juliette turned to the noise with a soft cough. "We're decent, you can come in," she said.

Hush opened the door and peeked in with a cautious glance before fully stepping inside. "So...we good?" he asked.

"Well, she's-"

Queenie ran over and socked her brother in the pit of his gut, causing him to double over with a wince. She might've been much more physically weaker than her brother...but even he had to hunch with a wheeze. She glared at him with a flurry of emotions. "You...are an *asshole.*"

"...yeah," he said between wheezes. "Fair enough."

"Whatever happened to taking our time with...all *this*?"

Hush looked up with a pained grin. "That isn't your style. We both know that," he said. "You would much rather rip the band-aid off in these kinds of scenarios, right?"

"Shut up." she said with flushed ears. After a few seconds, she quickly threw her arms around his hunched body with a tight squeeze. "You *suck*...Thanks, though."

"If you were...really thankful...you wouldn't have punched me." The barkeep, Hutch, coughed as he stepped out from the kitchen. "Sorry, Hush," he said. "Sometimes you gotta get punched...even if you don't deserve it."

"*Not* helping."

"Let's talk over food, you Misfits. Hutch...get us...ah, some jerky and booze. Thanks."

. . .

After dinner, Queenie and Hush quietly walked back to their dorms with crickets softly chirping into the cool night sky. The meal had been mostly silent, with everyone either eating food or sipping spirits. Once everyone had eaten, Juliette had placed some coin on the table and stayed behind as the siblings left the bar with full tummies. Queenie stared up at the stars with a busy mind. She wanted to work towards rectifying her mistake with Juliette...but she still had a long way to go. Hell, she couldn't even properly swing a blade without flinching. Every time she did...the image of the chimera just popped in her head. Her hand *still* tingled from the poison whenever she swung any weapon. Most likely, it was all in her head...but it was a memory that continued to haunt her.

She frowned and suddenly slapped her cheeks, causing her brother to flinch. That was a good first step to work on, Queenie thought as she turned to him with a determined stare. "Hey, you have any plans tonight?" she asked.

"Maybe, maybe not. What's up?"

She nodded to the park. "Spar with me. I need to get jitters out."

He raised an eyebrow. "Hm. Sure, why not?" he replied.

They walked over to the park and each took a respective stance in preparation for combat. Queenie firmly planted her feet on the wet grass and took a shaky breath, unstoring a familiar dagger. As she held the worn handle, imaginary eyes darted in her mind, causing her to go clammy with slight sweat. With trembling fingers, she flexed her forearm and stared at her brother with a wavering gaze. Hush, in turn, took a slight step back with his hands in his jacket pockets.

Queenie immediately jumped forwards...and stumbled as an imaginary screech echoed in her mind, causing her hand to tremble so harshly that her weapon fumbled out of her hand. She cursed loudly as she scooped her weapon off the floor and continued to run with strained resolve. Hush narrowed his eyes as he focused on the incoming threat. She lifted her arm and swung downwards, forcing her arm to strike with an unusual amount of effort. Her brother easily side-stepped the telegraphed attack as Queenie took sharp inhales, trying to steady her mind from her haunted memories. Hush took note of this, and said nothing, simply lunging forward and grabbing his sister's arm. With a single twist and pull, he flung his sister over his back and Queenie was thrown onto the floor with a solid *thud*.

She groaned as her hand's muscles strained to hold onto her dagger, forcing herself to not let go. Hush took a step back and observed in silence. After a few seconds, she stumbled onto her feet with deep breaths, pointing her blade to her brother once more.

"The Queenie I knew wouldn't have even been caught by me. Hell, she would've blocked my strike with chains, then counterattacked with a kick to the gut," said Hush.

"Shut it," she snapped. "I'm gonna stab you now, so you just stay there."

He smiled. "Go for it. I would love to see you try."

She roared and stepped forward yet again, determined to triumph over her failures. She would stumble for as long as it was required to eventually be confident in her blade once again.

Queenie would not fail the others again.

. . .

Once the siblings left the bar, Juliette took a sharp breath as she hunched over in her seat, pins and tingles slamming into her skull harshly. Hutch took notice and sighed, bringing over another bottle of alcohol. She took it with sincere gratitude, slamming the drink down to null her pain.

"You're doing too much, Juliette. You need to be resting," he said with a sigh.

"The Overseer herself asked me to help rebuild Queenie's confidence. I can't really say no to that, can I?" said Juliette.

"You could. You've done enough. Hell, you *continue* to do enough. If you keep moving around and using your soul…"

She waved him off as she finished off her bottle with a hiss. After pushing the empty bottle away, she rested her entire upper body on the table with a wince. Every movement felt like she was being stabbed. Every step felt as though her muscles were about to collapse. That wasn't even getting into how it felt whenever she tried to use her blessing. With each passing day, Juliette felt as though she was one day away from not waking up…but if she didn't act, who would?

Hutch walked to the front of the bar and flipped the sign from "open" to "closed". He turned to her with a disapproving frown. "You know, my wife doesn't like seeing you drink like this. She keeps asking me to cut you off," he said.

"It dulls the pain, Hutch. You know that."

"I know. That's why I'm still serving you. You're lucky." He blew out the candles hanging from the walls and reached under the bar counter to pull out a fuzzy blanket, placing it next to Juliette's head. "Sleep. The wife wouldn't like it even more if I kicked you out while you're like this."

She yawned silently, not even bothering to take off her mask. "…thank you, Hutch."

"Mhm."

As she nestled into her arms…she could imagine Gureke's disapproving stare. She imagined he would scold her again, saying she was pushing herself too harshly…that she should be more selfish with her time and efforts. Maybe he was right. Still…it was that same mentality that had resulted in his-

She tightened her lips. Never again. She didn't deserve rest. She would spend the rest of her life atoning, if it was the last damn thing she did.

. . .

Queenie opened groggy eyes from the stiff bed, exhaustion hitting her like a sledgehammer. The two of them had sparred all night, only stopping when they noticed the night sky turning a bit brighter. After a few hours, Queenie had forced herself to do simple thrusts and slashes with mediocre success. It would probably be a while until she would be able to be in top shape, but it was a good start.

She freshened up in the bathroom and stepped out into the empty hallways. Normally, Hush would be outside to greet her...but he had probably exhausted himself yesterday. That was fair: he had listened to her requests without even a word of complaint and earned the rights sleep in today. She glanced outside and noticed a familiar boy taking a brisk jog around the town hall.

Queenie stepped outside with a wave. "Yo."

Taba slowed his steps with heavy breathing. "...Hey. You're up early." he said.

"Yeah. No idea why my body decided to roll out of bed, but may as well get a head start on the whole soulscale issue," she said. "Is Juliette discharged yet, or is she still in the hospital?"

"Actually...I saw her heading to the eastern walls a few minutes ago. Why? You wanna go talk to her?" he asked.

"Kinda," she said. Queenie shuffled her feet, a bit uncertain as to how to approach the topic of asking him to accompany her. She always struggled in asking others for help or for even the tiniest of favors.

Taba took notice and gave a small smile. "You wanna go together?" he asked. "I could use a break."

"...Yeah. Let's. Thanks."

The two of them casually strolled through the quiet city, not really exchanging much words. As they walked, Queenie pulled out a dagger and tried to slowly twirl it in her hands as she always did, trying to ignore the shutters that flicked in her mind as the numerous eyes stared her down.

The more they walked, however, the more the sounds of...screeching rang out. Slashes and pained cries wailed through the air, forcing Taba and Queenie to exchange glances. The two hurried over to the castle gates and exchanged nods with the city guards. Taba nodded outside with a furrowed brow. "Is she outside?" he asked. The men nodded, gripping their spears with slight worry. Queenie rolled her eyes and pushed past the men, glancing outside to witness Juliette's fight.

The Drunken Fox darted around the dirt field, striking the air with her paintbrush at seemingly random intervals as the mutant she fought flailed with stutters and wails. The mutant bird she fought was missing a wing, clearly being cut off from one of Juliette's attacks. The beast stumbled around with a massive beak, clumsily pecking at Juliette with relatively little success. She rolled through the air, gripped her brush with both arms, and slammed into the sky with malicious intent. The attack seemingly missed, causing the bird to cackle with joy as it dived towards the Dancing Painter, lunging with an outstretched jaw. Right as it was about to clamp down on Juliette's head, the mutant suddenly split into two, heartless beady eyes widening as it collapsed to the floor in two pieces. Juliette limped over to the beast, paintbrush in hand, raising her weapon to deliver the fatal blow. The mutant, in response, slowly opened its mouth to croak its deep, dying cry.

"Jules...why?"

Juliette flinched, her weapon instinctually lowering as her blue eyes widened from behind her mask. *"Why? Jules, why? Why, Jules? Still a calamity? This is why we DIED. JULIETTE. SLEEP WITH US,"* it screeched.

As her hands wavered, the bird darted its beak forward to snap at Juliette's leg. She flinched as her knees bent to leap out of the way, a small wince etched on her mouth as her legs suddenly buckled. Queenie suddenly blinked back into reality and summoned a chain around her mentor's waist, dragging Juliette backwards as the mutant's beak failed to snap her leg off, instead only chomping on her Achilles tendon. The Dancing Painter grit her teeth as blood spurted out from her ankle, the mutant tilting its head upwards to gulp down the woman's flesh. Before it could swallow, however, a hidden slash suddenly slammed into the bird's throat and decapitated the creature.

Juliette tumbled to the floor with heavy breaths, clutching her calf as she struggled to stand. Taba squeezed Queenie's shoulder. "The mutant is dead. Let's go," he said.

The Misfits darted over to lend their mentor a hand. Juliette, seemingly slightly surprised at their appearance, gratefully took the assistance. "Sorry you kids had to see me like this," she said, wincing as she hobbled over to the city. "I'm getting rusty." She turned to Queenie, nodding with respect. "Thank you for saving me."

Queenie tightened her lips. It didn't feel right to accept the praise, seeing as Juliette still got wounded. The Dancing Painter took note of her pursed lips and rolled her eyes in response. "Oh, were you responsible for my fight, too? Stop feeling needless guilt," said Juliette.

"Yeah, yeah, shut up," muttered Queenie. "Why are you even here? Shouldn't you be resting? Hell, wouldn't the guards be able to stall for this until the Gatekeepers got here? Why even-"

"I fought because I wanted to," said Juliette, a vein in her neck bulging as she spoke. "Plus, danger is danger: be it for a guard or a Gatekeeper. If my involvement can reduce casualties, I'm going to step in."

Queenie frowned and said nothing, silently lending her shoulder to her wounded mentor as they hobbled through the silent city. As they drew closer and closer towards Juliette's room, Queenie steeled her resolve. When they eventually reached the hospital, Queenie blurted out a simple question with rapid speech without eye-contact.

"*Do You Think You Could Let Us Help In Getting The Soulscale?*" asked Queenie, eyes fixated on the stone flooring, afraid of the looming rejection that hung in the air.

"Sure," said Juliette, not even batting an eye towards the girl.

Taba raised an eyebrow but said nothing. Queenie blinked and looked up at Juliette, surprise plastered on the girl's face. "Wait. Really? Just like that?" she asked.

"Of course. It's beneficial for the city if we get the soulscale anyhow, I see no reason to decline," replied Juliette. "I'll come pick you guys up when I'm recovered. Get ready in the meanwhile."

She limped back into her room with a casual wave to the two and gently closed her door.

CHAPTER 5

When Hush woke up, the sun had barely crept over the sky-line. He groaned: how did Taba do this *every* day? He rolled out bed with stiff joints, freshened up in the bathroom, then quietly stepped out into the dark hallway and into the still morning air. He made his way through Malapace until he eventually reached the eastern gate, where a spunky girl waited with two baskets hanging around her neck as she impatiently tapped her feet.

"You're late," said Alexandria, a mixture of annoyance and relief spread on her face.

"Yeah, well, sorry for not having the drive in me to wake up before sunrise," said Hush while stifling a yawn.

"Well, we need to wake up early to make sure we can gather stuff before the mutants attack," said Alexandria. "Thanks for tagging along, by the way."

Hush tightened his lips as he stuffed his hands deeper into his jacket pockets. Honestly? He hadn't planned on helping her out. Rather, he was put in an awkward spot after she had asked him in front of her parents...and he had found it to be *extremely* difficult to turn her down in front of Alexandria's starry-eyed mother and stern father.

"I...wasn't really given a choice," he admitted with a defeated sigh, shaking his head.

"I know," she said with a grin. "You're too good of a guy to turn me down in that situation. Thanks, anyway." She rolled her eyes upwards to 'point' at the goggles resting on her head. "Could you...?"

Hush walked over and gently lifted up the goggles and placed them over Alexandria's eyes. She gave a small wink in return with lightly flushed cheeks. "Cheers. Let's go foraging now, shall we?" she said.

The two of them exited the city while greeting the guards. From their nonchalant reactions, this wasn't the first time Alexandria had done this. As they walked down the road, Hush couldn't help but notice how her shoulders moved in a way that made it seem as though her non-existant arms were moving wildly with each stride.

After a few minutes, they reached deeper foliage and Alexandria rolled her neck to adjust the basket that dangled in front of her. She stomped her feet onto the floor and the dirt slowly crumbled up into swirled chunks, forming around her shoulder's nubs as they grew longer and longer until she had two dirt arms. Hush couldn't help but slightly admire the detail of each limb: it was as if he was looking at a normal arm with a dirt texture plastered on top of it. Hell, he could even see the creases in the joints and the manicured fingernails.

Alexandria knelt down and hummed softly as she slowly tugged up carrots and placed them in her basket. While her arms worked seemingly independently, she turned to Hush and glanced downwards at her neck. "Grab the other basket and get to picking those herbs by those roots." she said, one of her arms daintily pointing towards a nearly dead tree.

Hush scooped the basket up from her neck and got to harvesting. He wasn't really sure what kind of herb he was plucking: it was a funny little leaf with smoothed edges that flourished out into a rectangle. It wasn't anything he was familiar with, even during his time with the clan. After a few seconds, he glanced up with a frown. "What herb is this? I don't really recognize it," he asked.

"I tried looking it up, but couldn't find it. Either means the book with its info was destroyed, or this is a new sprout," she said over her shoulder. "Picked...well, 'picked' it up one day, chewed it because I was bored, and it made me feel less hungry...kinda like energy-less caffine without the urge to pee yourself. So, now we mix that in with our food to make customers more full with less food."

"That feels dishonest."

"Eh, all restaurants cut their corners: you know that. Trust me, this is *way* more honest than some of the practices other places use."

"You ever think of giving it a name? It could be a new species."

"Nah. Seems...dumb to name something when people are starving, y'know?"

"...fair enough."

"So on that note, let's call it...whilimf?"

Hush stifled a laugh. "That's...certainly a name."

Alexandria grinned, flush on her ears. "It makes it sound like a smart person named it, no? Whilimf. Whilimf. Eh, it'll grow on me," she smiled.

The two of them continued to quietly pick at their own piles. After a few minutes, Hush's ears perked up as the crunch of dry leaves stepped close next to him. He turned around to see Alexandria stooped down to pick at the herbs herself, a small hum tracing her lips as she worked.

"My bad," he said, standing up. "Did you need me to...?"

"Nah, stay," she said, eyes focused on the floor. "We can get our work done faster if we stick together here."

Hush stared at her for a moment, noticing the slightest tinge of red on her ears. He shrugged and knelt on the dirt to begin digging once more. If it helped her out, he had no reason to decline.

The silent morning passed as the sunlight slowly peaked through the trees. Suddenly, Alexandria's voice called out from behind Hush. *"Come over here?"* it said.

He turned around with a slight frown, turning to the trees where the voice came from. A tingle in his fingers put him on edge: something felt...off. This was further emphasized when Alexandria herself turned around to stare at the treetops, her dirt fingers frozen in place.

"Now...Alexandria," said Hush, eyes fixated on the dense trees. "Did you...?"

"No. That wasn't me."

The pair silently got up and backed away slowly in the opposite direction of the voice. Suddenly, the two of them heard Queenie's sniffles from the branches. *"Hush...why?"* it sobbed.

"Count of three...we run. Ok?" said Hush.

"I mean...we could...*fight* it."

"Be real. *Not* the time for jokes."

Alexandria tilted her neck slightly towards him, a hint of a smile traced on the action. "Hey. You're strong. I can hold my own. I don't see a reason wh-"

Suddenly a mutant bird exploded from the treetops, its slender beak opened up in a screech as it chomped down on one of Alexandria's arms. The dirt crumbled away into the floor as she cursed, stomping her feet once more to draw stone and dead roots from the floor to wrap around her remaining arm. While the colorful mutant spat out the clod of dirt from its mouth, Alexandria reeled her entire body back as she threw her entire weight into a singular punch, crashing her weaponized arm into the mutant's head. The impact threw the bird back into a tree, its feathers shining a near metallic glint as it seemingly shrugged off the powerful blow.

"Oh. I...hm," said Alexandria. "I didn't think it would survi-"

Her words were cut off short as she yelped, Hush tackling her into the floor as the mutant dove once more with conviction, its beak snapping at where Alexandria once stood. When it missed, the bird unfurled its sturdy wings and flung itself into the sky, the outline of the creature hidden in the backdrop of the sunrise.

Hush scrambled to his feet and dragged a stunned Alexandria up. "Get *up*. We're running," he said.

"Yeah. I'm ok with that now."

As the two fled, the mutant flew closer and closer. Suddenly, a deeper voice rang from the mutant. "*Failure. Mistake. Disappointment.*" it boomed.

Alexandria flinched, her legs stumbling slightly as cold sweat suddenly beaded from her brow. Hush held her up while he gritted his teeth. The damned thing was imitating Alexandria's father, prodding at her insecurities. He flexed his fingers, using his blessing to nullify her hearing. She suddenly flung her fearful eyes towards Hush, confused and frightened at the sudden change of atmosphere. He nodded to her with a firm look, squeezing her shoulders with a clear message in his gaze. *"Keep running. Trust me."*

She swallowed and forced her feet forward, clearly shaken but determined to flee. After a minute of sprinting and dodging the mutant's telegraphed dodges, the guards of Malapace noticed their retreat and quickly opened the city gates, waving their arms to gesture the two inside.

Hush pushed Alexandria in the city as he nodded to the guards. "Get the Gatekeepers. I'll hold the line," he said.

The guards hesitated for a split second, but understanding that even the slightest indecision could be fatal, they nodded and slammed the city doors shut. He gave the worried Alexandria a reassuring nod just before the gate shut in his face. He exhaled softly as he stared down the mutant in front of him. Hush wasn't a combatant: he was at a *major* disadvantage. He had no chance of actually beating the mutant...but he *could* stall the beast out until reinforcements arrived.

The mutant simply tilted its head with a disturbing smile etched into its beak. *Could* the thing even smile? The bird opened its mouth, a more elegant, yet arrogant, voice quietly spoke from its hollow throat:

"I hate you. Disgusting."

Hush flinched, his muscles relaxing as his eyes widened. That voice. That wasn't Queenie's. That was...

His thoughts were interrupted as the bird tucked its wings in and suddenly lunged towards him like a spiral bullet. Hush slightly rolled through the air, using his hands to push off the mutant and roll across its course back, wincing slightly as the feathers cut into his flesh with each rigid roll. As expected, the beast's feathers were metallic-like, each one acting as a blade.

Hush flexed his fingers, eyes narrowed as the bird opened its mouth to imitate *her*...but reeled its head back in puzzlement as no voice rang out. Hush used the confusion to dart towards the mutant, focusing his soul into his fist as he slightly exhaled, trying to remember the sensation of his soul manipulation training, throwing his weight into the punch. The mutant stumbled back slightly, taking some damage, but not enough to truly hinder it in any way. On the other hand, Hush winced as he clutched his hand, a dull throbbing echoed in his hands. It felt as though he had punched a solid metal wall. For all he knew, he may have just done exactly that.

Hush flexed a few fingers and the bird suddenly flinched as its vision was robbed. It clicked its forked tongue around cautiously, tilting its head as it bounced its voice around. After a few simple clicks, the mutant suddenly flicked towards Hush with a twisted grin and darted forward with an open jaw. Hush sidestepped the jab, his mind racing as he planned his next move. Suddenly a sharp pain screamed from his leg as he collapsed to the floor, his leg losing more warmth by the second. He tumbled to the floor with a gasp and looked to his leg to see a nasty gash running through his calf. He tried turning his ankle slightly, but the low movement and the thrums of pain that boomed from his leg made it evident that he was effectively crippled for the remainder of the fight. Sweat dripped down his temple as he switched which fingers he flexed to nullify his pain, breathing a sigh of shaky relief as the agony vanished. Unfortunately, this meant the mutant regained its sight, and locked its beady eyes onto Hush.

The mutant quickly jumped up into the air with a mighty flap of its wings, then while its movement was partially obscured by the rising sun in the backdrop, it tucked into a bullet and dive bombed into

Hush. He forced all his weight into his remaining good leg and leapt towards the foliage nearby, using the shriveled shrubs to break line of sight. He cursed and looked down at his wound, trying to gauge the severity of his wound. The tear had grown even further with his last movement, and his body temperature was slowly going down. At this rate, he might actually die from the blood loss alone, let alone the mutant.

Right before the mutant went in for a fatal blow... a faint *whoosh* blew past the battlefield, and a familiar kimono flapped in front of him. The new combatant pulled out her paintbrush, gently twirling it across her arm and wrist. Her blue eyes peaked out from behind her fox mask, staring down the creature with slight curiosity and complete malicious intent.

Hush struggled to his knee with a strained breath. "You're late. Couldn't you have gotten here faster?" he rasped.

Juliette turned to him with a monotone expression. "I'm not in the best shape and it's the morning. I think you can afford to cut me some slack, no?" she said.

"Sure, whatever. Thanks for helping," he huffed, leaning against a nearby tree as he balanced his weight on his good foot.

Juliette took clear notice of his staggered movements. She turned to face the mutant, tracking its movements as she spoke to him. "How bad is the injury? Can you make it inside the gates?" she asked.

"I can get there. Issue is the bird...it's *kinda* in the way."

"That isn't a problem. Just keep running: I'll cover you."

Hush nodded slightly, inhaled sharply, then hobbled forward as quickly as he could. He used soul manipulation to alleviate some pressure on his wound, throwing himself as far as possible with each stride. The mutant slammed in front of him and unhinged its beak to snap into Hush's organs. However, it only succeeded in chomping onto the numerous sharpened steel bristles of Juliette's paintbrush. With a single strained exhale, she lifted the beast over her shoulder and flung the mutant *far* past Hush. When the creature stood up with a defiant scream, it was suddenly met by numerous pre-planted slashes raining down onto the mutant's wings, forcing it deeper into the ground. Using this, Hush scrambled to the gate where the two guards from earlier quickly opened the doors to let the wounded man in. Once safely inside, he flopped down onto the ground, barely being caught by soft...*moist* hands.

He looked up with tired hands and locked eyes with the tear-filled goggles of Alexandria. Her tender, dirt hands clenched tighter onto his frame. "You...are an *idiot*. An absolute *fool*. Do you think I would appreciate it if you died for me?" she snapped with a quivering voice.

Hush raised a hand to crack her goggles open a bit, allowing the accumulated tears to spill out freely onto the floor and his face. After ensuring her eyewear was empty, he chuckled...and promptly passed out.

· · ·

Juliette sipped from her gourd while Hush quietly sat with crossed arms. After a minute of awkward sips, Juliette finished drinking and dabbed at her lips with a napkin. 'Now...why did you want to see me? Scratch that: how did you even know I was here?' she asked.

'You weren't in your room. This was the next possible guess,' he shrugged.

'Hm. Fair. So what can I do for you?'

Hush squeezed his hands before rubbing his sweaty palms onto his pants. After a few seconds of quietly deliberating his words, he looked up with a nod. 'Could you talk to my sister tonight? I feel like you could really give her the push she needs to be 'herself' again.' he said.

'...a few questions,' she said, as she placed her gourd down and lifted up a few fingers. 'One, why come to me? Aren't you her brother? Why not handle it yourself?'

'I'm her brother, yeah. Doesn't mean I'm going to always be the right solution,' said Hush. 'Surprisingly, there's going to be a ton of times where what's best for Queenie isn't my direct involvement. This is one of them.'

'I see. Well, two: Queenie hates me. Furthermore, she suddenly feels guilt for my...condition. Why would a confrontation with me suddenly fix her?' asked Juliette.

Hush shook his head. 'She doesn't really hate you. Well, it's complicated,' he said.

'I have time.'

'Well...don't tell her I told you, but she's always looked up to the idea of the Dancing Painter as a kid. To her, you were a dictionary definition of a heroine who inspired her to be, as she would put it, a 'punk-ass, kick-ass, badass.' A good reason she's very movement oriented during her fights is because of your nursery rhyme. So...when she saw you in real life as a drunkard enemy? It kind of...conflicted with the perfect image she had in her mind. Plus, not to mention how much your personality clashes with the tales she heard of.' said Hush.

Juliette chuckled as she twirled her gourd along the table, the spirits sloshing inside. 'Yeah. Whoever wrote that nursery rhyme is an absolute buffoon. He didn't even fully capture me as a person.'

'...right. Well, you can kinda see Queenie's conflict, right? Her child-hood legend is an enemy. The tales of charismatic bravery don't match up with the personality behind the real thing.' Hush then leaned in and rested his elbows on the table. '...and she's the reason why her hero is now a cripple.'

'Mm. You don't think it's your sister's fault I'm like this?'

'No, that's dumb,' he said with a scoff. 'She didn't force your movement. You moved on your own. Your physical injury is on your own shoulders...plus, your current status is soul-related, right? In which case...Queenie really isn't at fault.'

'Clever. Slightly cold, but I can respect that,' said Juliette as she silently tapped her fingers on her arms, an odd expression plastered on her face. Even behind her mask, Hush could see her furrowed brows as she pondered...something. 'Well...lastly...let's say that you're right in the previous points. How do you know that this is the most correct action? What if this all backfires and makes your sister crumble irrecoverably?'

'Please. I know Queenie. I'm willing to bet my own life that this will help her,' he said.

Juliette traced her finger across the smooth, yet slightly sticky, table. 'Well. Shall we make a bet then? On the off-chance that-'

'You don't need to play the villain,' cut off Hush. 'It's been paining you to see Queenie like this for months too, right? This will help: I just need you to trust me on this.'

Juliette tightened her lips, clear hesitation written on her face. After a few seconds, a low voice escaped her red lips. '...are you absolutely certain...?'

'On the honor of the Family, yes.'

'...'

'Please.'

'Fine. Bring her here tonight. Let's pray this works, you Misfit.'

. . .

Hush woke up on a hard mattress covered by a thin bed sheet. He struggled to sit up with a mild groan, feeling fairly sleepy but much warmer than before. The bald man next to him sighed in annoyance. "Kid, you *really* gotta stop taking fights you can't win. You're still weak," said G.

"Well, if no one held back the mutant, it would have flown over the walls," said Hush. "Bigger question: where the hell were *you* guys? I was fighting for my life out there."

"Patchy was surveying the nearby villages. I was heading on over to Juliette's room for a checkup. Sana was-wait, why the hell am I telling you? Doesn't matter what we were doing, just know we were busy."

"Uh huh. Sure." Hush sat up with a stretch as he rolled his leg. As expected, the wound was gone. Though he wouldn't explain, G had a weird pill that seemingly cured any injury. G refused to give stockpiles of the pill to others, so the wounded would end up having to come to him to be healed...making the Gatekeeper a weird sort of "nurse" who tended to the extremely ill.

Hush looked around the room with a slight frown. "Where's Alexandria?" he asked. "She was with me, last I remembered."

"Who do you think dropped you off, nitwit? She was a crying mess as she dragged you in," said G, shaking his head with a frown. "Men shouldn't make women cry. Apologize to her later."

"Why would she be crying? *I* got injured, not her."

"Good heavens, you're dense. Just...just apologize to her. Let her buy you a drink. Ok?"

"I-"

G leaned in with a snarl. *"Ok?"*

"Got it. Will do."

G got up and opened the door. "Don't use your soul for the rest of the day. Your wound wasn't bad, but you lost a bit of blood. Take it easy for now."

"Oddly considerate of you," said Hush.

"Shut it. Now go. Spend the day with Alexandria, you dumbass."

Hush left the building with a careful stride. Sure, the wound wasn't there, but every time he took a step, he flinched in anticipation of a surge of pain. He forced himself to take a few brisk strides, and once comfortable with the pace, he burst out of the building's front door and ran straight into a nervously pacing Alexandria.

She immediately darted her head to the front door and took brisk strides towards Hush. She stomped her feet, formed an arm made of crumbly dirt, clenched her fist...and froze. She grit her teeth, sighed, and allowed the limb to hiss back onto the floor. "You...you have *no* idea how much I want to punch you. Hell, if you didn't come out from the health ward, I absolutely *would* have socked you." Alexandria said.

"Thanks for the consideration," said Hush, turning his head to see Alexandria's harvesting baskets laid against the wall. "Did you find everything your family needed for the night?"

Alexandria's nose twitched as she took a sharp inhale. She quickly turned from Hush, muttering "He just got discharged. He just got discharged. He just got discharged," quietly under her breath. After a few seconds of this, she turned around with a dull smile and sharp eyes. "Let's go grab some lunch. Yeah?" she asked.

"I...uh...sure. Yeah, I could do lunch," said Hush.

"Cool. Grab the two baskets, and let's go," said Alexandria.

The two quietly walked without exchanging a word. Hush wasn't sure why, but it felt as though Alexandria were angry at him...and he had *no* idea why. Had he done something wrong? After shuffling down the street, he coughed into his hand. "Hey...so...are you...mad?" he asked.

"Noooo, why would I be-" she cut herself off, exhaling softly and turning to face him. "Sorry, I'm...I'm being unfair. I was just worried, alright? Could you imagine: I ask someone ou-someone for *help*, they nearly die, and when they wake up, asks if they can go back out into the same danger I threw them in? I just feel crappy, and it isn't fair to take it out on you. Sorry," she said with a bitter tinge of regret in her voice.

"Well, for what it's worth, we're both alive. May as well make the most of it and move on, right?" he said."

"Ok, but you nearly *died*. I can't just...brush that off."

Hush stared at her with a bit of curiosity. Though she seemed extremely uncomfortable, Alexandria seemed to be working with great effort to look him in the eyes. From his upbringing, danger and death was an expected risk he took every day. After a while...the looming threat of death didn't really carry the same weight, so he couldn't fathom why Alexandria felt so much guilt. Still, he understood that she was deeply concerned about his wellbeing. He might not understand *why*...but Hush wasn't inconsiderate.

"Well, make lunch for me, and we'll call it even. Hell, we can go foraging another day to redo today's...circumstances. How's that?" proposed Hush.

Alexandria's eyes suddenly lit up for a split second, before she composed herself with a cough into her shoulder. "Yeah. I...yeah. I'd love that. Cheers...and sorry once again," she said.

"It's nothing, really."

. . .

Taba and Queenie walked into the bar as Alexandria and Hush were making a simple rice bowl with steamed veggies. Taba's mouth opened slightly as a small smile curled on the edges of his lips, Queenie tilted her head with mild confusion, and Alexandria suddenly looked towards her bowl with flushed ears. Hush simply stared with mild confusion at everyone's differing reactions.

"So...could we order lunch?" asked Taba.

"...sure. Yeah. Go sit down," said Alexandria.

Taba and Queenie scooted over to a booth. Hush hesitated, a bit unsure if he should follow suit. He took a small step towards the direction but stopped as he felt a small, yet firm, foot step on his shoe. Hush looked down to see Alexandria pressing her foot against his. "Not you, idiot," she muttered.

"I...guess we should make two other rice bowls?" he asked.

"Something like that, sure."

The two silently made extra food before Hush walked over and placed it in front of the others. Queenie turned with a frown. "What are you doing here? Didn't see you in your room earlier," she said.

"Alexandria just asked for some help foraging, that's all," said Hush. "What were you guys doing?"

"Dropped Juliette off to her room. Sun was up, we were hungry," said Taba, an odd glint in his friend's eye. His eyes darted slightly between Hush and Alexandria, eyebrows slightly raised as he did so.

99

Hush had no idea what was happening...but it felt as though he *should* understand. He would have to ask Taba later.

Alexandria sighed overdramatically from behind him, scooting into the booth next to Queenie. Hush shrugged and sat next to Taba. As everyone slowly began to dig into their meals, Queenie noticed Alexandria not making any attempts to eat. "Youf nof goffa eaf?" she asked with a full mouth.

"I...didn't think about eating a rice bowl without arms."

Taba grinned slightly. "I mean...you could always have Hush *fee-*"

"Hey Queenie," said Alexandria a bit louder than usual. "Feed me."

Queenie slowly chewed her mouthful of rice before shrugging, spooning up some rice and holding it in front of Alexandria. As the two girls slowly ate their meals, Hush shot Taba a confused look. Taba shook his head and waved his hand slightly, in a *'I'll ask you later'* sort of gesture.

After a few bites of rice, Alexandria cleared her throat. "Y'know...I have to ask, why haven't I seen you guys around before? The city is fairly small and I've grown up here my whole life. Were you guys outsiders or something?" she asked.

The Misfits slightly stiffened at the sudden question. They hadn't really told anyone that they were part of the Family or that they had initially tried to kill the Gatekeepers. It wasn't a topic they weren't trying to hide, but after a year? It seemed like a sudden bombshell to drop on their new friend. The trio exchanged a small glance before slightly nodding. Taba nodded to Alexandria as he casually scooped up some more rice. "Kinda. Former group of merchants ditched us outside the city last year because of a mutant. Sana took pity on us and brought us in," he said.

"How did you guys enter the mentorship program without applying for years?" she asked.

"I don't know, but Sana saw potential in us, apparently," Taba coolly replied. "She let us cut the line."

"Ah. What mutant ambushed you all? Just curious."

"A...uh...frog. Yeah."

Alexandria raised an eyebrow. "Really? Around these parts?" she asked.

"Hey, I don't get it either. Queenie almost got eaten."

Queenie scowled as she flipped Taba off. "Shut it. We won, didn't we?"

"Barely," muttered Hush. " I nearly got sprayed in acid."

"A win is a win, dumbass."

"Yeah? Well y-"

Suddenly, their conversation was cut short by the sound of a chair scraping against the floor drawing closer to their booth. They stopped talking to see a sickly figure draped in a dark cloak gently put the chair in front of their table, dusting off his seat before sitting down. While Alexandria wrinkled her nose in slight disgust, the Misfits quickly drew their breath in as their eyes widened in confusion and fear. The man quietly pulled out a small note card and a stub of a pencil, writing down a few scribbles without saying a single word. Once finished, he gently slid the note in front of Taba, locked his sunken eyes with Taba's wild stare, nodded softly, and lifted his hood over the sides of his face as he quietly walked out the bar.

Then, everyone blinked.

They all stared at each other, a bit confused as to what they were conversing about. Queenie suddenly flinched and looked at her hand, eyes widening as she opened her mouth. Taba stared at the notecard in front of him, reading the contents of the paper. After a few seconds, he firmly squeezed Hush's shoulder. "So...we need to go. Sorry, Alexandria, but thank you for the meal," said Taba.

Queenie silently got up, both of her arms tucked into her hoodie pocket. Hush wasn't *too* sure what was going on, but judging from the reactions of his sister and Taba, he had a general idea. He stood up and nodded to the confused Alexandria. "I'll come to you when I have the time and we can set up that second foraging thing. Cool?" he asked.

"I...uh...yeah? Sure. I mean, cool, cool. I'd like that."

The Misfits all silently exited the bar and turned into a back alley. Taba handed Hush the note card and nodded to Queenie. She grimly nodded and pulled out an oily, discolored marble. Hush read the contents of the paper with a furrowed brow. There wasn't too much on the paper. Just a few coordinates and a Z.

Zanshin had infiltrated Malapace yet again.

. . .

When they saw him, they had mistaken his dark cloak for a trash bag. Probably because he had chosen their meeting spot to be next to a dumpster. He looked up with tired eyes, softly nodding as he slowly stood up to extend a handshake. *"Taba. Queenie. Hush. I'm relieved to see you doing well,"* he rasped.

"Well, as fine as we can be," said Hush as he tried to ignore the shudders in his spine as he accepted the handshake. "Why are you here? Wait, first off: when was our last meeting?"

Zanshin scratched his chin as he pondered the question. *"It's...been a while. Over a year, maybe. I've occasionally checked in on you guys from time to time, but this is our first meeting in a minute."* He reached

102

into his cloak and pulled out a small tweed goody-bag, *"I found some berries on the way here. Would you care for some?"*

Queenie hesitated, but succumbed to her taste buds as she gingerly scooped up a handful from the bag. Taba took two berries out of respect. Hush politely declined, rubbing his stomach as he did. Zanshin popped a small strawberry in his mouth before he tightened and pocketed the bag. *"Now...I understand you must have recently spoken to Geralt, yes?"* he asked.

The siblings frowned in confusion, but Taba nodded. "Only yesterday, yeah. I haven't had the time to tell Queenie and Hush yet. Is this in regards to Limbo?" he asked.

"Correct," said Zanshin. *"So, you know the next... 'spawn' will be using Malapace as the base."*

Queenie and Hush exchanged confused glances, but Taba nodded grimly. "Yeah. I'm...not the most aware of what will happen to Malapace's citizens when it happens. Will they be assimilated? Destroyed? Ok? Do you have any information as to what-"

"The people will be fine," replied Zanshin. *"Only those with soul above a certain level will be able to interact with Limbo. The average citizen, or even soulbearer, will not notice anything significant."*

"Then...why come to us? From the sound of it, it seems like Geralt's got it all under control."

"That's why I'm here," sighed Zanshin. *"He...doesn't. That man acts like he can do everything himself, but he's going to die at this rate. The only thing he's accounted for is the climb. I doubt he has planned for the time limit, much less the descent. My role is to ensure everyone gets home safe and that includes Geralt."*

Hush frowned. "What do you mean? Are you worried he'll lose a fight or something? Because I can't see that happening," he said.

Zanshin tightened his cracked lips and scowled, causing the Misfits to unintentionally flinch. The older man noticed their reaction and hid his pained eyes with a bow. *"My...apologies. This frustration isn't directed towards you: it's him. He didn't even divulge all of Limbo's properties in his talk with you,"* he said.

Queenie raised a finger, to which Zanshin nodded. *"Yes, Queenie?"* he asked.

"Elaborate on this...Limbo in general. I know Taba knows, but me and Hush are a bit lost."

"Ah. That was my oversight, apologies. Limbo is where the soulscale is. Think of it as a mountain that changes when you aren't looking at it. When the current soulscale begins to... 'die out', Limbo slowly anchors into this reality. It's only during this time tha-"

"Nevermind. I'm even more confused. I'll just ask Taba later."

Taba cleared his throat. "Anyways...could you elaborate? What's this danger that Geralt faces? Why are you worried for him?" he asked.

"Limbo...only exists for those with a strong enough soul. Limbo also only anchors while the current soulscale is near depleted. If you were to obtain the soulscale, you'd need a lot of soul: the tasks required for just one person are near impossible," Zanshin replied. He then rubbed his dry hands together and stared at the floor with deep concern in his hollow gaze. *"I have no basis for it...but I fear he plans to sacrifice himself to obtain the soulscale for the Family."*

"...and the reasoning for this basis...?"

"He's launching this entire mission by himself. He hasn't told anyone, nor has he ran it by Father...though I imagine he's pretending like he

has. Geralt wouldn't do something so utterly ridiculous unless there was tremendous risk in the task."

Hush tightened his lips. It...sounded *very* much like something Geralt would do. The more dangerous a mission was, the more he tried to do it by himself. There was a time when nine mutants had attacked the caves while everyone was sleeping. Instead of waking the others up, he had fought tooth and nail for hours with nothing but four pebbles and a hand rolled cigarette. When the Family had woken up from their peaceful slumber, they saw a bloody man kneeling next to five carcasses, his head raised to the sky in an attempt to not pass out.

"Ok...let's *say* that Geralt was doing this by himself because of the danger. Sure. What can *we* do? I feel like there are tons of other Family members who would be of better help than us," said Hush.

"I'm already doing what I can to recruit as many from the Family without Geralt's knowledge. It's...a task, considering my curse," admitted Zanshin. *"Still, it is an effort worth pursuing. That man has sacrificed so much for us: why shouldn't we repay that kindness?"* He shook his head. *"I'm disorganized today, apologies. My fear is that we don't know enough about Limbo. Worst case scenario, it will 'unanchor' once the soulscale is taken off, taking a weakened Geralt with it."*

"Whoa," said Queenie, holding her hands up as she frowned. "So, if I'm correct, Limbo is a mountain. That much I get. Why would it unanchor? It's a mountain."

"Limbo doesn't really exist in our world. Well, it *does*: we just can't comprehend it," said Taba, pinching his brow as he tried to organize his understanding of everything. "The soulscale, if it helps, is like a little middleman between what we can and can't understand. Remove that from a mountain we can't fathom? Suddenly, everything about the unfathomable mountain becomes unstable, and *poof.* Did I miss anything, Zanshin?"

"No, that's a fine understanding. Well done as usual, Taba," said Zanshin. *"I believe in a possibility that Limbo would destabilize if there isn't enough, ah,* understanding *of the landscape. So, what if we had enough soul on the mountain that we could understand?"*

The understanding slowly dawned on Hush. "Ah. Did you want us to serve as "paperweights" of a some sort for Limbo?" he asked.

"Correct. I do not know if your presence is fully needed, but I would rather be safe than sorry. I wish my own self were enough...but my curse limits my capabilities."

"Do...do we need to do anything else? I don't really get how to really be an anchor."

"Simply standing on the mountain should suffice. Like...like holding up a pencil next to a tree to understand the scale for both, your existence should work to make the unfathomable...fathomable. Of course...obtaining the soulscale while ensuring Limbo is stable is one ordeal. Descent is another, yet that is a bridge I will personally cross once we arrive. I have already prepared myself for when that time comes: you need not worry about that." He pulled out three pieces of paper from his pocket and handed a slip over to each of the Misfits. *"I've written down my thoughts and reasoning on each of these, that way you'll sort of remember our conversation...at least, indirectly."*

Hush did a quick glance at the slip. It was a meticulous and well articulated plan and guideline on the plan, the time frame, and reasonings, but written in a way that an outsider would discard the paper as rubbish. It was a guideline that would've taken hours to fully craft out.

"So...if you had this the entire time, why didn't you just give this to us?" asked Queenie. "Same results, less effort for everyone, right? After all, we're just going to...forget all this, right?"

Taba and Hush winced and glanced at the nonchalant Queenie. As reasonable of a question it was...

Zanshin turned around quickly, but not before Hush could see the absolute agony worn between his eyes. He walked through the alley, but just before he turned the corner, Zanshin muttered dialogue to himself that only Hush's enhancing hearing could pick up.

"*I'm just...so...lonely. How would you get it? Everyone forgetting your existence. Fearing your arrival. Asking why you're meeting up with them. Do I need a reason to talk, to love? Do I need a reason to sacrifice, to cherish?*" he whispered as he turned the corner.

Then, everyone blinked.

CHAPTER 6

Taba sat on his bed, sitting at the paper that Zanshin had supposedly given him. It was an extremely detailed listing of what the Family had planned to do and by what deadline. To any of the Gatekeepers, and even Babs, this was gibberish. Honestly, he was both impressed and worried about Zanshin. Taba could never remember the man's face. For all intents and purposes, they had never met. Father had told them all that if they saw a man wearing an exaggerated dark cloak, it was Zanshin, but Taba had never seen such a figure. Or...maybe he had. The whole Zanshin situation was a headache.

The plan, from what it seemed, was heavily focused on Limbo appearing around Malapace in three weeks. There were too many "what ifs" that Taba had to consider. What if the Misfits weren't ready to climb Limbo? Would Limbo really appear in three weeks? Which members of the Family would appear and climb Limbo with Geralt? What would Malapace do in retaliation? Which...which side should Taba help?

Maybe...maybe I can just coast in the middle and not pick a side. It isn't like my involvement will really he-

You are the cornerstone of this plan. Your allegiance dictates the failure of-

"Could you shut *up* for just one second?" snapped Taba.

He heard a cough from the front door and locked eyes with Hush. Hush raised an eyebrow from the bedroom entrance. "Didn't say anything, man. You good?" he asked.

Crap. "Yeah, yeah I'm good. Just tired," mumbled Taba while rubbing his face. "What's up?"

He walked in and sat in a chair, holding up his own paper from Zanshin. "Well, I kind of wanted to discuss this. Before that, you've been off recently. Surprised and caught off guard *way* more than normal. This is a bit of a reach but...are you not using your blessing as much?" Hush asked.

"Look, man, it's not that big of a dea-"

"It's a yes or no question, man."

Taba hesitated...and Hush's eyes softened. "You wouldn't hesitate if it were simple," Hush said.

"...I guess you're right. Sorry...it's just...*really* complicated," said Taba.

"Today, we learned about an imaginary mountain that becomes fathomable by simply choosing to exist in our plane of reality. Enlighten me."

Taba tightened his lips...but sighed deeply. "Look, promise you won't tell anyone else. I don't need others to be worrying about me," he said.

"Sure," said Hush.

"Alright...well, I think my blessing is talking back to me. Randomly."

"Huh? That can happen?"

Taba threw his hands up, a massive weight lifted from his heart. "I genuinely don't know, this is a first. It gives me the same feeling as when I use my questioning, but it feels as though someone is just peering inside my head at all times and randomly booms in with prophecies of grandeur. I don't know why and I'm *so* over it," he said.

"You try using your questioning on it?" asked Hush.

"Duh. That was the first thing I tried. Now, it just randomly pops in my head with no rhyme or reason."

Hush crossed his arms and frowned. "Hm. Alright."

"...You're taking this awfully well," said Taba.

"I mean...you don't have any reason to lie. Plus, it isn't like your life is in any danger, right? What's the issue?" he asked.

"It just feels like...I'm dancing in the center of someone's hand, where all my thoughts and actions are being dictated by some other-worldly being. I haven't been so uncertain about something so massive in so long."

Hush shrugged. "You aren't wrong, I guess. Wish I could do something to help...but this is beyond me. Still, I won't tell anyone." He lifted his arm and offered a fistbump to Taba. "If you ever need to talk more or need me to do anything, let me know."

Taba met his fistbump with gratitude. "Thanks, man." Suddenly, he snapped his fingers and looked up at Hush with a small twinkle in his eyes. "That reminds me...how do you feel about Alexandria?" he asked.

"That seems random. Is this about the bar thing?" asked Hush.

"Yeah. What were y'all doing? How do you feel about her?"

"She's a good person. I promised to help her out in some foraging, I got attacked, and-"

"Wait, you got attacked?"

Hush winced. "Ah. Uh...yeah. Don't tell Queenie, but a mutant got me pretty good. Alexandria felt really bad so she made me lunch," he said.

"Ah...that explains why you were together," said Taba. "Still, no feelings for her at all? None?"

"Do you mean like, platonically? Or-"

"Romantically, Hush. Do you think she's cute?"

Hush coughed, taken a bit off guard by the question. Taba grinned as his friend seemed to be organizing his thoughts. "I...uh...I mean..." he stuttered.

"Look, do you like her? It's a simple question: a 'yes or no', if you will."

Hush stared at the table with a long gaze and a faint smile. "I don't know. It's...hard to say. I don't think I'm really deserving of romance, nor do I know where to go about it, so I wouldn't push it myself. You feel?" he said. Taba opened his mouth to respond, but Hush cut him off. "Plus...she's part of Malapace. The Family...well..."

Taba winced. Yeah, that *was* a bit tricky. He understood Hush's struggles, so he dropped the topic. "Fair. Anyways, you said you wanted to talk about Zanshin's plans?" asked Taba.

Hush perked up and cleared his throat. "Right. Well, I was just curious as to what you wanted to do. Did you want to follow his roadmap? It seems pretty straight forward," he said.

Taba turned back to his paper with a frown. Hush wasn't wrong: it *was* very detailed and straightforward. However...was it the *best* course

111

of action? Taba wasn't too certain. He looked up to Hush with a slight shake in his head. "I don't know, in all honesty. This plan seems to work if all goes well...but..."

Hush raised an eyebrow. "But...?"

"I don't know. My gut instinct is telling me that the plan is flawed," he said. "Something doesn't add up...but I'm not too certain *what*. I've been stumped for the past hour."

"I feel the same...but maybe the problem isn't logical," said Hush.

"...what do you mean?"

"Do you think there's a chance that you just don't trust Zanshin? That this is just a big trap?" he asked.

Taba blinked as he considered that possibility. No...no? Surely that wasn't the reason. Zanshin might, well, is *supposedly* a sketchy guy, but to not trust him? That seemed bizarre. Hush scooted in with a nod. "Think about it. He's forming a perfect plan involving *us*, some hostages from Malapace...and there isn't a backup plan. After all, why should there be? The plan is perfect," he said. "However-"

"...Zanshin doesn't plan for best case scenarios," realized Taba. "He's the kind of man who plans for the worst case scenario, and creates numerous plans depending on the situation. That's what makes him scary."

"Bingo. That's what caught my attention: this isn't like Zanshin. I might not be as smart as you...but I tend to notice a person's habits. This doesn't match up with the previous plans Zanshin has made. Something is up," said Hush. "That's why I want to ask you what to do...because *technically*, Zanshin isn't wrong. If left to his devices, Geralt could very well die upon harvesting the soulscale. How did you want to proceed?"

Taba stared at the roadmap that Zanshin had crafted. What was Zanshin thinking? What was his goal? Once he understood that...Taba could make a plan to use Zanshin's plans for everyone's benefit. "Honestly...if I were him," he muttered...

.　.　.

Normally, Taba dreamed about fuzzy patches of memories or conversations with Father. Tonight was different: he sat in a blank infinity...yet also felt claustrophobic. He clutched his chest and forced his breathing to slow...except his lungs failed to expand. All he could do was dryly cough as he clawed at his strained throat and-

"Boy. You look pathetic."

Taba turned around and stared at a...thing. It was a featureless human, like someone had wiped out a person's uniqueness and turned it into a blank slate. And yet...it was exceptional. It had no eyes, yet could see far more than Taba could. It had a limited form, but could move and be anywhere *it wished. Its joints appeared to be melted into each other, yet was inescapable. It was an impossibility, yet a certainty. It was like-*

The thing raised its arm. "Yes," *it boomed without vocal cords or a mouth to speak from.* "I'm the voice." *Taba tried to open his mouth to speak...yet nothing happened. He rubbed his face...only to discover no features. No mouth, no nose, not even eyelashes. He was featureless. Taba had so many que-*

"To answer, I am the embodiment of your blessing. I would be cautious in asking your questions; you don't have infinite soul," *it said as it gestured to Taba. He looked down and noticed a small portion of his torso was hollowed out, fully transparent. He panicked, slapping his chest and feeling his stomach sink as his arm phased through the cavity as though it wasn't there. Was he-*

113

"You are soul. In here, anyways," *it said. Taba watched in real time as a bit more of his soul chipped off into the surrounding land. Taba had so many questions...but he forced himself to calm down. Mindless panic and fear would throw away this insane opportunity. He* had *to make the most of this. It tilted its head as it emotionlessly grinned without changing facial expression.* "Very good. I was correct in choosing you, naturally," *it said.*

Taba stared intently at the being, hesitant on which question to ask. He had to be cautious: the more precious a question, the more soul it would take...and yet, a meaningless question would simply waste soul without any gain. He couldn't afford to waste his blessing on questions that he could eventually deduce. So...the most important thing to ask was:

"...Was my arrival correlated to the chimera? Fine question. Brilliant," *it said with applause echoed in its soundless voice.* "For that wonderful selection, I'll throw in a freebee: my recent arrival was tied with the chimera's erasure *and* your soul maturity. The chimera's existence unintentionally held Limbo back due to how scattered the soul varied across the landscape. With her defeat, Limbo began to reform."

Taba suddenly fell harshly to the floor. He glanced downward, only to realize that his entire lower body had vanished. That question had taken more soul than usual...which means it would have been difficult to deduce. Taba began to focus, his mind swirling on what question he should ask next. However, there wasn't a single thought that fully came into mind: he had no direction to ask for.

"Are you lost? Boring, but predicted. Let me give you some drive."

Suddenly, hundreds of thousands of frames blurred into his mind in an instance. Taba wasn't sure of how much time passed as he stood still...but his body exploded in frigid perspiration. Millions of 'yes or

114

no' questions flooded his mind. So many timelines flooded his mind. Queenie's death. Hush's death. Malapace crumbling. The Family being razed. Taba witnessed the end of everything and everyone.

The being leaned forward, its hands resting behind him. "Do you know what sparks all these timelines and futures?" *Taba looked up, body trembling, afraid to even move.* "Every one of these have a chance of occurring...as long as you don't interfere. If you want to save *any- one*...climb Limbo alone. Reach the peak before anyone. Do so, and you can save everyone...and I do mean that. *Everyone.* However...if even *one* person reaches Limbo's peak before you? People close to you will die. The more you lag behind to get to Limbo's peak, the worse it gets for everyone around you."

Suddenly, the white infinity slowly crumbled around him as his mind began to flutter. The being looked down at Taba. "You best hurry: you're waking up. When you do, there is a good chance you won't remember this...or even decide if this was a dream or reality."

The fear vanished, turning into desperation...which morphed into frightened rage. Taba glared at the being, a single question booming in his mind as he stared up at the unfathomable. His face vibrated until a crude mouth suddenly crusted into place, baring its gums as it demanded a single question. Though the mouth had somehow been formed...Taba still had no tongue, no voice box, not even a brain to properly speak. And yet...the being crouched down and observed.

"Am I good or evil? What an obviously boring question: that isn't even a 'yes or no' question. Furthermore, *you* don't even know what good or evil is: how could I answer something so stupid?"

Then, the infinite became finite...and the finite became void.

. . .

115

Taba's eyes slightly fluttered as he felt the rush of wind right before he slammed into the ground. He rolled up from his bedroom floor, wincing as he rubbed his face to check for blood. When his hand came back dry, he sighed as he climbed up to his feet. His mind and eyes were still shaking wildly...but why? His dream must have been something intriguing, if he could remember it. He craned his neck to peak outside his window and was met with darkened skies. It appeared as though it was still early morning: may as well begin his workout. He threw on his usual outfit, stepped outside into the brisk morning mist, and began to stretch in solitude. Once properly warmed up, he began his jog around the city hall. After a few laps, his mind would clock out and he autopilot his workout...so he appreciated the little bits where he was focused. The mist kissing his cheeks, the out-of-time cricket chirps that slowly died out the more he jogged, the small chittering of birds that crept up: these were moments that could only be enjoyed in solitude.

The more his feet slapped against the stone pavement, the more his mind slowly began to worry about, well, everything. Incoming Limbo, the war, his friends, his allegiances, and so on. As much as he hated these topics...it also helped him appreciate some of the other leader figures in his life: both from the Family *and* Malapace. It was suffocating to have worries stacked on top of each other, yet everyone seemed to fix these issues while also pushing on to the future. Oddly enough, he didn't know if that skill became easier with time...or if the others simply grew used to that stress and anxiety. He hoped it wasn't the latter. Probably was.

After a few rounds, he rolled his shoulders and stopped to stare at the slowly brightening sky, simply to just...admire the silence of the day. Suddenly, he heard the slight crunch of stone approaching, and Taba glanced over to stare in surprise at Babs shuffling over. She noticed his gaze and waved with a bland face. "Morning, brat. You ever consider a resting for one morning?" she asked.

"Oddly enough? I'd feel more antsy if I *didn't* do a morning jog," he responded. "Still, why are *you* out? Aren't you typically in your room at this time of day?"

"*Most* people are in their rooms during this time of day, fool. It's called sleep," she said. "Anyways, I'm out because...ah, I imagine I can't hide anything from you. Just checking in on Juliette and also wanted some morning air. Walking around the city while it's silent is...nice. It's a refreshing change of pace." She brushed some of the dust off the stone ledge Taba was resting on and sat next to him. "You look deep in thought. What's a brat like yourself thinking about?"

"...you're blind. You don't know what I look like."

"And you'd be surprised," she chuckled. "Anyhow, tell me what a runt such as yourself worries about."

"Limbo. My friends. The Family. The war. All that fun stuff, as usual," he said, a bit of hesitation on his lips. He couldn't remember his dream...but an odd sense of unease fluttered in his veins. He had the urge to climb Limbo alone, but he shelved the idea for now. Taba suddenly leaned forward and nodded to Babs. "Random question: so the outer villages don't know squat about you, right?"

"Pretty much, yes."

"What about Malapace? Do they know about your appearance?"

The Overseer's mouth morphed into an odd shape as she shrugged. "It's...tricky. Some do. Most don't. Everyone is aware of 'the Overseer', but they can't really fathom it to be a frail, blind hag. To them, I'm more of an idea and philosophy," she said.

"So...you don't exist in their eyes?"

"Kind of. That's completely fine: I've never been one for prestige or attention."

Taba rested his elbows on his knees, a bit unsure of what to really say. He oddly trusted Babs...despite her being the biggest cornerstone of Malapace. Even more bizarrely...she trusted him as well. Did they mutually trust each other to such an extent to expose Zanshin's plans/intentions? That much...he wasn't sure.

The Overseer stared at his eyes before calmly clasping her rickety fingers. "When Limbo comes to wrap around Malapace, I fully intend to include you Misfits in my defense plans," Babs bluntly babbled.

"Oh. That's...stupid and random. Where did this come from?"

She shrugged, her glossy eyes staring at his heart. "Felt like sharing that, since you seemed so torn on something. Figured it would help," said Babs.

Taba chuckled as he shook his head. "You wanted to soothe me by, what? Giving me more burdens? What kind of leader are you?" he asked.

"A reluctant one, obviously," she responded. "Now...I promise to help you find a middle ground in your plans. Do you trust me enough to share your worries?"

Taba weighed his options, then reached into his pocket to pull out a coin. He flicked it into the air, caught it, checked the coin, then pocketed it. Babs raised an eyebrow. "You really based your trust on a coinflip? I figured you better than that," she said.

"No, that's not it," said Taba. "It's something dumb that Hush taught me, but it works. You do the whole 'heads is X, tails is Y', then flip. While it's in the air, what side you want to see land is the side you're leaning towards more. Then, you check the coin's face to confirm those feelings."

"That's flawed, and you know that."

"Yeah, but it helps organize my head...sometimes. Anyways, I'll compromise. I'll share a portion of the Family's plans, but I want your help to execute certain things. Deal?"

"Will this sabotage Malapace?"

"On the contrary. It'll help your city."

Babs cracked a hideous grin. "Intriguing as usual, brat. Very well: you have my word. What's the plan?" she asked.

"One of our Family members plans to do a self-sacrifice to obtain the soulscale. Another one of our Family members doesn't want that, and neither do I. So...I want your help to prevent the self-sacrifice."

"Hm. Who gets the soulscale then?" asked Babs.

"First come, first serve. Deal?" said Taba as he extended an arm.

"That sounds fine with me," she said as she gently met his hand in a firm handshake. "We should discuss plans, then."

Taba's gut nagged at him, his 'shelved' idea blinking brightly in his brain. Before he could hesitate longer, he blurted his worries out. "I...don't know why, but I think I should climb Limbo. Alone. My gut tells me bad things will happen otherwise," he stammered.

Fear was a foreign emotion for Taba, and Babs knew this. She raised her eyebrow with concern. "I see. You don't need me to tell you how that is foolish, yes?"

"Yeah. I know it's dumb."

"Very well. I'll create an opportunity for you to either scale Limbo alone or with your friends."

The Misfit appreciated the kindness, his heart warmed with relief. She got up and gestured to him. "Let's talk more in my room," she smiled with somber eyes.

The two made their ways into the grand chambers of the Overseer. For such a humble woman, the room was draped with tons of grandiose fabrics and colors. Taba's blessing confirmed that the decor wasn't her decision, so most likely someone had decided to elevate her on a pedestal. Taba sat on a mat in the center of the room as Babs pulled out a small tea table with a bizarre teapot. Taba immediately recognized the container: she had pulled it out previously, before the Misfits had gone on their chimera hunt. It contained some weird liquid that wasn't *just* her soul. It had previously shown off visions of the Overseer's past: why was she pulling it out now?

Babs muttered something as she caressed the air, small bits of dull rainbow liquid pooling out of the spout. It *should* have been similar to oil...but looked far different. After twisting her hands gently into small circles, the liquid pooled into a single ball midair. Babs gently picked up the solid orb and placed it in front of Taba. He stared at it before looking at the Overseer with a confused look.

"Limbo may change eternally...but it's still a good idea for you to at least *experience* that impossibility in real time. That way, you'll know what to expect when it happens to you." she said.

That...was a fair point. Still, he hesitated to touch the orb. The last time he had done so felt not only jarring, but intrusive. Taba didn't feel too good peering into Bab's personal life...even if she was an enemy. She noticed his indecision and rolled her eyes. "Brat, I wouldn't offer this if I didn't want you to witness it...but I trust you're mature enough to absorb this. So, go ahead," she said.

Taba cautiously opened his hand, took a deep breath, and clasped the solid orb. Suddenly, the world around him disolv-

He was suddenly running with no shoes, leaving bloody footprints across a purple trail. His eyes didn't properly work...but he could still see. Colors weren't *quite* what he was familiar with, nor was the landscape...but he couldn't tell if that was due to Limbo or the Overseer's blindness. He continued to pump his legs forward between gasps, left arm gripping onto someone tightly. Every few seconds, she would squeeze the hand tightly and the hand in return would squeeze back. Something behind him was clambering with rickety limbs, shrieking something that sounded like a mix between the rustle of leaves in the wind and the sound of two metal blades scraping against each other. Despite the clattering limbs echoing closer and closer, Babs never turned around, instead focusing on navigating the terrain in front of her.

Suddenly, the grip of the person she was holding tightened, and in a split second, the person was yanked away. She quickly whirled around and was confronted with the trunk of a stained-glass tree. She cursed and whipped her head back to the direction she was running towards and was met with a...fish tank full of clear sand with fish shimmying their way through the organized dunes. Taba couldn't *quite* read her mind...but he could feel the Overseer's emotions. Suppressed panic, rational thinking, and slow breaths without closing her eyes. Without taking her eyes from the sand, she took slow steps backwards and groped the air behind her, feeling for *anything*.

Suddenly, a prick of pain exploded in her palm, causing her to flinch and nearly close her eyes in pain. Babs exhaled, grit her teeth, and whirled around to look at what she was holding. Without moving her eyes too much, she blindly stared at the tusk that had sprouted through her hand, drops of blood trickling down her arm. She cautiously glanced upwards an inch and took in her new environment: a dingy cave full of shiny, metallic bones, each one emitting just enough light to work as an impromptu torch. Babs calmly tore off a chunk of her sleeve and began to wrap the cloth around her hand, squeezing her hand for good measure. She then wiped the bloody tusk on the front of her shirt and held it up to her surroundings. Despite being blind, the new shine served to illuminate the darkness from her eyes. She ignored the throbbing from her hand, slowly exhaled, and-

Taba scrambled back from the tea table, sweat coating his entire body. He quickly clutched his hand to check for any wounds and took quick glances around, afraid that he was in Limbo. The orb that he had been clutching bounced on the soft padding of the floor mat he was sitting on. Babs quietly rubbed her fingers and the sphere turned back into ooze and slurped back into the teapot it had come from. "So...how did you enjoy Limbo?" she quietly asked.

"...Enjoy? Is that the word you'd use?"

The Overseer sighed as she gently placed her teapot by her side. "No, I suppose it isn't. Still, now you know what we're dealing with. Limbo is not something I recommend you climb, but if you insist...at least climb with a partner. A solo climb would drive you mad," said Babs.

Taba closed his eyes and tried to recall everything he saw...as well as all the actions Babs had taken. Holding hands. Not blinking. Feeling around instead of turning her head. "So...Limbo only changes once you aren't looking at it. However, it doesn't change if you're touching something. Is that right?" he asked.

"Not just something: some*one*. Progress is tricky to track in Limbo. As long as you continue to move forward, you're climbing the mountain," she said. "As such, I can't recommend you climb Limbo in a group larger than two people: any more than that, and you'll be hindered tremendously."

Taba frowned. Initially, he had planned to climb Limbo along with his friends. However, after last night...his gut told him that was a bad idea. In a world where people had magical abilities? He tended to trust his gut. Though splitting up the Misfits into one group with the siblings and another by himself seemed like it all worked out, climbing Limbo alone seemed like suicide. Taba would also need to help Queenie and Hush as much as he could. Maybe a tether to tie them together...?

He could plan for that later. Taba nodded to Babs as he slowly caught his breath. "So...do you have an estimate for when Limbo touches down?" he asked. "I would like to know how long I have to make a plan."

The Overseer shrugged. "I wouldn't know when it touched down...but there *is* a way to get the upper hand on the Family...something I imagine would help in thwarting their plans," she said.

"Oh? And that is...?"

Her blind eyes twinkled with mischief: a gaze Queenie donned right before brashly diving into danger. "Well...why not kill enough mutants to the point where Limbo touches down *sooner* than expected? That would work, no?" she proposed with a cackle.

CHAPTER 7

*O*ne of Queenie's earliest memories was when the clan was cele-
brating her sixth birthday. She distinctly remembered that day,
because while they gave her generous cuts of goat meat, her brother was
nowhere to be seen. The burly and cunning clan members all had thick
deceit under their faces that even she as a child could decipher.

She hated them all. But...they also housed her brother, so she tolerated
it, acted dumb. Queenie believed that as long as she was obedient, her
brother would live comfortably too. Maybe it was naive, but she was still
a kid: innocence was unfortunately expected.

After the massive celebration, she ducked out of the cave and found
her brother sitting next to the lakeside, staring at the reflection of the full
moon. He heard her approach and turned to face her. She couldn't really
tell...but one of his eyes looked weird...puffy, even. Maybe it was because
it was dark.

He quickly sniffled and turned his face away from her. "Why are
you here? Go back to eating, Queenie," he said with a wobbly voice.

"But what 'bout you?" she asked. "Did you eat?"

"I'm busy guarding the entrance. I'll be fine, go eat."

Queenie took a deep exhale and tried to use her blessing like she had practiced. Surely enough, the plate of meat she had stored was slowly drawn out. She grabbed it with her grubby paw and handed it to her brother triumphantly. "For you! Eat," she said.

Her brother flinched as he saw the food, a shimmer of fear flickering behind his good eye before quickly composing himself again. "Queenie...I can't eat this. Jin said so," he said.

"It's my birthday. I want you to eat it. Please?" she asked.

He hesitated, but tore off a small chunk of meat with his fingers and threw it down his gullet before handing the rest back to her. "It's...good. Thanks. Now go back before Jin notices you're gone."

She nodded and turned around, but suddenly stopped. "Hey," she said.

"Yeah, Queenie?"

"What's your name?"

The boy blinked, a bit caught off-guard by the blunt question. He cleared his throat and smiled, ruffling her hair as he did. "Uh...Hush. Named after the clan. I'm a pretty important guy! I'm so important that they put me in charge of tons of secret things. Now, go back to the party, ok?" he said.

"Oh...ok!"

She trotted back to the caves with a light heart. Years down the line, she would come to heavily regret that. She wished she had spent time with her brother on that moonlit night, instead of being spoiled by the scum that was her clan.

. . .

Queenie suddenly roused by the loud rapping at her door. She sat up in her bed, static buzzing in her mind as she tried to orient herself.

125

After a few seconds, the urgency of waking up slipped away and she quietly slumbered once once again...

...only for her eyes to fling wide open as she heard her door unlock with a distinct *chk*. Adrenaline pumped through her veins as she quietly unstored a revolver, staring at the entrance, the alarms in her head silencing when she stared at the blue eyes behind a fox mask. "...seriously? You had to risk getting a slug between the eyes? Couldn't just...*wait* for me to open the door? What if I was indecent? Hell, who gave you the key to my room in the first place?" snapped Queenie.

"First off...I heard you sit up about ten minutes ago. I imagine you just fell back asleep, so I figured this was the best way to wake you up.. Secondly, I bandaged your wounds before: even if I were to see you 'indecent', it would be nothing new. Lastly...no one gave me a key. I opened each of your bedroom doors once, so I can just retrace that motion with my blessing to open your locks," said Juliette.

The adrenaline wore off, forcing Queenie to grumble in alert sleepiness. "Fine. Whatever. What did you want?" she asked.

"The Overseer wishes to discuss some plans regarding Limbo. Even if you were to fall asleep during the strategy meeting...I imagined you would want to at least get an invitation."

. . .

When she stepped into the town hall's conference room, Queenie locked eyes with various mentors. A bit weirded out by all the stares, she nodded to numerous turned heads as she quickly scanned the room. She noticed her brother and Taba sitting in the corner, raised a hand in greeting, and walked over to take her seat. Babs sat at the head of the table, nodding to everyone as they all quietly stared at her direction. Once all the seats were filled, Juliette closed the conference room door as Babs cleared her throat. "Thank you for coming at such short notice. I know it wasn't easy waking up so suddenly...but this was an issue I wished to discuss quickly," she said.

The mentor who had rebuked Queenie a while ago, Banase, raised his hand. "That's all good, Overseer. Still...what was so important that it couldn't wait a few hours? We would've happily met up with you over noon. Why rouse us when the sun hadn't even risen?" he asked.

"Fair question, Banase," she responded. "It was in regards to a topic I had wished to keep secret...but as it stands, everyone will be dragged into its conflict. So, I figured bringing you all for an unplanned morning meeting was the best way to hide this from the average civilian." She nodded to her right, in the direction of Sana. "Could you explain a bit more, Sana?"

Sana cleared her throat as she took off her sugegasa, letting it rest on her back with the hat strap relaxing on her neck. "Well, do you guys remember a few years ago when G and I brought back the soulscale?" she asked. The entire room quietly nodded with small murmurs. "I appreciate you all for keeping the existence of the soulscale private...but it was quite an ordeal in retrieving it. It was on top of a mountain called 'Limbo', which is an imaginary mountain that tends to move around and pop into our existence when a few conditions are met." Naturally, people began to mutter at Sana's absurd statement, but she didn't slow down. Sana continued to speak, "As it turns out, those conditions are going to be met...*really* soon. When they are, Limbo will construct itself around Malapace," she said.

The room fell silent for a few seconds before erupting in a flood of concern, confusion, and questions. Sana winced, obviously expecting the reaction, but lifted up her arm and waited for the rabble to calm once more. "I truly understand your worries and confusion...but Limbo will *only* appear to those who are truly proficient in their blessings. For the mass population of Malapace, they will not see the mountain...as they can't comprehend it. The problem is that Limbo's arrival is brought about by killing mutants. Once Limbo appears, the city will be a mutant hotspot: and *that* is the biggest concern for the citizens," said Sana.

A mentor in the front raised his hand. "If this is such an issue, why can't we march into Limbo right now? The sooner, the better, right?" he asked.

"It isn't possible. As I've mentioned, Limbo is an impossibility that has to be witnessed, not forced. *Normally*...all we can do is wait for Limbo to arrive, but we don't have that luxury. So, we will speed up the process to bring Limbo to *us* sooner. That is the most we can do," Sana explained patiently.

Babs nodded. "So...I wish to have two groups. Group A will solely be in charge of dealing with mutants. Group B will be in charge of conquering Limbo. The majority of you all will be in Group A. As for Group B..." she glanced around the room. "...there are a few candidates I would wish to ask to climb Limbo. They may decline, of course." The Overseer began to list off names while holding up fingers for each member. "Taba. Queenie. Hush. Banase. Sana. I would like four of you five to go."

G scowled, arm flexed as he seemingly held back from raising his arm. Sana rubbed his shoulder with sorrowful eyes. She whispered something in his ear as his gaze softened. Banase frowned as he raised his arm. "Overseer? I'm flattered you've chosen me...but why?" he asked. "I'm not as strong as the Misfits and Sana."

Despite the tense atmosphere, Babs surprisingly let out a chuckle. "You? Not 'as strong'? Please."

"You know what I mean, Overseer. No disrespect intended."

"Well...you're one of the few mentors whose blessing is centralized on their own being. Combining that with your rational mindset, I have no doubt you would be irreplaceable in the everchanging Limbo," she said, pointing her finger to Patchy and Juliette. "For example, Patchy and Juliette, while strong, their blessings are nearly useless on the mountain."

Something in G's eyes snapped as he raised his hand. "Then why can't *I* go? I could conquer Limbo faster than *anyone*. You know that, Babs."

Babs stared at him with a stern, yet sympathetic, gaze. "I know you could. I imagine you could single-handedly climb Limbo faster than anyone...yet you also know why I *can't* send you," she said.

G grit his teeth, but his eyes darted downwards as he stared at the conference table in palpable frustration. Queenie stared at the bald man with a bit of curiosity. Why couldn't he climb Limbo? Was it because of a limitation? A restriction of sorts? It felt weird, knowing that there existed a restraint for the immortal man.

Once she ensured that G had settled, she turned to Banase. "Sana has already agreed to climb Limbo. What about you, Banase?" she asked.

"...well, if I am required, how could I say no?"

The Overseer tightened her wrinkled lips and turned to the Misfits. "And as for you three? Only two of you need to go."

Taba spoke up for the trio. "Yeah, we'll do it. No worries," he said, his eyes a bit zoned out. He seemed concerned about something...Queenie would have to ask him about it later. Babs seemed to notice his worry too, but disregarded it with a small nod. "Moving on," she said. "There is the matter of the Family. I'm certain you all are aware of their existence by now, yes?" Babs asked.

The room muttered with small nods, making Queenie feel uncomfortable. Everyone seemed to hate their Family. Well...that was fair: she couldn't really blame them for hating someone who had declared war against them.

"We have information from a reputable source that they plan to climb Limbo for the soulscale."

Suddenly, the sound of squeaking chairs rattled across the room as everyone swiveled their heads in the Misfit's direction. Though it was never officially announced, rumors had circulated that the Misfits were from the Family...and since none of them actually denied it, all the other mentors were openly wary of the trio. Malapace's citizens didn't seem to know the true objective of the Family...but they seemed to at least be aware that the Family's goals could not be met without trampling on Malapace. So, the accusatory glares were expected. Still, the three of them glared back at the numerous staring eyes, holding their chins up to defend their Family's honor.

Bab's noticed the obvious condemnation from the mentors and snapped her fingers "*Hey*. Focus. Stop suspecting your allies," she scowled. Everyone muttered as they faced Babs once more. "As I was saying, the Family plans to scale Limbo. We have few means of actually intercepting their plans, but it *is* possible."

"...And if you could elaborate a bit more on how that is, ma'am?" asked Banase with a furrowed brow.

"Simple. As Sana mentioned, we bring Limbo to Malapace...sooner than the Family expects," she responded curtly.

"...and how do we do that?"

Patchy stepped up while lifting his hand. "So...hi, gang. The idea is I *swoosh* the soulscale out of here, the 'mutant-repellent' vanishes, mutants swarm the city, we kill 'em all, their soul fizzles and ebbs at a much faster rate since we're bumrushing their deaths, their accumulated soul piles up as they die, then Limbo's descent is accelerated," he stated bluntly. "That is the fastest way we can climb Limbo. Any questions?"

A tall woman in the front raised her arm. "Yeah. Uh...*everything*? You guys haven't explained the entire situation. Limbo? Mutants? Family? This might be common knowledge to you, but *we've* all just woken up and are utterly confused," she snapped.

Patchy frowned. "I mean...we *could* explain it, sure. What's the point? It doesn't change what we have to do, and if we *did* explain it, a big chunk of you guys would be even more confused than before," he said.

"...*Seriously?* You just want us to...*obey* without any questions? What are we, lap dogs?" she scowled.

"Ooh, that would be nice, yeah."

The tall woman grit her teeth and swiveled her arm towards Patchy, the woman's arm suddenly morphing into what looked like a cannon made out of flesh and blood. Before she could fire, Patchy blinked behind her and slammed her face into the conference table. The lady roared as her shoulder blade slowly began to morph into weaponry. Before she could fire, Sana stepped in and yanked Patchy away, dragging him by the collar to the front of the room. Patchy whined as he

131

was pulled, but his face morphed into a monotone expression as Sana hissed something into his ear. He sighed and lifted his hands in mild surrender. "Alright, *geez*," he turned to the woman and slightly bowed. "Sorry, Becky. But uh, the whole Limbo thing is complicated. Going into all the nitty gritty would be too exhaustive, so here's the quick summary: Limbo is a mountain that kinda pops into place when soul is used. Dead mutants count as 'used soul'. So, by killing mutants, Limbo comes faster. Limbo comes faster, we nab the soulscale before the Family reacts. Cool?" Before Becky could answer, Patchy clapped his hands. "Cool. Let's move on, yeah?"

Becky 'disarmed' her blessing, scowling as she plopped back into her chair. An older man frowned as he lifted a shaking hand. "'O, 'hen can 'e 'spect this plan to 'ome into play?" he asked through a thick accent.

"Two days," said Babs. "Enough time to mentally and physically prepare, but not enough time for news to leak out to the Family. Any questions?" she asked. Everyone seemed tremendously uncomfortable, but motivated. After a few seconds, she smiled with sorrowful eyes. "I'm so sorry. I'll...make it up to you guys, somehow. Those in Group B, please head over to my chambers to discuss further pairings and plans: remember, two pairs of two is ideal in scaling Limbo. The rest of you, stay here and we can think about formations."

. . .

Queenie slammed her hand on the table with a scowl. "Me, Hush, and Taba in one group. End of discussion," she snapped.

"No," frowned Banase with crossed arms. "Inefficiency aside, three Family members, unattended, during a raid to disrupt the Family? Be real."

Queenie grit her teeth in frustration. The two of them had been bickering about team formations for the past fifteen minutes with neither side budging. She didn't see a world where she went on a mission without Hush and Taba, yet Banase refused to compromise the safety of Malapace on the off chance they betrayed the city. Well...she had to admit that his concern was fair, but she still didn't like it.

The oddest part, however, was Taba's silence. His eyes were quietly vibrating the way they did when he was using his blessing...but why? No, *what* was he questioning? Team formations...or the overall plan? Whatever it was, he wasn't divulging his secrets to Queenie and Hush...and that worried her. Taba's silence typically involved self-sacrifice, meaning it was up to Queenie and Hush to make sure he didn't do something stupid. Her ears perked up as Taba muttered under his breath: "*...how would I even enter Limbo alone...?*"

Sana interrupted Taba's thoughts by clearing her throat. "Well...I fully trust you guys, but how about a compromise? I really don't think climbing Limbo as a trio is smart, but we can entertain the possibility. I imagine Banase, or the other mentors, will settle for anything less," she said. The Gatekeeper pointed two fingers to Queenie and Hush. "You two, in a team. Taba will be with me and Banase. Fair?" she proposed.

In all honesty...it was a fairly good compromise (and *much* better than Queenie had anticipated), but this time, *Taba* shook his head. "Sorry, Sana. I can't do that," he said.

"Oh? Why, may I ask?"

"You've navigated Limbo. I've *seen* Limbo. In other words, you and I need to be in each of the groups. If you and I are in one group, the other group will have no info upon entering Limbo," he said.

"Fair," said Sana with a slight nod. "How's this? Me, Queenie, and Hush. You and Banase. Would that work?"

Taba hesitated...but also shook his head. "That won't work, either. It *needs* to be me, Queenie, and Hush in one group," he said.

Sana opened her mouth to protest, but Taba got up and gestured her over. She raised an eyebrow but the two of them walked over to the corner of the bedroom. Queenie raised an eyebrow as Taba pulled out a notepad and a pencil stub and jotted some things on a piece of paper. While speaking, he held up both hands with two fingers each. Sana took note of this, tilting her head in equal confusion. After a few minutes, Sana scribbled some things in return, to which Taba solemnly nodded and the duo returned to the center. She exchanged a concerned look with Taba, her eyes laced with borderline pity. "Very well. Taba, Queenie, and Hush. They'll be one group," she said.

"What? Bu-"

"I know, Banase...but trust my call as a Gatekeeper. Please."

The big man pulled at his suspenders while obviously deep in thought. After a few seconds. He sighed and snapped them to his chest. "Whatever you say, Sana. Just know that I *don't* agree with this," he muttered.

Sana smiled gratefully as she clasped his hands warmly. "Thank you." Taba lifted his hand, and the Gatekeeper nodded to the questioner. "Yes, Taba?

He snuck a small glance at Queenie before looking away. "So...how do blessings work in Limbo?" he asked. "Like, do they work as normal, since it's technically a mountain of soul?"

"Well...it's situational. It all really depends on the fundamentals of your blessing. For example, Taba: your blessing would probably be unaffected," she said. After mentioning it, Sana tilted her head and frowned before glancing at Queenie. "...hm. Now that you mention it... *your* blessing might get impacted negatively."

Queenie frowned. It made sense, but that would really suck if that were the case. After all, the majority of her strength came from the fact that she could pull out whatever tool she needed the most, adapting to the situation on the fly. "That stinks. So should I pull out a dagger beforehand?" she asked.

"Probably," shrugged Banase. "We have two days until we execute the plan. If you want, we can spar without blessings just so you guys can all get a hang of it."

Sana clasped her hands with a illuminating beam. "That sounds fabulous! Let's go to the field and tussle, yes?" she twinkled.

Taba's eyes wobbled as he silently made calculations. After a few minutes, he shook his head. "Sorry, Sana. We need to make preparations so we don't have time," he said with an unfocused voice.

Sana opened her mouth to protest...but closed it upon seeing Taba's furrowed brow. "I see. Shame, it would've been a wonderous experience for you to fight with Banase: his hand-to-hand combat is extraordinary." She then walked over to open the chamber doors to dismiss everyone. "Well, we'll see you guys when the time comes, alright?"

Banase nodded respectfully to everyone as he headed back into the conference room. The Misfits excused themselves and stepped out from the town hall. Once outside, Queenie turned to Taba and Hush with a nod. "So...what are these preparations that you need to do for the big day?" she asked. "I don't really know how to plan for Limbo, but..."

Taba was silent, staring at his toes. After a few seconds, he cleared his throat and looked up. "Alright, so...we need to make some equipment. I don't exactly know how to go about it, but we could probably ask a smithy. We need-"

. . .

"Two gloves that are stitched together by rope to be eternally holding hands?" Harrison's father scoffed. "Boy, in what *world* would you *ever* need such a foolish thing?"

Queenie and Hush exchanged looks. Harrison was, in short, someone Queenie beat up. His father respected that, and he also happened to be a smithy: someone who was able to craft anything using their soul (as long as they had the corresponding blueprint). Furthermore...he was a *really* good smithy. Now, she would frequent his shop to craft more ammunition, tools, weapons, and whatnot. Weird how life worked out. What baffled her was Taba's insistence on the glove without explaining to her or Hush *why* they needed such equipment. If anything, it seemed like a hindrance.

"A golden tether to bind the gloves, if possible. Also, something to maybe clamp on the wrist of either glove. Is it possible?" Taba asked.

"Boy, I might be the best in the business...but freestyling something without a blueprint?" he said with a frown. "That's a really high ask, even for *me*."

"We can pay you handsomely upfront."

"Yeah, I can do it. Do you have a hand size for each glove, or something unisex?"

Taba jerked his thumb to Queenie and Hush. "Take their hand measurements. Queenie's left hand and Hush's right hand," Taba turned to nod at Hush. "Are you cool with being left handed for a while?"

"I...don't know what that means, man," said Hush.

Taba smiled with a weird twinkle in his eyes, something Queenie wasn't too familiar with. Was it...wistful? Apologetic? It was fairly foreign to someone as certain as Taba.

The smithy waved his hand with a chuckle. "We can talk 'bout price later. I'll get this to you by tomorrow morning, fair?" he asked.

"Yeah, that's fine. Thank you, sir."

"Aye. Now get out of here, you lot."

The Misfits left the smithy, grabbed a quick bite at a food stand, then parted ways to do their individual tasks. Queenie, in particular, was swirling with questions. Zanshin's plan. Limbo. Taba's whole...aura. So many things to address and fear...but, well, she was just one girl. One at a time.

She stepped into the park, peeked over her shoulder, and unstored her dagger. As she casually gripped the handle, the unhinged jaw of the Chimera flickered in her mind, the rugged scales, the hand slamming o-

Queenie shuttered, exhaling softly. Two days. Two days to get over that damned memory.

With moonlight flickering off her blade, she swung into the night.

CHAPTER 8

H ush quietly placed the peanuts into the basket, his mind circulating on a few different topics all at once. Executing Limbo's arrival in less than thirteen hours. The fact that his sister had been 'secretly' swinging her daggers in the park for the past day. Juliette's condition. Most of all...Taba's unnatural reclusion. During massive plans like this, he would *always* involve Hush and his sister...but Taba had slunk away somewhere without even a notice. It honestly worried Hush, but he trusted Taba. If Taba wasn't spilling the beans, there was a good reason.

As his mind nonchalantly reached for a spotted plant, a dirt-y hand smacked his arm. "Hey. Not those, those'll give you a rash," snapped Alexandria. He blinked back to reality and watched dumbfounded as she plucked the leaves, stuffed them in a little sack, then tucked them away in her basket.

"So...why can *you* touch the leaves, when I can't?" he frowned. She simply stared at him with a blank expression as she slowly raised her arm. He watched as the arm crumbled away back into dirt, Alexandria's facial expression maintaining a nasty balance of monotone and borderline mockery. Hush held up his own arms in retreat. "You're right. That was a dumb question. My bad," he said.

She snickered as she stomped her feet, her dirt arms reforming around her nubs once more. "You're good, relax. If anything, I consider it an honor that you're desensitized to them," she said. Alexandria nodded over to a darker tree coated in fluffy moss. "Go scrape that off, it's ok if some bark comes off with it."

"You're serving moss in your bar?"

"Nah, but it serves well to dampen smells, so we usually chuck 'em in with the garbage."

Hush shrugged and began to scrape away at the tree. Though soft, it was surprisingly firmly attached to the tree. After a few seconds of tugging, Alexandria walked over with a humored sigh. "*Scrape*, you nimrod," she said, immediately wincing after saying it. "Sorry, that came out meaner than I meant. You pull-" she said while yanking, "grab the base, then shimmy your fingers through."

Hush tried, but his face twitched in slight discomfort as the tree bark scraped against his fingertips. "You make this look easy, ow," he said.

"Advantages of not having, well, *arms*, I guess," she shrugged. After a few silent minutes of prying at the moss together, she cleared her throat. "So...why'd you so suddenly take up my offer to forage again?" Alexandria asked.

"What do you mean?"

"Like...*everything*. Why so suddenly? It's only been a few days since the last one. Also, aren't you scared?"

Hush chucked the last bit of moss in his basket as he pondered her question. "A bunch of things just piled up...so I figured I should at the very least do *this*," he said.

The response oddly seemed to rattle Alexandria. She shifted uncomfortably as she stared at the tree stiffly, a whisper of silence passing by. "...am I just something to check off on a checklist?" Alexandria asked quietly.

"Of course not," Hush said as turned to face the short girl. "I made a promise with you and I fully intend to keep it. If I didn't care about you, I would continuously put this off. Hell, I doubt I would've even *made* the promise."

"O...oh," responded Alexandria, her ears reddening. "Ok, but well, what about the mutant? You aren't scared it'll happen again?" she asked.

"I'd be an idiot to not be afraid," he frowned. "Still, a promise is a promise, and if someone has to protect you, I'm arguably one of the better candidates." Alexandria turned away slightly and continued plucking some acorns that fell on the floor, and Hush absent-mindedly counted on his fingers. "I mean...the Gatekeepers are all busy. Same with the mentors. So, me, Queenie, or Taba are your best bodyguard candidates, right?"

"That's what you meant?" she asked, turning to face him with a flushed face.

"...yeah? I mean, do you know someone in Malapace stronger than me, Queenie, and Taba that *isn't* a Gatekeeper or mentor?" he asked, a puzzled expression on his face.

Alexandria closed her eyes, mouth pressed into what seemed like a frustrated sigh, before inhaling sharply. "No, you aren't wrong. I feel kinda goofy now," she muttered. She inhaled deeply and stood up with a determined smile. "Whatever, I'll just consider this a new hurdle."

"Huh?"

She flicked her fingers, a clod of dirt coming off and gently crumbling against his pants. "Get back to picking acorns, you...Misfit, was it?" she said.

"Ugh. Not really a fan of that name. It feels...cringy," he groaned.

"What a shame. Misfit it is," Alexandria cackled. "Come on, let's get these acorns before a mutant caterpillar steamrolls us or something"

· · ·

After dropping off the ingredients and waving a goodbye to Alexandria's parents, Hush walked through the morning city and stopped by the city park. Normally, his sister would be swinging away with her daggers, trying to overcome her implanted fears...yet today? Queenie sat on a tree stump, staring at the single dagger in her hand blankly. Normally, Hush would leave her be...but she looked lost. So lost.

Hush used his blessing to deafen Queenie. Most people would only notice something off after a few minutes, but Queenie immediately perked up, glancing around as she looked for Hush. One they locked eye contact, her eyes flickered downward slightly, almost hiding her dagger in embarrassment.

He walked over and undeafened her, raising his fist. "Taking a break?" he asked. She didn't meet his fist bump, hesitantly covering her weapon with her hand. Hush raised an eyebrow and sat on the ground next to her. "Out with it, what's on your mind?"

"I...I don't know."

"Are you being dodgy, or-"

"No, like, I *literally* don't know anything. Why am I fighting? Why *should* I be fighting? Why wield a dagger if I'm afraid? Why even try to overcome a fear in an unrealistic amount of time? Why should I try anything? Why should I *live*?" Queenie suddenly shut up, pale sweat dripping down her back. "I...I'm sorry, that got dark, *really* fast. Ignore it."

Queenie got up, her head staring fearfully towards the ground, but Hush instinctively grabbed her leg. She flinched, and he used that momentum to pull her to the ground, sitting her next to him. Hush pulled her in for a hug, warming up her cold sweat with his jacket. Queenie said nothing, simply trembling softly, as though she were expecting a universal answer that would magically unravel all her problems.

Hush gently pulled her away, stared at his younger sister in the face, and softly spoke. "I don't know," he said plainly.

Queenie blinked, a bit stunned by the answer.

He leaned back on the tree trunk. "I don't know tons of things, myself. Why do I care for Malapace, when I love the Family? Why am I willing to die for Alexandria, when she's my enemy? Why am I jumping into hell, for a foolish sister who blew her nose into my one good shirt?" he glanced over with a wistful smile. "...and what could I say to comfort that sister's heart? I don't know. All I know is that it hurts to see you struggle like this."

A flare of frustration rose on Queenie's face, pushing away and punching Hush squarely in the nose. A flourish of red splattered the field, the sound of Queenie's outraged panting rising. "You're *pitying* me? After I *trusted* you like this? *Really*? And I thought I *knew* you," she spat. "I would prefer if you said *nothing*."

Hush slowly got up, blowing bloody snot from his nose. "I know that's what you would prefer. Sadly? I'm a dumbass who ended up cherishing his dumbass sister...and small words of comfort isn't what you need right now." He pocketed his hands, hiding which fingers he was flexing, and prepared for combat. "I might not know what the right answer is...but I know for sure what's the *wrong* answer."

Queenie's eye twitched as she snatched up her dagger from the tree trunk. In an instance, she lunged at her brother, the rage flashing into fear as she stumbled, her hand trembling as it dropped the dagger. Before she could pick it up, Hush flexed his fingers to amplify her hearing to the highest degree. Immediately, she twitched as the miniscule sounds she would normally ignore flooded her mind. The crunching of feet on the ground, chattering in the marketplace, birds squealing in the treetops, leaves rustling in the wind. The sensations overloaded her brain, causing her to look up with infuriated annoyance.

...staring in bewilderment as she watched her brother silently pick up her dagger. Hush twirled the blade in his hands, nodding in slight approval at its upkeep.

Was this the right answer? Probably not...but he trusted Queenie.

Hush held the blade in a backhanded grip, pointing it to his chest. He closed his eyes, and in a swift motion, he plunged.

In response, Queenie executed three steps in immediate succession. First, she summoned a chain to hold back Hush's arm. Secondly, she withdrew the dagger back into her storage. Lastly, she stepped into her storage to "unstore" herself right in front of Hush, just to immediately slap him into the ground.

"**What is wrong with you?**" screamed Queenie with a cracked voice.

Hush rubbed his cheek, but shrugged. "A bunch of things, honestly. Still, why did you stop me?" he asked.

Queenie raised her foot to kick her brother...but dove to the ground and hugged him instead. "Why the *hell* would I want you to stab yourself?" she said frantically.

"So you *do* get it. Cool."

Queenie pulled back from him with frenzied eyes. Hush struggled up and smiled with a swollen nose, the blood still dribbling out. "You have a bunch of worries in life. Hell, you're questioning *life* itself. And despite contemplating the end...you're certain in wanting to keep me alive."

"You don't *get* to sound profound, the *hell*? Just because I have these...these *thoughts* doesn't mean I want you to get *hurt*," Queenie spat.

"I don't think you would get it if I didn't go this far. Sorry, I'm not good with words: this was the only way I could think to explain it." He sat up and wiped his nose on his sleeve. "Focus on one thing at a time: if you aren't certain on one thing, focus on what you *are* confident in. For example, I care for Malapace because it's full of good people. Doesn't mean I can't show stronger loyalty to the people who raised me. I don't know who I'll side with...all I know is I don't want to fight against *you*." He got up and extended a hand to Queenie. "I don't know *crap* about a ton of things, and I'm not going to pretend I do. All I can do is do my best to protect you as much as possible, because I don't think I could live with myself if I didn't. Doesn't mean

I can pamper you forever. Wish I could, but I can't. Still, I'll be here for you for as long as I breathe. Ok?"

Queenie stared up at him before grabbing his hand, pulling herself up. She clenched her fist, and Hush braced his abs for impact...yet the punch never came. Instead, she hugged him tightly, stuffing her face into his jacket.

"*Don't* ever *do that again.*"

Hush chuckled. "I'll try, just as long as you continue to live. Ok?"

"*...Dumbass.*"

"Love you too, Queenie."

. . .

G looked up from his book with a raised eyebrow. "You look...rough," he said.

"I got beat up bad," Hush winced. "You got a pill?"

G patted his pants, reached into his left pocket, and pulled one out. "I'm feeding you, get over here," he said.

Hush rolled his eyes and walked over. G was super skeptical of someone taking the pill and refused to even let others take the pill of their own accord. It was odd, but Hush wasn't complaining. G slapped his hand over Hush's mouth, tossing it into his gullet. Shortly after swallowing, Hush suddenly felt rejuvenated, stretching with a yawn. "Thanks," he said.

G put down his book and Hush couldn't help but notice the title: '*The Anatomy of the Brain, edition four*'. Before Hush could ask about the book, G spoke up. "So, kid."

"Yeah? What's up?"

"Are you prepared to climb Limbo?" G asked.

"Not...really, no. Still, I doubt all the planning in the world could prepare me."

G hesitated, scratching his biceps as he did. "Look. Kid. So...Limbo is..." he shook his head, twitching his nose with a sigh. "Forget it. Sorry, I'm not good with words. Just know, if you want to tap out, no one is gonna judge you, alright?"

G...showing sympathy? It was an odd sight to see. "I'll...no, *we'll* be fine. Thanks, though." said Hush.

The Gatekeeper silently folded his arms, staring down at his table. After a few seconds, he shook his head. "Nah. You won't be fine," G muttered. "Even if you *do* hold hands with someone...that mountain is disorienting if you and your partner aren't on the same wavelength." He looked up and nodded at Hush. "You ever do a three-legged race?" he asked.

"Uh...not really. Never had the freedom to do so as a kid."

"Damn, you had a crappy childhood. Well, imagine you're holding hands with someone. You see fire approaching you from your right, but your friend is running in the same direction. What do you do?"

"Stop...them? Is this a trick?" Hush frowned.

G rolled his eyes. "No, kid...but *that's* Limbo. Now, imagine that fire being directly behind you, and your partner is dragging you through the flames. In their perspective, they're drowning and fighting to keep both of you afloat. Even if you may not be experiencing the water, your partner could abruptly drown on dry land, simply because where *they're* at is different from where *you're* at," he said, sitting up a bit more straight. "I don't know what fresh hell you'll go through, but communication is key. Make sure you have a way to talk to your partner...no, *partners*, at all times, got it? Last thing you need is to unintentionally cause your friend's death, or vice versa." Before Hush could fully process those words, G gently, yet firmly, pushed him out the door. "Now, git. Leave me alone."

.   .   .

Hush spent the next few hours quietly making preparations for the climb, and he suddenly stood shoulder-to-shoulder outside Malapace's gates with Queenie, Taba, Banase, and Sana. Everyone seemed equally nervous, but composed. Taba looked around and frowned. "I know we're the only ones climbing Limbo...but where are the other mentors?" he asked. "I thought we were all gathering for this."

That question was indirectly answered when they heard the soft sashay of sandals from behind them, accompanied by the sound of bare feet slapping against the paved path. They turned around and saw a weary-eyed Juliette trudge over to where they stood, a solemn G following closely behind. Hush had seen her dance around the city here and there the past two days, but looking at her slouched walk, he now wondered if she had even stopped to *sleep*. Sana walked over to her and gave a tight hug, the exhausted Juliette not offering any resistance. Her blue eyes blinked slowly behind her fox mask. "Did Patchy move the soulscale?" she yawned.

"Not yet. He's going to move it once Babs gives the signal. When it's gone...we'll know," responded Sana.

Everyone silently stood next to each other, a bit unsure of what to do to pass the time. There was a small chorus of birds chirping in the trees, with light mist sprinkling onto all their clothes. If they weren't so tense from the incoming mission, the day would've been perfect weather to relax.

147

Suddenly, a ***thwa-koom*** rumbled the atmosphere, the ground trembling for a split-second before calming once more. Hush would've assumed he had just imagined the phenomenon, had it not been for the abrupt silence of bird chirps. Juliette took off her fox mask, with G suddenly clasping his hands as he closed his eyes with a clenched jaw. The Drunken Fox uncorked her drink, took a hearty swig, hissed in satisfaction, and tied the flask to her hip as she took a stance with her paintbrush. The air was tense as the party tensed up for what felt like an eternity. After about forty minutes of awkward silence, Juliette's blue eyes pierced the sky and nodded to Sana. "So...the other mentors are on the same page, right?" she asked.

"Mhm. They'll catch whatever mutant slips through your dance."

"Don't call it a dance, San-san."

Sana chuckled. "But it's *so* pre-" the Gatekeeper's eyes suddenly turned stern as she took a deep breath. "***Below,*** Jules."

Everyone had a split-second to jump away as a mutant erupted from the ground, its shiny claws reaching for the closest target, Banase. He scowled and drew back his fist, muscles flexed in preparation to counterattack. Before he could punch, the beast exploded into fine mist as Juliette's blessing eviscerated the creature in an instant. Before she could even exhale, two winged-mutants swooped from the skies with mindless chatter, a mixture of tentacles and talons reaching down. They suddenly tucked in their appendages and swiveled mid-air to dodge Juliette's numerous invisible prelaid slices. Just as Juliette turned to focus all her attention to the airborne creatures, an invisible mutant appeared from what seemed like thin air to swipe at Juliette's back...but howled in defeat as one of Sana's sickles sprouted from its head.

The Dancing Painter stayed uncharacteristically still, her glowing blue eyes closed as her fingers twitched randomly. They couldn't see it, but Hush's enhanced hearing could make out the cries and wails of fallen mutants from all around Malapace's exterior. Sana turned to face them, the glow in her eyes fading as she nodded. "Limbo won't appear instantly: tons of mutants will need to die first. Until then, try to avoid combat. You'll need the energy," she said.

"What about you?" asked Taba.

"I'll be by Juliette to cover her weak spots until Limbo appears. You guys, however, should hide. Go."

Banase raised his arm and slammed it against a mutant centipede, the insect easily cracking against the blow. He turned back to the Misfits and frowned. "I don't like the idea of leaving you guys...but get into the city. Make your last preparations, and *maybe* we'll see each other on Limbo's peak," he said.

The Misfits all scrambled into the city walls, the guards ushering them in as quickly as possible. Queenie muttered to herself as she mentally checked her storage for some tools to preemptively take out. Taba, however, seemed unfocused. He was counting on his fingers as he took hesitant breaths, seemingly uncertain of something. Hush took notice and tapped his fist against Taba's shoulder. "You good, man?" Hush asked.

"I...uh...yeah. I'll be fine," Taba said before nodding to an alleyway. "Let's start heading that direction. Put on the rope glove thingy."

Queenie pulled out the unique clothing from her pocket, slipping it on her left hand as she offered it to her brother. Due to the nature of Limbo, Hush had advised his sister from storing it in her blessing (much to her annoyance). Hush tugged it on himself, clasping the straps around his wrist and tightening the drawstrings around the interlocked fingers. It was snug, and the gloves were designed in a way that Queenie and Hush were making direct skin contact. Something about how "skin-contact worked, but leather didn't", according to Taba. Hush didn't fully get it, but he trusted his friend. Queenie pulled out a dagger and held it in her right hand, taking slow breaths before squeezing Hush's hand. "You sure you don't need a weapon? I can give you a gun if you want," she offered.

"No. I need free fingers to use my blessing. Holding something in my one free hand is detrimental: I'm stronger holding nothing than if I were holding a weapon," he responded.

Taba stared at his toes, an odd emotion on his face spreading more and more evidently until Hush recognized the look in his eyes. Taba looked up with notable guilt. "Look. Guys. I'm sorry, but I can't climb Limbo with you guys," he softly said.

The siblings blinked, exchanged glances, and looked back at Taba. Hush cleared his throat. "We knew, man. We knew," he said.

"...how'd you find out?" Taba asked with a sorrowful grin.

"The glove you gave me and Hush, duh," Queenie said with rolled eyes. "If you were really tagging along with us, there'd be three hands on this, right?"

"Ah."

"Was there a reason you couldn't tell us?" she asked.

"It's for a selfish reason. Nothing more," said Taba.

Hush raised an eyebrow. "Mhm."

He hesitated. "Fine. I made a promise to someone and didn't want to drag you guys into it."

"And that someone is...?"

Taba threw his arms up in slightly-forced exasperation. "Toukie. You happy?"

That wasn't the entire truth. Hush saw it, but didn't push. Ignorance was the better choice, sometimes.

Queenie rolled her eyes. "Obviously not. We'd rather you be with us...but you have your reasons," she said as she lifted her fist clenching the knife handle. "We trust you."

Taba tapped fists with her and Hush. "Thanks, guys. Sorry," he muttered.

"Don't sweat it," Hush said. "Just don't do something you'll reg-"

Then, everything stopped. Not instantly. Not eternally. But unmistakably, everything paused for the most brief of moments. Hush and Queenie froze in their tracks as what appeared to be a broken glass shard dangled in front of them, as though someone had broken a window in the air itself. Taba spoke from out of view. "That's Limbo, guys. If you touch that, you'll begin your climb. If you look away...well, no guarantee it'll appear again," he said.

Hush kept his eyes concentrated on the little shard. It was fascinating to look at...as though he were peering through a different universe, except the crack wasn't exactly transparent: not in a traditional way, no. Rather, it was as though he knew what *wasn't* on the other side of this window...so by hypothesizing what *could* be on the other side, he could fathom *everything*. Hell, if he weren't holding Queenie's hand, he most likely would've subconsciously touched the little shard.

"...If you aren't climbing Limbo, then-"

"No, I'll climb Limbo," said Taba. "My way is a bit...different, I guess. My blessing confirmed it...I just need to take care of something here first."

"So...if we climb Limbo, we'll see you at the peak?" Queenie asked with a trembling voice.

"Yeah. You guys could...climb slowly, if you want. It'd make my job easi-ah, nevermind. Just run as fast as you can: I'll catch up. On my count of three, touch the shard. You guys ready?"

"Kinda."

"Sure."

"Good. Don't forget why you're climbing. Three..."

Hush squeezed Queenie's hand with a quick pulse.

"Two..."

Queenie returned the favor.

"One."

The siblings touched Limbo...and began to climb.

CHAPTER 9

Just as Taba's blessing had predicted, the shard of Limbo appeared in front of him a one-hundred and ninety-six minutes after noon. There was no way he could resist the Limbo's allure. So, the millisecond the shard flashed in front of him, Taba turned away. Just the act of not sating his curiosity hurt his head. Without a doubt, the booming voice in Taba's mind was connected to Limbo: the excited chattering that rang out in his brain confirmed it. Though Taba was on a time crunch to climb Limbo as quickly as possible... there was *someone* he needed to address. After Queenie and Hush vanished, he locked eyes with the girl in front of him. Her expression was snooty, with pointed brows and an upturned nose, yet her eyes were fearful. Her entire body seemed composed and certain...yet her shoulders were hunched to her ears.

He glared at the girl, his nostril twitching in slight rage. "So...you're the mutant magnet, right?" he asked.

She narrowed her eyes, fists clenched as she took a conscious step backward. "Who are you? What do you want?" she snapped fearfully before her eyes widened. "Are you...Taba?"

"So are you? Answer the damn question."

Without answering, the girl turned on her heel and sprinted away. Despite her physique not being impressive whatsoever, she made a surprising distance in a matter of seconds. Taba immediately took off after her, closing the gap and slamming her into the ground with his knee, the anger in his chest rising even further. "I'll take that as a yes," he grit, his muscles clenched in raw malice.

The girl struggled feebly for a few seconds before she snapped at Taba, her eyes glaring at him. "Shut up. What do *you* know about me?" she asked.

"Not much. I don't know your name, your age, your history, hell, I don't know what Dad saw when he picked you. All I know is you tried to pull a fast one on my friend...and apparently, your curse vanishes when you die," replied Taba. "Don't get me wrong. This isn't just business: this is *very* personal. You don't get to screw my Family over, bastard."

The girl's eyes were flickering in fear, but her mouth opened against the dust of the floor to laugh heartily. Taba froze, still holding her in place firmly as he tried to decipher the sudden humor...until he realised it was *mockery*.

"Oh...you're *so* dumb. My curse doesn't just go away after I die. It simply fades away once the host vanishes: I'm sort of a 'return point', if you will. My curse will still linger on that kid until he dies, sorry," she said with a smile. "There *is* a way to save him, however."

Has she said a single lie in the past thirty seconds? **X**

Taba's blood ran cold. It would've been easy to kill her while there was no hope of saving Toukie...but if there was an *actual* way to save him? The intoxicating sensation of hope after having already succumbed to despair was something Taba loathed. Still, he couldn't ignore potential salvation when dangled right in front of him. He inhaled slowly to steady his pulse before softly exhaling. "Alright, explain," he said.

"Let me sit up first. I'm not gonna talk with dirt in my mouth."

Taba released the pressure off her spine but firmly held a grip on her left ankle to ensure she couldn't easily scramble away again. She sat up and dusted the dirt off her shirt before speaking in an awkward kneel. "So, you at least know Dad-"

"*You* don't get to call him 'Dad'."

"Fine. *Father*'s end goal. You know how he's planning to dismantle the entire s-"

Taba slammed his free hand over her mouth with a scowl. "Yeah, just go announce it to the whole world, why don't you?" he snapped.

The girl slapped his hand away with a scowl. "Whatever. You get the gist of it. If he were to succeed...well, my curse wouldn't be a factor anymore, so your friend would be free," she said.

Her logic...wasn't *wrong*. Taba frowned, slightly loosening his grip on her ankle. "So...why are you even here? I doubt you were here the same day as Malapace planned to bring down Limbo by sheer coincidence," he said.

The girl seemed confused, tilting her head as her brow furrowed. "Huh? What do you mean?" she asked. "Zanshin told us in his memo that today was the day we were climbing Limbo."

Taba froze, his mind calculating every single possibility before swearing internally. He had asked so many questions over the past few days and determined that this girl would be here at this exact location at this exact time. He had foolishly never asked *why* she would be here,

155

especially since she had no *reason* to be here. Taba was getting rusty. There was a good chance that Zanshin never *left* Malapace and continued to eavesdrop on every conversation, giving updated itineraries to the Family. If that were the case...how much did Zanshin hear? How much had he planned for? What incorrect information had Zanshin fed the Misfits? Taba couldn't help but feel as though he were being manipulated precisely: something that rarely occurred. "That doesn't answer why *you're* here. You already tagged Toukie, and Dad needs tons of soul for his end goal. Why put yourself in danger any further?" he asked.

"Well...I hear the Overseer is weak but has a crapton of soul," the girl responded. "If everyone is busy fighting off the mutants, then surely...no one will be defending her, right? And if I bring her to D-*Father*, well..."

None of her statements were wrong. Taba could even argue that her plan was genius. And yet...

He tightened his grip on the girl's ankle with a cold face. "Can't have that happen, sorry," he said.

"Why?" she whined while squirming. "It works for you too, right? Helps the Family and cripples Malapace, so what's the harm?"

Taba leaned in with clenched teeth, his vision slightly turning crimson. "I don't think you get it. Your plan isn't wrong. Your calculations are all good. I just *loathe you as a person*. I've never met you before, and it's already clear that you just shove your problems onto everyone else because you don't want to deal with it. Backstabbing whoever you can. Ditching whoever is inconvenient. I *despise* **all** that you stand for," he said with a trembling voice.

He raised his fist and swung with all his might. The girl yelped and reached her hand forward into the middle of the air. Taba's mind froze for a quick second. What was she doing? Why wou-

...he didn't even have enough time to question her actions before he stumbled into Limbo. As his mind was processing what had just happened, the girl kicked him away, causing Taba to stumble backwards a few feet. He scowled as he whipped his head around to where she once lay...only to look up to the humid rainforest...except instead of trees, the area was littered with mushrooms.

Taba cursed quietly: sure, he knew he would be brought into Limbo by someone else...but he hadn't expected he would be kidnapped like this. As he resisted the urge to glance around, he quickly racked his brain on the rules Babs gave him about Limbo.

Do I need to eat food while inside Limbo? **X** *Do I need sleep while inside Limbo?* **X**

For starters: Taba's body was on "pause". Just as Babs had told him, he wouldn't need to blink, eat food, use the bathroom, and so on.

Secondly, Taba couldn't look away, or the scenery would change. *Extremely* slow glances left and right seemed to be fine, but things like turning his head or blinking would change the scenery.

Third, each time the world changed, it would be "worse". Defining how a terrain became "worse" was tricky: from Taba's time talking with Babs, there didn't really seem to be a pattern. However, each change indisputably became worse. So, Taba would have to do his best to deal with the cards he was dealt.

Fourth...Limbo's peak would eventually be reached just by marching onwards. The progress across all areas would be shared, so *technically* it should be possible to reach the peak without changing realms.

Taba wasn't sure what the peak would look like...but Babs said he "would know".

Lastly...Limbo should not be traversed alone. Entering a world where everything was designed to trick and trap you, all while you weren't allowed to look around? Doing so was the equivalent of a death sentence.

Taba couldn't do much about that last point. He stood up slowly, careful not to turn his neck or eyes, and tried to take in the world around him through only his peripherals.

This region was full of tree-sized mushrooms. From each of the mushroom stalks, miniature trees sprouted perpendicularly, each one colored a pasty white. The sun wasn't "warm"...but the heat that rained down felt sticky against his skin. The ground felt squishy, as though he were walking on a toadstool. Just standing around made Taba feel nauseous. Still...there was no immediate threat or danger, so he would be foolish to look away in an attempt to change his landscape. So, he took a small inhale and trenched forward.

Everything about Limbo was centered around moving forward as fast as possible. He pushed past some spores, careful to not let his eyes wander too far. Taba felt something squirm beneath his shoes, but he dared not look down. One of the spores molded around a mushroom stalk just outside of Taba's peripheral view. He kept a careful stare and watched in confused horror as the stalk slowly reached a hand out, slamming its slimy palm against the tree with a warbled gasp, tumbling to the floor as its naked self freed itself from the mushroom stalk. Just as the creature rose from the floor with what could only be described as an inverted face, numerous other beings slowly purged itselves from scattered mushroom stalks.

'No matter what, don't turn around to escape your environment. Limbo can, and will, get worse,*"* Babs had warned him.

'*What should I do if I can't win a fight then?*' he had asked.

As the fungal beasts stomped towards him with shocking agility, Bab's white irises shone brightly in his mind. '*Why...you run,*' she said. '*You run forward without blinking or turning back.*'

Taba cursed and sprinted forward, keeping his eyes open in the pungent air as he ducked around the various fungi that slowly closed onto his location. He darted around the mushroom stalks, swinging between "branches" as he leapt from mushroom to mushroom. Once he had slowly gained a solid rhythm, he accidentally stepped on a squishy pocket, which blew a puff of orange spores into his face. Instinctually, Taba closed his eyes, unaware of his mistake.

By the time he had flung his eyes open, all the fungus had vanished. In its place, a vast array of void. It wasn't dark enough to really get in the way of his eyesight, but the atmosphere was similar to a forest's last minute after sunset, with dark skies rapidly overtaking golden light. The air smelled like stale paint thinner, dry as though Taba were standing right outside of a kiln. However, the forest seemed...off. After Taba stared at his surroundings, it clicked: the trees seemed painted, like the portrait of a hyper-realistic artist. The detail was so intense, that Taba imagined Hugh, an artistic member of the Family, would take this environment as a challenge.

...yet the scenery wasn't just detailed. The world softly swirled, independently of any other input or life. The longer he stared, the more odd images flooded in his mind. Laughter of children, pencils scratching on tables, the ringing of bells, and chattering of peers.

A school? Taba thought, carefully walking forward. Against common sense, he cautiously extended his hand towards a murky boulder, subconsciously asking a question to his blessing out of habit. *Am I in danger?*

O

Adrenaline pumped through Taba, his eyes widening as he leapt backwards. Just in time, as a melting hand splattered out of the rock, barely missing Taba's fingertips. He stared in horror as a man sludged outwards, gulping in air like a fish would wheeze when pulled out of a pond. Unlike the mushroom monstrosities from earlier, this man wasn't slimy. It was as though someone haphazardly splattered paint on a mannequin, clothed it, and then breathed life into it. The man stepped forward, his face, like melting paint, locking him in the eyes. To Taba's horror, there was no savagery in the man's gaze. There was sorrowful intellect.

The man lifted his hand, slamming it into his own throat. His skin muddled, before he yanked out a wriggling object. From the wriggles, a voice emerged. *"He...ll...o. It...hasbeen...so...long....since we...saw-someone,"* he sputtered.

Taba's fight or flight was kicking in, urging him to flee...but the questioner was curious. "Who...no, *what* are you?" he asked.

"Tee...tea...teacherrraugh." it croaked.

Teacher? That would've slightly explained the images that flooded Taba's mind. "So, those memories. Were they yours?" he asked, his foot positioned to flee at any moment of hostility.

"Nooooooo...No."

Taba frowned. Before he could ask who, the teacher pointed upwards. The gloomy sky suddenly began to drip, like pigments trickling down an easel. The sky splattered all around Taba, each glob about the size of a tiny boulder. Each chunk, flooding Taba's mind of innocent memories.

Childish memories.

Taba's blood ran cold, the urge to scramble growing larger. The teacher splattered forward, clutching his wriggling tongue in his hand as he did. "*Please. They...neeeeeeeeddd...bod...body. The...lasttt-person...centuries...ago,*" the teacher whined. He then pulled his chest aside. The murky colors split apart, revealing a rotting vessel, the color of a dead seal. In an instance, the teacher lost control of his hand, tearing a portion of his face off. Behind the murk lay the dilated pupil, full of sleepless dread.

"*Ki*ll. Me. Please," he sobbed.

Suddenly, the blobs that lay around Taba echoed in desperation, flinging sludge towards him with distress, cries of children filling the painted woods. Wordless wails, the woeful echoes demanding mothers and fathers, and sobs requesting hugs.

Fear vanished from Taba. On pure instinct, he sprinted. He would've loved to say it was because he was on a timecrunch, and had to reach Limbo's peak before anyone. Taba would've loved to say he pushed forward, for such a noble reason to save everyone.

In reality...his emotions failed him because his body had abandoned it to prioritize survival. Nothing more.

Taba sprinted, without veering his eyes left or right, deeper into the painting. It got darker and darker...but never to the point of pure blindness. The blobs kept melting from the sky, each one splashing more vivid memories into Taba's head as they all reached for him desperately. No malice, just pure sorrow and lonliness.

After a few minutes...Taba's sprint died down. Hundreds of lives had flashed in his brain, each one robbed of their innocence. It made his heart throb, killing his will to flee. In fact, he had half a mind to just...turn around, reaching to grab one of the muck piles, to soothe even one poor soul.

"You know...if you look away, all of the memories these kids implanted will vanish. If you stay any longer, this is where you die."

Taba didn't even question where the voice came from. Before he lost his sanity and sense of self, he blinked away a tear.

As the howling easel vanished, an endless library with wooden shelves and flooring took its place, all covered in lacquer coating. Despite no hanging lights or flames, the halls were well lit. Just as the random voice had said, the memories of the children vanished...though the images of melting paint remained. Ignoring the jarring juxtaposition of emotions, Taba frowned as his eyes very cautiously trained onto a nearby bookshelf. The spines just contained various names. Janice Lee. Thomas Flex. Rin Yamaoka. Without swiveling his head, Taba cautiously approached a book to his right and lifted it from the shelf, flipping the book open to a random page. To his surprise, the pages contained nearly no words, just a phrase: *"I didn't mean to"*.

Right above that phrase was a human tongue stapled on the page, still wriggling.

In his shock, Taba dropped the book onto the floor, a soft clatter ringing through the numerous halls. In an instant, the lights dimmed in the grand building, a cloaked figure suddenly appearing where the book fell. The faceless woman was easily nine feet tall, her thin limbs wrapped by her dark cloak. Her skin had the texture of hardwood, yet breathed softly with humanesque consistency. Before he could even flinch, the lady slammed her arm onto the book at hypersonic speeds, a resounding **crack** echoing from where she obliterated the floorboards. Taba stood deathly still, a single bead of sweat trickling down his nose. Even fearing the sound of sweat falling onto the floor, he slowly raised his chin as the sweat rolled downwards, if not to delay the droplet's fall for even a second.

After the being shattered the floor, she carefully picked up the fallen book, dusted off the cover, and reshelved it. Once in its place, the woman vanished, the library's lights turning on once again. Taba couldn't stop his spine from shuddering: the woman was closer to a wooden marionette than she was a sentient creature.

Can...can she see me?

"No, she can't."

Taba almost did a double-take as his blessing's voice manifested right next to him, taking slow, condescending steps. It was the same voice as the one from the painted world, speaking with methodical declarations. He rubbed Taba's shoulder's with a gentle, yet chilled, touch. "Boy. You're in *my* realm, now. Aren't you lucky to have a guide like me?" it cackled.

"Who...are you? Can that lady hear you?" Taba whispered with a trickle of fear in his throat.

It stroked its chin with an imaginary frown. "Who am I? Not a yes or no question, boy. To answer your second question...yes, she can," it responded.

"Fine. Are you my blessing?"

"*There* we go...and yes. Yes I am."

163

Taba's mind flew in a flurry. Who was the lady? Where was Taba? Why was he still alive, if the lady could hear Taba's blessing's voice? Was there some sort of trigger?

"Yes, to that last one," Taba's blessing said with a nod. "The others weren't yes or no questions...so I'm not answering them."

Taba resisted the urge to swivel his head to glare at his blessing. Despite this new development, he was still in Limbo: any slip of eyesight would change his environment for the worse. He *really* wanted to dissect the nature of the manifestation of his blessing's voice...but Taba couldn't afford that. So, he ignored his new guest and picked up another book from the bookshelf from his peripheral view. Just like the last novel, this one had a name on the spine: Richard Jamison. Upon flipping open the book, the phrase, *"No, wai-"* was printed right under a flailing tongue as though it were still alive. Taba resisted the urge to look away, carefully examining the contents of the book without covering the entirety of the library before him. The same pattern repeated. Flick, flat, lift, pause. Flick, flat, lift, pause. Every few seconds, the tongue repeated the same actions. Taba carefully shelved the book and picked up another novel. Likewise, a phrase with a tongue that repeated the same actions. Where...*was* Taba?

Without much answers, Taba decided to simply walk down the halls silently. Apart from the various colors, lengths, and widths of the books...the library didn't really change much. Honestly, if he hadn't seen the faceless woman from earlier, Taba would be sleepy with boredom. After about an hour of silent walking, Taba reached the end of a bookshelf. Attached was a simple poster with some finely printed text.

Library of Final words
Please obey the following rules!

Please, lower your voices. The librarian will not tolerate any whispers above thirty decibels.

Respect the library's selection! Any who vandalizes or desecrates the books will be persecuted.

Do not stay in the library for more than one hour. Other guests are waiting for their turn.

Any visitor caught violating these rules will be dealt with posthaste.

Taba stared at the poster with a frown. Guess that explained the faceless woman from earlier. However, the phrasing of these rules was perplexing. Ignoring the violent threats...rule one specified voices. *Only* voices.

Am I allowed to make noise in the library, as long as it's not from my voice? "Yes, boy. You're catching on."

The little itch in Taba's mind grew. Was it stupid? Yeah. Was it worth attempting? Probably not. Still, he took a slow inhale before clapping as loud as possible, flinching as the sound echoed throughout the halls. Cold sweat dripped from every pore in his body as he fully prepared to be crushed to fine pulp...but nothing happened. His hands were trembling, but he couldn't help but let out a grin.

He grabbed two books from his left to test another theory, chucking one in front of him and another far behind him. Both landed roughly around the same time, clattering across the wooden planks. Immediately, the light died down as the librarian slammed down on the book behind her, the ground gave way to the force of her palm, crunching loudly as it did. Once her long, pale fingers wrapped around the book, she vanished. Though she was out of Taba's field of view, it

165

was clear she repeated the same actions to the book he had chucked behind himself. He could hear her slender fingers rub the leathery covers of the books, as well as how they slid back onto the wooden shelves. Then, the lights turned back on in the library.

Taba felt as though his lungs were trying to cannibalize itself, but he couldn't suppress his grin. It was meaningless, but he had found small loopholes in the rules. Rule one only worked on voice. Rule two would summon the librarian around the damaged book. Rule thre-

Blood drained from his face. How long had he bee-

The lights dimmed, just as his blessing cackled. "Bit too late on the uptake, boy," it said with a grin.

Taba immediately took a stance, his eyes wide as he asked as many questions as possible. *Am I in danger?* "Yes." *Will she strike above?* "Yes." *Is her strike avoidable?* "Yes." *Can she be incapacitated?* "Yes." *Could I beat her in a fight?* "Absolutely not."

He tucked in his legs and dove forward stomach first, making sure his eyes were wide open and facing the same direction. Just as he leapt, the librarian slammed down on his prior location, her blank face *clicking* upwards to Taba. He scrambled to his legs and bolted forward, grabbing at the various books surrounding him and blindly flinging them into the ground. Though he couldn't see her, it was evident the librarian couldn't ignore his actions, judging from the scraping of fingers against the floor and the rustle of books slipping back on shelves. Still, it was everything Taba could do to ask questions to predict the librarian's movement as he slowed her down.

Is she going to strike at me within the next two seconds? "Ye-"

Taba's blessing was cut off mid-response as he dove to the right, slamming his body into a bookshelf. Just as he did, he could feel the librarian's fingertips graze his left rib cage, a wet gash slowly appearing on his side. Pain exploded in his side but Taba gasped hollowly as he forced his eyes open, scrambling to his legs to continue his sprint. His blessing floated along in his peripheral view, obvious amusement emanating from his skin. "Run, boy, run!" it laughed.

'*Shut up,*' Taba thought with exhaustion, gripping the bookshelf to his left and pulling himself upwards, dodging a wide swipe. He failed to pull himself up fast enough, wincing as the librarian nipped his heels. Taba kicked backwards on instinct, planting one of his feet onto the librarian's face, a hollow clunk ringing with minimal effect. Using the force of the kick, he dove forward to continue his run.

. . .

As the mud golem slammed its fist into Geralt, the dapper man clenched his teeth as he stumbled forward, his gait interrupted by the blow. He reached into his pocket to pull out a pair of dice, letting them whirl around in his hand before they careened backwards to embed themselves into the lifeless puppet. Just as he did, the hot spring geyser to his right exploded with boiling fervor, water hot enough to crack stone. Unable to fully avoid the hazard, Geralt swore as he focused his soul into his soles, gritting his jaw as the scalding liquid tore at his legs. Immediately, he could feel his pants burn to tatters, his skin bubbling with heated boils. Geralt felt his skin turn clammy as he huffed, the strength in his calves being tested. For all his years practicing soul manipulation...he could just *barely* handle the agony of Limbo. Still, this was the best outcome to protect the Family. If anyone could climb Limbo solo...it was Geralt.

The sizzling water breathed life into the ground, four new mud golems sludging up in front of Geralt. At least he could *see* these ones. Geralt extended his palm, dice and marble whirling around with buzzing fury. "I don't have *time* for you, damn it," Geralt snapped. "*Move.*"

. . .

Zanshin stumbled onto Limbo, his sunken eyes glancing around the blank canvas with mild worry. As expected...his curse seemed to also impact Limbo. So far, everything had gone to plan: Malapace removing their soulscale early, the city being raided with Mutants, and the children entering Limbo. Zanshin...*really* didn't want to include the trio, but this was the solution that seemed to preserve the most lives.

He winced as he stood up, his eyes squinting as Limbo's soul slammed into his brain. The mountain, unable to create a domain for him, was forcing him to witness hundreds upon thousands of sectors all at once like flittering light through a kaleidoscope. Should he lose focus for a second, Zanshin would crumble. He focused on his ascension, trying to track the children amidst the infinite settings. After feeling his soul tug slightly, he glanced to the "future" and saw Taba scrambling away from...a woman? No, it was closer to call it a mannequin.

Zanshin took a slow exhale as he began to jog. "*Hang in there, Taba,*" he rasped.

. . .

How long had Taba been running for? Five minutes? An hour? It was hard to say: time was a secondary concern while his entire being was pushed to its limits. His muscles screamed with lava, his mind creaked with cries, and his eyelids begged for rest despite not needing to blink. His entire body was littered with nonfatal wounds, coated with scrapes and near-misses. The wounds ranged from mild annoyances to genuine hindrances. His right leg was growing more fuzzy with each aching step, his left eye blinded by the downpour of blood spilling out of the cut on his forehead, and his posture crooked due to the first cut on his rib cage. As Taba ducked and avoided a blind decapitation, he knew his body was running out of options. How much further could he run? How much more could he dodge? How long could he think of questions?

It also didn't help to hear the silent cackles of his blessing. Sure, it was keeping him alive by answering Taba's questions...but the gloating just irritated him. It frustrated Taba further even further as the librarian didn't even *attempt* to stab his blessing. Did his blessing not count as a guest? Could only Taba see the blessing, even while they were in Limbo? If he weren't running for his life, he would've loved to find out the specifics.

"You're reaching your limit," his blessing said.

'Shut it.'

"Wah wah, you hate me. Sure," his blessing said with a shrug. "Doesn't change the facts, boy." It swooped in front of Taba with an empty face, but it seemed as though the blessing were grinning and frowning at the same time. "You hate me? Get revenge by proving me wrong. *Use* me, boy. Swallow your pride and soar higher."

'I've been using you this entire time, have I not?' Taba mentally complained as he dove through an opening on a bookshelf to avoid another blow from the librarian. *'What else did you want me to do?'*

"Who knows?" it shrugged. "By all means, anyone else in your boots would be dead, no doubt. Still, is that enough for you? To be *better*? To be *alive*?" It leaned close to Taba's ear with a wordless whisper. *"Doesn't all this just **piss you off**?"*

'Not really, no. I'm just tired.'

"If you insist."

His blessing finally shut up, but Taba really was running on fumes. Sooner or later, the librarian would catch him off-guard, piercing a vital organ or limb. Then, he would be rapidly dispatched. Taba *needed* rest...but if he stopped moving, the librarian would gut him. The only escape Taba could think of was turning his head to change the landscape...but Limbo would get worse and worse with each setting change. Could he really risk that?

His eyebrow twitched, a tinge of blood trickling out as he did. Risk? Why did that word annoy him? No..."annoy" wasn't right. It felt wrong. It would be smarter to say the word felt uncharacteristic. If Taba could ask the right questions, everything that unfolded was a guaranteed outcome. There was no risk in that.

So...what was the point in fearing Limbo's scenery change?

From a more energized and logical standpoint, Taba could probably list five different reasons why he shouldn't change his current scenery. Unfortunately...he was just so, *so*, tired.

With the librarian skittering behind him, Taba reached his mental limit, turning on his wounded heel with an undignified yell, his arm throwing a punch as he turned.

As the library vanished immediately, Taba was met with utter dissatisfaction as his punch didn't connect with the librarian. Instead, his punch slammed into a familiar bed frame. Instead of shattering, the headboard wobbled slightly: proof of shoddy work done by an amateur smithy. Taba resisted the urge to blink in surprise. This was all...*disturbingly* familiar, but he couldn't recall this. It was as though someone had gotten an eraser and rubbed out a portion of his mind where this memory *should've* been.

A creaking door opened behind him. He should've been on high alert, but for some reason...he was calm. He couldn't even bring it to himself to ask whether or not he was under attack: he *knew* he was safe. A woman gasped behind him, rapid steps approaching his location. "You're wounded!" she said, cold hands touching his leg. Taba continued to stare at the wall, his mind racing in confusion. What was going on? Who was this? Where-

The room he sat in swiveled around, and Taba found himself staring at a familiar looking woman. He...he had *seen* her before. Where...?

She softly touched his cheek with a frown. "How did you get injured this badly? Stay here, I'll go get some bandages," the lady said as she ran out the room. Taba heard some whispers from the hallway, and soon she returned with a bigger man following closely. His left eye twitched upon seeing Taba's face, kneeling down to examine him carefully. "Hoo boy, yeah. This is gonna be rough. We're a bit low on supplies...but we'll see what we can do, ok kiddo?" he said.

The two adults began to plaster poorly-made bandages around his body, all while wiping off any excess blood. After a few minutes of dabbing and care, Taba sat in the bed relatively clean. It felt odd. Not the sudden warm welcome, but the fact that this all felt so...scripted.

The man and woman pushed him flat onto the mattress and pulled the covers over him. "Get some rest," they both ordered. "You're too young to be working this hard."

"I'm...sorry, but what? Who...?" Taba stammered, confusion blending with exhaustion and familiarity.

Before he could get any words in, the room faded to dark. Just as quickly as the bedroom turned black, it brightened up with morning light trickling through the windows. Though he hadn't closed his eyes or slept, Taba felt strangely invigorated. He wasn't fully healed, but felt comfortable enough to get up. Wincing at the soreness of his wounds cracking open, he stepped out of bed and hobbled over to the bedroom door, peeking out to prepare for the worst. Instead of ambush, however, Taba was greeted by the sight of the woman's back, humming away as she stirred a pot by the kitchen counter. The man from earlier was sitting at the dining room table, chewing a piece of slightly burnt toast. The two of them looked up at Taba, putting down their things to hurry over to where he stood.

The woman gingerly rubbed his cheek. "You feeling better, hun?" she asked.

The man elbowed her away. "Easy. Give him some space," he scolded before nodding at him. "How you feeling, son?"

"...son?"

Am I...their son? "...Yeah. Well, not *quite*, but close enough." his blessing responded mentally.

It was odd. Everything made sense: his familiarity of his surroundings, the coaxing nature of these people, similar physical features. By all means, it shouldn't be a surprise...

...so why couldn't he remember anything about this? His childhood home, his parents, *any* of this? Where the memory *should* have been...was just blank. It was as though a record were skipping over a chunk of his life, resuming after it had skipped five songs.

Taba hesitated before reaching out and grabbing his "mother"'s arm. It was warm, soft, squishy, and fragile. She stared at him with a blank from, squeezing his wrist in return with her free hand: a sensation that was all too familiar. His "father" rubbed his shoulder with a calloused hand, the bumps of rough skin scratching all the right places.

Is this a memory? "Well...eh, I'll give it to you, boy. Yeah, it is. To be more specific, it's how your version of your parents in your memory would act to the current you," the blessing confirmed.

Taba had to manually resist the urge to glance around the room. Somehow, Limbo had switched the region from the library to, well, a non-existent memory. He would've loved to take a look around to see what he could recognize, but-

Before he could even finish the thought, the kitchen swiveled around and suddenly Taba was staring at his living room. His mouth slightly opened in surprise as he walked forward. Just as it had yesterday, the entire house had rotated on Taba's pure whim. What even *was* this place?

Am I in danger here? "No. If you want to rest, this place is your best bet," Taba's blessing said. "Time limit doesn't mean a damn if your body breaks down at the peak, after all."

He walked forward into the living room to rub his hand over every surface possible. The chair with one leg that was a *bit* off center, the carpet that was slightly green in the corner from the one time he had thrown up, the aloe plant with the tips clipped off. All new to Taba's experience, but all so...nostalgic.

Out of curiosity, Taba attempted to swivel the room again. *I want to be facing the bathro-*

Just as it had before, the house rotated to face the bathroom before he could even finish his thought. Seems as though the place was reading Taba's desires and intentions, adjusting itself to cater to his entire need. This was a memory of Taba's childhood that didn't exist, where he could rest up without any looming danger. If Limbo always changed its environment to something worse every time...why did it choose something so comfortable? He *much* preferred this over the fungal forest, gloomy painting, and the library.

Taba rotated the house so he could walk back to the kitchen to sit down. His "parents" followed suit. He had time to recollect himself here. Taba could rest up, try to uncover any secrets here, then be on his way later. For now? He had no reason to leave.

Taba reclined in the chair and began to slowly strike up a conversation with his...parents. The more they talked to him, the more he laughed and slumped into his chair. If Limbo had no time limit, with no requirement of food, water, or necessities overall...yeah. Why *should* he leave?

As he talked, the day changed four times...but he didn't care. The mystery of this forgotten memory, the comfort of the home, the love of his parents. They all tickled his fancy. By the sixth day, the concept of "escape" felt wrong. Why would he leave his parents?

By the twelfth day, Taba was eating some slightly stale gumbo with his parents, tossing banter as he slurped away. His father was complaining to his mother about how the gumbo was colored brown instead of orange, to which his mother rolled her eyes and threw an extra meatball in his bowl as a peace offering. While he wasn't looking, Taba stole the meatball from his father and quickly threw it in his mouth. His mother, having watched the entire scene unfold, laughed heartily while the father turned back to his bowl with utter confusion.

174

Taba swallowed the meatball, laughed for the first time in a long while, and gave his father a piece of lamb in a gesture of apology.

Taba could not hear it anymore. Taba could not hear his blessing laughing in the background as each day passed.

Taba was truly at home.

CHAPTER 10

For a place deemed an "impossible mountain"...there was surprisingly not as much climbing as Queenie expected.

She landed down in an odd bog, her lower body submerged in the muck. Staring ahead, she tried to take in as much information as available. The sludge was a vibrant orange, bouncing light off in all directions. The sludge also seemed to pool into highs and lows, like a toddler's poor attempt at making massive cities in a sandbox. When she tried to move forward, the syrupy liquid seemed to grip at her legs and whine, pulling back at her progression with active resistance. The air was humid, but with some odd density, as though she was constantly moving through thin spiderwebs. She rubbed her cheek with her free hand to see if there was some muck in the air, but her hand came back with no abnormalities. Hm.

"I'm in this weird bog," Queenie called out to her brother. "It'll be slow to move, but I'm safe. You?"

"I...man, I don't like this," she heard Hush mutter. "I'm in this dim cave. Tons of eyes are staring at me...but that's it. Still, I can see all their eyes move at any action I take. I can't tell if the eyes are from the same creature or not. Let's go."

Queenie squeezed Hush's hand and took an uncomfortable step forward. Moving felt like a crossover between swimming and manual trudging, all while the sobbing bog filled her ears with wailing as it pushed back at her movement. She tried to summon chains from her storage to hoist herself up...but her blessing felt different. Normally, her storage felt as though she were pulling things out of a back-pack...but now? When she "reached" for her "backpack", her hand groped the air. She could still feel the items in her storage rattle around, but she wasn't able to easily access them as normal. Hell, even the dagger she had pulled out before entering Limbo had vanished back into her storage. So much for entering Limbo "prepared".

Queenie fished around her pockets in hopes of forgetting some-thing useful inside. Though she felt no tool that could be of actual usage, she felt a soft fabric trace itself on her fingers. Queenie frowned as she pulled out a handkerchief. When did she...? Eh, didn't matter, she supposed: whatever she had at her disposal, she would use.

She shrugged as she dabbed at her face. Oddly enough, the hand-kerchief was soothing to the touch, the dense humidity seemingly floating away from her face. She raised the handkerchief to her eye level to fully examine the fabric, raising an eyebrow to see no notable changes. She passed it back to her brother, subconsciously nodding as she did. "Yo. Feel this. It feels nice," Queenie said.

She felt Hush pluck it from her fingers, followed by the sound of fabric dragging across his skin. "Whoa. That *is* nice. What's in it?" he asked.

"Dunno. Found it in my pockets, go figure."

"Huh. Go figure, indeed," he said, passing it back up to her. "You should probably hold onto it. I think you would need it more than me, since you're in a bog."

She took the handkerchief back and placed it in her pockets, pushing forwards. The siblings walked silently for what felt like eternity without making much progress. Queenie was constantly on edge, partially because of the unfamiliarity of the environment, partially because of the constant cries of the muck.

After some time, Queenie felt Hush grip her hand tightly. "Hey. Not to alarm you...but I think the eyes are getting closer," he said.

"What do you mean?"

"...what do you want me to say? The eyeballs in the dark are growing more clear and bigger. I...my spine is getting chills from this. *Not* a fan."

Queenie tried to push through her sludge faster, but it felt as though the bog were pulling at her even further with each step. Hush said nothing, but she could feel her brother walk with a *bit* more urgency than before. Desperate to break the silence, Queenie cleared her throat. "So...can you blind the eyeballs?" Hush took a small inhale to answer, but another thought crossed Queenie's mind. "Wait. What happens if you blind *yourself*? Would Limbo just endlessly shuffle different areas?" she asked.

"Well, first off...I'm not blinding myself. I don't want to find out what happens if I do. Secondly, I tried blinding the eyes. When I do, the eyes disappear...but the second I stop using my blessing, the eyes come back. I don't see a point in doing it. How is it for you?" Hush asked.

She glanced downwards slightly at the orange sludge as it wailed into the abyss. "The gooey stuff won't stop screaming. It's slowly getting to me, can't lie," she admitted. "The air sucks, too. All in all, it's super uncomfortable here...but I don't think I'm in danger."

The pair continued to walk forward. Queenie didn't want to say anything to worry Hush, but the bog was slowly starting to bubble in unfrequent chunks, like air bubbles escaping a swimmer's nostrils. The sobs was slowly growing, turning from whining to harrowing shrieks. The air, which used to be clear, was slowly growing more thick and brown. It wasn't really impeding her progress, so she tried to ignore the changes.

Queenie didn't really get Limbo. If the region changed everytime they looked away...how did that work if she was holding Hush's hand? He wasn't in her world, neither was she. If that were the case...the eyeballs in Hush's world should be visible for her. Likewise, the sludge in Queenie's world should also be slowing Hush down, but judging from his steps...he didn't seem to be impeded whatsoever. Plus, she had glanced down slightly, but the world hadn't changed when she looked back up. Was it because she was holding hands with Hush? If so...

She decided to take a gamble, took a deep breath, and twirled to look at Hush. Just as she suspected, she saw Hush's backside walking easily through the bog, as though the sludge were just a hologram for him.

Their worlds would stay the same...as long as they held hands. That was amazing intel. She poked her brother's cheek, eager to share the news. He flinched, but kept his head facing backwards. "That you, Queenie?" he asked softly.

"Mhm. Guess what? You can turn your head to look at me," she said.

"I'm not following you."

Queenie sighed and grabbed her brother's cheek to swivel his head forcefully. He flinched as his head turned, his eyes alarmed as he locked eyes with Queenie. She raised an eyebrow. "See? Told ya. I bet you still see a dark cave with eyeballs behind me, right?" she said.

"I...how did you find this out?" he asked.

"I turned around. Duh."

Hush locked his jaw, his eyes flashing a tinge of anger. "Seriously? Why?" he scowled.

She rolled her eyes and waved a hand. "Gut instinct, relax. My train of thought was damn good, but this is good info. Now, we don't have to have our head and eyesight locked onto one location for the entire climb. I don't even know how you'd manage that...like how would you even dodge if something were to attack you from the back?" she said.

"Eh. Taba could probably do well in this kind of environment," Hush shrugged.

Queenie slightly nodded. Yeah, if anyone, Taba could probably climb Limbo by himself. She turned around and trudged on ahead. Suddenly, Hush gasped and Queenie could feel his grip on her hand tremble slightly. Queenie turned around and saw sprouts of blood prick up from his jacket sleeve. She cursed at the sight and turned to run...but the sludge was slowing her down even further. It felt like she was pushing through a wave of syrup, with the shrieks turning into howls of laughter, the light brown air turning into a murky fog that had fully obscured her view. There was still no danger...but the

180

longer she toiled through, the more danger Hush was in. She needed to change her domain...*now.*

Fueled with desperation, Queenie closed her eyes for two seconds. Once open, the swamp had vanished. There she stood, in an endlessly vertical room with a ceiling that melted into the darkness. On the ground there were countless rows of padded seats, each one housing a person, with a clear aisle down the middle. Oddly enough, the people seemed to have clothes from different regions...or maybe time eras? From imperial garbs to baggy jeans, each one slammed their eyes into Queenie when she appeared. They all held fearful expressions, as though they knew what was coming next.

Queenie didn't give a damn. She didn't know these people, and her legs were free. So, she ran without batting an eye.

After a few strides, a spotlight sparkled from the looming heights onto Queenie. She looked up with a frown, squinting into nothingness. As she did, another spotlight shone onto a random spectator, the fear in his eyes melting into awe. Suddenly his skin morphed as an indecipherable language trickled from his lips. Two other heads began to sprout from his neck, his suit and tie tearing as his flesh bulged with warts and slime. Queenie stopped running and stared, her flesh turning cold as the gibberish turned into croaking, the screams of the nearby spectators being drowned out by the crunching of bones, as the numerous legs that sprouted from the former man pushed into fragile ribcages around it.

A bit over a year ago...the Misfits barely succeeded in taking out a mutant. Even then, it was only with the help of Juliette. So...how was it here? How was the mutant frog that nearly wiped them out, standing before her? Queenie cursed and instinctually tried reaching into her storage, her trembling fingers failing to pull out anything.

"Oh...piss off," she muttered, turning to flee down the aisle. Hush kept up her pace, his breathing indicating that he was getting bitten less.

More spotlights rained down, each one morphing into something from her memory. Be it members of her former clan, regular animals, hell, even *buildings* from Malapace. The transmorphed creatures seemed to pose no major threat, each danger choosing to focus on the more vulnerable captives strapped down in the chairs. If anything, the only hurdle seemed to be the shrinking space as Queenie swiveled around bloating victims. After a while, it got to the point where the aisle was too narrow to maneuver, the floor turning into a bloodbath with a symphony of screams. Queenie had bigger problems, so she scrambled over all her former memories, pushing off walls and beings in the newfound labyrinth.

...until she felt a deathly familiar claw grab her head, crashing Queenie into the floor. It was instantaneous, but Queenie could never forget that texture. Soft, yet scaly. Fluffy, yet slimy.

The same sensation of the mutant that physically scarred Juliette...while traumatizing Queenie.

Queenie slowly got up, nervous sweat dripping down her brow, as she stared at her former Family member, the chimera once named Linda, in her eyes. Just as Queenie remembered, the chimera stood one head taller than her with a lumpy body, its "human" skin shimmering with tiny embedded scales, each one adorned with their own patterns of spots and stripes. From her behind was an impossibly long tail coated in coarse fur, tipped with a spike at its end. Her skin shed droplets of liquid, sizzling as it rolled down onto the seats next to her. Tiny eyes littered the chimera's forehead. Normally, the eyes would be scanning every detail of the environment...yet right now? They all clacked into Queenie's skull. The thing had massive fur-tipped ears, each one bigger than its own head. The nose was squished into the face, and her mouth was split open vertically at the chin, each "side" of the mouth covered in square teeth with jagged flats. Drool escaped from her mouth, its forked tongue lapped at her tongue and cheek, wiping a smear of sloggy venom across her face. The spittle burned slight scars in her face, yet left no lasting damage as she would quickly regenerate any injuries. Any spit that landed on the woman seemed to sizzle meaninglessly against her scales.

A creature that eagerly thirsted for strength, absorbing the strong to gain further heights. If this was an accurate recollection from Quee-nie's mind, it would make sense that it ignored the helpless victims and gunned it for the strongest being in the area.

Running was logical. Some could even argue that it was the correct psychological response. And yet...Queenie felt a mixture of dread and rage. She stopped running, staring her failure in the eyes, and screamed a flurry of many emotions.

Before she charged in recklessly unarmed, she felt a squeeze in her left hand bring her back. "Queenie. What's the scenery you're in?" Hush's collective voice asked.

She whirled around, wild eyes brimming with unrestraint. How-ever...that fervor shackled itself when she saw the numerous bitemarks across Hush's body. Even as he calmly spoke, a spurt of blood bubbled from his shoulder. Queenie's brother betrayed no emotion as he fo-cused on his sister, a look of concern evident.

Queenie closed her mouth. Queenie's pride demanded she face her woes, tearing the chimera's head from its body. And yet...there were some things far more important than her vainglory. The soulscale and redemption? Sure, they were reasons to climb Limbo...but there was more than that. She just wanted to be someone who could proudly hold her head up next to Taba, and more importantly, Hush.

Against the natural order of her mind and body, she turned around. Queenie felt bitter hatred and rage, frustrated at her own weakness. And yet...she knew fighting here would create greater regrets. Queenie needed to obtain the soulscale, not just for redeeming herself in front of Juliette, but to prove there was nothing she couldn't overcome. The chimera hunched down, limbs swelling, fangs dripping, eyes twitching, tail flicking, and harrowed a war cry as she dove onto Queenie. Before her legs buckled, Queenie closed her eyes and exhaled.

"None of your business," she said with a tremble. "Don't worry about me."

When she opened her eyes, the seats and memories vanished. In their place, existed countless glass boxes. Queenie stood fully enclosed in the center of a glass box, with *that* box fully enclosed within numerous other glass boxes. She pressed a hand to the glass wall, a bit baffled at the sudden change. There was no door, no opening whatsoever. To her feet lay a single steel hammer, but to Queenie's surprise...she felt a surge of her own soul gush through her arm as she picked it up. It was a sensation similar to when she withdrew something from her storage. That meant this was *her* hammer...but why was it here?

She gripped the handle tightly. Queenie could ask questions later, but right now she had a duty to run. She reeled her arm back and slammed the hammer into the glass box, the wall shattering without too much difficulty. As shards rained around her, Queenie winced as her body slowly got littered in tiny cuts. As she burst through the box, she quickly ran forward for ten seconds before reaching the wall of the secondary box. Before even reaching the wall, she had already reeled her arm back to shatter the glass wall. Since *this* box was bigger than the first one, the glass shards were naturally larger as well. Queenie did what she could to avoid the more dangerous chunks, but she couldn't avoid many of the cuts that rained down on her arms or legs. Gritting her teeth, she pushed forward in desperation, determined to save her brother.

After about the eighth box, Queenie felt Hush firmly grip her shoulder. "Queenie, *stop*," he said.

She turned around, exhaustion plastered on her face. "You...you safe?" she gasped.

Hush expression was...pained? Was he hurt? Of course he was: his jacket and jeans were coated with multiple, uneven bitemarks. Still, her brother pulled his jacket sleeve to his hand and brang it up to Queenie's eyelevel. "Queenie," Hush said softly as he dabbed at her face with his jacket. "What the hell happened to 'there was no danger' or 'don't worry about me'?" he asked.

She looked down at her body. She was littered in wounds, blood seeping from numerous cuts everywhere. Hell, there was even a chunk of glass embedded in her right shoulder that she had been ignoring. Queenie winced as she yanked it out, the shard clattering to the floor. "I'm fine," she muttered, fully aware Hush wouldn't buy such a statement.

Her brother said nothing. Instead, he sat on the floor and patted the ground next to her. "Sit, let's get you patched up," he ordered. "Give me that handkerchief."

Queenie swept away some glass before plopping down next to him, pulling out the cloth from her pocket. Hush took it, flexed a few fingers, and Queenie felt all her soreness vanish. He reached into his pockets, pulling out some bandages as though he had been expecting something like this to have happened while on Limbo. Hush, using his teeth and his only free hand, began to tightly wrap around her more serious wounds. It was a bit shoddy, but after a few minutes, Queenie's wounds were fully patched up. She still felt sleepy, but the bandages were oddly soothing. He nodded to her firmly. "Better?" he asked.

"Eh."

"Good enough for me. Let's sit down to catch our breath. Once you've got enough gas in your tank, we'll take our time moving forward, ok?" he said.

"...sure. Thanks." Queenie said softly.

. . .

Queenie, Taba, and Toukie were hiding behind the boulder, both of them trembling at the sound of padded footsteps and screeches. They heard approaching footsteps which ended up belonging to Nancy holding Hush in a piggyback. He was covered in sweat, huffing as crimson hues stuck the insides of his shirt to his stomach. Nancy grimaced as she held her arms out, the blood from his shirt slowly seeping back into his open wound. Once the majority of his blood returned back to his body, she rolled up his shirt to examine the wound firsthand. It was a nasty gash, the result of an attack that was a mixture of a burn and a slash. She hesitated, but drew out a bit of the blood attached to some of Hush's loose skin, using it to amateurly suture his wound shut.

An attack, that was entirely Queenie's fault. She had insisted they enter mutant territory, with her tromping ahead before they could protest. Taba had noticed the mutant first, but it was Hush who had tackled his sister to take the blow. Toukie, in turn, bombarded the mutant in explosions to flashbang the creature. As Taba dragged the stunned Queenie to shelter, Hush and Nancy had stayed behind to hold off the mutant. The five of them weren't prepared for this. The Family wasn't aware of this sudden excursion, so reinforcements weren't coming anytime soon.

Nancy peeked out from behind the rock, a visible tremor shimmering across her septum piercing. 'Hush, on my signal, you can null your sense of pain. I'll hold off the mutant while you get back to camp. I'll see you there, ok?" she said with an obviously forced smile, her freckles slightly twitching.

'No. You can't take it on alone,' Hush said with ragged breaths, forcing himself up. 'Plus, it'll track us anyways, since it marked me. I'll support you,' he said with a determined nod.

'It...it's my fault you guys are in this mess,' Nancy said, shaking her blond hair. 'Let me at least take responsibility. I'm not letting you guys fight any more than this.' She stood up with clenched fists, removing the scalpel strapped to her thigh to make small incisions to her hands, drawing trickles of blood. 'Don't worry,' she said. 'I'll make sure it doesn't get past me.'

Nancy took a sharp breath, but before she could dive out from behind the boulder, a sickly hand firmly gripped her shoulder. The entire party turned around in surprise as a dark-hooded figure turned to face them, a thin frown stretched across his stretchy skin. 'We told you guys not to venture out without permission,' *he scolded.*

'Who are y-wait...Zanshin?' asked Taba.

Another hand suddenly ruffled Queenie's head in a familiar fashion, causing her to look up with mild annoyance and relief. A well-suited man took the cigarette from his mouth as he examined the mutant before him. 'Hm. I think that's a...skunk? Right?' Geralt said without looking at Nancy.

'Geralt. Look, I-' Nancy stammered.

'Relax. Time and place for everything,' Geralt said calmly, putting out his cigarette with his shoe. 'On one hand...you really should've told someone before heading out. On the other...good on you for offering to hold the line. I can respect that.' He jutted his thumb behind him, to the direction of the camp. 'Still, you guys are all out of your element. Get to the cave, we'll talk later. Ok?'

The mutant skunk sniffed into the air, locking its beady eyes onto their spot with a hiss, swiveling its butt towards their spot to fire an acidic spray towards their boulder. Right before it could fire, Geralt furrowed his brows and quickly twirled a marble around in his palm before shooting it at the skunk. The marble zipped faster than any of Queenie's bullets, slamming into the mutant's back leg, causing it to lose footing with a screech. Geralt reached into his pocket to pull out a small pebble, massaging it between his fingers before nodding to the party. 'Seriously, get back to camp. It'd be hard for me to take this thing down while also protecting you guys. Zanshin will be close behind you all. You're in good hands,' said Geralt.

Nancy got up, but instead of running, she looked to Geralt with her chin held high. 'Geralt, please. Let me fight. I ca-'

Zanshin touched her shoulder, causing Nancy to flinch. 'You have a good heart...but sometimes, you need to learn when to fall back. Swallow your pride: your priority right now should be protecting the kids,' he said.

She bit her lip, but nodded as she scooped up Hush, looking at Queenie, Taba, and Toukie. 'You three can follow, right?' she asked. They nodded. So, the party fled from their first mutant encounter, with Geralt cleaning up their mess.

. . .

"Feeling better?" asked Hush, tucking her handkerchief into his pockets as he slowly unflexed his fingers.

"No...but I'm sick of just waiting around," said Queenie, wincing as she stood up. "Let's get this over with."

As far as she could see, it was a prismatic void, the only thing in her way being an infinite number of glass boxes, each one enclosing her. Queenie frowned as she turned to Hush. "So...whatever happened to the eyes?" she asked.

"Ah...they stopped...staring. Don't worry about it," Hush said.

She didn't trust that answer. It felt as though her brother were hiding something, but prodding wouldn't get them anywhere, so she nodded and continued onward, her brother in one hand and a hammer in another. The more boxes she shattered, however, the further the distance between each box, removing a big chunk of the urgency.

"Hey, Hush?"

"Yeah?"

"I've been thinking about this for a while...but once we get to the soulscale, how are we gonna extract it?" she asked.

Hush squirmed, looking around him nervously. "Well...if it's small, I figured it would be a good candidate for you to store in your storage. Do you think it'll be possible?" he asked.

"I...I'm not sure. The weaker version I saw in Malapace already seemed impossible. I don't think I could handle a fully charged one," she admitted.

"Well, we'll figure it out. In the meanwhile, change of topic: when's the last time you've danced?" he asked with a bit of urgency in the trickles of his voice.

"I...don't dance? I've never danced in my life. Why do yo-"

"What about that time with the whole 'Dancing Painter' rhyme? You would always hop around wh-"

Queenie's face flushed violently. "Hey. I was a kid. Shut up. Anyways, why are you suddenly bringing this up?"

"Trust me, but follow my lead."

He suddenly swiveled Queenie around, holding her close to his chest. Queenie was about to protest, but she noticed his shirt damp with sweat. Judging from how much his eyes seemed to dart around him, it appeared to be nervous sweat. Wordlessly, Queenie held her hammer tightly but wrapped her arm around his back to rest on his shoulder. They extended their gloved hand forward, twirling around as though they were in a ballroom, an unnatural level of formality overtaking Hush. His breath was tight, but as Queenie rested her head against his chest, his heart was beating at an unnatural speed. After a few minutes of this waltz, he suddenly let Queenie go from his chest, bowing to the nothingness around her. He let out a shaky breath before nodding to her. "Alright. Sorry about that, let's go on," he said.

"Ok, yeah. What the *hell*?" she hissed while jogging forward. "What are you not telling me?"

"So. I blinked. Big whup, it happens," he muttered while darting his eyes around.

"You dumbass, why would you...fine. Whatever. What's your setting?" she asked through a scowl.

"Ballroom. There's random guests and stuff, none of them human. When the spotlight is on you, you dance. If you fail, your partner eats you. That's the gist of it," he said.

"...partner? Wait, how do you know all this?"

"I've just been observing as it happened. Didn't want to alarm you, that's all."

Queenie groaned as she broke out into a full sprint, ignoring the aches of her body. Of course her brother would do something so selfless. What an *idiot*. "Alright, I'm guessing the spotlight is off you. When is it going to shine on you again?" she asked.

He glanced upwards, silently counting. "It seems to be shining in the order of where the dancers are standing. I don't know when it'll be my turn next, but for now I'm safe," he said. "...Sorry for not mentioning this."

"I'm smacking you after all this," she snapped, smashing through the next glass wall, flinching as the shards scraped the bandages wrapped around her. What concerned her more than the injuries, however, were the boxes. The further they went, the more sturdy the glass walls were becoming. Her hand continued to sting as the handle reverberated against her squishy palm. While it had initially only taken one hit to shatter each cube, now it was taking five or even six swings. They were slowing down and Queenie feared it was her fault and-

She scowled. That was a loser's mentality. She channeled her soul through the hammer, feeling it hum with a familiar coolness in her hand. Before even reaching the next wall, she began to wildly swing her arm before chucking the hammer, putting her entire back into the throw. The hammer left a sizable crack into the wall but bounced off towards her. Determined to make the most of it, she caught the hammer midair and slammed it into the crack, shattering the next wall.

Unfortunately, since she was so focused on catching the hammer to break the cube, her positioning left her facing upwards as the glass rained down all around her. As glass rained on her face, she closed her eyes with a cry, but not before a tiny shard slightly embedded itself into her right eye.

She crumpled to the ground and clutched face, gently pulling out the shard and flinging it to the floor. Her right eye burned with pulses, a pain she had never experienced before. Her brother was yelling something, but she was so focused that she couldn't hear his concerns.

It hurts. It hurts. It really hurts. It hurts. It hurts so much. It hurts. Can I see? Is my eye gone? It hurts. It hurts. Ow. Ow. Why? I...

I need to get up. I need to **move**.

Through tears, she pushed up on the floor with closed eyes. The first thing she noticed was how she couldn't feel any glass shards at her feet anymore. The next was, well, the fact that her hammer had vanished from her hand.

Lastly? The cold crunch beneath her fingers.

She opened her left eye, blinking away her tears as she glanced at the icy terrain around her. A blizzard blew harshly around her, but her body didn't feel any colder. Even while she rubbed her free hand on her cheek, the friction generated no heat. Instead...her bones chattered. It was as though the ice were pelting her soul over her body. Shame, since the ice would've been *wonderful* to put over her right eye. Queenie took a step and flinched as her foot sank down with a *snap*. She glanced down with her good eye and noticed a snapped...cylinder?

No...a *finger*.

Queenie slowly turned around, the knots in her stomach thickening with each look. The floor was a mold of piled, frozen humans. From how their faces and limbs slightly twitched here and there...Queenie wasn't sure if they were hanging onto the dredges of life or if their corpses was expelling the last of its energy. The trees, from a distance, seemed to be coated in layers of powdery frost. However, upon closer inspection, the trunks were birthed of twisted spines, the roots of braided ribs, and branches of eternally reaching arms, groping at nothing. The snow that pelted at Queenie's face was flakey, rubbing off her skin without melting. She looked up at the clouds and saw a myriad of hung bodies strung onto infinity, skin flittering off their frozen, yet rotting, corpses onto the floor. Queenie looked back forward, feeling a surge of nausea flood her throat. She...*really* wished she hadn't glanced up. Or down. Hell, this entire landscape as a whole made her feel queasy.

She suddenly felt Hush swivel her around and pull her in for another dance, this one with a faster tempo than before. He locked eyes with her, the blood draining from his face. "Holy sh-*Queenie*. What happened to you?" he asked with frantic dignity.

"I got hurt," she snapped with a watery voice. "It happens. Whatever. Focus on your dance first, ok?" she sniffled.

193

Hush was *obviously* distraught...but he pushed forward with a rapid tempo, the siblings taking swift steps across an imaginary dance floor. Each of his movements would cause one of her numerous wounds to split open, causing Queenie to flinch with every jerk. Her brother noticed and was trying to slow his tempo down as much as possible, but Queenie was jostled around regardless.

One of Hush's movements caused Queenie's ankle to trip over a corpse's neck, the *crick* of their throat forcing her to yelp and stumble to the ground. As she landed in the pile of frozen bodies, Queenie felt her brother's hand turn clammy. He proceeded to roll with her, flipping her onto his back before breaking out onto a sprint. She couldn't really tell if they were moving forward or backwards, but it was evident that anywhere was fine...as long as it wasn't *here*.

Queenie's breath was short, her head spinning. She wasn't sure if it was from exhaustion or from the new snowy atmosphere. Judging from how her lungs felt numb...it honestly could've been both.

Without warning, Hush lurched forward and a warm puddle started forming under Queenie's stomach. She put her free hand where the puddle formed and pulled back a sticky, red handprint.

Queenie's shirt and stomach were intact. The back of Hush's shirt was in tatters.

Despite it all, Hush got up with a groan and continued to run faster. Oddly enough, all of Queenie's pain had vanished, allowing her to concentrate more on the scenery around her. It was desolate, with the only colors in sight being white, pale blue, and grey. From the peripherals of her vision, she could *barely* make out a humanoid creature standing at an odd crook from beyond the snowstorm. There was no way it was human, however. Its knuckles dragged across its toes.

It was hunched over, yet easily stood over eight feet tall. The last detail she noticed was its knees: they were far too high up on its legs, with the joints bending awkwardly outward, as though it had broken each leg from the inside-out. Whenever she tried to focus on it, it vanished and reappeared wherever her new peripheral was.

She...*really* didn't like how it was facing her direction. The last time she felt similar uncanny chills was, well, the chimera.

Queenie glanced down at her brother's haggard eyes. His face was pale, cheeks sunken, and his ponytail was undone, matted with blood and oil. His head darted to his left as he jumped a bit backwards, Hush's face contorting into pure agony as a sudden hole the size of a golf ball appeared in his left ribcage, the force of the blow throwing him to his right. With his free hand, he clutched his chest with a wheeze, yanked an imaginary pole from his body, and continued to sprint. After a few minutes of scattered movements, he reached his arm out and grabbed an invisible handle, swinging it open and diving through an imaginary room. He leaned against the "door", huffing as he grabbed his side.

"...Queenie, what's your current setting?" Hush asked through gasps.

Worry and bile bubbled up her throat, but Queenie choked out a response. "Snowy mountain of corpses. Something out there is staring at me. It's cold, but not physically: I don't know how to describe it," she stammered out. "Nevermind that, are you ok? You're-"

"I'm *fine*," he snapped, before closing one eye and exhaling softly. He glanced back at her with a nod. "It looks really bad...but I can move. Trust me, you're in a worse spot than me. How's your eye?" Hush asked.

"It used to hurt, but not anymore," Queenie responded. "I don't think I can see out of it, though. Dunno how that'll affect my depth perception, but I think I'll be fine."

Hush nodded slightly, but his eyes were fixated on something in his domain far past Queenie. His mouth was slightly ajar, not out of fear...but disbelief? The look Hush had on his face was the same one that someone might have upon seeing someone they hadn't seen for decades...but *far* more wistful. He shuffled a bit on the floor, his face morphing into something that could only be describes as unimaginable agony. His nose twitched before sighing, looking at his sister with wistful resolve.

"Queenie. Do you trust me?" he asked calmly.

"We've made it this far. Don't think I would've made it this far with someone I didn't trust, y'know?" she scoffed weakly.

"Good. Think you can move?"

They got up to their feet and Queenie prepared to walk in the same direction Hush had ran from. Hush gave his sister's hand a tight squeeze. "Hey. From now on, no matter what...don't look back. Ok?" he said.

"Uh...can I ask wh-"

"Sorry, I'm out of time," he muttered with a watery cough. "I *swear* we'll see each other again. Trust me."

Suddenly, the ropes around their glove loosened and the strap that tightened around their wrists became slack. As her wrist became limp, the last thing Queenie felt was her brother's hand slip away...and just like that, he was gone.

Queenie couldn't even afford to turn around in shock. This wasn't just betrayal. No, the sudden waves of pain that began to flood back into her system told her that this was something far more agonizing.

All she could do was clutch her suddenly throbbing right eye, screaming pained wails into the rotting, howling storm.

CHAPTER II

E ver since the chimera, there was a thin siren in Juliette's head, a tiny ringing that didn't serve any purpose but to nettle her existence. Whenever she used her blessing, that annoyance grew with each slash.

So...with thousands of pre-laid slashes raining down across the entire outer walls of Malapace every second? It felt like her head was about to split open. If it weren't for G, her brain would've collapsed upon itself hours ago.

Juliette did what she could to ignore the headache and sprinted across the perimeter of the city, manually dicing whoever she could. G was following close behind, finishing off mutants that she failed to eviscerate in only a few kicks. His hands were tied down since he was using his ascension...but that was fine: she could make do.

Her glowing eyes twitched to the side as suddenly crouched deeply towards the pavement, feeling the *woosh* of a mutant's tail flying over the back of her neck. The mutant chattered back at her with vibration, lunging its gaping maw towards Juliette. She pushed down on the ground, but felt something slightly snap in her leg. Bursts of sweat bubbled out from her forehead, causing her to groan and collapse to the floor. G leapt over her fallen body and slammed his heel into the roof of the creature's nose, forcing its upper jaw to crash through its neck, decapitating it in the most unusual way Juliette had ever seen.

He kept his hands together as though he were praying and nodded to her. "What happened? Explain," he ordered.

"...small snap in my left achilles. Not broken, though. It hurts to move my ankle."

"Got it," said G, muttering as he closed his eyes to concentrate. Almost immediately, the burning sensation in her foot vanished and Juliette stood up with relative ease. She patted his bare shoulder. "Thanks, G," she said with slight concern. "You sure you don't need a break? It's been a few hours, an-"

"You sound like Sana, and *both* of you are dumbasses," he snapped. "I'm fine. What about you? You're overusing your ascension in a weakened body. I don't even know how you're even conscious."

"Neither do I," admitted Juliette, rubbing her forehead. "Still, if I can protect everyone, I don't mind. W-"

"Huh, toots be darned: Father was right. Guess you *are* weakened," a female voice rang out.

The two turned around to lock eyes with a girl wearing a cropped shirt and knee-length skirt. Her tiny earrings shimmered behind her blond hair, her sneakers twisting into the floor. She unstrapped the scalpel from her thigh and tilted her head with a frown. "Father said you took a *nasty* hit from Linda. Didn't think it'd be this bad. How ya holdin' up, sweetpea?" she asked in a slightly mocking tone.

Just as Juliette was about to dive towards Nancy, the small ringing turned into a bombastic screech within an instant. Her face crunched up in agony as her mouth twisted into a wordless cry, body stiffening as she stumbled into the floor. Juliette cracked open an eyeball towards G and noticed his hands were separated. What had hap-

The pain exponentially grew to an unbearable level. Juliette's eyes rolled to the back of her skull before she passed out.

. . .

G was stunned silent. His ascension had the condition of clasping his hands together, but his hands were suddenly dragged apart by something internal...like his veins were tugging against his muscles. Moreover, he couldn't freely move his arms: as though some imaginary force were holding him back. Without his blessing, Juliette couldn't function. And if she wasn't conscious...

The sound of crashing walls echoed throughout Malapace, the burden of the numerous soulbearers within the city drastically growing without Juliette's aid. The average soulbearer could barely survive an encounter with a mutant, let alone *defeat* one.

It was happening again. G was letting everyone down. His family's blood would once more be on his hands. He-

G clenched his jaw, took a deep breath, and roared in defiance, focusing all of his soul into his arms. Like straining machinery, they slowly began to move back down to his sides. It would be impossible for him to ascend once more...not while *she* existed in front of him. Judging from her appearance, she seemed to match Patchy's description perfectly.

"Are you Nancy?" he asked through forced restraint.

"Gosh darn! I'm *that* famous?" she cooed.

She was a bloodbender: one of the worst matchups for G. Still, he had no choice: if he didn't take her down *right now*, Malapace would fall to the upcoming swarm of mutants. He was heavily handicapped, with his arms essentially being useless duds, but that was fine: he only needed his legs to secure victory.

Suddenly, a big shadow loomed over him. G barely had time to turn before a massive swing cracked his neck, throwing him into the foliage to his right. If it were *anyone* else...they would be dead, no doubt about it. G pulled himself out of the tree with just his legs, his neck cracking into place as he stared at his new foe. It was a big man wearing a white tank top, tropical shorts, and a bathrobe. He had long locks and wore a big smile. He looked fat, but the way he moved? G suspected he secretly was just as built as Banase.

"Who are you? Don't recognize you from the reports," said G.

"Aw. Guess I'm not as famous, huh?" the big man frowned.

"Silly Maggle, not everyone is as popular as me!" giggled Nancy.

"Maggle, hm?" said G. "That's a new name."

The two Family members slightly froze, wincing at the small slipup. The man named Maggle shrugged. "Eh, whatever. Corpses can't spill the beans," he said.

Nancy glared at him. "Wait. The phrasing of that sentence means you're about to merk *me*, toots. What do ya mean by th-"

"Wah, you know what I mea-"

Their conversation was cut short as G's legs exploded with power, closing their distance in a single leap. Maggle's eyes widened as a thin blue layer suddenly appeared in front of his face, stopping G's knee from crushing Maggle's windpipe. The big man grinned as he grabbed G, raised him up into the air, and slammed him into the ground. Before G could get up, Nancy joined in, her arms coated in her own blood as she pierced all of G's joints and organs with pinpoint precision.

It wasn't enough to do any meaningful damage...but it succeeded at pinning him down.

"Sorry, shnookums," Nancy curtly mocked. "Our job isn't to beat ya. Only an idiot would try to kill an immortal man. No, we were tasked with holding ya in place."

Maggle raised an eyebrow as the ground below him tremored. G's massive shoulders pushed up from the ground, the bald man clenching his teeth as he strained all his muscles. In response, Maggle simply slammed his massive leg downwards onto the Gatekeeper. "You sure are strong," muttered Maggle as glanced at the motionless Juliette on the floor. His gaze softened slightly. "The poor rose. Who trampled over you?"

Nancy took shallow breaths as she focused her blessing onto G. "Well...*technically*, she was already crippled before we got here, darlin'," she gasped. "If she were healthy...hoo *wee*. Don't think we woulda had a chance."

. . .

Sana continued falling through the sky, the wind whipping around her proving to be a hurdle in keeping her eyes open. Still, it was something she needed to tolerate, lest Limbo change once again. She tightly held Banase's right hand, with her own right hand serving as guide to navigate past the numerous ruby stalactites that jutted out around the sides of the hole. Behind her, Banase was swiping away frantically. According to him, there was a murky fog that was seeping closer and closer to his eyes, dampening whatever it touched with extremely dense purple molasses. The more that was packing onto him, the harder he found it to move, let alone *breathe*.

In short, it was a really difficult landscape for the two of them, but Sana hesitated to close her eyes. Limbo had a way of creatively making things worse...and she didn't want to find out what was more irritating than splattering against a ruby pillar at one-hundred and twenty miles per hour.

"*How is it on your end?*" Sana screamed against the wind.

"I...some of it went up my nose," Banase responded nasally. "It's getting really hard to breathe and my arm is getting heavier. I don't know how much longer I can keep this up," he gagged.

The further she dived, the more scattered and massive the stalactites became. Sana's curse was ineffective in this domain, so she was depending entirely on her eyesight. She suspected there was something in the air to make it even harder to keep her eyelids open, but Sana wasn't one for excuses. The freefall was also an *excellent* way to speed through Limbo. The longer she could stay here, the better.

She twirled past as many obstacles as possible until she accelerated to a point where she was dodging things with pure luck. With minimal warning, her eyes widened as she was suddenly centimeters from splattering against a ruby spike. Since she had no other option available to her, Sana closed her eyes and felt both of her feet plant onto firm, yet slightly spongey, soil. She hesitantly opened her eyes and blinked to a yellow tinged atmosphere, the bright morning sun bouncing off numerous blades of grain. To her right was a tall stone castle, with grapevines trickling towards the left window-

Her eyes widened. This was...no.

Sana instinctively took a step back, but her sandals popped on something. It was a familiar texture: one Sana was deathly afraid to confirm. Regardless, she held her breath and lifted up her foot. It was the velvet splotch of blackberry pulp. And...and right next to that...were two burnt-

The Gatekeeper immediately fell to her side and vomited. Too familiar. This was all too familiar. This was surely an illusion cast by Limbo, but the pieces that the mountain had plucked from her mind were just *too* accurate.

A firm hand gripped her shoulder. She looked up with monotone eyes, nostrils twitching with crimson dread. Banase looked at her with a reassuring face, his mustache wriggling as he sniffed. "Not sure what you're seeing, but I haven't seen you this distraught *ever*. You need a breather?" he asked.

Sana spat out the remaining bile from her mouth and curled up in a ball, her eyes fixated on the stone castle up ahead. Banase sat with his back leaning against her, sighing as he did. "I had to blink, sorry. I was actively suffocating with each passing second," he said as he looked around. "This new area is just, well, a sea of white, silky curtains." Banase reached his hand out to touch the imaginary textiles. "Feels like fabric, flows like water. I think it'll function like quicksand. I'm on a small patch of mud, but it's shrinking each passing minute. Still, we have time to rest up...so I'll let you know when we *have* to move, alright?"

Sana nodded with slight appreciation, her fearful, yet infuriated, eyes piercing the building in front of her. Most likely, that was her next destination for this region. Limbo would probably ensure she never got close...but if she could burn that damned place down...

She took a deep breath and slapped her thigh with her free hand. This wasn't like her normal, peppy self. '*Smile. Smile. You* have *to,*' she told herself. *'You're the positive, bubbly one. No one cares for your sob story. Let's go.'*

Sana stood up and dusted off her dress with more strength behind her actions. She squeezed Banase's hand with gratitude. "Sorry about that, Banase. My new setting is this grass field. No upfront dangers as of right now. I'll be fine," she said.

Banase lifted his foot hesitantly and dipped his toes in the imaginary silk in front of him. "It sinks right through," he muttered. "I think if I go completely under, it'll be hard to pull myself back up. I should treat this like a one-way tarpit."

Sana crouched down and slowly exhaled. "I'm about to run. Hold tightly," she smiled.

"Welcome back, Gatekeeper," Banase grinned.

· · ·

The cursed girl yelped as she fell face first onto the ground. She had only heard *stories* of Taba...but meeting him in person? It was oppressive. Everything she did, anything she thought: it was as though he saw through it all. Not to mention, Taba's pure physicality: there was no way anyone would be able to easily overpower him. When she saw the glass shard randomly appear in front of her, pure instinct let her know that *this* was her ticket out of here.

It was always so hard to find strong scapegoats to pass the curse along to. The weak ones died too fast, and the strong ones had no openings. Shame she transferred the curse over to...what was that boy's name? Cookie? Maybe she should've passed it along to Taba instead: she wouldn't mind if he died, and he most likely would've survived longer than the exploding brat.

The cursed girl got up with a frown. So...was *this* Limbo? It was more friendly than the others had warned her about. She sat on a patch of moss, little flies buzzing around the rainforest as random birds chirped off in the distance. For a mountain, it was awfully humid. She hated it.

A fly buzzed next to her eye, but when it landed on her cheek, suddenly her perspective changed. The cursed girl found herself sharing eyesight with the insect, numerous eyeballs glancing up at her nose through a red filter. Alarmed, she shrieked and swatted away at the bug, her eyes closing as she shook her head wildly.

Suddenly the humidity changed into pure heat. She cried in agony as she sharply looked down at her feet. Where there used to be moss, now was a bubbling line of furnaces. Her feet were steamed raw, her skin slightly bubbling due to the blistering heat.

The air above her head suddenly pelted down on her neck. The cursed girl swirled her head back and felt the blood drain from her face as millions of fleas blotted out the sun, jumping into every single open crevice available. She wailed, swallowing thousands of insects as a result, turning away to spit them out. As she did, the scenery changed once more.

The cursed girl spent the next minute spiraling in a fervent circle, each time her eyes shifted away from what was in front of her, the scenery would change. There was no pattern in how the scenes changed. The only recognizable pattern was how each time she swirled her head, things got *exponentially worse.*

After snorting out a noseful of lava, the cursed girl blinked away tears of heat and suddenly teleported into a...well, it was hard to say what this new area was. A cave of dust? All she knew was the air stopped hurting. So, she stared forward and cried.

The last thing she felt was her flesh being warped...no, *assimilated*, int-

. . .

Nancy felt her veins trembling. She hated this feeling. *How* was he *this* resilient? Sure, Father had always said the Gatekeeper named G should be treated as though he were immortal...but he was still wriggling with full force after twenty minutes. The more the Gatekeeper struggled, the more her blood strained to pin him down. Maggle wasn't having an easy time, either. He had shifted from standing on-top of G to essentially pushing down on the bald man with both his arms. Even *with* Maggle's blessing, G was pushing back ferociously to such an extent that Nancy feared the ground may give out.

The two Family members had stopped their mocking quips and had now focused all of their attention to pinning G, but it was evident that he would eventually break loose. Nancy didn't even want to *think* what would happen once he was free. '*What a monster,*' she shuddered.

The crunch of gravel echoed from behind them. "Boy, G. You look dumb right now," someone said with a yawn.

Nancy and Maggle whirled around and locked eyes with...no one. They squinted at the air with confusion until a massive amount of pressure vanished from below them. Their blood ran cold as they quickly turned back to the ground where G no longer lay pinned.

The lazy voice coughed once again. "No, over here, slowpokes."

Maggle barely had time to turn around to block a nasty elbow strike from Patchy. Just as his arm was raised, Patchy blipped out from in front of him and Nancy suddenly felt a sudden force slam into her spine, knocking her to the ground.

"You...you know, that isn't any way to treat a woman," she whined as she rubbed her back.

"Really? Because all the women I know in my life could kick my ass," Patchy said with a frown. "Equality, and all that."

Maggle cursed and turned around to where Juliette lay, but it was too late. G was already there, his hand cupped over her mouth as though he had fed her something. His entire body was red with all his muscles strained, but surely enough, Juliette's blue eyes suddenly fluttered open.

"...Shi-"

. . .

'What's your name?' he asked with a chirp.

'...I just need a new weapon,' Juliette responded coldly.

The smithy smirked as he held the splinters of her spear. 'Who even made this? *It's crappy,' he frowned.*

'I don't remember, nor do I care. Can you make me a weapon or no-'

'Yeah, but it'll take time.'

'How long?'

'I don't know.'

Juliette sighed as she stood up. 'It appears I've wasted my time here. I'll take my business elsewhere,' she responded curtly.

The smithy tapped the splintered handle. 'Hollow wood. That's why it cracked when you gripped it. When it cracked, I bet the spearhead tilted to the right. It made your final blow miss, and that caused the cut on your shoulder, right?' he said with a focused stare.

Juliette blinked as she shifted her bandaged shoulder back, caught a bit off-guard by his accurate analysis. 'How do yo-'

He waved a hand. 'Eh, of course *that's what happened. It's shoddy. Plus, smithies now-a-days only craft for bulk. They don't make specialty tools for the client anymore,' he sighed, tilting the dented spearhead towards the sun. 'Give me a chance, ma'am. I'll craft you an unbreakable weapon that fits your fighting style* and *your blessing. You won't find higher quality anywhere else.'*

'...but you don't know how long it'll take?' she asked with a frown.

'Nope. But hey: I'll loan out some free weapons until I finish. How's that sound?' he offered.

'Well, how much will the finished product cost?' she asked with a narrowed glare. Juliette was in the middle of a campaign: she couldn't exactly spare tons of time or resources.

'It'll be free,' he said with a wink.

Juliette felt a twitch of anger. He was messing with her, why did he even entertain his ideas? 'Oh? What's the catch?' she asked sarcastically.

The smithy placed her shattered weapon back in the repair bag and tied it up. 'Nothing, really. I get to talk to a beautiful woman and perfect my craft. It's a win-win for me, no matter what,' he smiled.

Juliette's nose twitched in irritation...but when she glared at the smithy to tell him off, she noticed his eyes. They were earnest. Excited. No malice, whatsoever...like looking at a child running up to their mother or father while clutching a fistful of daisies.

It...really wasn't like Juliette to trust a stranger. Not like this.

'...what's your name, smithy?'

'Gureke! Yours?'

'...Juliette.'

His mouth opened softly. 'Oh, like, 'The Looming Calamity', Juliette? That Juliette?'

Her lips tightened as she subconsciously darted her eyes to the floor in shame, but before she could respond or storm off, he grinned wildly. 'Ooh, that's kinda cool! Glad to be of service, Miss Calamity!' he chuckled.

Juliette hesitantly looked upwards, her azure eyes holding slight confusion. 'Do...do you not fear me?' she blinked.

'Nah,' he said dismissively. 'You're just another customer. Just promise not to kill me after I'm done, and we're all good.' Gureke walked back into his workshop and came out with a spear, handing it over with a nod. 'Ok, lemmie see a few swings. I want to get an idea of how you fight.'

That was Juliette's first impression of Gureke: the source of her greatest regret.

. . .

The Dancing Painter slowly roused, her head pounding furiously as she sat up. How long had she been out for? She felt something heavy cupped over her mouth, and upon glancing to her right, noticed G kneeling next to her. His muscles all seemed heavily strained...but his eyes glowered with fierce determination. A bit to her left, Patchy was fighting the girl named Nancy and the spa owner, Maggle. The more she observed his movements, however, the more obvious it became that Patchy was just buying time. It was evident that he was fatigued...but that made sense. He had moved the soulscale by himself.

Maggle noticed Juliette waking up, his eyes flicking between relief and alarm. He yelled something towards Nancy, who narrowed her eyes and reeled her arm back, trickles of blood quickly pooling at her knuckles. She punched the air and a few scattered bullets of blood

210

zoomed to her location. G dove in front of Juliette, blocking the buckshot flying in her direction with his body. He exhaled sharply as he looked up at her. "Can you ascend?" he asked with surprising composure.

Juliette tried to relax her mind, but the sharp screech jumped back, causing her to wince and clutch her head. "No, I...my soul can't take it," she said.

G cursed under his breath, eyes closed as he tried to think of a plan. As he did, an enormous, mutant spider skittered through the trees with its numerous legs, each bristle containing little webslingers to drag anything closer. The mutant lifted its fangs to slam down on G but was intercepted by Patchy, who suddenly appeared on its head, crunching down on the spider's head with his arms, before vanishing to continuously tussle with the Family members.

G had already ascended once...but what he needed to do was obvious. He clasped his hands once more, his heart and mind straining as his eyes glowed brilliantly. The Gatekeeper screamed as his body trembled, a surge of energy flowing once more in Juliette. The Drunken Fox wasted no time, her eyes glowing once more as countless cuts rained down all around Malapace yet again.

Maggle noticed the endeavor, his eyes widening as they also began to glow. He held Nancy close, holding her into a tight bearhug as a thin bubble wrapped around the two of them. All of Juliette's slashes rained down at once, but Maggle's bubble held up with utter resilience. Any solid bits of soul that chipped off were regenerated immediately. The big man looked up at the Drunken Fox with awe. "Thorny, indeed," he said. After admiring her for a few seconds, he glanced down at Nancy. "We're falling back: we did our part. Now, it's Luong Xiaoli's turn."

Nancy opened her mouth to protest, but held her tongue. Maggle's blessing, let alone ascension, wasn't designed to wrap around others. Despite his composure, she could feel all of Maggle's muscles straining under his thin layer of fat, his heart pumping overtime to keep up with Juliette's onslaught. Nancy grit her teeth, but nodded. "Damn it, Zanshin's plan better work," she hissed. Accepting this answer, Maggle scooped her up, and the two of them trotted off as far as they could away from Malapace.

Patchy watched the Family run away...but decided to let them go. What was important right now was the wellbeing of the city, but more important, of Juliette and G. Geysers of blood rained from G's nose, his eyes twitching red as he struggled to even stand up straight. Juliette was fairing even worse: she had slouched on the ground, the only proof that she was conscious being her hand that limply grasped her paintbrush.

Patchy himself wasn't doing so hot, either. Moving the soulscale was, to say the least, draining. It was tricky finding a place where the impossible fragment couldn't be retrieved...let alone *relocating* it there. The whole ordeal had taken far more hours than he had expected. Ironically, he had taken it back to where Limbo had appeared last: the coastline. There, it could quietly sift back into the unknown without outside interference...hopefully.

Patchy jogged over to his friends while heavily breathing. They were both alive, but barely conscious: it seemed as though they were staying awake through sheer willpower. Patchy clenched his teeth as he balled his fists in frustration. He...he couldn't do anything to help them. If only he were useful like his brother, he-

The Gatekeeper sighed as he took off his jacket, draping it over Juliette. He pulled a handkerchief from his pocket and wiped away the blood on G's face. Patchy couldn't do anything meaningful, sure. Still, his brother would do whatever he could...that was for sure. So, he would do the same.

There was the sound of numerous legs scurrying across the floor along with the crackling of expanded earth. The commotion that Patchy's fight with the Family had attracted a few other Mutants. Insects, birds, and even a few fish that swam underground. Patchy was so...*so* tired. Still, if he could move...

He grabbed a rock from the floor and twirled it in his hands, glancing up at the mutants.

Patchy took a deep breath, leaned back, and threw the rock.

For the city. For his friends.

For his brother.

CHAPTER 12

*T*aba *really couldn't remember a lot of things. When his blessing manifested, what age specifically he met Father, or what happened to his biological parents. However, whenever he tried to focus on the topic...he felt his mind slipping away to other topics. Eventually, he stopped thinking about his past. Taba was never sure if that was his choice or not.*

Father suddenly began to speak, forcing Taba to zone back in. '...is Geralt. He'll be in charge of training and supervising you three, for the most part,' he said as he pointed to a well-suited man with finely trimmed hair. He donned sunglasses and had the slightest smell of tobacco on his sleeves. He seemed to wear a constant sneer, but the crease of his eyebrows seemed delicate, concerned and gentle for those around him.

'These guys?' Geralt frowned. 'Father. They're kids. You can't be serious.'

'...would honestly prefer to keep them out of fights, if I could,' admitted Father. 'Still, considering their history and the world around us...it's

impossible to make them pacifists. So, may as well make sure they're safe,'
he said.

'Ugh, kids,' Geralt grumbled as he crouched down to their eye level.
Queenie shuffled behind Hush, who held his hand out in front of his
sister nervously. Taba himself wasn't too sure what to think: he had only
seen Geralt in passing, and every time they did, Geralt was puffing a
hand rolled cigarette.

Geralt took his shades off and tucked them in his pocket, locking eyes
with each of the kids. His eyes were mismatched: with a scar across one of
his eyes as a white iris peered back. 'So, kiddos. How old are each of you?'
he asked.

'12.'

'Uh...10.'

'...14.'

'Cripes. Y'all are...' Geralt cut himself off, shaking his head. He stuck
a hand out in front of each of them. Nervously, they all shook his hand
limply. The older man frowned. 'Practice your handshakes. It sounds
dumb, but a proper handshake goes far in building confidence and trust.'
He stood up and gave a slight bow to the three of them. 'Anyhow, I am
Geralt. I don't know squat about you or your backstories, nor do I care.
Just know I will do whatever I can to raise and protect you all.'

His eyes slightly lit up before he jutted his thumb to the oak tree behind
him. In response, the slight crunch of leaves echoed out. 'Behind that
tree is Zanshin,' said Geralt. 'You can't see him, nor will you ever fully
remember him. Just know he's equally looking out for you. If any of you
kiddos stumble, one of us will catch you. Got it?' he asked.

The three of them awkwardly nodded. Geralt shrugged and clapped his hands. 'Excellent. Now, I'll put some beans on the fire. Dinner is in an hour, until then...stay out of trouble.'

. . .

Taba laughed as he heartily crunched on some toast that had no sustenance, texture, or density. It was hard to fully wrap his head around it, but his "parents" felt so comfortable. He couldn't really recall ever meeting his mother or father, but this all just felt so...*right*. How long had it been since Taba had just indulged, carefree? It felt...

~~wrong.~~

Taba discarded the afterthought. It was irrelevant. He indulged himself in the forgotten memory some more, and just as quickly as the others had, another day zipped by, the light outside the window dimming and brightening once more.

Suddenly, Taba felt a cold, almost *hesitant*, hand touch his shoulder. *"Taba. Get up,"* a sickly voice hissed. *"You know deep down this isn't right."*

Taba almost blinked from how sudden the mood shift occurred. The hand on his back was...foreign to this memory. It threatened to shatter this peace, yet Taba didn't dare turn around. Why...?

'*Oh, that's right. Because if I do, Limbo will change,*' Taba thought. How had he forgotten about Limbo? It was such an important mission. Mission? What exactly *was* his mission? Did it even matter? Why would he abandon something so safe and comfortable? His mission be damned, Taba sh-

"No. Think of everyone. Queenie. Hush. Father. Toukie. Geralt." the raspy voice reasoned, the cold hand desperately pushing down on him. There was a slight pause before the voice spoke again, this time with

the slightest tinge of regret and bitterness. *"I...I really wish you could stay here. However, if you do, your friends and Family will all die. I don't want you to live with that denial or regret,"* he said softly.

Taba stopped chewing his meaningless meal and put down his useless napkin. "Who...*are-*"

"Don't ask that," he hissed. *"The second you do, you'll forget. The moment you look at me, you'll forget when you look away. This is the closest thing I can get to a loophole, and even* then, *there's too many limitations,"* he said.

Taba had a sneaking suspicion who the voice belonged to. The fact he had never heard this person before, how they only listed off the Family, and the kind sadness behind all those words. Only a small handful fit those descriptions...and if it *was* **that** person...

The Misfit shut up. Instead, he silently extended his left hand out into the nothingness. As he anticipated, a cold, withered hand clasped it firmly. "How do you know about my setting?" asked Taba.

"Limbo impacts me differently...and for some reason, it's decided to prod at a memory of yours that I've stolen," he whispered regretfully. *"It was the only way for you to grow up as normally as possible."*

"That doesn't answer my question. How were you able to locate me? Limbo is infinite and everyone has their own individual settings."

"As I've said, Limbo impacts me differently," he said. *"Since people forget me, it slightly also applies to Limbo. Ironically, Limbo becomes more difficult for me to avoid when I hold hands with someone else. As to how I located you in all of Limbo...I'm able to always see the positions of anyone I steal memories from. Combine that with the fact that Limbo struggles to make different settings for me...it's just a matter*

of me making my way to you as fast as possible. I'm...sorry it took so long," he apologized.

"Why did you steal this memory?" Taba asked carefully. "It's...so *happy*."

"It...it wasn't out of ill intent. I'm sorry, that's all I can really say."

Taba stared at his "mom" and "dad", both of them chortling in their imperfect house and lifestyle. The sunbeam flickering between tree leaves outside their window. The stove that never produced enough heat to properly cook meals. The shoddily crafted table. The bland meals. The mismatched carpet. The off centered wall-candle. The worn-out sofa. The mildew-y doors. His...home. Childhood. One that was stolen from him, for a hidden reason? Now that Taba had it back, he was expected to tear himself away from it? A mixture of rage and frustration filled his gut.

Taba's eyes twitched...frustration? Why was he frustrated? That was such a bizarre emotion in this context. It was only after a minute of contemplation did Taba realize why it felt so fitting yet incorrect: he couldn't bear to live in comfort, knowing his friends and Family were suffering elsewhere. He had already made peace with the fact that he was going to lose his childhood once more...and felt suffocated by this fact. Why...couldn't Taba just be happy? Comfortable? Could he not just *rest*, even for a moment? Why was everyone allowed happiness but him?

Taba clenched his fists and hesitated...before closing his eyes for the first time in days. He was being selfish: *only* him? How idiotic. Queenie, Hush, Nancy, Toukie, Maggle, Little Stuart, Zan...*Geralt*, Father, and many more. They were agonizing far more than Taba was: how *dare* he step away from his duty?

"You'll...explain this all to me later, right?" Taba asked aimlessly, his eyes still closed.

"On my word, honor, and life: yes. I'm so, so sorry for it all." the heartbroken voice responded.

Taba felt the creaky chair underneath him vanish, his comforting childhood fading once more. He felt like tearing his throat out in unjust sobs...but that would be for another time. In the meanwhile...

The tired Misfit felt another wrinkle crease under his eyes as he opened them. In place of his comfortable memory was...dust. That was the best description of this new region. It was a series of caverns, potholes, and cavities. Though the tunnel seemed to have sculpted shapes, the floor shifted under his feet as though he stood on sand. With each step, the air rose up with a *poof*, flying up his nose and threatening him to sneeze.

It was...annoying, but nothing worse than the library he was trapped in "weeks" ago. Taba wasn't sure how this domain was worse than the others. He was afraid to find out. After a few steps, his blessing reappeared next to him, floating an inch off the ground as it silently observed not the region, but Taba. It was similar to how a Queenie watched his face to capture the moment when he fell into a trap or prank.

If Taba hadn't caught his blessing's looming foreshadowing, he would be dead. What saved Taba's life wasn't his blessing or experience. It was a mixture of instinct, as well as the person holding his hand suddenly yanking him back slightly.

The creature made no sound as it stepped out from the ceiling, nor did it leave any footprints on the ground. Footsteps did not echo through the tunnels, breathing didn't whistle through imaginary nostrils, chatters stayed muffled through non-existent mouths. The creature didn't even stifle the air or raise up dust as it moved: it was as though a hologram shifted past them. Taba struggled to fully fathom this creature. When it moved, it walked with animal-like anatomy, like a cow or horse that had between four to nine legs. However, instead of hooves, the limbs ended in seven fingered human hands. Whenever the creature lifted its limbs up to walk forward, it seemed to zip up back into the main body. To take a "step", an arm would grow from its central blob, stretching out from the skin like an arm pushing against air-tight fabric. There was no face, no eyes, no nose, no discerning features to truly identify something as a "face". However, it was obvious that it was looking around from the way the skin twisted around at various angles. More than anything, however, what truly shook Taba was the skin. It was mismatched, like someone had slapped together various materials onto a sticky canvas. While the creature had no discerning features, the *skin* had distorted facial features, with the faces becoming even more warped with each of the creature's movements.

Half the atoms in Taba's body screamed to run. The other half begged him to freeze and pray for the creature to pass.

The creature stepped into the ground, silently walking towards its unknown destination. Just as it stepped through the floor, Taba noticed one chunk of skin looked a bit more...new. Familiar. It was heavily burned and swollen, but unmistakably, the skin of the cursed girl. The cursed girl who had passed her curse along to Toukie. Her mouth distorted into a warped plea, just before being sucked into the main body and into the dust walls.

220

Questions. Questions. Questions. There were hundreds he wished to ask, yet sweat dripped from all his pores as he froze in fear and dread. His blessing leaned next to him with a soft whisper, something aligned with amusement tinged on its voice. "You need not worry, I'll do you a fine service and answer the questions you're barely able to think of. Yes, that was the cursed girl who cursed Toukie as a mutant magnet. Yes, she's alive and conscious. Yes, *all* of that creature's skin is alive and conscious. Yes, if it touches you, you'll share the same fate. No, it leaves no traces of its existence: no residuals or sound, nothing. No, it can't see you: the senses it uses aren't something any living creature on Earth has. Yes, it can die." His blessing paused before crouching in front of it, seemingly just to savor Taba's facial expression. "No, you can't kill it."

Taba exhaled a shaky breath, but decided to push on ahead. He tiptoed through the dust-carved pathways towards the first of hundreds of caves. However, he didn't make even ten paces before the creature's hands gently pushed through the ground, pushing up to the ceiling a mere few centimeters from his face. It was all the Misfit could do as he stared at hundreds of morphed mouths, either cursing him for living carefree or begging for death. The second the creature slunk into the shadows of dust, all residue of his existence vanished once more. There wasn't as much as disturbed dust.

Taba's spine trembled, but he was determined to continue his climb. Despite this resolve, his body suddenly slunk onto the floor, the pressure in his knees giving out as he suddenly collapsed into the dust. The dust cloud that puffed up stuck to his skin as all he could do was tremble in despair. The more he tried to stand, the more his legs failed to muster strength. The withered hand holding him pulled at him with a hiss. "*I get how you feel, but you need to move. Let's go,*" he ordered.

"...How? You saw that thing. No matter where we go, it can just...*appear*. We can't hear it or predict it," Taba said weakly. " If it touches us, we die. However, if we close our eyes, then things get *worse*? I...I shouldn't have left the memory. This is *so* much wor-"

The grip of the man behind him tightened. "*Things **always** get worse, Taba. That is no excuse for you to stop. If you're in hell, why stop? Why give up in hell? Run, walk,* crawl... *but don't stop moving. If you fail,* others *will suffer,*" he said with controlled anger. He took a sharp inhale...but stopped, exhaling softly. "*Taba. I...I understand despair. I face it every day. There is no salvation for me. That doesn't mean I should give up. If I do, others will share my fate. That is why I move on. It's fine to feel afraid. By all means, it's ok to despair. Still, don't stop doing your best: just know I will help you in the background, ok?*" the sickly voice said in a kinder tone.

"...I...I'm scared, Za-"

"*Don't say my name: too risky.*"

Taba sat in the dust, knowing that his lack of action risked both their lives more and more with each passing second, yet he failed to find the energy to even twitch. The hand Taba held trembled slightly...but it tightly gripped Taba. Of course Za-*he* was scared too. Despite that...he waited next to Taba. What a selfless man: Taba was ashamed to do such a good man an incredible injustice.

It was this selflessness that inspired energy in the Misfit. With trembling legs, Taba crawled to his feet, a tremble in his throat silencing the whimper that threatened to escape. It was a pathetic appearance, but the man behind him gave his hand a firm squeeze. It wasn't much...but enough. With shaky legs, the pair slowly made their way through the dusty cave. After a few minutes of intoxicating silence, Taba opened his warbly mouth to ask a question, *anything* to try and keep his mind off what he just saw. "...did you see the creature, too?" he asked.

"Yes. I'm in the dust-cave, too. Since Limbo can't make a setting for me, I'm joining you for yours. Don't you worry, I'm keeping a sharp eye behind you. I'll let you know if I see it, ok?" he said.

"Thanks....and sorry fo-"

"Your reaction is more than reasonable. Others would've gone insane. Don't worry, I don't think any less of you. In fact...my respect for you has grown tremendously," he said, a freckle of a smile echoed at the end of his statement.

The two of them shuffled their feet through the caves, trying not to make any sudden movements. Whenever they moved, the ground had the density of sand, yet rippled like water. Each step caused tiny puffs of dust to rise up, threatening to make Taba sneeze if he moved too quickly.

After a few minutes of silent walking, Taba lifted his foot but felt the blood tingle in his leg as the creature's leg crashed through the ceiling. Taba jumped backwards and lifted his arm to warn the person behind him. Just as before, the creature made no noise or gave no indication that it was only a few inches in front of them. Sure, he knew that touching this thing meant instant assimilation...but Taba was morbidly curious about the creature. The way it shuffled about, how it had no stable central mass, how it was faceless yet had a face. The being was a walking paradox, existing with rules and laws that existed outside of Earth.

As the creature slunk away to the ceiling, Taba's blessing appeared and stared at the being as well. "You humans...your perception of infinity is so...*limited*," it sighed. "You hold onto odd emotions such as fear and dread to the point where many of you can't fathom existence without it. You run from death because you can't understand what's beyond." Taba's blessing waved its arm, a slight ripple appearing through the nothingness before stabilizing. "Though...I suppose that ignorance makes your life all that more fascinating. If you saw things like *we* did...I wonder if you could bear it."

Taba swallowed dryly as he forced himself to walk stiffly forward, trying to keep his mind off the creature. "You're awfully talkative now. Why didn't you speak up months ago?" he asked.

The man from behind coughed. "*Taba? Who are yo-*"

"Oh, that man can't hear me, boy," Taba's blessing said. "If you want to avoid appearing even more idiotic than usual...you can always think your questions."

"Nah, I don't know if I'll get this chance again. I'm talking to you verbally," Taba said. He then gave a slight squeeze to the man behind him. "Sorry, Za...sir. I'm just talking to my blessing. Long story, bear with me." Taba turned back to his blessing with a frown. "Anyways, answer the question."

"Boy, who do you thi-"

"Your existence is bland, right? I can't imagine you'd throw yourself in the thick of all this if there wasn't a catch for you. You clearly have the power to ignore me...so the fact that you're conversing with me has to be of your own volition. You're bored, aren't you?" Taba asked.

It was honestly a guess. Hell, his blessing was probably reading his mind and could see the cogs turning...but instead of ignoring

Taba, the blessing slowly turned to face Taba with amusement. It had no facial features (none that Taba could recognize), yet it obviously grinned. "I knew I was right in choosing you," it cackled.

"Choose?"

"I'll entertain you, as you've entertained me," it said as it floated casually next to them. "You're partially right: I'm doing this out of entertainment. However...beings on *my* level don't understand boredom. It's below us, so we don't care about it. We blessings choose the user, whomever we think we'll mesh the most with."

"Wait...blessings are sentient?" Taba asked. This was a first: how come he'd never heard of this?" As Taba spoke out, he could feel the hand he was holding grow cold. Odd.

"A small handful of people know, and *none* of them want to share that info," his blessing said with a shrug. "*We* personally don't care, but I suppose it makes sense for a human to not want to divulge secrets. It isn't for any malicious reasons, however. On the contrary, actually."

"How do people figure out blessings are sentient? Do *I* know anyone who knows blessings are sentient?"

"Boy, quite a few people in your life know that blessings are sentient. I'm not telling you names, however: that's on you to ask."

"Dad?"

"No."

"Babs?"

"Mhm."

Taba frowned. Babs wasn't a fighter by any means. By all accounts, Dad was stronger than Babs. What was the difference between the two leaders?"

"Geralt?"

"Mhm."

"Juliette?"

"Yes."

The gears slowly clicked in his mind. Maybe...?

"Toukie."

"Nope."

"Maggle."

"Yep."

Just as Taba expected: people who had ascended knew about sentient blessings. He wasn't sure what ascension was, all he knew was it seemed to be a stronger version of one's blessing. From how everyone seemed to shush up about it, there was most likely a heavy downside attached to it.

Well...that was one clue to ascension, Taba supposed. Another thing bothered him however, a specific phrase his blessing mentioned. "So...what did you mean you *chose* me?" he asked.

"I'll tell you that when you ascend," his blessing said with an odd tone. Something about that sentence didn't make sense, but Taba couldn't really place what it was. Whatever, he got good info about his blessing and ascension. All he needed to do was survive Limbo, and he could go from th-

Suddenly, a raspy gasp echoed from behind him and the sensation of what could only be described as a miniature black hole built pressure behind Taba. Instinctually, he turned around and locked eyes with Zanshin as his right leg was suddenly pulled backwards. Behind him, the creature had manifested itself, one of its limbs already molded together with Zanshin's flesh. He gritted his teeth as sweat popped

226

out of his sickly skin. He looked up at Taba's horrified face with a determined nod. "*Taba. You don't worry about me, ok? I'm going to let go of your hand when you turn around, and when I do...run. Ok?*" he said. "*You'll forget about me, that's fine...as long as you continue to run. Now turn around.*"

Taba's back was drenched in sweat, but he did as instructed. Already, his memory of...someone was slipping. What was slipping? Taba wasn't sure. He wasn't even aware that he was holding someone's hand: it felt numb in his grip.

"***Now, Taba. Let GO.***"

Taba flinched, unsure of who or why, but he let go and ran forward. It was an undignified sprint, dust kicked up behind him as he scrambled forward. His normally sharp mind faded blank as a primal instinct caused a surge of energy through his legs. He dashed through cracks and tunnels, keeping his eyes focused in front of him the entire time. Even as dust sprinkled into his dry eyes, he kept his eyes strained forward. The movement of both his arms pumping as he ran felt off. Why didn't he run before? What was the danger? The danger was...a...creature? What was so threatening about the creature?

Taba squeezed his empty hand. It was brief, but there was a sliver of body heat. Was he...*always* alone?

. . .

Taba glanced at his little postcard and looked up. Brick watchtower, rusted fence, rotted carcass. This should've been the meetup spot. Dad was against the idea, but Taba's blessing confirmed it was possible to execute: there was no reason to doubt it.

A crunch of leaves rang out from behind him, causing Taba to turn around. As expected, there stood a man wearing a dark cloak. He had never seen this man before, but the description matched: Ominous cloak, sickly skin, and a sorrowful stare. Taba had most likely met this man before, so he needed to choose his words carefully so as not to hurt the man's feelings.

'Zanshin?' *he said with slight hesitation.*

The tired man nodded silently before looking up at the brick watchtower. 'I surveyed the entire outskirts of Malapace,' *Zanshin said softly.* 'This is the highest point that is closest to the city that you can climb without attracting attention. Any closer than this and you'll grab their attention.'

'Got it. Thanks, Zanshin,' *Taba said with slight hesitation.* 'Also...don't tell th-'

'I won't. Your request is safe with me,' *he said. His cracked lips tightened with disapproval.* 'Still, I don't recommend this: I've spied on the Gatekeepers in the past, and one of them keeps glancing at my direction every time. These guys are strong, Taba: they're beyond your blessing's expectations.'

'My blessing is never wrong,' *Taba said with a frown.*

'Maybe...but that female Gatekeeper...I think her existence will foil your questioning.'

Taba shrugged. 'I might fail: it's possible. Still, even if I do...I trust the Family. You'll get us out if we fail, right?'

Zanshin hesitated, his eyes darting downward for a split second before he dryly swallowed. 'I...I can't guarantee it this time. However, on the off chance you guys do fail...just know I'll work tirelessly to get out. You'll never be alone, I'll be there to back you up,' *the sickly man said with determination.*

'No matter what?'

'No matter what.'

       . . .

Time was tricky to calculate in Limbo. How long he spent scrambling through the tunnels, Taba wasn't sure. Oddly enough, though the dust looked and felt exactly the same, Taba could distinguish the various tunnels. It was tricky to navigate his surroundings while only facing forwards, but his blessing helped him in that regard.

There was a blank spot in Taba's memory. From somewhere in the memory of his house to a little bit in the dust cave...he couldn't recall what had happened. The more Taba tried to recollect what had happened, the more his blessing twirled in the air with odd glee. It was disturbing, as though it was mocking Taba in a way he would never understand.

He had asked a few questions to his blessing, and it had arrogantly answered with an air of pleasure. Taba was indeed running from a monster. It wasn't a mutant. It was killable, but Taba couldn't kill it. The creature could kill him in one touch. Lastly, it emitted no tell. No sound, no heat, nothing. If Taba couldn't see it, he had no actual proof the thing wasn't directly behind him. So, Taba assumed the worst and kept running. He occasionally asked his blessing if the creature was within his area, but his blessing simply shook its head with an odd level of amusement. Taba tried to ignore his gut feeling that something was off, and pushed forward.

The more he traveled through the tunnels, the more dull the air became. Not due to a lack of light, no. Instead, it was as though the concept of light was becoming more irrelevant the more he tunneled downwards. Everything turned to what he could only describe as a "slow purple", the dust under his feet losing its density. He wasn't falling, he wasn't walking, he wasn't floating. It was a form of movement that Taba genuinely could not fathom.

Then it clicked: it was a kind of movement similar to what he experienced his blessing do earlier. Taba had only seen it as floating, but maybe that was simply because it was all his brain could perceive it as. Having experienced this himself, it was closer to...well, the world moving forward as he stood still in the air. Sure, it probably would've looked like he was gliding along, but it was closer to Taba controlling the world with his mind, and falling in the direction he chose as everything rotated to his will. Odd.

Suddenly, the dust cleared up and Taba touched down on the ground. Everything blew away, and what remained was a cracked glass shard in the air, similar to what he had seen when Limbo had initially appeared in Malapace. Reality seemed to warp itself around the opening. Was this...it? Was this the end of Limbo?

O.

Fatigue and relief dripped through Taba's brain, his veins pumped with adrenaline as he felt excited to end it all. He reached up to touch the shard...

...and just as swiftly as a reader would turn the page to a book, the landscape warped.

There was no light source, but the air glowed softly enough to allow no source of darkness. Crystals jutted out randomly from the terrain, each one shimmering a different color as it popped up. Bushes with liquid berries floated along the skies like jellyfish. Entities that had impossible anatomies crept along the edges of existence, yet unlike the ones in his previous areas...these ones had no malicious intent as their unfathomable eyes scanned through the skies, peering through time like a slideshow. The ground crunched under Taba's feet with each step, yet just as easily as it shattered, it also sprang back up with a burst of pebbles, healing itself instantly. All of the things he witnessed seemingly pointed towards a singular point in the sky, far above him.

Upon looking up, he flinched as he suddenly realized he had been unconsciously glancing around Limbo's peak. Before the question appeared in his mind, Taba's blessing popped up next to him to answer the unspoken question. "No, boy. This is the peak of Limbo. You can look around now. Things don't get much better, or *worse*, from this point. Brace yourself: you still need the soulscale," it said with an air of curiosity in its voice.

Taba probably should've asked for where the soulscale was: after all, that was the point of *all* of this. And yet...he couldn't help but be absolutely captivated by everything. The ground, the atmosphere, the creatures, hell, even the air he breathed was unique. Taba felt a tingle in his soul, a similar feeling to how he propelled himself towards the end of the dust cave. However, when he tried to "float" as he had before, he remained stationary. Taba frowned. Why wasn't he lifting up off the floor? What had changed?

"I won't answer that...but you should look up," his blessing said, a finger sprouting up towards the brilliance above the two of them.

Just as Taba looked up, a blurry shape crashed down next to him, cracking the ground with an explosion of soul. The shape groaned in an oddly familiar voice. An oddly familiar...*female* voice. Wearing a brown hoodie. With her hair thrown in a mess. Holding two daggers.

Taba hesitated, but he reached out and touched the petite woman's shoulder. "...Queenie?" he asked cautiously.

She flinched, looking up at Taba. She was battered to a similar extent to when they had all fought the chimera. The difference was the stream of tears flowing from her eyes.

...from her *glowing* eyes.

CHAPTER 13

Queenie had been trudging through the "snowy" plains for a while. No matter how much she rubbed her hands or pulled the hoodie tightly over her head, her bones and soul chattered helplessly. The chills were so intense that she couldn't even worry about what had happened to Hush. Frost slowly built up in her airways and veins, threatening to sap her life with each creaky step. The worst part of it all was how she had to keep focus in her peripheral vision for the clunky creature. The one positive was how her storage seemed to "reappear" in this environment. She didn't have access to her full arsenal, but she was able to pull out a pistol with four bullets. She loaded her weapon up and held it close to her chest, unsure if she should fire at the thing or wait for a counterattack.

Every so often, a hand on the floor twitched more than the rest, a tree twisted out another spine, or a *bit* more "snow" fell than expected. Queenie really tried not to focus on any blob or direction. Even the sensation of squishy flesh below her heel made Queenie's entire ribcage creak with discomfort. The hands hadn't tried to grasp at her feet, the trees did not charge at her, and the bodies in the sky did not fall. Oddly enough: she suspected no danger would derive from these aspects. The main concern she had was towards the lunky husk that stayed out of her direct sight.

...the same one that suddenly lurched in her direction and broke out into a full sprint.

Queenie flinched and raised her gun diagonally from her direction. She wasn't the biggest fan of shooting like this...but it wasn't anything she was unfamiliar with. She pulled the trigger and had to avoid blinking in surprise as the sluggish-looking creature held its hand up, catching the bullet between its fingers. Before she could decide what to do next, the creature suddenly appeared next to her, rubbing its squishy, fuzzy, yet coarse, hands across her cheek.

"Odd. Fascinating. First time I've seen you so up close, human."

She darted back and swiveled her head to the being. Her arm was pulled upwards, her eyes gazing down in alarm as the being held her bare hand. "A bit jumpy, but I knew that," it said. "I've been watching you for years now, I know you more than you know yourself. Had I not held onto you, Limbo would've warped."

Queenie cursed and fired another round at the being. This time, the bullet stopped midair, as though it had been blocked by a syrup forcefield. Now that she was face to face with the humanoid, she stared at its face with uncanny horror. It had a human face, but similar to how a child might draw a face with incorrect proportions. The eyes were slightly too front facing. The nose was a bit too low. The mouth was too long. The ears were front-facing, like a cat. In fact, everything about the humanoid was just *slightly* off. Too long arms and legs, Incorrect joint locations. Abnormal height. Sausage-like fingers that held a horrifyingly powerful, yet controlled, grip on her hand. The skin was slightly blue, but Queenie wasn't sure if that was due to the environment or its natural hue.

It stared back at her with mismatched blinks. "I'm sorry, humans have names, yes? I do not have one, but I know yours is...well, I do not know the rules of names. Is it the first one you're given? Is it the one with the strongest desire? Is it the one others call you? Should I call you Olivia or Queenie?" it asked curiously.

The humanoid was so casual with her, that Queenie's "fight or flight" response shut down completely. "I...uh...my name is Queenie. I'm sorry, who...? Aren't you going to kill me?" she said blankly.

"Why would I kill you? That's a waste of resources, and the search for another user would be unsatisfying. You have the highest potential out of everyone," it said with a disturbing frown.

Queenie was about to blink in utter confusion, but the humanoid swiftly pulled her eyelid open with a shake of his head. "No, do not close your eyes. That will change Limbo."

The boorish fingers scraped against her skin as well as her open cuts, causing her to cry out in pain. "Owowowow, stop. *Stop*," she said.

The humanoid released its fingers. "Apologies. Humans are so fragile. I thought I controlled myself well, but you are weaker than expected," it said. "Still, avoid closing your eyes. I do not know if we will have the chance to talk like this again, and this is, to be frank, exhilarating for me."

"Who...are you, anyhow?" Queenie asked cautiously.

The humanoid stood up taller, its uncanny look having an odd sense of nobility. "I have followed you since you were born. I know your character traits, your history, and capabilities. I am your blessing."

"...huh?"

The humanoid waved dismissively with a free arm. "It might be a lot, sure, but the whole 'storage' you have? It's not quite that simple. Well, no. It's actually simple, but you have the wrong idea about it. Let's walk, it isn't good to stay here for long," it said.

The two of them trudged along the snowy mountain as the humanoid talked to her. "I apologize for my appearance. I figured you would feel most comfortable around a human so I've tried my best to replicate human's appearance, but I struggle at the finer details. Anyhow, I am your blessing. The ability you've had since you were a child? That is all thanks to me."

"Are you saying the storage, no...*blessings*, are alive?" asked Queenie.

"All of them, yes," it said. "Many humans don't know it, because, well, being able to recognize that blessings are sentient means the soulbearer is closer to ascension."

"Ascensi-"

"The thing where the soulbearer's eyes glow and their blessing gets stronger."

"Oh. Isn't this a good thing then?"

"That is subjective. In terms of power? Yes, by all means: ascension is an incredible boon, and many ascensions can be utilized in combat...even for soulbearers without combative blessings," the humanoid replied. "However, it also has drawbacks. Harsh drawbacks. I do not know if you wish to know them."

Queenie frowned. "Why would I not want to know? Information is good...at least, that's what Taba would say," she muttered.

"You are on the road to ascension. It is near undeniable you will ascend. However, ignorance is bliss. The burden of knowledge can be an anchor for your soul. Are you certain y-"

She rolled her eyes, already getting used to this odd being before her. "You said you've known me since birth. You should know my answer. Now get to it," she snapped through chittering teeth, flinching as frost slowly began to build in her teeth's roots.

"Very well," her blessing said as it crawled up some jagged rocks, ignoring the cuts formed on its skin. "Ascension is a bit misleading of a name: it is the normal state of one's blessing. However, the human body can not withstand one-hundred percent of a blessing...so it hard-caps itself. At all times, no matter what, humans are limited to using ten to twenty percent of their blessing's capabilities. This limitation is lifted, however, if the soulbearer fulfills two requirements."

Her blessing lifted one finger. "One. It needs to have complete control and understanding of its blessing. Even if the soulbearer fulfills the latter condition, there's no way it can handle one-hundred percent if it can't even fathom ten-percent, right?" it said.

"I...guess? That doesn't really answer the question in regards to downsides," she frowned.

"We are getting there. The second requirement..." it said as it ducked through a crack, shimmying through a tight crevice. "...is tied directly to one of the downsides. You see, the human body compensates for such an explosion of power by allocation. It shifts resources from one part of the body to another...or rather, one part of the soul to the other."

"I don't get it," Queenie frowned. "Soul is soul. There isn't an organ that 'has' soul to shift over, right? You can't move around soul that doesn't exist."

"For humans, yes. However, for us blessings...we perceive everything differently. For example, time. You humans live through the passing of time, but us blessings can flip through time the way you humans can turn the pages of a book. The past, present, and future is constantly available to us. Every single branching path, every choice, we observe it all."

"Oh, is that how you found me?" Queenie asked with slight curiosity, pushing away the thick lump in her heart. She wasn't much of a thinker, but this was all so new and bizarre to the point that she wanted to learn more.

"Precisely. Out of all humans in all stages of humanity, you are the best suited soulbearer for my capabilities," the humanoid responded with an incorrect-looking smile. "Anyways, back to the topic of soul. The second requirement needs the soulbearer to have passed a certain threshhold for their soul: otherwise, an infant could ascend without proper maturity. Even if a person matures, the human body still can't withstand the entirety of a blessing. So...we simply shift blessing from the future of that human's life to the present. That is the only solution."

Queenie was not a smart girl...but the gears turned in her head slowly. "Wait...so one of the downsides is-"

"Correct. Ascension compresses a soulbearer's lifespan drastically. It heavily increases their soul capacity, allows them to fully utilize their soul, yet tremendously shrinks how long they have left to live," it responded casually.

The numbness in Queenie's brain was loud. She wasn't sure if this was due to her blessing's response, the fact that she was apparently close to ascending herself, or the fact that the cold of Limbo was nipping away at her life.

Queenie's blessing continued speaking as though it hadn't dropped life changing news. "...naturally, the human body is designed for preservation. Even for the sake of strength, it will not sacrifice decades of life for a powerup. That is foolish by everyone's standards...except under one condition." The blessing turned its neck one-hundred and eighty degrees, a sickening *snap* echoing as it made eye-contact with Queenie. "This exception is if the soulbearer faces a pain far worse than death. An agonizing level of torture so intense that the soulbearer is willing to give up *anything* to obtain their goals."

Queenie shuddered as the uncanny blessing stared her down. "Like...physical pain, if I got stabbed a thousand times? Would that work?" she asked.

The blessing shook its head, a nauseating *crick clack* echoing with each movement. "No. Physical pain has its limits, even if you were to be clever with the limits of torture," the humanoid said as it swiveled its head back forward to look down the crevice they were wiggling through. "No. The only level of pain that is enough, the thing that can generate enough agony to reach ascension...is regret."

"Regret?" Queenie had to resist rolling her eyes. "Seriously? That's vague. I once regretted not eating the last strawberry in a plate, yet I haven't ascend-"

"I do not think you understand the weight of regret. These would be regrets so strong to the point where you wish you could die to reverse the outcome," it said as the two of them stepped out into an opening that resembled the depths of a frozen ocean, the world expanded over their heads in an endless layer of crackling frost. Numerous eyeballs stared at the opening, eternally preserved to observe the newcomers. "Regrets, like your weakness being the reason your entire platoon dies. A purehearted child accidentally killing their loving guardians. Losing a brother, and your own identity..." Queenie's blessing stopped walking and calmly turned around, resting its free hand on her shoulder. "...being so weak that her brother dies in her place."

All the water in Queenie's body turned to sand as she stumbled slightly. She had been trying to get her mind off what had happened, but there was a gnawing thought in her head as the lump in her heart was fully realised. Was Hush ok? Was he alive? He was injured, but surely he could run off. Why did he let go? Did he betray her? Did he save Queenie? What did he-

Queenie blinked away blood-stained tears from both her healthy eye and hemorrhaging eye. She *desperately* wanted to not think about it, yet was also plagued by what could have happened. Everything regarding Hush was tearing her apart, but she wasn't sure what to do. Run? Face the truth? What...what should she-

Her blessing squeezed her hand softly. "*That* is true regret. Knowing if you were stronger, he wouldn't have made the choices he did. If you moved differently, maybe he wouldn't have had to worry about you. If you hadn't tripped during your dance, maybe he wouldn't have needed to run. If you were uninjured, maybe your brother would still be holding your hand. Does he love you? Does he hate you? That tearing, wretched feeling? That dull sludge? *That* is the regret

240

that causes people to ascend. It's this pain that makes people sacrifice *anything* to never feel again...even if it means a premature death."

Her blessing lifted her up and carried her on its back, cradling her softly as it walked forward. Queenie's heart hurt. It didn't stop hurting. Even when she saw the glass shard in the sky, the aching did not stop.

"Is...is that the end of Limbo?" she said weakly.

"It is. However, before you touch it...I want to give you some hope." Her blessing set her down and held both her hands. "Your blessing does *not* create a storage to store and access things at whim. It allows you to access Limbo. The things you store and withdraw? They're thrown into Limbo, coated in your soul. Since they are not living beings, they don't suffer any damage," the humanoid said. "Because of the nature of your blessing...I know your brother is currently alive. I only know this, because I, in some odd arrangement, am far more aware of the inner makings of Limbo than most blessings."

A flicker of light ignited in Queenie's eyes. "Wait. Hush is alive? You're Limbo? Wh-"

Her blessing held up its hand. "It may sound slightly contradictory to my prior statement, but I am not Limbo, nor do I have *absolute* control of Limbo. I am closer to a landlord or surveyor, in your human terms. Yes, your brother is alive...for now. He is on death's door, but he is alive...if just for another second, anyhow."

"Take me to him. *Now.*"

"No."

Queenie instinctively pulled out a dagger from her storage and held it through her blessing's neck, rage flickering through her being as she left a thin cut on his throat. "That wasn't a *suggestion*. Take me to him, **now**." she ordered.

The humanoid frowned deeply, and Queenie suddenly felt the tips of numerous blades prod across her entire body. Her good eye glanced around and she saw hundreds of blades surrounding her, flying in a circle around her body. They were delicate, tracing her arms to only cut the thinnest layer of skin: nothing that would even leave a scar. It wasn't exclusive to daggers or swords: chains were wrapped around her ankles, a cannon was pointed at the back of her head, and numerous firearms filled their chambers with rounds, ready to fire. The message was clear: her blessing had utter control of the situation. It could kill her at any moment on a whim.

The humanoid cautiously slid the knife away from his throat, a trickle of blue, syrupy blood ebbing out.. It was slow, but it easily pushed back against Queenie's slash. She should've been afraid, and she was, yet that fear was fully eclipsed by her worry and rage for her brother. All the weapons and tools that surrounded her were familiar. After all, they were all items she had personally stashed away. The chips and nicks of numerous blades, the worn tape on handles, and the stains on the triggers of the guns. These were all patterns that she had grown accustom to. Guess it made sense that her blessing would have ownership over all her things.

"Queenie. Even if I could take you to him, it would lower his chances of survival. He needs to be alone for this," her blessing said. "I assure you, the biggest thing you could do to help him is to obtain the soulscale. The humanoid flicked its wrist, and all of Queenie's stored weapons and tools vanished. "Someone you know has already reached the peak of Limbo. At the peak, you will have normal access to your 'storage'. It is up to you to claim ownership of the soulscale. If you need the push to ascend...call for me. I will give you the greatest regret that will stain your heart forever," it said somberly.

Queenie tried to ignore the undertone of the blessing's statement. She pushed the advice to the back of her hand and nodded grimly as she tried to ignore the aches and chills that ran through her entire being. With a trembling finger, she touched the glass panel and watched as the terrain twirled into the chip, just before exploding into...something mesmerizing.

All of her wariness vanished instantly as she gazed around in awe. There was so much to focus on. Shimmering air, bushes that bubbled across the sky as though it were alive, mountains that steadily grew as though it were bamboo, numerous beings and beasts that drifted through the air as they casually glanced through flickering timelines. Pebbles endlessly popping up from the ground every second, like bubbles emerging from a bog. Furthermore, Queenie could feel her spine shudder as though it were adjusting to new senses and feelings. It felt as though her arms were wrapping around the entire domain, everything under her awareness. Was it because this was her "storage", wrapping everything subconsciously in her soul? Perhaps this was due to the nature of her blessing, that wasn't cer-

Her eyes widened as she twirled around. Her blessing had vanished and was no longer holding her hand. She wasn't sure what emotion she was feeling, but Queenie couldn't help but look around to look for the humanoid. It wasn't as though she liked the blessing's presence, but rather the blessing gave her a sense of familiarity and security. Still, maybe it was for the best that it wasn't here.

She tore her eyes away from the immaculate scenery and walked forward towards the heights of infinity. Everything seemed to be pointing to a pinpoint far beyond her gaze. Queenie tested her blessing out, reaching into her storage to see if she could pull out a dagger. When her hand comfortably rested on the worn tape of a handle, she sighed in slight relief.

Relief was an odd emotion to feel, especially since her hand still slightly trembled from the memory of the chimera. Still, after the events of Limbo? Losing her brother, talking with her blessing, and reaching Limbo's peak? The chimera seemed so small now. It was anyone's guess as to whether she had gotten over the chimera...or if the recent events had just made the trauma seem tiny by scale.

She summoned chains above her, grabbed on, and flung herself up higher and higher, swinging between summoned chains as she ascended. The further she rose, the more Limbo bloomed. Flowers made of clouds sprouting from tiny, stone fireflies. Waterfalls of sparkling amber, pouring out from nothingness into the past. Spiderwebs of dancing music, the sounds twirling in time with the rhythm of eternity. Nothing made sense to her, yet she found that impossibility tremendously difficult to look away from.

Nonsensical. Bizarre. Beautiful.

Eventually, the burning fervor she felt vanished, all emotion except awe slipping away from her shoulders. Queenie touched down on a floating quartz pillar and blinked away bloodied tears, a mix between agony and beauty swirled in her mind.

Fascinating. Your passion allowed you to climb far.

Her single eye widened as she looked up, watching as Limbo's peak suddenly lowered itself next to Queenie. At the peak, there was

244

a...being? Being wasn't a correct word. Neither was God, nor god. As Queenie stared at ___, she found herself struggling to fully name who, or *what,* she was looking at.

___ had no mouth, yet could frown. ___ had no eyes, yet had such sympathy in ___'s gaze. ___ looked humanoid, but the more she looked at ___, the more ___'s form changed, similar to how light would shimmer and bounce off a silk dress. Even when Queenie closed her eye, she could clearly see ___ in her presence. Unavoidable. Inevitable. Omnipotent.

You cannot fathom me. The majority of what I am consists of things humans are not aware of. Do not try to comprehend something you do not know. Instead, let me lower myself as much as possible, so you may guess what I am.

___ toned itself down, and suddenly Queenie found herself staring at the sun. Not the literal sun, but it looked like a human composed of flames, as well as outer space, the ocean, the mountains, and everything that was unfathomably stronger than Queenie. There were a few other parts of ___ that she didn't recognize, but Queenie's instincts told her to avoid staring at such spots. Queenie wanted to reach out to touch ___, but she knew in an instant would mean agonizing death. And yet...

Correct, though not in the way you imagine. Touching me means losing soul. You would not burn up, be crushed, or drown when touching me. No, your existence would vanish...but that isn't why you've climbed to Limbo's peak, no?

___ extended ___'s hand, and in the center twirled magnificence. It was nothing like the soulscale Queenie had seen under the Overseer's chambers. Just by looking at it, Queenie understood the power and protection it could provide to anyone who held ownership of it. Protecting the entire city of Malapace. Healing a damaged soul. Rewriting reality. It would all be possible, if you could utilize it. Before Queenie could rationalize a plan, ___ clenched its hand and turned around.

Of course...you'll have to compete with that human. He still climbs, and his drive is incredible.

Queenie forced her eyes away from ___ and went slack as a familiar man jumped from obstacle to obstacle, rising through the heavens with fierce determination evident through his shades.

"...Geralt?"

___ vanished and reappeared next to Geralt. He stopped climbing and stared. There was understandable awe in his face, but after a few words, his jaw locked as he pulled out a few marbles from his pocket. They floated around in rapid circles before being thrown at mach speed. Despite the power behind a blow, ___ didn't as much flinch upon the impact. ___ twirled ___'s limbs, and Queenie flinched as the pillar she rested on suddenly rotated next to Geralt.

From far away, Geralt looked fine. Up close, it was evident he had gone through his own struggles. His trimmed hair was disheveled. His shades were cracked, with the lens split at various places. He was barefoot, with heavy burns and tatters all the way up to his mid-shin with his necktie wrapped around a red blotch on his left calf. His right sleeve was barely held up by various threads, clear cuts etched out over nearly every square inch. His left sleeve was torn off, tied up onto his bicep over a very obvious wound. There was stubble lined across his immaculate jawline, cheeks slightly sunken in as he took shallow breaths.

His eyes widened upon seeing Queenie. "...Queenie? What in the blazes are you doing he-" his gaze rested on her right eye. "...no." Ignoring his burns, he rushed over and clutched her face, eyes widening as he stared at her wounded eye. "Nonono. Queenie, *why the hell are you here?*" he snapped, more fearful than angry.

She pushed him off gently. "Same reason as you, honestly. I need the soulscale...and I made it to the peak. Would you let me have it?" she asked quietly, knowing well what his response would be.

Geralt flinched, hesitation clear on his lips as he shook his head. "I...the *Family* needs it. This is far beyond you and me. I'm sorry," he said with a pained expression.

___ interrupted by pulling the ground beneath their feet away, choosing to exist between them.

Two beings want the soulscale this time for different reasons. I am indifferent as to who obtains it. So, here is what I will do.

___ extended the soulscale out, allowing it to twirl in the air rapidly, before sending it flying miles up into the sky.

Strike each other. The last one standing owns it. Show me your devotion: how far you'll go for this.

Queenie locked eyes with Geralt, both of them trying to read each other. She needed the soulscale to repay Juliette: to make up for Queenie's shortcomings. Geralt needed it for the Family, to help *everyone*. This was a situation where neither one could compromise their desires, and the first one to act would gain a massive advantage.

...And despite it all, Queenie couldn't help but feel relieved when Geralt sat on the floor, gesturing Queenie over. She summoned some chains and leapt over to where her former mentor sat. He was exhausted and desperate for his goals, but Queenie was so relieved to see he kept his dignity and honor. Before he could open his mouth, she dove into his arms and hugged him tightly, warm tears stinging the gash on her wounded eye. Geralt let out an exasperated breath as he patted her head.

"It's been rough, yeah?" he said gently.

Queenie sniffled and blew her nose into Geralt's ruined suit. He didn't as much as flinch, instead pulling her face away to wipe her tears with his dirty thumb. He looked at her carefully, a crease appearing on his brow. "...Where is Taba and Hush?" he asked softly.

Her eyes flicked a spark before looking down. She was ashamed to even mutter what had happened, and she could feel Geralt's hands tense up. "No...*both* of th-?"

"...Taba isn't in Limbo. Hush...he...he let go." she said with agony. Before Geralt could even take a breath, she looked up in a frenzy. "But...but he could be alive. Hush wouldn't die. He's too strong. He's gone through worse, no way he'll...he'll..." her voice trailed off. She didn't want to even finish the sentence. She shoved that doubt and fear far away, into the crevices of her mind. If she considered the possibility right now, Queenie could very well shatter and never recover.

Geralt's face morphed from utter despair to immense fury...but the rage wasn't focused on her. His jaw trembled as he looked to his right, eyes burning malice into ___. He hugged her tightly once more before gently letting her go, ruffling her hair as he stood up to ___.

"How many more must suffer until you're satisfied?" Geralt said with an unusual tremble in his voice. "How many children must die for your entertainment?" he asked as he stepped forward. "How many mutants will you throw into the world just for the sake of 'creation'? When will you let us *be*?"

You seem to be mistaken. We are above malice or joy. Would you shake a fist at the skies if a tree falls on your child, or if thunder strikes your homes?

Geralt screamed, his eyes glowing as all of Limbo trembled. Numerous pebbles and marbles lifted up as they all rained down an infinite barrage onto ___. ___ vanished and stood behind Geralt, placing a limb on Geralt's right shoulder. In an instance, his arm swelled up four times the size, before shrinking and fizzling out of existence. He cursed and leapt, throwing a kick enhanced with soul manipulation into ___. Upon making contact, his leg also fizzled away. He collapsed onto the ground, holding himself up with his remaining arm and food, sweat beading on his face.

He looked up, his anger stronger than ever. "You're beings above us, yet you can't comprehend us? Our love? Our suffering? Our bonds? To *hell* with you, the Family will see you all blown to embers and ashes...if it's the last thing Father does," Geralt belted.

Comprehend...is an odd word. I cannot speak for all blessings, but I understand you humans. All your connections and pain. However...when handling absolute power, you will find that it is meaningless.

___ opened ___'s body, revealing the soulscale once more.

...consider this a gift. Partially for the damage I have done to you, partially out of respect for your drive, and mostly because I am curious as to how a human will react to absolute power.

___ placed the soulscale on Geralt's neck...and the effects were instantaneous. His entire body crackled with soul, his obliterated limbs immediately regrowing into their prime condition. His regenerated arm grabbed at his neck, ripping away at his flesh to hold the soulscale in his palm. His entire body trembled as all the marbles and dice floated out of his pockets, whirling around him rapidly like agitated bees. Geralt's body twitched as his right hand twitched into a fist. His eyes were glowing, but through what seemed like tremendous effort, they snapped back to their usual color. Velvet poured out of his sweat glands as he looked down at Queenie with fear.

"...*Run,*" he rasped.

All of the marbles and dice splashed outwards into an explosive firework. Queenie barely had time to summon a shield in front of her to block the blows, and even *then*, they tore through the metal with utter ease. Though the shield damped the impact, her skin was pelted with numerous trinkets as she was thrown off the marble pillar. Through a wince, she summoned a chain and lassoed herself onto a floating grass ball, balancing on the tiny planet as she clutched her ribs. Judging from the pain, it was obvious either a rib was broken or an organ was internally bleeding. She looked up with a hunched look at what looked to be an omnipotent Geralt, descending gently on top of a platform of pebbles.

The situation had changed. She not only needed the soulscale for Juliette and Malapace...but also to bring Geralt back. She unstored a sniper and aimed it at the hand clutching the soulscale. After adjusting for distance and falloff, she exhaled slightly and fired. Unfortunately, as expected, the bullet twisted midair and screamed off into the distance.

...of course bullets were useless. Geralt's blessing heavily countered them, after all.

Queenie threw the sniper off to the side and pulled out a dagger as she unpocketed the one she had pulled out earlier. She held one in her mouth as she summoned two chains: one far above Geralt and one reaching up to him. As the chain behind Geralt snaked down in a sneak attack, a marble that blurred around shattered it within a single strike. Queenie cursed and yanked herself up, raising her arm to cut off Geralt's soulscale-studded arm. Five pebbles zipped from Geralt instantly, each one aimed at a vital organ. She responded instantly, summoning a chain to pull her downwards, rotating her below Geralt in a U-turn as she swung upwards behind her former mentor.

Had Queenie not been trained by him, she would've been minced.

Her eye widened as she instinctively summoned four chains to yank her backwards, seven marbles and dice flinging themselves blindly at her. She ducked into a ball, clenching her teeth as the tiny projectives cut deep cuts into her flesh. The momentum flew her into a bubble made of molten glass, her head ringing loudly as it slammed into the structure. She struggled to her feet, but rested on her limbs, gasping with exhaustion and agony. Her skin slowly burned and melted across the surface, but she was too drained to note it.

Geralt's blessing was simple. Within a certain diameter...he could control anything smaller than his hand. There were a few specific guidelines to follow, but for Queenie? He may as well have utter dominion. Queenie's bullets were tiny, so they were useless. The only projectiles she could use were her chains or her cannon, but the chains were too brittle and the cannon was too predictable. So, she *had* to fight melee...but that was also a specialty of Geralt.

Proficient at range. Untouchable in close-quarters. Geralt was impossible to conquer. There was no way she was winning in her current state...but if she failed, not only would she die...but she would be failing Geralt. Failing Taba. Failing Juliette.

Failing Hush.

She closed her good eye, calming her mind and soul, building up the courage to take the step forward to level the playing field. *'Hey. Blessing. You there?'* she asked.

I am.

'I'm ready for that ascension. Give it to me.' she said.

Your heart will collapse. Are you sure?

'...I need power. If I don't...everyone will suffer.'

Silence. Suddenly, time stopped for a split second, but it was enough. Just as her blessing said, her heart died.

And there he was. Hush. Lying on a ballroom floor. Numerous javelins littering his body, which sprouted thin blue vines. Eyes as dead as a fish.

His heart stopped beating...the second you stepped into Limbo's peak.

Queenie thought ascension fill her with overwhelming power, like being zapped with electricity. She didn't expect to feel...deflated. The life left her arms. Her healthy eye stared blankly into the ground. Swirls flooded her mind. Oddly enough, there was no sadness: she was simply...stunned. There were numerous explanations for that imagery. An illusion, a "worst case scenario". This was something she physically couldn't comprehend or explain...so she sat blankly. Even as Geralt grabbed her head and threw her from the mountain onto the ground of Limbo's peak, she careened motionlessly. When she lay in her little crater, she cursed that his attack failed to kill her. Water steadily flowed from her eyes like an unclosed faucet. The aches of her body vanished: physical pain didn't matter anymore. She simply lay where she was thrown, motionless.

Oh. How she wanted to die.

She loosely clenched the dagger in her hand. One quick plunge, and it would all be over. She could wake up from this nightmare. Yes, that's what this was: a nightmare. No other explanation.

Queenie lifted the dagger, and-

. . .

The two of them sat by the lake. Hush had a tissue plugging up a bloody nose while Queenie kicked dirt up in the water, cackling as tiny dragonflies lifted off from their water reeds. Jin had been bringing her on so many missions, none of them containing her brother. So, she really appreciated the tiny bits of time she could spend with him. It was odd, because while Hush also seemed to enjoy her company, he always kept darting his eyes around. There was always danger, be it animals or whatnot, but Queenie didn't care: she felt safe around Hush.

He crinkled a leaf between his fingers, throwing the tiny flakes into the lake. 'Hey, Queenie?' he said.

'Yeah?'

'Is everyone treating you well? No one is-'

She rolled her eyes. 'They're all super nice to me. You always ask that question. What 'bout you? What does Jin make you do?' she asked.

'I...ah, some stuff in the caves. Usually moving merch and goods around. Stuff you don't need to worry about,' he said in a hurry as he turned away. He dropped his ruined leaf and picked up a little pebble, throwing it into the lake. As the rock sank into the lake, the ripples caused the sunbeam across the water's reflection to vibrantly bounce.

The siblings sat in the morning sun, a bird chirping in the branches of a dead tree. The wind blew a cool breeze, making the sunbeam's heat a bit more tolerable. Queenie picked up a pillbug that scampered across the floor, forcefully curled it up into a ball, and balanced it on Hush's knee. She giggled as it rolled off, bouncing into the grass. Hush frowned as he dusted some dirt off her shoulder. Once she was clean, he smiled and ruffled her hair. He turned back to face the waters, staring silently in the calm morning. Queenie giggled and did the same.

. . .

The tears dribbled out of her eyes, but she forced her legs up. Everything ached to the highest hell, but she spat blood to the floor. Her soul craved death, but she stood with her chin up. Anything less would belittle Hush, his death, and everything he stood for. She lost her major reason to fight...but standing still felt *wrong*.

Her blessing felt...tiny. Well, what she was using before, anyhow. Now that she had ascended...she realized how little she had been utilizing it. Wrapping her soul to put them in storage was the limitation of her soul, but if she were to compile all the soul in her life...what was to stop her from dragging Limbo onto Earth? Of course, that wouldn't matter right now, since they were already in Limbo. Still...a blanket of her soul draped over Limbo's peak. Everything here was hers...and she wouldn't give it to *anyo-*

"...Queenie?"

She flinched and looked up. To her right was Taba, staring in disbelief. Queenie frowned in return: how was Taba here? He shouldn't be in Limbo. Wha-

Queenie blinked. Her vision was...normal. She touched her wounded eye and a burst of pain caused her to wince and withdraw. No, it was still damaged: guess ascension didn't heal her. Though her left eye saw everything clearly, her right eye (the one that had gotten damaged) saw things...more fuzzily. No, what she had mistaken for cured sight was instead a misty outline of her surroundings.

254

Taba crouched next to her and carefully examined her face. "You...are you alright? Where's Hush?" he asked.

Queenie's heart split open, the raw insides exposed to the void. Still, she stared at Taba with hazy eyes. "He's dead. I confirmed it," she said.

Taba's eyes widened as his eyes twitched slightly, before a puzzled expression rested on his face. He opened his mouth to speak, but changed his mind as he shook his head. "We can talk details later," he said while looking up with a frown. "Is that...Geralt?"

"Yeah. He has the soulscale embedded in his right hand. We need to take it out, or he isn't going to be himself ever again."

Taba nodded solemnly, questions obviously swirling in his mind, but he stayed composed as he murmured questions into nothingness. He suddenly flinched as he grabbed Queenie by the hoodie and yanked her backwards, a grapeshot of marbles crunching into where Queenie stood. Geralt crashed down, his eyes twitching red as he took ragged breaths, veins pulsing through his arms as they creaked upwards like a malfunctioning puppet. Taba exhaled softly as he held a defensive pose, nodding softly to Queenie. "Do what you can to back me up. I'll play around you," he said calmly.

Queenie nodded as she pulled out a gun. It was odd: by all means, his blessing had proven her bullets to be ineffective...and yet, she felt oddly confident. She fired four rounds to Geralt, and as he had before, the bullets careened off into different abysses. Out of instinct, she tugged at her soul, and each of the bullets swirled around midair and back towards Geralt's location. His face twitched into a snarl, marbles flying up to collide into each of the bullets midair. Though he was uninjured, Geralt *had* to make a more active input against Queenie's shots. She could d-

Geralt's legs pulsed with soul, with Queenie and Taba having a split second to react before he closed their distance in a single leap. Queenie yanked herself backwards with her own soul, while Taba dove to the ground. As Geralt's kick barely swung over them, Queenie swung forward with both her daggers as Taba swiveled upwards, his legs being thrown into an axe kick into Geralt's face. Their former mentor twisted his body midair, his arm flying towards Queenie in a backhand punch. She grit her teeth, and instinctually raised a pillar of stone from the ground to block the blow. The three of them stared in bafflement as Geralt's fist cracked through the pillar, none of them expecting such a development.

Capitalizing on their unanimous bafflement, Taba leapt up and threw a right-handed hook towards Geralt. Even though he was caught off-guard and was being borderline brainwashed, Geralt would *never* be caught by surprise. He caught Taba's wrist with one arm and flicked his other arm, pelting Taba with a barrage of shrapnel scattered around Limbo. There was no surprise on Taba's face, his face twisted in agony as tiny holes started to form in his skin. Not wasting the opportunity, he lashed out and grabbed Geralt by the waist, pinning him down.

"QUEENIE."

She immediately understood, dragging her arm across the sky to summon her cannon at point blank. Her eyes glowed with vigor as the cannon exploded next to Geralt's right wrist. The impact caused smoke to explode into the atmosphere, throwing the three of them back.

As the dust settled, Queenie staggered upwards, coughing as she fanned the sky with her arms. Taba, having been directly next to the impact, lay unconscious on the floor, a blood splatter painted across his entire body. Queenie hoped it wasn't his blood: she didn't know if she had it in her if she lost someone else close to her.

Queenie wiped the trickle of blood from her damaged eye, staring at her hands. Everything hurt. Her body, her heart, and her soul. Whenever she thought about her friends and Family...her chest ached. It was torture to even think of others...and it felt as though there was only a tiny thread separating her from empathy to utter apathy. If being so close to others hurt this much...maybe it would be better to be alone and uncaring.

Geralt coughed as he clutched his wrist, staring at his soul-stone-embedded hand that lay on the floor. He seemed to still be suffering from the aftereffects of the odd possession, but his brow was creased with agony and regret. Just from his gaze, it was clear he had a million apologies that he wished to say to the two of them.

Queenie took a step forward...and groaned as fell to her knee. Her eyes flickered gently as the throbbing in her heart grew tremendously. Geralt noticed the reaction and raised his arm, worry plastered on his face. Still, he stood back, obviously worried that he would lash out again. So, he did the next best thing he could and called out to her.

"So...you've ascended?" he asked sadly.

Her head spun as her eyes buzzed with weak light. She struggled to formulate words as she looked up with a wobbly head. Geralt tightened his lips, obviously torn between fear, worry, and anger...but he simply sighed instead. "When you ascend, there's a few heavy draw-backs. One of the ones that your blessing doesn't ever mention is that as you use it, you feel the pain your body first felt as it initially ascended. In fact, the longer you use it, the worse the pain gets. It's enough to crumble even the strongest of veterans," he said. Geralt twirled his good hand, the marbles on the floor shuttering before calmly flying towards him. After gathering them up, he stuffed what he could into his pockets. Once his weapons were tucked away, the two of them stared at the pulsing soulscale.

"So...now what?" Queenie asked weakly.

Geralt said nothing but walked slowly to his hand, pausing right before it. As he stared at it, the sky rippled as two others slammed down into Limbo's peak: a woman and a man. The woman winced as she rubbed her elbows and adjusted her hat, while the man projectile vomited onto the immaculate floor. The two of them let go of each other's hands and glanced around with a mixture of awe and alarm, glancing at both the scenery, Queenie, Taba, and Geralt.

"Queenie? Taba?" Sana asked with a hesitant frown.

Banase wiped his mouth and stood tall, holding up his fists. "Sorry that we were late. I...something...someone? Well, whatever it was, it was holding us back from touching the last shard," he admitted.

Suddenly, the two of them noticed Queenie's gentle, glowing eyes. They also noticed how Hush wasn't in the area. Sana opened her mouth, horror plastered on her face. "Oh. Oh. *Oh.* I'm...oh," she said.

The Gatekeeper walked over and gave a gentle hug to Queenie, stroking her head gently with her calloused hands. As she did, Banase walked forward to where Taba lay, carrying him gently in his arms. However, before he could return, Geralt flicked a marble towards Banase, cutting him off.

"Let him *go*. He isn't yours," snapped Geralt.

"You don't get to decide that," said Banase with a raised eyebrow.

Geralt took off his cracked shades, throwing them onto the ground. As he did, his eyes glowed quietly, shaking all of Limbo once more. "Put him *down*," he said quietly.

Banase gently laid Taba next to Queenie, patted her shoulder, and stood up to adjust his suspenders. Once they were taught, he hunched over with his arms up, his disheveled mustache twitching in anticipation. Sana glanced over, patted Queenie's back, and stood up to face him as well. Geralt was exhausted and outnumbered. And yet...

He lifted his hand, and the scattered debris from all of Limbo's peak lifted upwards, swirling into a typhoon of destruction. Sana and Banase simply stared in slight shock at the looming spectacle as it blotted out the impossible sky, raining death onto them all.

Queenie had no reason to step in, yet she recalled how she had raised the pillar of stone to block Geralt's swing from earlier. If her ascension allowed her to control Limbo...then maybe...

Her eyes flickered once more as the ground erupted upwards, forming a glass shelter as it protected them all from endless hail. As she thought: her ascension allowed her to quite literally control the aspects of her storage: Limbo. Sure, it sapped quite a bit of soul...but Queenie was tired of death and suffering. She didn't want to think anymore. No more.

When the rain finished, Geralt remained standing with a pained expression. "Queenie...really?" he asked softly. Queenie couldn't meet his eyes, looking down in shame. "They're our enemies, Queenie. We...you..." he sighed as he shook his head. "Fine. I can't force reason: not now, anyways. Still, you also can't stop me from what I'm about to do." He reached into his jacket and pulled out a hand-rolled cigarette, a lighter hovering slightly as it lit his tobacco. He took a deep inhale before puffing out soft smoke. "What are your names?" he asked the guests with a calm voice.

"Sana, Gatekeeper of Malapace," said Sana.

"Banase, a mentor from Malapace," said Banase.

"I see," said Geralt, putting out his cigarette with his bare foot. He put his remaining hand in his pocket and held his chin high, a tornado of scattered rubble rapidly forming behind him. "You face Geralt. A former debt collector, the right hand of the Father, the strongest mentor of the Family, and the one responsible for those damn kids," he said, the tornado of pebbles behind him blotting out the infinite sky. "I will not leave Limbo alive, but neither will *you*," he thundered.

CHAPTER 14

A fter Geralt's declaration, Sana's eyes immediately glowed as she glanced over to her allies. As expected, they were all standing wary of the man...but were mistakenly bunched up. Tightening her lips in worry, she clenched her legs and slammed forwards, pushing Banase and Queenie away. They looked back with slight alarm right before the hurricane of miscellaneous debris coated both her and Taba's unconscious body. As she stood in the eye of the storm, Sana drew her sickles, twirling the handles in her hands as she channeled her soul through the blades.

Just as quickly as it had formed, the hurricane suddenly began pelting objects at her direction, each pellet being shot fast enough to act as a bullet. Sana inhaled sharply and sliced the first stone cleanly in half, the impact of her strike cutting through Geralt's soul and severing his connection with the rock. Then, a marble zipped towards her right thigh. Then, a woodchip to her left rib. Then, like a hound-ing cloud of locusts, a swarm of black crashed down at her, all the items flying at random intervals, random times, and random targets. Sana began to hack through the endless attack, her blades cutting everything seamlessly, all while ensuring the sleeping Taba next to her feet remained unharmed. The attacks seemed to alter their paths and intensity when flying near Taba, and Sana took whatever advantage was given to her. Of course, she would never put the young man at risk...but Sana needed to reserve as much focus as possible to simply survive the onslaught.

Outside of the hurricane, Sana could feel Banase, Queenie, and Geralt all fighting in melee range. Geralt still had numerous orbs full of murderous intent swarming around him, but Queenie seemed to be using her blessing to counteract this, turning a one-sided masacre into a fistfight with obstacles.

Sure, Geralt was clearly exhausted...but if Sana weren't dragging so much of his attention away, Banase would've been eviscerated. All she could do was swing, dodge numerous fatal blows, and pray the others could take Geralt down.

.   .   .

Queenie was sweating harshly, taking deep breaths as she continuously continued to hinder Geralt. Her blessing summoned a barrage bullets and chains, each one flying towards her former mentor. She wasn't aiming to harm him, but Queenie knew anything less than a fatal blow wouldn't serve to even bother Geralt. If she could knock him unconscious, this would all end. Still, that was a tall order. Geralt was summoning a hurricane of debris to keep Sana away (and knowing him, also ensuring Taba wasn't getting hurt), focusing his blessing to fend off all of Queenie's summoned projectiles, all while fighting hand-to-hand (with a missing hand) against Banase and Queenie.

Honestly, if she didn't feel so dead inside, Queenie would've gained a new level of respect for Geralt that she didn't know existed.

Banase was throwing a flurry of punches at an astonishing speed, considering his size. Geralt was ducking and parrying all the blows, responding with casual jabs or kicks whenever an opening presented itself. Banase was doing a good job bobbing and weaving, yet he was smacked around a few times. Queenie was hesitant to be swinging a blade...but eventually turned her brain off, allowing only static noise filter through her thoughts. After a few stabs that only struck the air, it was clear Geralt wasn't getting hurt anytime soon.

Geralt tucked in low and threw a solid elbow into Banase's chin. As he did, he also did a slight leap to whirl his legs into Queenie's arm, twisting her hand and efficiently disarming her. Banase reeled back, but tightened his core and slammed his right leg back to stabilize himself, smashing his head into Geralt's shoulder with a heavy headbutt. Geralt slammed into the floor, but immediately pushed his bloody stub into the floor to push up into a handstand, twirling onto Banase's shoulders. Queenie pulled out a thin ice pick from her storage, leaping high to sink it into Geralt's arm. Banase saw the opportunity and gripped tightly onto Geralt's leg, flipping him into the weapon. Geralt grit his teeth as he glared at the assault, a marble flying out of nowhere to crash into the icepick, causing it to clatter into the floor. Right as it did, he stomped into Banase's face, only to scowl as the kick was caught by the bigger man. Banase lifted Geralt into the air, roaring as he began to slam him into the floor. Suddenly, a dice flew out from the tornado circling Sana and embedded itself into Banase's shoulder, causing him to weaken his grip before Geralt was thrown onto the ground. Queenie winced as he landed with a *crack*, not moving for a few seconds. As he lay still, the tornado slowed slightly...but picked up in speed once more as Geralt rolled away a few feet before climbing back up.

Geralt's nose was bleeding, his head was swirling, and he stood hunched at a slight angle. Maybe it was the slam. Maybe it was the blood loss. Maybe it was the literal tornado holding off one of the Gatekeepers of Malapace. Regardless, it was clear that Geralt was reaching his limit. If Banase and Queenie kept their assault, then surely th-

A figure hobbled up from behind Banase. She had never met him, but the sickly looking man gave an odd sense of deja vu. He wore a tattered t-shirt and muddied pants, with one of his legs missing, a black cloak wrapped around the stub. His face was ghastly, sunken cheeks outlining a determined face.

A spark of energy pulsing in her brain, Queenie barely had time to scream a late warning before the unknown man swung his dagger downwards towards Banase's neck. Banase, noticing something awry, took a small step to the left. While avoiding the fatal blow, the big man's face morphed into agony as the blade lodged into his collarbone. Banase leapt backwards and locked eyes with his assailant, who held an odd canister that seemed to be full of white powder. Flour, maybe? Her guess was confirmed when the man unscrewed the top and chucked the contents into the air, forming an odd sort of smokescreen in front of them and hi-

...Queenie's mind fluttered blankly. What was she doing again? She turned to face Banase, her face morphing into alarm when she saw a dagger embedded into his collarbone. Equally shocking was the confusion plastered in Banase's pained eyes. Geralt also seemed slightly confused, but after squinting a bit, something seemed to click in his mind as he scowled deeply. He was a bit away, but Queenie could clearly hear the mutter under his voice:

"*...damn it, Zanshin. This better not be you.*"

"*It's me. Sorry,*" a raspy voice echoed out from behind them all. Everyone whirled around and stared at a man missing a leg, leaning against a boulder studded with light. Sweat beaded across his face, but he nodded to Geralt. "*You need to stop shouldering the burden by yourself.*"

Geralt nodded to Zanshin's missing leg. "Were you always missing a leg?" he asked.

"*...Yes.*"

"Somehow, I don't buy it," Geralt sighed, standing up a bit straighter as he took a deep breath. "Queenie's not on our side at the moment. Can you help me detain her?"

"*I saw. We can focus on the big man, first.*"

Queenie felt like her lungs were about to implode, but her arms twitched with anticipation. Her emotions were everywhere: despairing from Hush, desperate to stop Geralt, determined to protect Malapace, exhaustion from ascension, and the creaking desire to end it all. Still, a bit of string tugged at her heart, screaming for silence. Too many people, too many events, why couldn't it just all...go...*away*? With desperation, her heart screamed, and Limbo bent around her. Geralt noticed her agony and dove towards her, extending his only good hand to hold her.

Queenie clenched her fists, and Limbo warped her and Geralt away.

· · ·

There's a ranking system of exhaustion. First, there's groggy. Then, tired. Sleepy. Drained, battered, wired, twitchy, slogged. Lastly, and

265

oddly enough, it loops all the way back around to being just…tired. It becomes impossible to fathom any fancy word or phrase to describe one's exhaustion. Desperately wishing to crash into bed, yet being completely awake, yet feeling that adrenaline fading away, yet manually forcing your muscles to stay taut in fear of collapsing altogether.

Geralt, by every name and definition, was *tired*. It wasn't just the tornado he formed around the Gatekeeper, no. Nor was it the two-on-one fight he had with Banase and Queenie. Hell, it wasn't even the numerous regions of Limbo. The… the ___ that had obliterated Geralt and jump started him with the soulscale? It was the equivalent of trying to cook a potato in a puddle of lava. After that whole episode, Geralt wasn't sure if he was drained or rejuvenated. Maybe he was both.

…but more than all that, the biggest commotion of events was Queenie. His heart was torn everywhere. Attacking her, seeing her ascend, and watching her keep up with him in combat. It was an odd mix of emotions, from heart-break, despair, grief, worry…and pride.

That pride expanded even further when Queenie managed to kidnap him into a foreign piece of Limbo. Geralt had known Queenie ever since she was a child. Hell, until today's recent events, she was *still* a child…yet she continuously kept surpassing his expectations.

Queenie stumbled around, wheezing dryly as trembling hands clenched two daggers. The landscape was purely white, as far as Geralt could see. That was unfortunate, since there was nothing in the area that could be used as part of his arsenal. He also had no marbles and trinkets in his pockets, all while missing a hand. To top it all off…he was drained in every aspect: physically, mentally, and soul-wise. If Queenie were to fight him, she *might* actually come out on top.

266

Geralt took a stance and forced out a smile. "I can't remember the last time we sparred. Excited to see how you've grown," he said.

Queenie said nothing as she swayed. No emotion, no fire, no reaction. Her eyes were listless...*nothing* like Geralt was used to seeing. That was fair: she had just ascended. She probably felt suicidal.

So, Geralt's responsibility as her guardian was to reignite her will to live. Right here, right now.

Queenie blindly leapt forward, her arms seemingly swinging independently of each other. Her left hooked long arcs while her right tightly jabbed inwards. For the majority of fighters, this would be sloppy...but for Queenie? She was covering all bases and could easily shift her pressure to the biggest weak spot. As expected, when Geralt ducked the large left hook, Queenie immediately dropped down as well and immediately put her back into her right arm's stab. Geralt fell backwards and kicked upwards into Queenie's hand. Queenie tilted her blade flat into Geralt's heel, using the force to push herself backwards.

Before Geralt could even stand up, Queenie suddenly vanished into the air and suddenly reappeared behind him, her left arm once again raised to stab his shoulder blade. Geralt frowned, but slammed his elbow towards her palm. She responded by letting go of her dagger, using the momentum to lift up off Geralt's blow, twirling in the air to land squarely on his shoulders, wrapping her legs around his neck. He pursed his lips, tightly gripping her ankle and doing a front flip to throw her off with sudden force. It worked, causing her to flip off the floor into her starting position with only one dagger in possession, the other embedded into the nothingness of the floor.

Geralt quietly walked forward and yanked the blade from the floor, silently staring at the worn handle. He then looked up with a sorrowful expression. "Queenie, why exactly are you fighting now?" he asked.

She stared back blankly, causing Geralt to sigh. He calmly walked forward, making Queenie subconsciously flinch. He held her dagger up, handle first, calmly wrapping it around her left hand. "If you hate me and want me to die, that's fine. If you want me to live and are only trying to prevent me from killing the mentors of Malapace, that's also fine. However, right now? This fight doesn't make sense. As it is in this place you've brought me, I can't harm Malapace. I can't take the soulscale." Geralt leaned down and wiped her damp cheeks with his remaining hand. "No matter what your emotions are, I can take it full on...but you need to be honest with yourself. What is the point of our fight?" he asked.

Queenie's shoulders slumped, obviously unsure of life in general. Geralt understood her agony: he had faced it so, *so* long ago. When he lost Rebecca and his s-

Geralt sighed and shook his head. He was too old to reminisce and regret. All he could do now is fix the future. He gave her a warm hug, ruffling her hair as he did. "Life is ass, yeah. Wish I could give more comforting words, but this crappy feeling is why the Family fights. I'm sorry you had to experience this," he said.

As she dug into his chest, Geralt couldn't see her face. All he could feel were two, warm, wet spots form into his chest as she squeezed him ferociously. It stung to high hell, but was nothing compared to the suffering Queenie was going through, so he simply embraced her back.

As he cradled her, he hummed softly. He wasn't sure why...but it just felt right.

"...do you think I could've saved Hush?" she whispered softly.

"I don't know, that's for you to decide," Geralt responded. "Still, what would *Hush* say? Probably something lik-"

"...like how it isn't my problem. He would also probably use his blessing to shut me up so I can't cut him off," she muttered.

"Yeah, that sounds about right," he said. "He was always that kind of idiot, too selfless...but I guess that's one of his strongest points."

"...yeah. It is...no, *was*. It was."

. . .

The hurricane around Sana had vanished, but she was kneeling on the floor and taking deep breaths as she tried to quickly regain her stamina. Understandable, really. The ma'am had swatted off an endless barrage for what felt like at *least* thirty minutes all while protecting Taba. It was astonishing how she was untouched, much less *alive*.

As much as Banase wanted to rush to the ma'am's side, he was in a pickle himself. An older man he had never seen stood in front of him, balancing on his only leg. While Banase couldn't confirm it, he was *certain* this man was the perpetrator of his wounds. Numerous slices and stabs, each of them inches away from crucial organs or arteries. He held his fists up into a tight guard in front of his face, taking shallow breaths as he kept a sharp eye on the man.

"Could I ask for your name, sir?" asked Banase.

"*...that is your fourth time asking that question...and this is my fourth answer. My name is Zanshin. I'm not looking for a fight,*" said Zanshin.

Banase frowned as he flexed his forearm. "So...explain the cuts I have, would you?"

"...*incentive to keep your distance, and yet also to not look away. That is all.*"

"Why would y-"

"*I'm waiting for* them *to return. Second time you've asked, by the way.*"

"And by them, do you mean Queenie and the older man?"

"*Correct. Queenie is on your side, no? So our goals should obviously align. Let us await their return in peace. After all...I have yet to fulfill my purpose here.*"

Something rubbed Banase the wrong way. It was true he worried about the little girl, but his gut told him awaiting her return was Zanshin's plan. "You keep saying things that refer to how many times I've asked things. Have we met before?" he asked.

"*First time I've met you.*"

Good chance this was a memory relating blessing. Since this gentleman had emphasized how he didn't want Banase to look away...maybe it was sight based. Keeping a steady eye on Zanshin, Banase took a shallow breath and took swinging steps to close the gap between them, bobbing and weaving as he did. All the while, Zanshin leaned against a supporting wall until Banase was within an arm's reach. When the opportunity presented itself, Banase sucked in a tight breath as he threw a strong right-hook towards Zanshin. Zanshin moved his head out of the way, simultaneously striking with his palm to misdirect the blow to cause the blow to crash and shatter the wall behind them. While Banase immediately threw out a left jab, Zanshin simply held his other arm up with a trembling jaw. Banase's blow connected, causing the older man to slam against the crumbling wall with a painful-sounding whine. As Zanshin crumbled to the floor, he grabbed a handful of debris from the floor, throwing it at Banasc. On instinct, he covered his face, swatting it all away an-

Banase stood up, blinking. Why was he covered in wounds? Where was he? His mind clicked upon realizing that the sound of clacking debris had vanished. He turned around and saw Sana on the floor, gasping for air as she clutched her chest. Before Banase could bolt over, a blade sprouted from his calf, causing him to wince as he stumbled slightly. He turned around to find out what had happened, locking eyes with a battered old man. He was missing a leg, utterly battered, and leaned against what seemed like a giant snail shell made of rusted steel.

The elderly man, sweat beading down his face, nodded towards Banase. "*Before you ask...my name is Zanshin. Keep your eyes on me, but stay away,*" he said with a determined glare. "*Until it is time to descend, I cannot afford to perish.*"

. . .

Queenie and Geralt sat next to each other, each one staring at each other's wounds. Neither one was too certain as to what the correct call was.

For Queenie, her mind was jumbled. The safety of her Family, where she stood with Malapace, her ascension, her brother...it was hard for her to stomach it all. She just wanted to stop thinking and go on full auto-pilot, but doing so would be a massive disservice to Geralt and Hush. Still, the aching from ascension grew with each ticking second, like a drum slamming it's beat into her head. The longer she stayed here, the worse things would become.

Geralt, on the other hand, worried about the kids. Was Taba ok? How should he approach Queenie and her mental state? What about the soulscale? To what extent should he prioritize the Family over the wellbeing of these kids? Where did Queenie even take them? What was Queenie's ascension? There was no way she could maintain it for much longer: Geralt had to be prepared for when she slumped over.

With so much on both of their plates, the two of them should've been quick to take action. Ironically, with both of them being bombarded with worries and concerns, all they could do was sit down.

Geralt rubbed his wrist, trying to ignore the throbbing pain that rang throughout his entire body. Damn stump was burning like high hell, but he didn't want to worry the girl more than normal. Still, Geralt needed to act: before Queenie's ascension collapsed and the severity of his state became apparent. The one item that could resolve these issues was...

Geralt stood up and extended a hand to the girl, who took it with forced conviction. "How you feeling?" he asked.

"Ass," she sniffled.

"Fair enough," he said as he took a few steps back. "You're running out of time, so I'm going to treat you as an adult now. Get ready."

Queenie hesitated, her fingers twitching as she took an uncertain step backwards. "...Geralt?" she asked with a faltering voice.

"We both have our problems and goals. I wish I could fix them all for you...but I'm a flawed man," he sighed. "Still, both of us have crap that, unfortunately, can be fixed by the same item...and neither of us can compromise for it." Geralt took a lower stance, holding his good arm in front of him with a deep exhale, mentally preparing himself for what he had to do. "...You get what I'm getting at, Queenie?"

Queenie twitched, an obvious pang of agony striking her...but she picked up her daggers and took a stance. "Am I allowed to strike to kill?" she asked quietly.

"Go for it. I'll just ask Nancy or Father to patch me up," he grinned.

The declaration irked Queenie with annoying familiarity, causing her to subconsciously smile. "You think you'll win?" she asked.

"Let's find out."

Queenie stood stiffly, her puffy, red, eyes evident even past the glow of her ascension. Still, the light was flickering rapidly, proving that her soul was being whittled away. Soon, she would have no more soul to utilize her blessing, and they would warp back to where the others were. Both of them knew this...but instead of Geralt allowing this to naturally happen, Queenie was grateful. Her former mentor had given her a chance to live without regrets. She took a shaky exhale, jumping up and down to loosen up her aching body.

She had problems, major worries, and unending regrets. Those could wait until after this fight.

When her toes touched the floor, she slammed forward with explosive energy, even managing to startle the alert Geralt. He cackled with unnatural joy, using his good hand to catch her left swing. Queenie, expecting this, twirled her entire body and swung her right arm into Geralt's ribcage.

"Good! As taught, you exploit your enemy's weakness!" he roared with delight. Still, he kicked upwards a perfect one-hundred and eighty degrees, disarming Queenie and forcing the knife to twirl into the air. With his gripped hand, he yanked Queenie close and head-butted her nose. A solid *crack* rang out, a splatter of blood flowing through the air. Not wasting time to even register the wound, Queenie turned the wrist that Geralt had intercepted, flicking her fingers to throw her knife into his ribcage. It was shallow, but enough to cause him to let go. Upon hitting the floor, Queenie shook off her dizziness, pushing off her toes to dart at Geralt's legs. In turn, Geralt leapt high, snatching Queenie's other dagger out of the air, gripping it tightly to rush towards the floor. She cursed, slamming her palms into the floor and pushing backwards, completely killing her momentum and avoiding the stab by merely a few inches. She jumped backwards and took a defensive stance. Geralt placed the dagger he caught out of the air in between his teeth, using his now free hand to wield the other blade.

In an instant, Geralt had not only managed to disarm Queenie, but also take possession of her weapons. This was a tricky situation...and yet, Queenie felt the oddest pride for her former mentor, an unnatural yet familiar laugh creeping up on her exhausted face.

Geralt chuckled with clenched teeth, pushing his thumb tightly into Queenie's blade. It was small, but she could see the soul flow through his thumb, creating enough pressure to cause her weapon to snap. It was an action that caused her to frown, but the meaning of the self "handicap" became evident when he hurled the pieces towards her. The dagger, including the handle, was about eight inches. However...now that it was broken in half, the individual pieces were *much* tinier. Small enough to fit in one's hand.

The handle and blade picked up speed and sped towards her. Queenie cursed and darted to the right, feeling the blade whiz past her cheek. She wasn't even able to keep track of the weapon, because Geralt was now in front of her, twirling her blade in his fingers, swiping rapidly in ferverous swings. For Queenie? She saw the weapon as simple extensions of Geralt's arm, not losing her cool even when avoiding the weapon by mere centimeters.

It was odd. So much was weighing heavily on her heart...but as she fought with Geralt, barely avoiding fatal blows? She had the stupidest smile on her face. Maybe she was broken, insane...but the emotions that she felt as she threw two jabs at Geralt's cheeks? The stinging of her knuckles was a wondrous accompaniment to the brilliant smile her former mentor had. Hearing the fizzle of Geralt's blessing behind her, she grabbed Geralt's tattered shirt and took advantage of his strengthened core to effortlessly twirl around, putting him in danger of his own blessing. As the broken dagger whirled safely to the left and right, his boisterous laughter filled the empty chamber they scuffled in. Not letting up, Queenie took a deep breath and flipped upwards, flexing all her muscles to lift over Geralt to land on his arm. If he were energized and in perfect condition, this would've done nothing...yet to the *current* Geralt? His grip loosened the slightest bit, but it was enough for Queenie to seize the opportunity to snatch her blade back. She fell to the floor, but pushed up with her shoulder blade as she bounced, using the extra force to push back up. With an airy head, she joyously laughed upon landing on her feet, twirling her blade once more in her hand.

"You're stronger than me in nearly everything," she boasted. "However, for weaponry and hand-to-hand combat? We're equals. Hell, I might even be better than you," she teased.

Utter delight radiated off of Geralt's cheeks...with the most wistful eyes she had ever seen. Before she could register why, her ascension finally gave out, the sky shattering as the little pocket Queenie had taken the two into crumbled. Her consciousness flickered, all energy fading as she fell towards the floor. Before she could slam harshly into the floor, she felt sturdy arms catch her decent, lips pressing on the top of her head. Before her world faded to black, she heard a small phrase:

"Welcome back, Queenie. I'm so...*so* proud of you. No matter what you do or choose, just know...we will *always* love you."

. . .

'Queenie?'

'Eh?'

'You're special.'

'I know. The clan kept telling me that. That guy called Father says it too. I hate it. I don't wanna be special if it means I can't talk to you.'

'Really? I think the opposite. I don't care what happens to me, but seeing you *be showered in praise and gifts? Nothing makes me happier.'*

'...Why?'

'I dunno, I just think it's cool. I just feel...really, really *proud.'*

'...would you still love me if I weren't special?'

He laughed, ruffling her hair. Her face flushed, but she didn't swat the hand away. He looked towards the sunset with a confident smile. 'There isn't a world where you aren't special. Doesn't matter your blessing, looks, personality, anything. You'll always be special to me. I don't give a damn what anyone else says.'

'...You're gross.'

'Love you too, Queenie.'

. . .

Sana's head was spinning, the muscles on her body aching to high heavens. She hadn't exerted herself to that extent in *years*. Even considering how she was protecting Taba, she was out of shape. The Gatekeeper sharply inhaled rapidly to oxidize her muscles, trying to muster the strength to stand up. She could barely lift her head, but judging from the grunts and muttering, Banase was fighting with...someone. Whoever it was had no killing intent towards Sana: he wasn't even paying her any attention. Either this new opponent was an utter fool...or a genius who knew about Sana's curse.

The tingle returned to Sana's ankles, so she exhaled sharply before forcing her legs up. Her stance was wobbly, and she threatened to tumble at any time, but she pushed past her dizziness and looked upwards, her sugegasa falling off her head and being caught on her neck by its string. She saw Banase, holding his arms in front of his face in a tight guard, littered with numerous wounds. A man hobbling on a single leg stood in front of him, looking equally worn out...but with not as many notable wounds. Still, at this rate, Banase would fall first. Sana needed to be there to make sure that didn't happen.

Before she could even step forward, the sky shattered, like a fake window above them all, and out tumbled Geralt and a pale Queenie. Sana instinctively took a step forward, but had to stop to gasp, her head swirling with sickening colors. She fell to a knee, her dress becoming taut as she rested on the floor.

· · ·

Geralt looked over at everyone, obviously tremendously drained. Still...from the way he held himself, it was evident that he was the strongest one out of everyone...currently. Had he fought Sana without any hindrances...Geralt dismissed the thought. He didn't want to consider the possibility of loss.

Banase saw Geralt step out and roared, stomping over with thunderous footsteps, pouring all of his soul into his blessing to deliver a fatal punch into Geralt's skull. Geralt flicked his index finger, and a marble shot up from the floor and slammed into the soft, unprotected center of Banase's gut, making the big man lose all concentration as he tumbled into the floor, all the air sucked out of his lungs.

"If I had more soul…you would've been riddled in holes," muttered Geralt. "You all did a number on me, I have to commend you for that." He looked over at Zanshin, the slightest confusion crossing his eyes before impossible recognition flickered in his gaze. "Zanshin? Where's your cloak?"

"*…how can you recognize me without my cloak?*"

"Eh. Not many people can climb to the peak. You have no hostility to me, so you aren't from Malapace. I can't really remember you, either. So…"

Zanshin tightened his crusted lips, but nodded silently. "*We won. How will you transport the soulscale?*" he asked.

Geralt shifted Queenie from his front onto his back into a piggy-back. He then extended his fingers while closing his eyes, his entire hand vibrating as the soulscale suddenly shot up from his detached palm and swirled a few inches above his fingers. Geralt spat up bile from the sudden pressure of the soulscale, immediately lowering to one knee, but refusing to let Queenie go. In fact, he held onto her even *more* tightly, every vein in his body pulsing with agonizing constraint.

Sana forced herself up, tightly gripping her sickles as she trudged over to the incapacitated Geralt. As she lifted her arms to decapitate him, she suddenly flicked her eyes to the right as a blurry figure hobbled over to a fallen Banase. Her mouth twisted into an agonized screech as her eyes flickered with fading light. She darted backwards, expending soul she did not have to stop Zanshin from stabbing Banase's throat. Zanshin took this opportunity to let go of his dagger to backhand Sana, causing the weakened Gatekeeper to stumble onto the floor.

"*Omnipotent, my ass,*" he huffed. "*I guess it would seem that way to anyone without knowledge of your blessing...or should I say curse?*"

Sana didn't even have the energy to glare at him. How did this man know? Damn it, damn it *all*.

Suddenly, Limbo's peak concentrated into a flat stage, just as ___ appeared before them. ___ existed with an odd emotion.

So...the one who has claimed the soulscale is him who is named Geralt. That was to be expected. Now...how will you get back?

Geralt looked up with twitching muscles, not even able to properly open his mouth to verbalize his thoughts. Regardless, ___ understood it all, and replied.

There are two ways to exit Limbo. You can either climb down the same way you climbed Limbo...with all the difficulties and 'unpredictabilities' to boot. Or...you can intrigue ___. Put on a play, be the greatest fool amongst fools, and ___ will send everyone on Limbo's peak back to your planet and time.

Geralt mentally cursed. He had expected this. His initial plan was to quickly grab the soulscale, then use his ascension to defend himself as he climbed down. However, as he climbed, it became utterly evident that this was impossible: there was not a single person who could make the climb and decent...apart from Father.

To his surprise, Zanshin stepped up with a calm demeanor...as though he expected all this.

"*How is this? I will stay behind on Limbo if you let the others go.*"

Oh? Why would this entice ___ ?

279

"*My curse is that anytime someone looks away from me...they forget me. If I can not die in Limbo as all my loved ones forget my entire existence? As I am chained up, forced to watch them suffer? Would that not entertain you, to watch an endless and eternally agonizing performance, a broken man screaming helplessly into the void? Watching as his sanity slips away to despair?*"

___ *paused to ponder this.* ___ *stopped all of reality and time to consider Zanshin's words. Then...*___ **grinned.**

That is wonderful. Truly, truly, intriguing. This will be entertaining for what is beyond eternity. Your mind, body, and soul will tear itself to shreds as you stand witness to helplessness. You do not know the high bargain you have proposed. Are you certain you wish to plaster yourself with this regret?

Zanshin's face twisted into utter fear, yet he gripped his fists as he slowly nodded. "*Before you shackle me, however, let me release my ascension from Taba. Call it a last request,*" he said.

Why should ___?

"*I made a promise...*" Zanshin pointed to the unconscious Taba. "*...to him. I promised to explain things afterwards, and I am not a promise breaker. Plus...you'll see me suffer more when the ascension is lifted.*"

Very well. ___ *permits this.*

Zanshin hopped over, his eyes glowing softly as he clutched his own chest, yanking out a jittering section of soul. It bounced around rapidly in his hand before Zanshin calmly placed it on Taba's chest. The unconscious Misfit's body shuttered slightly before settling. Sighing softly with a sorrowful look, Zanshin looked up with a determined nod. "*I am ready.*"

Geralt scowled as he tried to voice his protest...but his lips failed him. Still, Zanshin took notice and smiled. *"I know what you wish to say, friend, and how you must hate this. Still...you have carried the burden for far too long. It is my turn,"* said Zanshin.

'My burden is nothing compared to yours!' Geralt desperately wished to scream, but it was all he could do to hold possession of the soulscale and Queenie.

Before Zanshin could speak further, chains of infinity and the unfathomable pierced Zanshin's sides, like a needle skewering a tapestry. The sickly man twisted with agony, before vanishing. Geralt scre-

Geralt blinked. What had happened? Why was he so tired? He looked at his good hand and saw the soulscale floating around his fingers. When did he obtain the soulscale...?

· · ·

Sana stared blankly into nothing. She was...staring at someone, wasn't she? Still, her curse told her something was about to happen...*very* soon. She pathetically crawled over to Taba's body, limply grabbing his wrist. She would protect the child, no matter what.

· · ·

Questions and exhaustion swirled both Geralt and Sana's minds, just as ___ stood up with thunderous glee.

It. Is. DONE.

And right before all their eyes, the peak of Limbo vanished, with Queenie in Geralt's grasp and Taba in Sana's.

CHAPTER 15

How long had her headache rung? How many had she vanquished? How many mutants were obliterated? ...How many more were left? Juliette did not know. It was all she could do to sit on the floor, propping herself up on her paintbrush, her mind long torn as it traced hundreds of thousands of slices all around Malapace's walls. Behind her, G had clasped his hands in a prayer, his head lull, swaying with the gentle breeze. Judging from the slight trail of drool from his lips, he was unconscious, yet actively using his ascension. Juliette was not worthy to be in the presence of such genius. She would do all she could to honor her friend's efforts.

The sky began to ripple. Directly overcast, the moon flittered towards the sun. Without anyone noticing, the sun blared against the moon. The solar eclipse, and in turn, Limbo, had begun.

And just as it had started, Limbo finished.

Without warning, the sky crashed, the shattering echoed all around Malapace. Juliette weakly turned her head and saw two figures falling from the sky. They were too far away for her to make distinct details...but even Juliette could identify a woman in a white dress, tightly hugging a person as they plummeted.

Juliette's baggy eyes lifted slightly in exhausted alarm. '*Sana.*' she wished to scream, yet when her lips opened, not even a croak came out. A figured blurred past her, and Juliette could've cried in relief upon seeing the man wearing a raggedy shirt accompanied with flip flops jump into the sky, only blinking short distances to reach the falling allies. Patchy was clearly tapped out, since he wasn't ascending like usual. Still, he scooped everyone up one by one, gently placing them on the rooftops.

...and yet, the mutants still arrived at a steady rate. What happened? Did they not have the soulscale? The situation was already dire enough: Juliette *was* the city's backup plan. If she fell...

Juliette hunched over, vomiting pure crimson bile onto the cracked pavement. Mustering whatever she could, she stood up with trembling limbs and stiffly walked closer to Malapace. With each step, her headache rang louder and louder, until she collapsed on the floor once more. It was pointless, without G's aid, Juliette was shackled to this one spot. No matter how much she willed it, she could do nothing but pray someone else found a solution.

She was not sure how much longer she would last, but Juliette would not rest until the city was safe.

· · ·

Babatiya sat in her chambers, her fingers tapping silently as her eyes scoured numerous cities and locations. The numerous cries and pleas reached her ears, yet she could only provide so little aid. Juliette was about to die, G was overexerting himself to ensure this didn't happen, Patchy was fighting without any ascension, and the other mentors

283

were very quickly getting overwhelmed. Not to mention how they had no one in the medical bay providing ample care to the others, ensuring the city's already dwindling forces grew weaker and weaker with each passing hour. Babatiya tried her best to lead her people to the route of self preservation, even if that meant forcing mentors into fights that were guaranteed losses. Her heart tore tremendously whenever a mentor fell, since their blood was on her orders...but she pushed through. There would be time for tears later.

The sky began to ripple, and amidst all the chaos, the solar eclipse rang loud. When Limbo crashed, hope surged through Babatiya's brain...but quickly died when she saw the condition of the survivors. Only an exhausted Sana and an unconscious Taba returned. Where was Queenie, Hush, or Banase? Were they...?

There would be time for tears later.

Babatiya's blind eyes glowed as she quietly whispered into Sana's ears. *"Sana. six-o-clock, four mentors are cornered in a building. One of them will die from blood loss. Protect the remaining three. I will be watching,"* the Overseer ordered.

Sana's arms were visibly twitching, but she subtly nodded, trying to force herself up before collapsing. The Gatekeeper bit her lit hard enough to sprout blood, and stood up with shaky determination. Exhaling softly, she powerwalked over to the location given. Patchy stood by, his face warped into worry and hesitation, but Babatiya whispered to him. *"Patchy. Two-o-clock, there are nine mentors cornered by three mutants. One hawk, two aardvarks. Save them,"* she instructed. Patchy grimaced as he watched Sana limp off, but nodded and turned around, sprinting to Babatiya's orders, leaving Taba on the rooftops.

Leaving people to die. Ignoring the suffering of others. It was a process that was maddening. Babatiya hated it...but would not wish this role on another. So, she would be as heartless as needed to ensure the minimal suffering.

Her chamber doors slammed open and Babatiya turned around to try and identify who had entered. It was not a soul pattern she recognized. Plus, judging from the sound of their footsteps, it was a heavier character wearing clothes she was not familiar with. Who was this...?

Suddenly, she flinched. The person was carrying her receptionist, Tabitha, in a chokehold. His cocky voice rang out with a smug undertone. "I'm sorry, I was told you were busy. Could you spare time in your schedule for a meeting?" he said mockingly.

"...release Tabitha first," she scowled.

He let go, and the receptionist tumbled to the floor with watery coughs. The visitor kicked her side, pushing her back to the entrance. "Get outta here," he snapped. Tabitha whimpered and scampered out, clutching her side. Once alone, Babatiya's guest cracked his neck as he examined her. "I don't get why they treat you like a god. You seem weak," he frowned.

"I never said I was strong. Who are you, and what do you want?" she asked.

"You aren't worthy of knowing my name," he sneered. "Instead...I'm here to cut you a deal. See, your city is about to fall. If I do nothing, my Family wins...but that's boring. I want to fight someone strong: winning by default makes an ass out of me."

"So...what's your deal?" Babatiya asked.

"Tell me where you're keeping Toukie. Since he's the one attracting the mutants, if we take him back to our base, your city should be mostly safe."

This was suspicious. The Family, cutting a deal to protect Malapace, even at the cost of a hostage? Something was off. "What are your terms? Why would you help us?" she asked.

"Eh. The Family needs the souls of your people, doesn't really help if you all are dead, right? Think of it like keeping cattle around, and killing 'em when the time is right," he shrugged. "As for terms...we get Toukie back *and* you owe us two favors."

"...that's quite a unique number. Why two?"

"That's what I asked, but *he* said that 'two was enough'. What a dumbass. Whatever, doesn't matter. Deal?"

Babatiya closed her eyes, her mind throbbing as she considered every possibility. There was not a single outcome where her people survived another day: the resources were already spread too thin. This was either pure luck...or...'Father' was looking out for her. What a buffoon.

She sighed, and to her guest's surprise, she knelt on the floor and bowed, her forehead touching the ground. "Save my people, please," she earnestly pleaded.

The man above her scowled, reeling his leg back, and kicking her with enough to send her flying, crashing her into her bedframe. As a thin stream of blood trickled down her cheek, she groaned. His nostril twitched. "What fool abandon's her pride so easily? Are you *that* weak? The leader of Malapace...bowing?" he snapped.

Babatiya struggled to her knees, but looked up with a blind glare. "Of course I would bow. This is not because I have surrendered or have abandoned my pride. It is me showing utter gratitude to a savior. It not matter how others view me, I simply act how I believe is correct. Is there any more appreciation I can give, apart from bowing with all my heart?" she asked.

He walked over silently before squatting next to the Overseer, simply staring at her blind eyes. "You...you're weird. Odd. At least, I can see why Father is doing all this," he muttered.

So it was *him*. What an idiot. "When you next see him, smack his head. Tell him he's an idiot," she snapped.

To her surprise, the man offered her his hand, to which she cautiously took. He helped the Overseer to her feet before walking to the main entrance. Before he exited, he turned around with an odd level of respect on his face. "My name is Luong. Luong Xiaoli. Remember it every waking minute as the man who spared your life," he ordered.

"Of course. I do not forget my debts," she responded, before nodding to the front. "Tell Tabitha to take you to where the hostage is being kept, under my orders."

The martial artist nodded...and left.

.   .   .

Luong Xiaoli and Toukie casually strolled out of the city with minimal interference. Occasionally, a mutant appeared, but the pair silently took out each creature that crossed their paths. After a while, the duo had successfully entered the woods outside of Malapace, meeting up with Nancy and Maggle at their designated rendezvous. Upon seeing the scrawny boy, Maggle stood up and exhaled sharply, extending both his hands to wrap a small bubble of his own soul around Toukie. A thin layer coated the powder monkey, hiding his presence from the mutants in the area. Once secured, Nancy let out a shaky breath and wrapped her arms around Toukie, squeezing him tightly in a bearhug.

Luong Xiaoli plopped on a nearby tree stump, grumbling into his chest. "I did as Zanshin asked, but I still think he's a dumbass. Why shouldn't we attack right now? Hell, I *alone* could steamroll the damn place: this is a wasted opportunity," he scowled.

Maggle shook his head, the bags under his eyes growing slightly. "Victory is assured: Taba's blessing confirmed it. What *isn't* guaranteed is achieving Father's goal. If we were to take the city out right now...there wouldn't be enough soul to execute his plans. Not to mention...Father himself needs the Overseer for his ascension. Too many loose ends to finish them off, so be patient," the big man said.

Nancy pursed her lips as she stepped a bit away from Toukie. "I'm...a bit worried. I don't know why...but something feels off with Zanshin's plan. Do you think he'll be ok?" she said with a tinge of worry in her gaze.

"Zanshin's plans never failed. I trust the man...but you're right. I'm worried that he's taken on a brunt of the burdens this time around," Maggle said. "Next time we see him, we should show him our highest gratitude."

Suddenly, the heavens flickered with the briefest of eclipses before the sky shattered, causing the Family to flinch as they looked upwards. Their eyes collectively widened in disbelief as they saw a half-conscious Geralt plummeting towards the earth as he tightly held Queenie. Luong Xiaoli quickly sprinted forward, diving to catch the two before they slammed onto the floor. Nancy wasted no time, her expression going monotone as she activated her blessing. Geralt's wounds stopped gushing blood, with gory patches of skin acting as impromptu sutures for open gashes. In his remaining hand, the twirling soulscale of impossibilities.

Silence fell over the Family. There was a dense disbelief that tainted the air, from seeing such a wounded Geralt to the unfathomable soulscale. However, perhaps the most unbelievable thing was how this was perfectly on schedule, in accordance with the plan given to them by Zanshin. How...how far ahead did that man think? What possibilities did he calculate?

...and where was he amidst everything?

. . .

After Luong Xiaoli took Toukie back, the city went from tens of mutants every minute to ten mutants every day. Though it was still a tremendous amount to defend against, many casualties were spared.

Taba, Sana, G, and Juliette were sent to the medical ward to rest up. Due to the lack of proper medics, the few merchants with able bodies and merchandise were scampering around to donate whatever they could. No one was allowed into their ward, apart from the Overseer and Patchy. However, Patchy rarely had the time to check in on the others, since he was the only able-bodied soulbearer who could consistently take out mutants. Whenever the other mentors would see him, he was either defending the city, sleeping, or visiting the medical ward. No one had ever seen him eat, much less drink.

Taba and Sana's vigor slowly returned over a day, but G and Juliette's complexions were worsening with each passing hour. Cheeks became sunken, muscles lost density, and their breaths became more shallow. It was all Babitiya could do to dripple the tiniest chunks of boiled rice into their mouths. Even if they *did* eat food...Babitiya had no solution to replenish their soul. It was all she could do but sit in

289

their ward, desperately scan every village nearby for aid, and curse her own weakness.

The Overseer sat on the creaky cot, blindly staring into the comatose Gatekeepers. Would they wither away? What about Banase, where was he? What of Queenie and Hush? Did they truly fail in retrieving the soulscale? What...what happened? So many questions...yet no answers.

Babitiya clasped her hands tightly. A miracle, mercy, *anything*. Anything to save her city.

. . .

Queenie woke up to the sensation of warm fuzz spreading through her head. She groggily opened her good eye and sat up. The first thing she noticed was how damp her surroundings were. Then, how her wounded eye was wrapped up in heavy gauze. It seemed a bit amateur, initially, but the careful weaves and ties spoke otherwise. After her good eye adjusted, she squinted in the dark and noticed dozens of eyes all staring back at her, each gaze curious, worried, and excited. Lastly, the warm, calloused hands on her forehead.

These were the same caves that the Hush clan used to operate...before they were purged. Now? It served as the Family's hideout.

The first to move was Nancy, who dove into Queenie with a sound that was a cross between a squeal and a sob. "Queenie, *gosh*, it has been *days*! Days! You are *never* going out again, you he-" she was cut off as she was pushed to the side with a grumble. "Move over. Let her breathe," Luong Xiaoli snapped. Nancy scowled and dropped some impressive combinations of slurs and swears to the fighter, while a smaller child grabbed her fingers. "Welcome back, Queenie!" Little Stuart chirped. As the little boy grabbed her hand excitedly, a middle-aged man wearing an apron and a braided beard chuckled, patting her shoulder. "Knew you'd survive, you fighter, you!" Hugh chuckled. As he did, another boisterous laugh echoed from behind him. "Told ya, the girlie wouldn't die too easily!" roared Maggle, with a hint of relief flickering between his eyes.

Lastly, a familiar, worn, yet comforting voice smiled from behind her. "Welcome back, Queenie," he said softly.

She looked up, and a whirlpool of emotions swirled in her chest as she choked. "...Hey, Father. I'm...I'm back."

Father looked down at her as his hands gently, yet firmly, pushed down on her forehead. "Don't get up: you still need to recover. When you feel better, can you tell us of your experiences?" he asked calmly.

Memories of Limbo flashed through Queenie's head, a muffled tear slashing through her heart. She...she didn't want to wait on the crappy feeling. So, she stared at the damp ceiling and began to speak to no one in particular, while her mind was numb to reality. The soulscale. Limbo.

Hush.

The Family stayed silent. The first one to break the agonizing stillness was Nancy, who balled her fists into her lap with heavy sniffles. "No...Hush? Really? Hu-" Nancy choked on her tears while Maggle also looked down in frustrated shame. The silence in the cave was excruciating, the Family torn between mourning and disbelief. Even the crude Luong Xiaoli was silent, his arms folded in silent respect. Father did not move, nor did his expression change. After all, he had seen thousands of deaths: it would've felt more fake if he had shown an expression. And yet...Father's eyes gained a deep wrinkle, a crease that spoke volumes of his agony. Queenie simply sat in the middle of them all, her arms limp with dead eyes. She wasn't really sure of how to react. Maybe if she slept, the day would pass faster. Unfortunately, she was well rested...which was odd, due to how sluggish her entire body felt.

She took a deep exhale and forced herself upright, slapping her thighs. "Whatever. It happened, get over it," she said with some forced agitation. "Where's Geralt?"

The already deafening silence grew louder as everyone stiffened up. After a few seconds, Father sighed and nodded to the corner of the cave. "He's..." he trailed off.

Queenie got up on stiff legs, crookedly walking over to the dark corner. There sat Toukie, coated in Maggle's blessing. Toukie's eyes donned heavy eyebags as he glanced over, nodding at her with a solemn expression. Right next to him lay Geralt, hunched at an unnatural angle, his body taking shallow breaths, beads of sweat dripped onto his ragged suit. His missing hand was tautly wrapped with leaves and bandages, but didn't seem to do much to completely stifle the bloodflow. His remaining hand was subconsciously flexed, the soulscale twirling a few inches above it.

Father walked up from behind her, shaking his head slightly. "I..."

"Fix him."

"I-"

"You fixed me. Fix *him*."

"His case is more...unique. The soulscale is interfering with my bl-"

Queenie rolled her eyes, walking over and immediately storing it. She felt the weight of infinity slam into her stomach, but the pure hatred and rage she felt at the universe gave her the energy to stand.

She exhaled through her nostrils and nodded to him. "No more interference, right? Now *fix him*," she snapped.

Father blinked before quietly walking over to place his hands on Geralt's head. Within minutes, where his missing hand should've been glowed a faint blue before spurting out a new hand. Geralt looked more refreshed, his shallow breaths turning more deep as he straightened his posture. After stabilizing him, Father turned back to stare at Queenie with disbelief. "How...how did you...?" he stammered.

"My blessing, turns out, is the place where the soulscale comes from. Whatever," she said tiredly. She turned around and began walking to the mouth of the cave, squinting as the sunrays hit her face. Father followed her with a hesitant step, unsure of her intent.

"...Queenie? Are you all ri-"

"I'm going back."

"To Malapace?"

She nodded silently, staring off into the distance. Father chewed the inside of his cheek, but ultimately gave her a tight hug. "I'm not going to force you to stay. Thank you for being in my life," he whispered.

She shook him off tiredly. "No, I'll be back. Don't worry. I just need to do something really qui-"

Her words were cut off as the rest of the Family exited the cave, a bit of worry on their faces. "Queenie? Where you goin'?" asked Little Stuart.

She crouched to his eye level and gave the boy a tight hug. "Get back into the cave. I'll be back in a jiffy, ok?"

"Oh. Ok!" he chirped, trotting back inside. As he waddled back, he kept turning his head back, obviously aware that something was happening behind the scenes. Still, he obediently ducked into the cave with some of the other members of the Family.

Nancy timidly approached Queenie. "Hun, you...you should rest. It's been a rough time for you. You'll feel quite better after some sle-"

Queenie pulled a revolver out of her storage, chambered a bullet, spun the cylinder, pulled back the hammer, placed it under her chin, and pulled the trigger. Everyone screamed as a quiet 'tuk' shattered the skies, frozen in place as the female Misfit pulled the gun from her chin with a disappointed stare. "Drats," she muttered.

Nancy slapped the gun out of Queenie's hand, before slapping Queenie, a wild and fearful expression in her eyes. "Why would you *do* that?" she cried, tears welling up across her trembling face.

Queenie rubbed her cheek numbly as she stared at her friends. "The more you guys question my decisions, the more I spin that cylinder. So, I'm going back to Malapace to do something, then I'll be back. Any objections?" she asked plainly.

Everyone stood stiffly, afraid to even move, in fears that Queenie would react unfavorably. Maybe they hated her now. That was fine: none of it mattered. Father gently grabbed her shoulders and nodded to a dead tree a few ways from the cave. "Stand by that tree for a bit, will you? The rest of you guys, back in the cave," he ordered calmly. The shaken Family members nodded as they walked back into the cave. Queenie shrugged and did as instructed, sitting by the yellow grass. Oddly enough, Father went back into the cave as well, not really giving much of a sign as he did.

To her surprise, a few minutes later he returned, with an exhausted man wrapped over his shoulders. Father grunted as he sat next to

Queenie, nudging the man he was carrying. "We're here, Geralt," he said softly.

Geralt cracked his good eye open, staring at the girl. "Hey. We're matching," he chuckled as he slightly nodded to her bandaged face. "Father couldn't fix it?"

"I guess not," she muttered, staring at Father. "I'm not complaining...but was there something wrong with the eye?" she asked.

Father shook his head, confusion plastered on his face. "I don't get it either. Whenever my soul tried to penetrate your eye...it was rejected. Maybe too much time passed, or maybe it's because it's a wound inflicted directly from Limbo. I don't get it...I'm sorry," he apologized.

Queenie waved him off. "Eh. It's not like the eye is gone completely," she said, cracking the wounded eye open behind the bandages. Her vision was dark and fuzzy, like looking through cracked glass. The color was a mixture of grey and red, her eyeball growing more painful the longer she kept it open, wincing as she shut it once more. "Back to topic, why did you want me here?" she asked Father.

"I...don't know how it feels to ascend," he admitted. "I know the activation conditions, but that's it. So...I at least wanted to give you some time with someone else who *has* ascended. I don't know where Zanshin is, Maggle is too emotional to think straight right now, so the only one who *does* know how to ascend is..." Father patted Geralt's limp body, who winced with each pat.

"I guess that's me," Geralt said, getting off Father's back to rest against the dead tree. "Didn't even let me rest, damn it. Can a man not sleep?" Geralt nodded to Queenie. "What was the regret? Was it Hush?" he asked.

295

Queenie stiffened up. Geralt noticed and rest his head on the tree trunk. "Bingo, I guess. Yeah, that...that will do it," he said softly.

Queenie tautly stared at her socks, her eyes desperately trying to focus on any detail apart from the facts. The little thread that was loose on the ankle. The color pattern. The little grass stain. The...

It was her fault.

Her shoes were battered. She needed to replace them soo-

If Queenie was stronger, Hush wouldn't need to carry her. If she had stronger pain tolerance, he wouldn't nee-

Her eyes welled up, but she forced the tears back into her dull sockets. Her hoodie sleeves were cut up. She would need to hire a smithy to remake it. Fortunately, she had a blueprint for it. She just needed-

Hush was dead. She saw his body.

Queenie cleared her throat. One of her fingernails was chipped slightly. She would need to cut her fingernails later. She always had a habit of biting them off, but Hush had tol-

Hush was not coming back. Queenie was alone.

Queenie's vision blurred as her eyes poured. Her expression did not change, she simply stared at the tiny waterfall that hit the dead grass. The chasm in her heart, finally realized, sat exposed to the sky as the air flowing through it forced the dead heart to pulse once more. Geralt scooched a bit closer and pulled her into his chest, patting her back softly as she stared into the black void. "Yeah. The feeling never goes away. It's all you can do to get used to it," he mourned softly. "I wish there was better news I could give...I'm sorry."

Father held out a hand, yearning to comfort the duo...but held back. Instead, he forced himself onto his feet to walk into the cave.

He...wasn't qualified to comfort the pair. His mere presence was an insult.

As he stepped back into the cave, the other Family members met him right at the entrance, concern written on their eyes. He shook his head and walked further in. His Family looked to the floor...and followed.

. . .

Banase woke up in a moist atmosphere, blindfold draped over his eyes. As his fingers touched the wet stalactite, he knew he was in foreign territory. Was he still in Limbo? No: he could blink, and everything stayed the same. He slightly shifted his wrists, feeling course rope rub against them: the same texture that smeared against his ankles.

The ropes themselves weren't a problem: he could easily break through them with his blessing. However...where *was* he? Who restrained him? No matter how much he racked his brain, the only answer that bubbled to his brain was...

Banase's thoughts were confirmed as he heard a pencil scratching away, another pair of footsteps entering the room.

"How is it going, Glen?" a deep voice asked.

"I...ah...he's slowly rousing, I believe," said a more timid voice. "The way he's been moving indicates recovery. I heard Queenie woke up, is she ok?"

Banase's ears perked up. Queenie. Foreign voices. His restraints. Yes, without a doubt...his captors were the Family. Banase did not doubt his ability in a one-on-one fight...yet against the whole Family? He doubt he would see the light of day if he did not plan accordingly. So, he feigned slumber as he tried to gather more information.

"...Queenie has ascended. I believe Hush is dead. I worry for her mental health, but there's nothing I can do to comfort her. All I can do is sit on the side. In truth...it's quite frustrating," the deep voice muttered with a sorrowful undertone.

"...oh dear. I...oh dear," the timid voice said with somberness.

Hush...was dead? Banase struggled to believe it. Even with his minimal interaction with the young man, he could not fathom such a tricky individual to perish. And yet...the sorrow in the deep voice was heart wrenching. Stern like a leader, yet tender like a parent: it was the voice of someone who balanced both roles with perfect tragedy.

Silence rang in the room, with only the soft inhales of the three men echoing in the moist caverns. After a minute of mourning, the deeper man cleared a warbled throat. "I...I will go check on the others. Please give me any update if the Malapace member wakes up."

"Of course, Father."

Banase's blood grew cold. Father? The boss of the Family? A vein in his neck bulged, yet Banase lay still to wait for his opportunity. Once the footsteps shuffled out of the room, Banase mentally counted out two minutes. Ensuring no reinforcements were coming, he channeled his blessing into his arms, silently grunting as he tore through his restraints and ripped off his blindfold.

He had only a few seconds to kill the timid voice from earlier before the alarm was sounded to alert the Family. If he could do so, Banase could escape...or better yet, take out Father.

And yet, when he ripped off his blindfold, his eyes blinked in rapid motion as they adjusted to a bright blue bubble that surrounded him. Outside of the bubble stood a lanky man wearing a raggedy labcoat, hunched in mild surprise at Banase's actions. Banase sucked in a quick breath as he clenched his right fist, pouring soul into it to unleash a dense hook in an attempt to shatter the bubble.

Despite his tremendous physicality, however, the bubble did not break. In fact, Banase's fist simply...stopped upon touching the bubble. All of the kinetic energy in his blow had vanished. He stared, stunned at the outcome. He...had *never* seen something fully withstand his blows. What on earth...?

"You...you aren't breaking that, I'm afraid."

Banasse turned to the timid voice, watching the scientist casually take notes with odd collection. "I knew you were awake for a while, since your ears perked, fingers rubbed the stalactite, and legs rubbed only slightly: behaviors that you did not exhibit for the past few days. Plus, the vein in your neck bulged when we mentioned Queenie." The scientist finished up his notes as he placed his clipboard on a rack next to him. "If we didn't force you to act, most likely you would've feigned unconsciousness for a few weeks, no? The only way we were going to prove you were awake was for you to take initiative. Unfortunately for you...this is a bubble that withstood Linda. You aren't breaking through this, ever. Sorry." He got up and then walked towards the entrance of the room. "I'll go tell the others. You stay put, we'll be right back."

It was all Banase could do but scream in rage, slamming away at his prison with no success, as the Family's scientist walked out with calculated perfection.

. . .

"Do you need me to come with you?" Geralt asked.

"Nah, I'll be fine. I...hm. Malapace is..." Queenie pointed to the left. "*That* way, right?"

299

"Yeah. Just walk straight for a day. You have enough food? Can you move with the soulscale? You su-"

"I'll be fine, Geralt. Seriously," she scoffed, a hint of a smile returning to her face.

"Alright. Well, if you don't return in a week, we're hunting you down. Got it?" Geralt frowned.

"Yeah, sure. Just make sure *you* guys stay alive, ok? Without the soulscale, the mutants are going to be attracted to Toukie for a few days."

" He's coated in Maggle's blessing; he'll be fine. Even if he weren't: who do you think we are? Get outta here."

The response was so nonchalant that Queenie couldn't help but stifle a laugh. Just as she turned to leave, a rumble of footsteps echoed out from behind her. She turned around and was stampeded by her Family, all diving onto her in a massive hugging pile. Each one tightly hugged her tiny frame, with the massive Maggle wrapping his arms around the entire group. Nancy pulled back with watery eyes. "You come back safe, ya hear?" she sniffed.

Queenie's heart tugged, but she softly grinned. "Yeah, got it. I won't die, ok?" she replied.

After everyone got their fill of hugs, they all waved as Queenie walked off into the woods. She had grown up in these parts, but it was the first time she had traveled here alone. Though the roads stayed the same, with all the usual landmarks and markings, the flavor of the journey felt different in solitude. Though it couldn't have been longer than a year or two since she last walked this road, Queenie still found herself becoming immersed in nostalgia. The blueberry bush that was always yellowing on the leaves, yet continuously managed to sprout a handful of blueberries year round. The odd mushroom circle that surrounded the massive redwood. The skull of a dead mutant dangling on a branch as a chipmunk balanced on it, rustling against the lightest of breezes. The marking of Xs on various trees and rocks, indicating mutant territory. As Queenie quietly crunched through the leaves, she nestled up next to a tree stump as the sun began to set. Right next to it was a pit of stones, used as a safe checkpoint for a campfire. She gathered a few dead branches and chucked them into the pit, grabbing a match from her storage to light the dull fire. Queenie pulled out the chipmunk she had hunted from earlier, skinning and gutting the critter before cooking it over the fire slowly. She was careful to not let the blood splash onto her clothes: after all, the nearest river wasn't for a while. After cooking the critter to a slight char, she chewed at remaining edible pieces before turning in for the night.

Her sleep, for the first time in a while, was dreamless. Queenie woke up to cold mist, stretching with a guttural yell as she scratched her stomach. She got up and continued her trek. The little chipmunk from last night was surprisingly filling, staving off her hunger even partially through the morning. She pulled off some outer bark from a nearby pine tree and peeled off some strips of the more inner, softer sections to chew on her walk. It was bitter, but it kept her mind busy as she climbed over the mossy boulders in the overhead sun. After a bit of clambering, she squinted down the mountain and was met with the familiar stone walls of Malapace off in the distance. She took a deep breath, spat out the wad in her mouth, bit off some more pine bark, and climbed down.

After a few hours, she was stopped at the city's entrance by Malapace's guards. "Halt. State your business," they instructed.

She frowned as she casually chewed her bark. "Seriously? I saved your asses a while ago, and you don't remember me?" The guards exchanged glances, a flicker of recognition between them. Queenie looked ragged, but her outfit was simple and familiar. She rolled her eyes and flipped them off. "Relax. I'm just here for a pit stop. I'll be out of your hair real quick...probably. Can you let me through?"

"Let her through."

The guards turned around in surprise to see a tired Patchy standing at the entrance, nodding at her. "So...you returned. Any particular reason, or..." he asked with moderate suspicion.

"Just fulfilling a promise, something like that," she said. "I'll head back after this."

Patchy yawned, but nodded. The guards uncertainly stepped aside, pounding their chests in respect to the Gatekeeper. Queenie nodded to Patchy. "Where's Juliette?" she asked.

"The medical ward. You know where that is, or..?"

"I got it."

She walked through the familiar city, glancing around the buildings. There was much less ruin than she expected, but many buildings were still crumbled away. The families and merchants of the city seemed more quiet, looking outside windows and stores with a nervousness that seemed fragile. Children gone from the streets, laughter and chatter silenced, and tension filled the air. Though Queenie's allegiance was with the Family...the death of peace really did hurt to see.

She walked into the medical ward and peeked around the rooms. To her surprise, many rooms were filled with mentors, not civilians. There were more injured soulbearers than she anticipated, to a level where she was confused. In her time at Malapace, Queenie had *never* seen this many patients.

After walking down the hall, she saw a door guarded by Gary, a previous combatant who lost against Taba. Though she wasn't there for it, apparently he helped dig up potatoes with Sana and Taba.

It would explain why he was in charge of protecting her ward when available hands were short. He glanced up with a flicker of recognition on his face. "You're...uhh...you're that girl who beat up Harrison, right? I forgot your name," he frowned.

"Don't worry about it. Patchy gave me permission to pass," she responded.

"Oh. Sure."

"You're not going to question it? No authentication? Anything?" Gary stared back with discomfort, shuffling his feet as Queenie crossed her arms. "*Man*, you guys are lazy," she muttered as she pushed past him.

The room smelled like stale ointment. Sana lay snoozing away on a little cot, with Taba adjacent to her in his own bed. Queenie sighed in relief, seeing Taba's overall wellbeing. She contemplated taking him back to the Family...but that was too risky. Even considering his exhaustion, Queenie wasn't sure she could beat Patchy while carrying Taba. She would have to rescue him later. For now...

She readied her spirit and pulled back some curtains that covered some beds. As expected, Juliette and G lay in them, both having lost so much weight that if they did not wear their distinct clothes, the pair would not be recognizable. Queenie reached into her storage and yanked out the soulscale, the impossibility twirling a few centimeters above her fingertips. She stared at it blankly: Queenie wasn't really sure what to do from here.

'Place it a few inches away from their heads' a humanoid voice instructed from her soul, causing her to flinch in surprise. Queenie wasn't sure if she was relieved or disgusted at the voice, but she did as instructed and placed it next to Juliette.. The fragment flickered and jittered the closer it got closer, until a threads of braided, faded soul wisped through Juliette's eyes. All time stood still as her entire body slightly shown blue...before fluttering with vitality. Juliette took deeper breaths in her sleep, even pulling her bedsheets over her body more tightly to preserve body heat. She repeated the action with G, a bit unsure of how to feel as the bald man shuttered back with spirit. On one hand...she was relieved that she managed to heal them. On the other...she had technically revived two of the strongest entities of Malapace, and might have unintentionally caused many hurdles for the Family. Oh well: she did what she felt was right, that was all.

"So...did that fix 'em?" Queenie asked out loud.

'Their soul is stable. As for their physicality...that is entirely on them,' her blessing responded.

"Great help you were," she muttered, storing the soulstone into her storage. She glanced over at Sana and Taba. They didn't appear to be in any dire condition: a bit of sleep would probably fix them up. She pulled out a piece of paper and pencil, scribbled a note, then stuffed it in Taba's pockets. She opened the door, and to her surprise, there stood an out-of-breath Babs.

The Overseer coughed as she held up a finger to catch her breath before speaking. "Why...why are you here? What happened? Why did you heal them?" she asked between pants.

Queenie subconsciously unstored a dagger, causing Babs to hold her breath. Queenie tightened her lips uncomfortably...and began to unravel and retape the handle of her blade. After a few seconds, Queenie shrugged. "I dunno. I just...don't think I could live with myself if I didn't. That's all."

And with that...she quietly left Malapace and walked back home.

EPILOGUE

Taba sat confined in a bubble, floating along the nothingness. If he hadn't just scaled Limbo...he might've been fooled. This domain, however, was plain and simple. It was the equivalent of seeing a coffee table in a coffee shop. Taba turned around with a slight frown. If this wasn't Limbo...

"You're here, aren't you?" Taba asked with annoyance.

A thin blue strand appeared from Taba's chest as it began to weave itself into his blessing. It stared back with a mockingly faceless grin. "Nothing can simulate the real deal: you see that now, yes?" *Before Taba could respond, it raised up a hand.* "You don't need to answer, human. I already know your answer," *it said.*

The bubble popped, sending Taba freefalling into an ocean. Upon crashlanding, he resurfaced into a humid forest, spitting up mud as he crawled up from the ground. After he rubbed his eyes clear, he looked around with slight familiarity. This was...

"Correct. This is the forest with the mutant trees, or rather...a memory of it," *Taba's blessing said as it flicked its fingers back and forther. With each movement, the trees sprung to live and shriveled back into stagnation, as though a recording were being rewinded and sped up back and forth.* "You may not know it...but your memories are now free."

"Free?" Taba asked.

"Your Family member? Zanshin? He had stolen some childhood memories, but recently he returned them. You should thank him next time you cross paths with him," *Taba's blessing said, malicious glee in its voice.*

Taba resisted the urge to roll his eyes. His blessing knew that Zanshin was impossible to remember...if he even existed. For all Taba knew, he had either never met Zanshin...or they had spoken five minutes ago. Whatever, Taba would make sure to show his appreciation next time. He leaned against the same mutant tree that had submerged him beneath the earth and nodded to his blessing. "Why am I here? What is the point of this talk? You never initiate anything without reason," Taba said.

Taba's blessing extended its hand, and the world swirled around it, melting the scenery until it was a moldy paintball. Once converged, it clenched its fist and the world exploded into a familiar bedroom. Taba looked around, slightly stunned, at the sudden change. "There are memories you've been robbed. They are not pleasant: in fact, Zanshin had his best interests for taking them. I simply wish to see your face as you remember it all," *the blessing said, laughter traced upon its solemn aura.* "So, I will give you the option. Do you wish to remember?"

"...why give me the choice?" Taba said suspiciously. "What trickery have you plotted?"

"No tricks: this is just the greatest way to hurt you," *the blessing said bluntly.* "Choosing something, and immediately regretting it. Nothing more agonizing than the rue of hindsight."

"*Why would I actively choose something that would hurt me in the long run?*" *Taba asked. However, it was a stupid question: even* he *knew the answer to that question.*

"The same reason I chose you for my ability," *the blessing said.* "You're innately curious. You hate it when you don't know something, and go to all ends to pursue knowledge. That same trait allows you to fully utilize me...and will also be your undoing. Best part? I doubt this will even ascend you: it is regret for the sake of regret," *it cackled.* "Nothing like an utter tragedy, no?"

Taba cursed as he turned away from his blessing...but knew it was inevitable. Already, he felt the urge to turn around and ask to see the stolen memory.

The blessing laughed humorlessly as the world fizzled away. "I'll see you on the other side, Icarus," *it cackled.*

.   .   .

Taba groggily sat up, rubbing his eyes. He glanced down at his stiff bedsheets before looking around. Juliette and G were in their cots, snoozing away as daylight traced their skin. Sana sat in a nearby chair, quietly peeling a potato with her sickle, flicking the skins into a wastebasket. She flinched upon feeling his gaze, glancing up at Taba. Upon seeing his open eyes, she dropped her sickle and potato, running over to tightly hug him with a shaky sigh.

"I'm...I'm so... I don't know what I would've done if you had..." the Gatekeeper stammered before she pulled herself away, quickly checking his face for any blemishes. "How are you feeling? Any injuries? How's your soul? Are y-"

"I'm *fine*, Sana," Taba said, his face beet red as he gently, yet firmly, pushed her away. He glanced over to the other two. "How's Juliette and G? Are they...?"

Sana glanced past them, a mix of relief and worry on her eyes. "They've stabilized. The two overworked themselves in defending the city, so they're just sleeping in. Me and Patchy have been taking turns feeding them soft porridge, but that's about it." She looked at Taba with a raised eyebrow. "You're pretty thin, yourself. Did you want some food?" she asked.

Taba's stomach growled, but he pushed the hunger aside. "I'm hungry, but I'll eat later," he muttered as he tried to not look at the peeled potato Sana dropped on the floor. "I need to speak with Babs. Is she in her room?" he asked.

"I...yeah, she is. You should rest up a bit more, though. You just woke u-"

"I said I'm *fine*," said Taba, standing up on shaky legs. He took a step forward and stumbled slightly, before taking a soft inhale and hobbling to the front door. Sana hesitantly reached out...but lowered her arm. Judging from the look in her eyes, it was clear she wasn't following Taba out of pure respect. He appreciated the gesture.

Taba's eyes were glazed over as he leaned on building walls and railings, limping over to the town hall. He already had a firm idea on where Queenie was: most likely, she was with the Family. Normally, Taba would've been relieved that she was back home...but this was the worst case scenario.

'You...are you alright? Where's Hush?'

Taba wiped his forehead with his shoulder as he pushed into the town hall. Tabitha was sitting in a chair, her neck bandaged oddly. She stiffly raised a hand to Taba, who gave her a small wave as he pushed past her.

'He's dead. I confirmed it.'

Taba slammed Bab's door open, the elderly woman kneeling on the floor in front of a small table. There lay two cups of tea with a bitter aroma, and a humble plate of celery. "I've been expecting you," she whispered with a rasp. "Sit."

Taba winced as he crashed on his butt, scooching forward as he gave a slight bow. His stomach gurgled as he stared at the celery, to which Babs waved. "Eat. I saw you approaching from a while away. Whatever you have to say can wait two minutes," she ordered.

Taba listened, scarfing down the vegetable as he sipped the lumpy tea. After a minute, he coughed and took a deep breath. "I just need to confirm...where's Queenie?" he asked.

She hesitated, but met Taba's fierce stare. "Back to her Family," she responded.

"Damn it. *Damn* it."

Babs wrinkled her brow with confusion. "Why so distraught? Isn't that good for you?"

"Hush is-

. . .

The boy once named Hush opened his eyes. Well, that was misleading. Rather, it felt as though his brain had...blinked. He looked down and stared at the bleeding vessel. As he rested his hand on its arm, he jerked his arm back. As expected...it was cold. Still, it was unnerving to witness.

The brother glanced around at his world. The ballroom was cut off from this area, a blue bubble coating the crystalized cavern. He walked

310

in a bit deeper, his legs not familiar with the lack of density in each step. After a few moments of time, he turned the corner-

-and there she was. The lady in blue, her hair fading at the ends in a aquamarine mist. It wasn't just her clothes: *everything* about her was azure...though in different shades. Ultramarine eyes, cobalt hair, cerulean skin, navy clothes, *everything*. More than the azure hue, however, the lady's personality was outstanding. Her eyes were calm, yet upturned in the most arrogant fashion. Her arms were welcoming, yet her chin was held up as though she were looking down at everyone. She was a short woman, and yet...her presence was tall. She held an elegant stance, yet her hands fiddled with a tiny pebble.

It was like looking in a mirror...and also, as though he were looking at his sister.

"...Mom?"

She glanced back with nonchalant eyes, a bit a of familiarity flickering between her hazy pupils.

"...Oliver?"

ABOUT THE AUTHOR

Seon Jung has *always* loved fantasy. He's adored diving into different stories, exploring their worlds, and theory-crafting numerous "what if"s for different abilities, lores, and so on. It's this admiration that's nurtured his curiosity and imagination from a young age. One day…he decided to share his world with earnest hopes to spark that excitement of fantasy in others. He truly thanks you, the reader, for the time you've spent indulging him!

Seon spends his time writing, playing games of all kinds, wondering about why his computer randomly crashes, and loving God. He believes that there is a fine balance of formality and goofiness that humans should strive to balance, and that everyone should "know when to lock in, and when to be a goober".

www.ingramcontent.com/pod-product-compliance
Lightning Source LLC
Chambersburg PA
CBHW021500110726
47899CB00001BA/233